Elephants, Bunnies & a Headless Giraffe

A NOVEL

SHANNA SARSIN

ELEPHANTS, BUNNIES & A HEADLESS GIRAFFE Copyright © 2019 by Shanna Sarsin

All rights reserved. This book may not be reproduced, distributed, or transmitted in whole or in part, except by a reviewer who may quote brief passages in a review; nor may any part of this book be reproduced, stored in a database or retrieval system, or transmitted in any form or by any mean, electronic, mechanical, photocopying, recording or other, without written permission of the publisher. Published in the United States by Self Publishing LLC. Printed in the United States of America. For information, address
www.SARSINS.com

ISBN 0-578-40049-5

Library of Congress Cataloging-in-Publication Data
https://lccn.loc.gov/2018912213
Sarsin, Shanna. Elephants, bunnies & a headless giraffe / Shanna Sarsin. Shreveport, LA : Sarsins LLC, 2018.
    pages cm
    ISBN: 9780578400495

Cover photo and design © Shanna Sarsin
Back cover design © Shanna Sarsin
Author photo © Shanna Sarsin
Book design by Shanna Sarsin

This is a work of fiction. All characters, organizations, and events portrayed in this novel are either products of the author's imagination or are used fictitiously. Any resemblance to persons living or dead is purely coincidental.

Contents

Preface 7
PART 1 Pink & Purple Elephants 9
1 D.D.S. or Better Yet 'Boo Thang' 11
2 Blink of an Eye 21
3 Cards on the Table 27
4 Jokers & Aces 51
5 Kings, Queens & Jacks 75
PART 2 The Brood & The Bunny 83
6 Face to Face 85
7 The Perfect Card 91
8 Gabby's Beau 103
9 Love Naked 127
10 Abracadabra: A Flying Dove 143
PART 3 Tuskers 165
11 House Keeping 167
12 Yoked 185
13 1224 Euphoric Lane 197
14 "ME" for "WE" a Tuskky Tango 217
PART 4 A Headless Giraffe 225
15 My Funny Valentine 227
16 Forty-Six, Thirty-One 285
17 It is What it Is Because… 305

Epilogue 317
Acknowledgements 319
About the Author 321

PREFACE

How hopelessly metaphoric. As I stare out the window of the plane focusing in on nothing at all, the heavy rain beating down the window mirroring the tears I'm unable to trap from streaming down my face. Flood lights, extra lights added to the runway because of the storm, to illuminate the tarmac so we can take off. "Please God, let us be able to get out of here," I pray silently to myself. Piercing lights, lights so intensely beaming they're blinding. Blinding like the reality that was just smeared in my face. I want, no I need so badly to just scream, but I cannot do that because I'm on this plane. I face the window hiding my tears and swallowing the sobs. As the plane pulls from the ground and ascends into the air, I feel my heart literally being ripped from my body because there are pieces of me that I'm leaving behind that I know I will never get back. Fragments of me left to simply rot away.

PART ONE
Pink & Purple Elephants

CHAPTER 1
D.D.S. or Better Yet 'Boo Thang'

It was the beginning of my favorite time of year here in the DMV. We were on the cusp of Cherry Blossom Season, which for me meant the beginning of the best nine months of the year. A true southern girl at heart, I didn't enjoy the harsh East Coast winters at all. I could live without any snow or rain for that matter. Other than work, social commitments and select black-tie outings I hibernated in the house and flew home as much as possible during the full ninety days of winter, but this was the time of year when I loved being outdoors. I could have been home half an hour ago, but it was so nice out that I wasn't ready to go in the house. I was literally like a kid during summer break before the streetlights came on. I was driving around the neighborhood rounding the thirteenth hole on the golf course, listening to smooth jazz on the Sirius XM radio Watercolors channel and just relishing in how grateful I was about the weather and to be in my neighborhood. It was only three years ago that I was first introduced to this subdivision and thought to myself, "What a beautiful neighborhood. I wish I could afford to live here," and here I was now a homeowner in the very neighborhood I'd so admired. God is so good. My thought was interrupted by the phone. It was Tiffany, my baby sister whom we affectionately referred to as Tippy, calling as she often did on her way home from work. This was another aspect of my life that I was truly grateful for, my familial relationships. My little sister and I spoke at least once a day, but often two to three times a day, and thanks to modern technology we regularly FaceTimed. She was definitely one of my best friends.

"Hey Tippy," I answered.

"Hey Girl! Whatcha doing?"

"I'm just driving, literally wasting gas. It's so nice here. I didn't want to go in the house just yet. You must be on your way home from work?"

"Yes Ma'am. It's been a long day, but I still have to pick the kids up from Kumon before heading home. I'm glad it's nice there because y'all have had some rough weather."

"Tell me about it. I am burned-out on winter after living here. I'll be so glad when I can move back down South. I don't necessarily want to move back to Georgia but maybe Birmingham. That will bring me a lot closer to home."

"Me too. You've been gone for so long. Boo to Birmingham, but that's better than you being all the way up there. Any hoo, I wanna ask you something." It was normal for Tippy to abruptly change the topic of conversation because her mind literally moved like she did, 150 mph.

I curiously replied, "Ok..."

"What's your age limit?"

"Huh?" I didn't understand the question.

"In a man. What's your age limit?"

"Hmm, I don't know...I guess fifty max fifty-five. He can't be drawing Social Security." I laughed, "Wait, why do you ask?"

She giggled a little both from being tickled by my response and from what sounded like slight nervousness. "Well there is someone who is one of my business clients that I think could possibly be a good person for you to meet." Tippy was in banking and specialized in wealth management. "I'm not trying to match make or anything like that, but if it turned into that it could be cool. He is someone you can Google. I was talking to him today, and every time I speak to him, he just reminds me of you."

This was a little awkward, however, intriguing because my sister had never introduced me to a man. We never even really talked about my dating life except that I didn't have one and didn't plan to have one as long as I lived in the DMV. This guy must have made a serious impression because this wasn't at all her style. "Ok. I'm listening. Tell me more." I prefaced before firing off a series of standard questions: "Like, well how old is he? What does he do for a living? What does he look like? What's wrong with him, meaning why is he single?"

She laughed, and I laughed with her. "Girl you are so funny. There is nothing wrong with him. At least I don't think it is. Well let me say as far as I know and can see, there is nothing wrong with him. I don't know exactly how old he is, but I believe he is in his fifties. If I had to guess I'd say around fifty-two. He is an attorney. He is single and has a daughter who is grown and out of college, so no kids and no college tuition payments," she giggled. "Y'all have a lot in common."

"What does he look like?" I asked again.

"I mean I think he is nice looking, but you should look him up online, and see for yourself."

"What about his teeth?" I asked. I knew it was shallow, but bad teeth were a problem for me, and I had no interest in partaking in a 'Build a Beau' project at this point in my life.

Tippy was laughing so hard she was losing her breath as she responded, "His teeth are fine. You are too funny."

"I may be funny, but I'm serious."

"I know with your picky self," she teased.

"Hmm," I thought out loud. On the surface he sounded interesting enough for me to allow my sister to continue.

"Like you, he pledged a fraternity while in college, and is a member of a couple of civic and community focused social clubs, which is something else you all have in common."

I interrupted her to ask, "What is it about him that reminds you of me?"

"Ok, I know you are into fashion, and you know that isn't really my thing but honey!!! Every time I see him, he is dressed to the nines. I'm talking about straight GQ, and you know if I notice it, it is really noticeable because I'm not into fashion that way." We both laughed in agreement, and she continued. "Well, he is always dressed very nice, neat and classy. He wears these really fashionable shades. You know I don't know the name brand or style, so don't even ask, but they look like something you would like. But what tipped it over for me on the fashion was this blazer he had on. It was super nice. I could tell he spent some money for it. Probably had it tailor made, but it's not just the fashion. Every time I talk to him, he reminds me so much of you. Just the things he says, and the words he uses. He is picky like you too."

"What's his name? How so, and how do you know he is picky?" I asked.

"Well he was at my office for a business meeting, and he was looking at the photos around my office and began asking me about Joseph and the kids. You know I love talking about my family, so I was telling him all about the kids and their activities and our family stuff. Well as we were talking his phone rang and it was his daughter calling. After he finished his conversation with her, I asked him about her. He said she is either thirty or thirty-one, not quite sure on that because I wasn't fully paying attention to what he was saying about her, but she is unemployed. He was a little fussy because she was asking him for money, and I told him he sounded like you when Brian asks for money." She and I both burst out laughing because my twenty-nine year old son Brian often made the same type of phone calls. In the midst of our laughter Tippy proceeded with the conversation, "He and I burst out laughing, just like we're laughing now, and then I said, 'I'm sure she asks you because your wife probably doesn't allow it. Children know which parent to hit up for money.' And he said, "Wife!? I don't have a wife. I'm single." I was shocked because I don't handle his personal affairs, and even though there is no wife listed on any of the business documents I just assumed all this time that he was married. So, I said, 'Well the second time is a charm.' To this he said, "I probably won't ever marry again. Besides there aren't any women for me here in Atlanta." I laughed and said, you sound just like my sister. At this point he said, "You have a sister?" I told him I actually have more than one sister, but you remind me of my oldest sister. She lives in Maryland and works in D.C., beautiful, single, and has an adult son, but she is very, very picky. Then he said, "Really? There ain't nothing wrong with that because I'm picky too." Then I said, yeah as a matter of fact let me show you a picture of her, and just so happened you posted that photo of you on Facebook today in the limo headed to your lecture, so I showed him that one. Baby I wish you could have seen those eyes light up!" That made me giggle, and Tippy giggled too. "Gab, after he saw that picture, he started asking me a whole bunch of questions, and you know me. I couldn't answer half of them, but it was so funny. Then he had to leave because his daughter had come to his office to get the money she'd called for. But check him out."

While Tiffany had been talking, I'd parked at the country club and Googled him to find a couple of photos and professional biography. He was handsome in his pictures and well accomplished per his bio. However, for me while that was nice it was like looking at a photo spread and reading an article about George Clooney in *Cosmopolitan* magazine. Once I finished looking and reading, I was indifferent.

We continued our conversation about this mystery man, which was funny but still a little awkward. "Ok. I just pulled him up via Google, and he is not bad looking. His bio is impressive. What questions about me did he ask that you couldn't answer?"

"He wanted to know what your job title was, and you know I can't remember that long title. He was asking where you went to college, what were your degrees in, what sorority and professional social organizations you were a member of and all that kind of stuff. I gave him enough, but he can get the rest from you. If y'all ever talk one day."

"I know you know where I went to school?" I questioned.

"Yes, but I don't know all your majors and minors, all those societies and organizations you're a member of, and I can't remember your job title."

"Tippy!? I'm a Deputy Director. Why can't you remember that?"

"I thought it was longer than that?"

"Well its Deputy Director of EEO, Diversity and Corporate Citizenship, but the main part is Deputy Director. Tippy that is all you have to say when someone asks you what I do," I chuckled.

"Like I said, I can't remember that long title. Besides if y'all ever talk you'll need something to talk about," she joked.

"Oh ok...that's funny," I said, and in what was our typical fashion our topic of conversation transitioned to sharing our evening plans, workout updates and deciding menus of meals I was going to prepare when I was home for my monthly visit the following week.

"Summer sun and summer fun all for a summer bunny."

Three months later while in the car on a sunny Friday heading home from work, my baby sister and I were again on the phone and the topic of conversation was once again, Mr. Dasht D. Spelbender, Esq.

"Hey Tippy!" I answered.

"Hey Girly, hold on one second let me close my car door and get out of the parking garage."

"You're just leaving the office? Is everything ok?" I asked.

She was laughing now. "Yeah, I'm just leaving. This was a long day because it's the first Friday of the month, but I didn't call to talk about work. I had to get out of the garage so he couldn't hear me."

"Who?" I asked.

Giggling she replied, "Your Boo Thang."

I literally burst out laughing. Over the past three months his name had come up in our conversations when she'd either seen him in passing or had business meetings with him. I'd learned his law firm was a tenant in her office tower, affording Tiffany the opportunity to encounter him on a regular basis outside of their quarterly business meetings. Now she'd began jokingly referring to him as my 'Boo Thang.'

"I was coming back in the building from a late lunch meeting with a client when who do I see walking in a little bit ahead of me. So, I called out, 'Hey Mr. Spelbender!' He turned around with a big grin and said, "Hey Tiffany! I haven't seen you in a while. How have you been?" He waited for me to catch-up to him, so we wouldn't be yelling across the parking garage, and when I got close, we exchanged a friendly hug, and both headed into the building. He was a few steps in front of me on the escalator, and I said, 'I've been doing well. It has been a while since I've seen you.' He said, "Yeah it has been a few weeks." I said, 'Yeah, you've been hiding, and it caused you to miss out.' At this point he was at the top of the escalator about to head to his office, but he stopped dead in his tracks and turned around and waited for me to get to the top of the escalator. Once I got to the top he asked, "What do you mean?" I said, 'Well I was going to introduce you to someone, but I hadn't saw you or heard from you, so I said oh well. I guess it doesn't matter anyway because that person is gone now.' He immediately asked, "Was it your sister?" Tippy and I both laughed at that. "I told him, 'As a matter of fact it was, but she's gone back to D.C. now.' Then he said, "Well when is she coming back, and how often does she come home?" I told him, 'Oh she is here at least once a month,' and he said, "Really?" I could tell he was excited. Then I said, 'Yes, I told you that awhile back. We love for her to come home. She comes home and spoils us with her cooking.' He stopped me before I could say another word and said, "She can cook?" 'Yeah!' I said. 'She is an excellent cook, and we love it. We can count on having gourmet meals every day she is in town.'"

"Why is it so shocking that I can cook?" I asked, not really anticipating or wanting an answer.

"Gab women nowadays don't cook, and if they do, they don't cook the way you do. It's really a big deal, and he was clearly impressed."

"I guess," I replied. I wasn't flattered that something as basic as the ability to cook impressed him.

"He said, "Well send me a picture of your sister." As if he didn't remember what you look like." Again, Tippy and I both laughed. "I told him, 'No, I can't do that without her permission. But I tell you what, you send me a picture of you, and I'll send it to her, and ask her if I can send you her picture.' He quickly said, "Ok, ok. That sounds good." So...what picture do you want me to send him?"

"I don't care. Send what you think is pretty, but don't send it until he sends his, and send a face picture and a full body shot. Don't send more than two pictures." I instructed.

"Substance is who you are; show is what you allow me to see."

Early the next morning I received two photos of Mr. Dasht D. Spelbender, Esq. better yet, 'Boo Thang,' and I must admit 'Boo Thang' was definitely easy on the eyes. His smile, Lord have mercy! I was still lying in bed when the text came through, and that smile made me sit straight up. It was clear that he had veneers, and it was money well spent because his smile was simply beautiful. It had the effect on me like an ice cold glass of well water on a hot summer day after an hour of child's play. He was bald, which I'd noted earlier when I'd Googled him. Not particularly attracted to a shaven head, I resounded the bald head was the result of a receding hairline. He appeared to be in great shape, not too small, not too large, toned, actually model like in stature. I'd guess he was about 6' 4", and no more than two hundred and ten pounds. The suits he wore in the two photos were clearly tailor made, so I could definitely see how Tippy had noticed his fashion sense. They were classic cut, adequately conservative and fit him to a tee. In one of the photos he was wearing shades, which I guessed were the shades Tippy had referenced a while back, Ray Ban Aviator Classics. Made sense. "Ok fly guy," I thought to myself. His nails were manicured to perfection. He was definitely attractive.

"She's pretty." This was his response to the photos of me Tiffany had sent him. She'd forwarded me their text thread, and I was mortified! The headshot was a recent picture that I liked. I'm being too modest; I actually loved it, which is why it was my profile picture on Facebook. However, the full body shot was, in my opinion, not a true representation of me. It was too old. It was from President Obama's last Inaugural Ball, which was almost five years ago! I'd gained a few pounds since then, actually thirteen to be exact. I called her immediately. "Hey Tippy."

"Hey Girl! Did you see your 'Boo Thang's' response? "She's pretty," she teased. Tippy was being a real little sister. She was truly tickled.

"Yeah, but Tiffany why did you send him this old picture? I'm not that skinny now."

"Gab that's a good picture. You look the same to me, and he thinks you're pretty, which we already knew. So when are you gonna call him?"

"Ok. I guess. You know we're our own worst critics." We both laughed in agreement.

"Yeah, I know, but Gabriella, you look fabulous."

"Thank you, but I'm not comfortable at this size so I've got to lose this weight. But I won't be calling him. In my world the dog still chases the cat. You can give him my phone number but tell him to call me next weekend because I have a lot going on this week. I won't have a lot of time to be on the phone. I'm determined to get my workouts in this week. After work, gym, and a couple of social obligations all I'll have energy for is a shower and it's off to bed."

"I totally understand you, this *Insanity* is kicking my butt, but I have to have my body right for my vacation in eight weeks."

"Yeah girly, you can't be flabby in bikinis and short shorts," I teased and in our typical fashion we both cracked-up laughing and transitioned to another topic.

At this point it was what it was. If he called fine; if he didn't call fine. Either way, it was no skin off my back. Best believe I wasn't going to be sitting waiting by the phone.

CHAPTER 2
Blink of an Eye

The week had been a taxing one. I'd traveled all week and was glad to be back at home for the weekend. As much as I would have loved to lounge around the house reading and catching up on my sleep, I couldn't because my weekend was filled with philanthropic and social commitments.

It was Saturday morning, and I was headed to an executive board meeting for one of the non-profit organizations I supported. As usual I was rushing because it was an hour drive without traffic, but despite it being 7:30am on the weekend I-295 was stalled. According to the navigation system there was an accident two miles ahead. "People in the D.C., Maryland, Virginia area really cannot drive," I thought to myself. I was guaranteed to see at least two accidents every time I left the house. I couldn't be late today, so I said a silent prayer that whomever was in the accident was not injured and that the traffic would ease up and at least start moving. My thoughts were interrupted by the phone. It was Tiffany calling.

"Hey Girl! What are you doing?"

"Hey Girly!" I replied. "As usual, I'm driving. Headed to my executive board meeting but stuck in traffic. What are you getting into today? I'm sure you have lots of kid birthday parties to attend."

She laughed, "You know it. We have three birthday parties today. One at 12pm, another at 2pm, and the last one at 5pm. You know my kids love to party, especially Benjamin. I don't mind though. I'm glad because these kids are living the life and will have great childhood memories when they're all grown up. Just partying all the time."

We both chuckled, and I agreed with her sentiment. "I know and that's awesome. We didn't have parties like that when we were younger. Brian didn't care too much for birthday parties when he was a kid. Shucks, by the time he was eight, he was over it. That's probably why he loves to party so much now," I half joked about my adult son. "Besides, you only get to be a kid once, and it should be a fun time."

"Yep," she said and continued, "I love that they have friends and positive, fun things to do. Keeps me busy, but I love it. But I was calling because I meant to call you last night, but by the time we got in and I got the kids all settled it was too late to call. I wanted to tell you I spoke to your 'Boo Thang' and I gave him your number. He said he was going to call you this weekend. So I wanted to give you a heads up."

I smiled, "Well I hope he doesn't call today before noon because I'm going to be busy. What did he say when you gave him my number?"

"It was a quick conversation. It was early Wednesday when I was on my way to work, like around 7:45am. I said, 'Good morning Mr. Speldbender,' and he told me to stop calling him Mr. Speldbender and call him Dasht. I said, 'My mother taught me to respect my elders, but ok, good morning Dasht.' He said, "You need to stop all that. I am not your elder." I didn't want to burst his bubble and tell him yes the hell he is my elder." She laughed, and it made me chuckle. "I told him, 'I meant to call you earlier in the week. I've just been so busy, but I wanted to let you know my sister received your pictures. She said you're handsome,' and Gab at this point I could tell he was smiling hard because he said, "Oh, really?", and I could hear his grin through the phone. So I kept talking, 'Yes, she said you're handsome, and she said I could give you her phone number. She asked that you not call until the weekend because she is super busy and traveling all week. Let me know when you're ready to write the number down.' Then I gave him your number, and he said he would give you a call this weekend."

"Ok. I will let you know if he calls. I just arrived at my destination. I'll chat with you later."

Saturday came and went with no call from 'Boo Thang.'

Sunday was another early, event filled day for me. My sorority was hosting its annual, signature spring fashion show and scholarship fundraiser, which was one of the premier affairs in a neighboring county. I looked forward to this event because it gave me an opportunity to catch up with my sorority sisters. This year it was both fun and work because I needed to scout out potential sponsors for the fundraiser I was planning and chairing in October for another social organization I was a member of. After the fashion show, I hung out and had an early dinner with some of my sorority sisters before driving the forty-nine miles back to my side of town.

I wanted to just relax when I got home, but my neighbor was hosting a jewelry party. I typically don't socialize with the neighbors, but Mrs. Emily had lost her daughter to cancer in February. I'd only encountered her daughter twice last September and would have never known she was even sick, let alone dying. Rachel was a tall, slender, goddess who appeared to be the picture of perfect health and fabulous life. Apparently, she'd had a bout with cancer a couple of years prior, which is what had prompted her mother to move in with her. Now that she was deceased her mother still lived in the house. Mrs. Emily would stop me from time to time when she saw me at the mailbox or pulling into the garage to chat because she said I reminded her of her daughter. Rachel and I were the same age, forty-six. I always felt sad now when I saw Mrs. Emily. I could only imagine how hard it was for her to have lost her daughter at such a young age. It was imperative I at least stop over, socialize briefly and make an obligatory purchase.

The jewelry was amazing and of course expensive. I'm not really a jewelry person, but I had to control my impulse to purchase several pieces. I was one to buy things and either give them away or never wear them. I narrowed my purchase down to two items, which was more than I'd planned or needed to buy. To my surprise the party actually turned out to be fun, and I really enjoyed myself. It was good spending some time with Mrs. Emily, but I'd been out and about all day and needed to go home and relax prior to kicking off another hectic work week.

I came home to find I'd missed a call and had a message from 'Boo Thang'. I immediately listened to the voicemail. His voice was deep but not overtly sultry. He had a strong, southern drawl that flowed like warm maple syrup and made him sound friendly. I could hear his smile through the phone. I decided to get out of my clothes and get comfortable before calling him back. Once I changed into some sweats and got situated, I dialed him up. What I'd anticipated would be a fifteen or twenty minute routine get to know you on the surface conversation actually ended up being almost two hours, one hour and fifty-seven minutes to be exact, of stimulating discussion about current social issues, politics, family and life in general. The time had literally flown by in the blink of an eye. He had been so easy and fun to talk to. He was surprisingly really funny. After we hung up, I sat looking out the window reflecting on the conversation, and I smiled. I smiled from the inside out.

We had so much in common it was uncanny, but oddly refreshing because it made me believe, at least initially, we were possibly compatible, he would be able to understand me, and we could be friends. He had been married and divorced. So had I. He had one adult child. So did I. He was active in the community and supported several non-profit initiatives. It was the same for me. He enjoyed and relished the opportunity to be home relaxing. Me too. I enjoyed classical music and the opera. He enjoyed them as well. I wanted to learn to golf. He did also. He enjoyed playing chess. I wanted to learn. We both loved dogs. This was bananas in a good way. He was a jokester, who apparently tickled himself, and his laugh was infectious. I loved to laugh and could be quite silly too. He cursed a lot; which I could tell he was trying to curtail because he quickly realized cursing was not my preferred vocabulary. It seemed he could clean it up when in certain settings, but I'd quickly concluded that when he wasn't in the professional arena, he could get a little wild. In spite of the profanity, he was very articulate and obviously well educated. On the other hand, he exuded a comfort and ease that conveyed a down-to-earth humility that was admirable. At this point I concluded he was potentially the type I could take to the White House or a college tailgate and we would be fine in either setting. At least that's what I was hoping.

"Choosing to see what you want won't necessarily protect you from what you really see."

I had to admit this was a first for me. It typically took several conversations for me to be this intrigued, but so far, he was different from anyone I'd ever met before. The next day I stepped out of my comfort zone and called him. He seemed genuinely happy to speak to me and most appreciative of my call. He told me he had driven to Savannah for a business meeting, which was about four hours away. I found it odd that he'd chosen to drive so I'd asked why. He said it was because he'd waited too late to have his assistant book the flight, and the timing made it cost ineffective. This didn't make much sense to me because it was a business expense, but I didn't spend any time pondering it.

I had begun the conversation with the standard, "Hello, how are you?" He told me his day had "been a little rocky" but it was getting better especially since he was talking to me. He was flirting already. I really didn't know how to feel about that, so I chose to not respond or give substantial thought to it. He told me his air conditioning had stopped working midway into his four hour drive.

"You won't believe this! My damn air conditioning conked out on me about half way through the drive down here. I was sweating like a pig, and I was pissed because I just got my car serviced last week. So, I called Mercedes back home and got knee deep in their asses. I told them they had to fix this shit and fix it quick."

"Oh my," was all I could manage to say. I wasn't sure if he heard me, but he continued telling me about his day.

"They made arrangements for me to drop my car off at the dealership here in Savannah, and they tried to offer me a ride to my hotel in a damn shuttle. That bear I had on me was growing."

"Bear?" I thought to myself but didn't interrupt him to clarify if I'd heard him correctly or clarify what he meant.

"I told them they were going to give me a damn car to drive because this was their fault. The lady at the customer service counter said, "Ok Mr. Spelbender, let me see what we can do." I told her, 'No don't see what you can do. You do something, and you do it quick.' So she went to the back and talked to somebody. When she came back, she told me they had a car for me to drive. Now you won't believe this because I couldn't believe it. She had the nerve to walk me over to a damn Kia. I almost lost my package. I'm not a doggone kid. That's a damn car you give a kid in high school or college to drive. There was no way in hell I was driving that damn Kia. I told her, 'I'm not driving that. You all are going to have to do better than this. This is an insult.' By now she was looking all stupid and shit and tried to tell me that was all they had. I told her she could either find me something else or give me one of those Mercedes they had sitting on the lot for sale. So she went back to wherever she had gone earlier and came back and offered me a Chevy Impala. I wasn't happy about this either, but I was hot, sweaty, had a strong bear on my back and needed a cocktail. So I just took the damn Impala. Now I must say, that bad boy has some power to it. It's not at all my class of car, but it can get up. I hurried and got to the hotel because I don't want anyone I know to see me driving a damn Impala. My buddies would laugh my ass out of the state."

"Wow that's a lot. Will your car be ready tomorrow?" I asked.

"Yeah, they said it will be ready tomorrow. It cost me $250, which I don't think I should have had to pay but whatever, let me finish telling you."

"Oh. My goodness, there's more?" I thought to myself as he continued to talk.

"I made it to the hotel and checked in, headed to my room ready to get a shower and relax. I go into the room, and the damn room hadn't been cleaned. I called the front desk and told them to get a manager up here now. The manager came up and apologized profusely. He called down and had them bring up a key card to another room and had the bellman come up to help me move to the other room. You won't believe this shit, hell if it hadn't happened to me, I wouldn't believe it my damn self. I get in the other room and it wasn't clean either. There was still trash in the bathroom and dirty towels on the floor. At that point I did lose my package a little bit. I said, 'What the fuck!? You've got to be kidding me.' I called the manager's ass back up to the room. He was so embarrassed. I told him I wasn't moving again, so he had the cleaning staff come up and clean the bathroom and bring me some clean towels. I made them change the bed linens and vacuum too because I didn't trust that either. The manager kept apologizing, and he comped all my meals for the rest of my stay. I feel better now that I've had a shower, and I'm relaxing with my cocktail. So that was my day. I'm going to order me a good meal after I finish talking to you and get prepared for tomorrow. How are you? How was your day?"

I was honestly almost speechless. We had been on the phone for at least fifteen minutes, and he'd shared a lot of information while potentially unintentionally revealing some not so flattering characteristics about himself. It was clear he was a little high maintenance and had a bit of a temper. I would definitely have to process this later, I thought to myself. "My day was fine, not nearly as eventful as yours," I answered.

CHAPTER 3
Cards on the Table

After that first phone conversation, Dasht and I talked every day, and we never spoke for less than an hour and a half. Sometimes we'd talk multiple times a day, and our conversations went well beyond the surface. So being one not to waste time, on our fifth conversation I decided to begin laying my cards on the table.

"Diamonds may be a girl's best friend, but sometimes you have to give up a few diamonds to get a handful of hearts."

"What is it that you're hoping to accomplish by talking to me?" I asked.

"Well, I want to get to know you?" he said rather matter of fact.

"Why?" I asked just as matter of fact.

"Well, I really want some companionship. I want to have someone in my life, a lady. Someone who is my lady. You know?"

"Hmm. Ok. I can understand that. Why? Do you not like being single?"

"I mean, I enjoy being single, but it gets old. I'm at a point in my life where I want someone to spend time with, travel. You know, someone I can do things and enjoy life with."

"I totally understand that. I have been single for quite some time, and I actually enjoy it, but I must admit that there are times when I miss being in a relationship. I am most conscious of my relationship status when I'm at black tie events, and I'm the only single woman at the table. All dressed up but alone because in those types of settings it's mostly couples. Sadly, I can't take a date because it's typically a situation that intertwines with my professional sector, and I don't want to have a different date every year because women get labeled negatively for things like that."

"I understand your position. A lot of times I don't go to big shin digs like that for that very same reason. There is this big holiday ball though that I have to attend every year for my firm, and I've never taken a date. They take pictures and shit too, and I don't want to have a bunch of different women in the pictures with me. Besides taking a woman to something like that can give her the wrong idea?"

"How so," I asked.

"You know, have her thinking it's more than it is, like she is your girlfriend or about to be your wife or something."

"Oh yeah, I get it. I was dating someone four years ago who had just assumed he would accompany me to an annual work gala, and his feelings were hurt when I told him he wasn't going. I actually had to explain to him that I couldn't traipse around with him in my professional arena because we were not engaged, nor did I see us together long term. Needless to say, that didn't go over well, and I ended the relationship shortly after that."

"Damn! Ok, I see you're a heartbreaker, just crushing men," he said both jokingly and seriously.

"I wouldn't say that," I said. "I try not to hurt people because I don't like to be hurt, which is why I actually have been by myself and celibate for the last two years. So, if you're looking for a sex buddy, booty-call, friends with benefits, or whatever else people call casual sex these days, I'm not your girl."

"Ok, ok. I hear you," he said clearly processing what I'd just said. "Well I'm not celibate. What's with that, are you waiting for marriage?"

"No, not necessarily. I know I'm marriage material, but marriage isn't necessarily my goal. I don't do random dating. I'm not designed for it. I'm a monogamous relationship person so I'm all for marriage, but I never want to experience another divorce. At this point my celibacy is not about marriage per say. What I will say is that I found myself in a situation where I was in a relationship with someone who wanted to marry me, but I didn't see him as marriage material. He was dating me with marriage as the end goal, but I wasn't dating him with the goal of marrying. No matter how unintentional, I hurt someone, and that wasn't fair to him. For that reason, I decided I needed to reevaluate my dating and relationship goals before dating again if for no other reason than to avoid creating bad karma. For the last two years, I've been taking time to figure out what I want for me. Not what the world says I should have or want, but just what does Gabriella want for Gabriella. I took sex out of the equation for a myriad of reasons. "Like," he asked?

First and foremost, I'm a Christian, not a Bible-thumper, but I am a Christian and I try to live right. I believe in and really want to go to heaven, so I can't just gallivant sexually. Secondly, I don't want to rack-up a large number of sexual partners. Call me old-fashioned, but I just don't. I can still count them on one hand, which from what I've learned as a single woman is definitely something to be proud of for a woman of my age in today's society. However, according to my Grandmother any number more than one is still too many, unless the previous one died. Besides when you're sexually involved with someone it clouds and changes things. I also don't want to catch an STD, and let's face it, it's dangerous out in this world these days. So many men, and women too, on the down low and the low down, and condoms don't prevent every STD. That's why I decided it was just best for me to practice celibacy until I figure out what, and who I want."

"Ok, I get it. I'm not celibate, but I get it. So how do the men you're dating handle this, this celibacy?" He asked rather slyly.

I'd told him in our very first conversation that I was single by every definition of the word, but since he was asking again, I made sure I answered and answered thoroughly so there was no confusion about my relationship or dating status. "I'm not dating anyone. I told you that already. I'm 100% single in the truest definition of the word. I'm not talking to or texting any man on the phone. I don't go on dates. I've never invited or had a man in my home where I currently live. I don't have men in my space whatsoever. I am truly single and celibate."

"Damn, ok. I hear you," he paused. "Well I'm actually single too. I'm not committed to anyone."

I dissected his last statement in my head. "Hmm so what you're saying is you have women you potentially date and occasionally have sex with without commitment." Part of me wanted to say this to him, but another part of me didn't want him to regard me as rude or condescending. After all, he was being open and honest, I reasoned to myself and decided to keep my interpretation of his statement and thoughts about it to myself. Instead I said, "I believe it's best to just be honest with people. Too many people dupe people into relationships with lies and presenting their representative as opposed to their true self. I don't want to meet another representative. I hate for people to waste my time playing games and misrepresenting themselves. What you see is what you get with me. This is me, take it or leave it. If a person can't accept me for me, I don't want them around me."

"You're really hardnosed, but I get it. I'm not trying to get duped either."

"I'm not necessarily hardnosed, but this is me. I'm quite matter of fact. I say what I mean, and I mean what I say. I am an honest person. I'm not saying I've never lied or that I don't lie. What I am saying is that I don't make it a habit of lying to people because I don't like being lied to, but being honest with you now, I can't and won't say that's always been the case in my past relationships."

"Really?"

"Yeah," I said sincerely. "I wouldn't flat out lie, but I have lied via omission or allowed someone to believe a conclusion they'd come to on their own about me that I felt was advantageous to me, but I knew it wasn't true."

"Like?" he interrupted.

"Like I grew-up in a rich family. Only to have it come back and bite me in the butt later."

"Hmph. I see."

"Like I said, that only comes back to bite you in the butt later or at least that's been my experience. So I don't do that now. My position is this is me. Take it or leave it, but I'm not lying out of fear of rejection. If a person can't accept me for me then he isn't the one for me. Simple as that."

"I've had people assume things about me too. You don't have to worry about that with me. I've never had a problem with lying. I'm a straight talker. I will always talk straight with you, and I want you to talk straight with me. So let's make straight talk our deal ok? Deal?"

"Deal. Straight talk it is," I replied. "The reality is no one tells everything because that's just the way it is, and sometimes people actually don't remember or don't think certain things are important anymore. On the flip side of that, there is also some stuff, irrelevant stuff, you just don't want to know."

"True, true, true. I don't ever want to hear details about your sexual past with another man," he interrupted.

I thought to myself, "Dang! How did we get to sexual past?" I thought to myself. Rather than respond with my first thought I said, "Exactly, and same here unless it's something that affects you in the present because I believe it is important to tell people about the things that will have an impact on them being in a relationship with you. So even though that is one of those taboo topics, if it has an impact on the present and future, I believe it should be discussed. I will tell you as much information upfront as I believe you really need to know to allow you to really know me, but if it's something you want to know just ask. I promise I'll answer honestly because not to be harsh, but if the truth about me runs you away, then run. Please run, so I can meet the man God has for me."

"Like I said, heart breaker, crushing the fellas and running them off," he said jokingly, but I knew there was some seriousness to his gist.

"I guess. Call it what you will. I just don't play games. I never have. I'm not good at it, and it's a waste of time. I'm too old for games and BS, and I don't like for people to waste my time."

"I don't like to waste time either," he said.

"Good. So, I ask that you don't waste my time or bring any foolishness to my life, and I promise I won't bring any foolishness to your life or waste your time."

"Ok. That's fair," he paused for what sounded like him taking a drink of something. "You know I'm at a place in my life where I just don't want any strife or drama. I want to be with someone and have it be easy. You know?"

"I'm all about having ease and peace. My life is quite peaceful. There is absolutely no foolishness. I love walking into my home and how quiet and calm it is. That's one of the pros of being single."

"Tell me about it. Hell, sometimes I wonder if I've been single too long. I've been by myself for almost twelve years," he paused again, and this time I could tell he was drinking something. "I enjoy the bachelor life. It's cool, but I want a woman in my life. I'm a hardnosed type of guy, but I'm romantic too."

"I've been single for a long time too, actually eight, almost nine years now, and I have a good, no I have a great life. I have a wonderful relationship with my family, which is why I fly home once a month. I have a blessed and awesome career. I have fabulous friends that are like family. I am genuinely happy with my life. There is absolutely no foolishness here, and I don't want any."

He took another long sip of whatever he was drinking before responding. "I understand your position. I don't like a lot of foolishness either and my life is peaceful too."

"My Grandmother always said, "It's ok to trust people, but count your own money and always cut the cards."

Later in that first week, Thursday to be exact, we dove even deeper into conversations of revelation.

Dasht had called me while I was in the gym requiring us to postpone the conversation. Once I got showered and settled in, I called him.

"Hey Gabby! I'm sorry, it is ok for me to call you Gabby?"

I laughed, "Hello Dasht. Yes, you can call me Gabby."

"Yeah, Gabby is going to be what I call you. Wait, does anyone else call you that?"

"No. No one else calls me that. My family members call me Gab or Gabriella."

"Ok. Good. Gabby is going to be my name for you."

"Ok. How was your day?"

"My day was good, but I don't want to talk about that. I want to talk about you." He paused, "You know I'm really enjoying talking to you."

"I'm enjoying talking to you as well. What are you doing?"

"I'm sitting here having me a cocktail, looking at some work and watching the news. Wait let me say that's what I was doing. Now I'm having a cocktail and talking to you."

"What do you drink?"

"Single malt scotch is all I drink. What do you drink?"

"I'm a big coffee drinker. I love coffee. If you want to be my friend buy me a cup of coffee and a book." I laughed.

He chuckled as he took a swig of his drink, "I'm not a coffee drinker. What else do you drink?"

"I'm not a drinker. I will have a glass of wine or champagne from time to time, but it's typically a cup of coffee in the morning and water for the rest of the day."

"Hmm. Why? Have you always been that way?"

"Yes. I've never been a drinker. I tried to drink when I was younger and ended up drunk and sick both times, which let me know it wasn't for me."

"Do you smoke?"

"Heck no. You don't smoke do you?"

He laughed, and it sounded like he was putting ice in a glass. "No, I don't smoke. I used to, but I quit about four years ago."

"Whew, thank God because that would have been a deal breaker for me."

"Really?"

"Yes."

"Damn! You're hardnosed as hell. Why?"

"I hate cigarette smoke. My parents used to smoke. Well my Dad still does. My Mom has quit, but they used to smoke in the house. My Mom was a rude smoker. She would blow smoke straight in your face, and cigarette smoke stinks. I never picked-up the habit. I won't even sit next to or dance with a person who smokes."

"Damn. So, do you smoke anything else?"

"Huh, what do you mean?"

"You know, marijuana."

"Absolutely not!"

"Never?"

"I have never smoked marijuana or partook in any illegal drugs," I said both matter of fact and with a tone that conveyed I was somewhat annoyed at the potential insult.

"Well, I can't say that I've never smoked marijuana. I don't smoke it now."

"When you were in college?"

"Hell yeah. When I was in undergrad and law school. We used to get stoned, especially at the frat house."

I could tell he was smiling at the memory of getting high in college; however, this didn't bring a smile to my face. "Hmm. Well a lot of people experiment while in college. I never did. I always thought about that commercial with the egg in the skillet, *"This is drugs. This is your brain on drugs."* So that was enough for me to say no to drugs."

"Well I didn't say no," he attempted to make a joke of it.

I wasn't at all amused. "I know a lot of people do smoke marijuana, but that is a no-no for me. I don't want to be around anyone doing that, and I won't date a man who does that," I said in a serious tone. "Have you ever used or experimented with other drugs?"

"Hell no. Just marijuana. Everybody smoked pot and cigarettes back in the day. That's just what we did."

"Hmm. Ok."

"So, what are your other deal breakers?" He seemed to be somewhat anxious.

"Cheating and hitting," I said without hesitation.

"I would never hit a woman. Hell, if I've got to hit you, then I don't need to be with you. Now I'm not a Boy Scout. Straight talk I've been with a lot of women. I mean a whole lot of women, but I'm a reformed bad boy now."

I dared not clarify nor quantify what a lot was. "Reformed bad boy huh?" I thought out loud.

"Yeah, I mean I have done some things in my past," he said rather defensively. "But I've long cut all that out."

"What prompted the change?"

"Nothing prompted me. When I turned forty-five, I just stopped partying and skirt chasing. I guess it just got old."

"Hmm. Did your skirt chasing contribute to your divorce?"

He took a long sip of his cocktail before responding. "Hmm. It probably did. I mean it wasn't a situation where I got caught cheating or anything like that. For the most part, I was faithful. I wanted it to work...," his voice trailed off as if he'd gotten lost in thought. He took a sip of his cocktail before speaking again. "Straight talk I did step out of my marriage towards the end. She stepped out too. We both stepped out, but I never got caught."

"Hmm. You don't think she knew you cheated?"

"Well, I wouldn't call it cheating. I mean we were estranged during the times I stepped out. I don't think she ever thought I had stepped out. I took care of home..." He paused and then abruptly added, "But all of that is in the past. I'm not like that anymore."

"Wait did you have more than one affair? Estranged? Meaning you all were separated?"

"No. I didn't say I had an affair. I said I stepped out. We were just doing our own thing. I don't want to talk about the past anymore. Have you been watching the news?"

"Ok, so you literally just changed the subject. It's ok I guess, but I wouldn't be me if I didn't point out that you just abruptly changed the subject because you no longer wanted to talk about what we were talking about."

He laughed a deep, throaty laugh that wasn't at all infectious. It was a different laugh from the previous laughter that was starting to become familiar. Then he took a sip of his cocktail before he responded. "Hmph. Yeah, so did you see all the hoopla over this Mueller investigation? It's getting really funky."

It was clear he'd taken a hard stance and was not going to talk about this topic anymore today.

"If you're going to build something in the air it is always better to build castles than houses of cards." - Georg C. Lichtenberg

For the first time in a long time I had a weekend that was free of travel or social commitments. I was elated to be at home because there was so much spring, now summer, cleaning I needed to get done. I'd started my day with a three mile walk through the neighborhood and was now organizing items in the basement when the phone rang, and his name came across the caller ID.

"Good morning Dasht."

"Hey Gabby! What are you up to?"

"I'm up and at it, being productive getting some things done around this house."

"Oh yeah?"

"Yeah. I'm cleaning out the basement and packing up stuff so I can have contractors come through in a couple of weeks."

"Contractors?"

"Yes. I'm remodeling."

"Oh yeah? Me too. I've been here in this house for four years, and I've been remodeling since I moved in."

"Oh wow. I've been here two years and it has been the same. At first, I was rushing to get it all done, but everything is so expensive here. So rather than stress myself out and rush to get it all done I'm taking my time. This also enables me to get exactly what I want."

"What are you having done?"

"Well it's all cosmetic work, but I'm basically redoing the entire house. Every doorknob, door hinge, light fixture, the entire house. I'm moving things now to have hardwood flooring installed."

"Oh, that sounds nice."

"So how are you today?" I asked.

"I'm good. I was just sitting here doing some work and you came across my mind."

I giggled a little, "Oh really?"

"Yeah. Why are you laughing at me? I think about you a lot."

"I'm not laughing at you. I'm smiling out loud."

"Smiling out loud huh?"

"Yes. So, you've been thinking about me. What exactly have you been thinking?"

"Well I enjoy talking to you. I look forward to talking to you, and I don't typically spend a lot of time just talking on the phone."

"Me neither."

"But it's something about you. I just really enjoy talking to you. There is an ease to it. You're easy and fun to talk to. I like looking at your pictures too. Something about your eyes. They tell a story, and you have some gorgeous legs. You're a beautiful woman."

"Aww. Thank you. Yeah, I can also be quite silly at times. Most people are surprised by my goofiness, but it's not something for everyone to know about me. I only allow people to see the parts of me that I want to be seen. Everyone doesn't deserve to know me."

He flirtatiously asked, "Do I deserve to know you?"

"Well you're getting to know me, but how much of me you get to know remains to be seen."

"I can tell you're quick to dismiss guys."

"Hmm, perhaps."

"Why is that?"

"Like I told you before, I don't like playing games or wasting time with foolishness. I actually hate dating. It's not like it was before I got married. People don't court or put forth effort. Just want to jump into bed. I'm not judging anyone. It's just not for me."

"I'm not into playing games either."

"Well since you say I run guys off, let me ask you the million dollar question that typically sends them packing."

Cautiously he said, "O...K...,"

"What value can you add to my life?" I asked without hesitation or reservation.

"Oh, that's easy. I can bring love, companionship, loyalty, commitment, faithfulness, stability and respect. I really want true love. I've been in a loveless marriage, and I don't want that again. I'm manly and all that, but I want romance too. I want to be in love with one woman and have her be in love with me. That's what I'm looking for. I've lived the playboy, bachelor lifestyle and that is old. I believe I'm the kind of guy you've been looking for. Bottom line is you can't run me away."

I was surprised, and I could tell he was smiling as if he'd hit a home run. In all honesty he'd definitely scored. Dasht hadn't hesitated to answer nor struggled to find the words to say the entire time. Even though it didn't seem he was in need of my confirmation that he'd knocked it out the park, I refused to let him know he had. Instead I asked, "Who said I was looking for someone? I'm open to a relationship, but I'm perfectly happy being single."

"No one wants to be alone," he countered.

"Maybe but I believe a person needs to first enjoy being alone before they can enjoy being with someone else. After all, if you don't like you how can you expect someone else to like you?"

"You make a good point. I guess I can't argue with that. As always, I enjoy talking to you, but I need to get back to this work. Want to talk again later?"

"Sure. I need to finish up in this basement too. I'm going to dinner with some of my girlfriends this evening, but we can talk prior to?"

"Ok. Talk to you later."

In this short period, it had become obvious to me Dasht was accustomed to having his way with women and was definitely putting forth more effort than he was accustomed to. In spite of that it was clear he'd decided I wasn't going run him away, which I found intriguing and entertaining. At this point in the getting to know you phase I'd typically been able to eliminate guys by requiring them to court me and asking the "value to my life" question, but he didn't seem to be bothered or deterred by that. Even though it didn't seem to be his norm, he didn't seem to mind putting forth the effort to court me, but only time would tell how willing he really was.

Later that evening while heading to dinner with my friends in Silver Spring, which was a little more than thirty miles away, I decided to give Dasht a call. After all, he'd earned a little effort on my part with that out of the park answer to my question earlier.

"Hey Gabby!"

"Good evening Dasht. How are you?"

"I'm great. How are you?"

I was a little surprised he'd asked because he habitually told me all about his day before asking me how I was. "I'm well," I answered.

"You're so proper. Are you really always this way?"

"I don't know if I'm proper, but this is me. So yes, I am always this way."

He laughed, and it seemed as if he was laughing at me, before saying, "Ok I hear you."

"Is that funny?"

"Not really. What are you doing?"

By now I'd noticed Dasht had a habit of abruptly changing the subject when he was uncomfortable. "I'm driving, heading to dinner with some of my girlfriends."

"Oh. Ok." He seemed to be at a loss for words, then I heard the ice hitting the glass, which let me know he was making a drink.

"How was your day?"

"My day was good. I got a lot of work done. Now I'm about to order me some dinner and watch a little *Lifetime*."

"You work a lot," I said pragmatically. "What do you do when you're not working besides watch *Lifetime*?" I was a little shocked that he watched *Lifetime*. Not a big television buff myself but I recall most of the shows on *Lifetime* were about relationships gone crazy on steroids.

"Yeah I'm a lawyer so it is what it is. When I'm not working, I'm typically at home watching television. I love my tube. I don't go out too much. I typically just keep to myself."

"What about your social organizations? Do you attend those events?"

"I try to go to meetings, and I do attempt to attend the key events."

"So work is your primary activity?"

"Yep!" he replied rather ecstatically while taking a sip of his cocktail.

"I totally understand working and working hard, but it's important to have balance. I learned that the hard way."

"Oh yeah? How so?"

"Well, this is embarrassing, but a little over three years ago I had a two week hospital stay because I was working too much.

"Really? What happened?"

"I had a very demanding job with an even more demanding supervisor, and I made it even harder by being available 24/7. The more I gave, the more was required. I was working on average twelve to thirteen hours a day. I was there two hours before her day began and left two to three hours after her day ended. I started feeling really bad, but instead of taking a break, I kept on pushing. I could typically rejuvenate enough to push through the next week over the weekend. Well this time I didn't make it to the weekend." I stopped to catch my breath before continuing. "I'd stayed in the office until midnight the night prior and arrived home around 1:30am only to have to get back up at 5am to be out the door by 5:45am to beat the traffic. At the time I lived fifty-two miles from work. When I got out of bed that morning I couldn't stand up. I took a step and hit the floor."

"Damn," he interrupted.

"Yeah. Needless to say, it scared the crap out of me. Rather than call in sick and go to the hospital, I muscled up the strength to shower and get dressed. Mind you I couldn't stand-up straight. I went in to the office, but my body wouldn't let me make it through the day, so I left and came home and got into bed. I called in sick the next day, which was a Thursday. It was the first time I'd called in sick or taken a day off in three years and my supervisor was angry."

"Angry? Wow, that's awful." I could hear ice hitting a glass signaling him making a drink.

"She was pissed. Thank God I was too sick to care. The next day I called in sick again. That Saturday a friend of mine from Texas called to check on me, and I was so weak I could barely speak. She was going to call 911 and have them send an ambulance, but I pleaded with her not to do that. She said the only way she wouldn't was if I went to the hospital. I didn't want to go to the hospital, so I went to Patient First instead."

"Someone had to threaten you for you to go to the doctor?"

"I didn't want to go."

"Why is that?"

"I don't like to go to the doctor, and I thought I'd be fine."

"Hmm. Well I'm not like that. I go to the doctor, but finish telling me what happened."

"It was the middle of July and it was hot, but I was freezing to the point I had on sweats, a jacket and a hat. On the way there, I realized I hadn't eaten a real meal in four days, so I stopped at McDonalds and got a shake. When I was at Patient First, they drew blood and the shake had caused my blood sugar to spike, but other than that my blood work was fine. The doctor gave me fluids because I had a temperature and advised me to go to the emergency room if I didn't feel better. What he didn't tell me was he'd called my best friend whom I'd listed as my emergency contact. By the time I got home, she was there waiting to take me to the emergency room. Once we entered the emergency room, they immediately took me to the back. My body was shutting down, and they couldn't figure out why. The next day after all my test results came back the doctor came in and told me the only thing that was wrong with me was dehydration and stress, and stress was going to kill me. Sadly, I was on my work phone answering e-mails when he came into the room. He took both my work and personal devices and kept me in the hospital for two weeks forcing me to rest and eat properly. I took an additional week off after I was released and quit that job a month later. Now I focus on having balance between work, leisure and rest."

"Damn. All of that was from stress?"

"Yes. Stress really can kill you. The sad part is we're all dispensable. God forbid you get hit by a bus. Your coworkers will be sad for a day or two but trust me two weeks later it will be business as usual. That's just reality, harsh but reality."

"I don't know if they'll forget about you that soon," he said in a way that conveyed he was both thinking about this and bothered at the thought of him being forgotten in such a short period of time.

"Well the two weeks I spent in the hospital were a reality check for me. Life is too short to not enjoy it, and what's the point in working if you never enjoy some of the fruits of your labor?"

"That's a good point."

"That's why it's important to have balance."

In a tone that expressed both intrigue and sarcasm he asked, "So how do you balance yourself Ms. Gabby?"

"I am conscious of how I spend my time. I like structure anyway, so that helps with managing my time. I'm not saying I don't ever just pass the time, but when I do it's intentional. I make sure I have time for spiritual and physical fitness. It's a must that I get eight hours of sleep. I still work long days, typically nine to ten hours a day, but I don't just work until I'm dog tired. I work when I need to. I prioritize so I can have balance. A key part of that has also been mastering the art of saying no and being ok with just being."

"Are you good at saying no?"

He was flirting again. "No. I'm great at it." I replied flirting back a little with a giggle.

"Hmph. Ok Ms. Gabby. Are you going to help me get balanced?"

I laughed, "I don't know. I guess I could try."

"I would like for you to try to help me be balanced. I need balance in my life." There was a childlike melancholy and sincerity to his tone that betrayed his typically suave character.

"I believe the best way to begin is to set yearly goals. Not New Year's resolutions, but goals. I try to do five things each year to make myself a better, happier more balanced person."

"Like?"

"Well I love to read, so I try to read something spiritual, something fun and something catered towards my professional development all throughout the year. I don't have as much time to read as I would like, but I try to read at least ten books a year. I try to attend a minimum of two shows and two concerts, and I try to learn something new each year. This year I'm supposed to learn to golf, but I'm not sure if that's going to happen. Next year my goal is to start getting more stamps in my passport. I want to travel out of the country twice a year."

"Ok, ok," he said while sipping his drink. "I like that. I read a lot, but I need to read more stuff that isn't work related. I've been trying to become more spiritual. I watch a spiritual broadcast every morning before I read the newspaper. That's how I start my day, and that helps keep that bear off of me throughout the day."

I laughed, "You and that bear." By now I'd learned that "bear" his personal colloquialism for anger or bad attitude was something he experienced often.

He was laughing in his hearty, infectious way, "Yeah! That's just one of my sayings, but I can get a bear on me and sometimes it's hard to get off. But back to what I was saying before you made me start cutting up. I'm trying to be serious." He was borderline giggling at this point. "I should learn to play golf because a lot of business happens on the golf course. I've gone to lots of shows in my day, but I love listening to live music and going to the opera. I need to travel more too. So maybe we should get some stamps in our passports together."

I had to give it to him, he didn't miss an opportunity to flirt. "Maybe," I responded with a slight smile on my face.

"Hey earlier you said you wanted to learn to play chess."

"Yes. I really do. I've tried to teach myself on the computer, but it hasn't worked out so well."

"Word is you're a pretty good cook?"

"Huh? That was random, but yes I can cook."

"I have a proposal for you."

"A proposal?"

"I want us to make a deal. Ok?" He sipped his drink before he continued. "I'll teach you how to play chess, and you make me some collard greens. Deal?"

I was stunned. Even though we were both Southerners and collard greens were a staple in Southern cuisine, I would have never imagined him to be a collard greens type of guy. "You like collard greens?"

"Yes, I love collard green. They're my favorite."

"That's easy. It's a deal."

"Cool. We have a deal."

"There is a myth that a spade card is a dark or death card, but in the game of life you can be dealt a handful of spades and still win. It's all in how you deal with the cards you're dealt."

It was late Sunday evening and as was quickly becoming my norm, I was winding down my day on the phone chatting with Dasht. I enjoyed talking to him, but I remained very guarded. I was still unsure about him and my willingness to attempt to embark upon a relationship of any kind, friendship or romantic, with him, but since we'd never met in person there was no pressure. Not having the traditional initial face to face meeting had removed all the typical warm and fuzzy. There was no physical attraction or sexual chemistry to cloud my judgment. That made it easy for me to talk to him because there was absolutely no obligation, and the conversations were meaningful, had substance, and I found him to be interesting. One thing that had long interested me was his name.

"Tell me about your name. Why did your Mom name you Dasht? Is that your Father's name, or did it come from somewhere else?"

"When I was born my mother said I had a veil over my face. You know what that means?"

"Oh yeah," I replied. "Its old wives speak for a baby born with the placenta over the baby's head and face, which is rare and superstitiously believed to mean the baby is a chosen one so to speak. I believe the proper terminology is caul birth."

"Damn! Ok, ok. Look at you. You're smart." He was noticeably both shocked and impressed causing him to take a moment to gather his thoughts and composure, before continuing the explanation about his name. "Mom said she wasn't in labor too long. I think she said from the time she had the first pain to when I was born was like less than two, maybe three hours."

"Wow," I interrupted. "That was fast."

"Yeah, I know, and because I was born so fast, she named me Dasht. As you know the "t" is silent, but she wanted the spelling of my name to be unique because of my being born with a veil. I didn't like having the "t" at the end of my name when I was a little boy. I actually really hated it because teachers would always mispronounce my name, but as I got older it grew on me, and now I like it because it is distinguishing."

"What is your middle name?"

"It's Damone."

"Hmm, Dasht Damone Spelbender. It's definitely different so I can see how it can be distinguishing. It has a nice ring to it."

"Why thank you. So that's the deal with my name."

Everything is a deal. That was another part of his lingo. He really had some funny sayings. For instance, if he was about to lose his composure, he said he was "about to lose his package" and if a person was short or curt in response, he referred to them as, "acting funny bunny." He also referred to himself in third person as the "Dash-Master" or "Diction". It was kind of weird but also cute and compelling.

"Why law school I asked?"

"Well I originally wanted to be an Air Force or Navy pilot, but my sister inspired me to become a lawyer. Camille and I were always really close when we were growing up. We were only fourteen months apart in age, so we were almost like twins. My sister was always very smart. She pushed me to be the best I could be. She always got straight A's, so when I would get a B I would feel bad. She always talked about being a lawyer and eventually a judge when we were younger." He paused just long enough for it to become awkward, and then continued. "When we were in middle school, she was riding her bike to visit with one of our cousins at my Aunt's house a couple of blocks away when a drunk driver jumped the curb and killed her." I could hear the pain in his voice as he said it.

"Oh my God," I gasped softly, "I'm so sorry."

"Yeah," he said. "It's been over forty years, but not a day goes by that I don't miss and mourn my sister. My life has been good, but I believe my life would have been so much better if Camille were still alive."

I was speechless at this point. This was heavy. "Do you have any other brothers and sisters?"

"I have a younger brother, Gary" he said, and his voice trailed off again.

I thought to myself, "Please don't let this man tell me his brother is dead too."

He cleared his throat and continued, "My brother actually had a bad motorcycle accident three years ago that left him paralyzed from the neck down."

"Damn!!!" I thought to myself. Here I was trying to lighten the mood and it was getting darker and darker, but the upside was we were putting our cards on the table and getting to know each other. These were definitely some significant events in his life that I needed to know about as I'm sure they've had a long-term impact on him. So rather than run from the conversation I decided to continue.

"Where is your brother now?" I asked.

"He is in an assisted living facility. I go and see him once a week, but I don't stay long because it's really hard for me to see my brother in that condition."

"Does he have a wife?" I asked.

"No, he never married."

Somewhat at a loss for words, I dared to ask another question. "Hmm, ok. Nieces and nephews?" I asked.

"No nieces and nephews," he said.

"You're from a small family," I said.

He answered, "Yes," in a somber tone.

I was desperate to change the subject. "Well I'm the opposite. My family is quite large. I have five siblings, two sisters and three brothers," I said. "As a result, my parents are currently blessed with thirteen grandchildren, and I have five nieces and seven nephews."

Somewhat snapping out of the funk he'd drifted into he said, "Oh wow. That is a large family."

Aware of his vulnerability and willingness to possibly talk without abruptly changing the subject I continued to ask questions that would give me more insight. "So why no more than one child?" I asked.

"Well, I never really wanted children, but the deal was she, my ex, was pregnant. It was my last year in law school, and I had planned to pursue a career in politics. My Mom said I had to marry her because, "there would be no bastards in the Spelbender family; we don't do that." Besides, I couldn't have a bastard child out there when I ran for office."

"That's life in the South for you. I totally understand that. Social pressure contributed to my marrying my ex-husband too," I said. "We hung in there for ten years," I volunteered. "How long were you all married?"

"We stayed married for eighteen years. I moved out the day after my daughter graduated from high school and filed for divorce."

"Oh crap! That is cold blooded," I thought to myself. Then I countered that initial thought with a reminder to not judge or jump to conclusions. He was talking, and I needed to listen. Hell at least he was being open. "Had you all planned it that way?"

"Well she knew I was going to file for divorce, but she didn't want it. Jewel tried to talk me out of it, but it was over. It had been over at least ten years before I filed the deal. We had long stopped having sex or interacting at all as husband and wife. She had her friends, and I had mine. I told you I was still going through my bad boy phase. I just hung in there for my daughter. I loved her I guess, but I wasn't ready to be married or to be a father when that deal happened."

CHAPTER 4
Jokers and Aces

"You may have all four Aces, but if you don't know when to lay them on the table it may as well be the four twos."

The more we spoke, the more Dasht revealed about himself. Sometimes his revelations were controlled and intentional while at other times his tongue betrayed his intent.

"Hey Gabby!"

"Hello Dasht. How are you?"

"You know, I'm really enjoying getting to know you. I told Velma about you today."

"Velma? Who is that?"

"I haven't told you about Velma?"

"No...?"

"Velma is my girl! I can't believe I hadn't told you about her. She is my executive assistant, but she is also my friend, my best friend. She is like a big sister too. She has been with me for over twenty-five years now."

"Oh wow."

"Yeah, she started working for me when I was in the District Attorney's office, and when I left public service for private sector, she left with me. She has followed me from firm to firm and stuck with me when I started my own firm too."

"Ok."

"I love Velma, so I told her about you today. In full disclosure she looked you up on Facebook and found your pictures. She said you have gorgeous skin, you're pretty and exotic looking."

He was barely pausing for air. Not only could I not get a word in, but this was a bit over the top. Why would his assistant look me up on Facebook? He could have simply shown her one of the photos my sister sent or one of the one's he and I had exchanged since we'd began talking.

"I don't know why she said you're exotic looking. Maybe it's your eyes and hair. There was a picture she showed me on your Facebook where you're wearing a red hat I really love. Will you send me that picture?"

"Damn!" I thought to myself. She had really gone deep in my photos to find that. I logged into my Facebook account and updated my privacy settings while I was searching for the photo he'd requested. "Sure. I'll text it to you. What made you tell her about me?" I'd managed to get the question in while he was taking a sip of his cocktail. By now I could tell when he was putting ice in a highball glass and popping the cork on a bottle of scotch.

"I tell Velma everything. She is five years older than me and is like my big sister and my best friend. Today while we were sitting in my office having lunch, I told her I've been talking to someone, and I really like you."

"Hmm, so what exactly prompted her looking me up on Facebook?" I can't lie, her looking me up didn't sit well with me.

"She did that after we'd finished our lunch. It was later in the day when she was at her desk. She called me over and showed me your pictures. She Googled you and everything. You really are a pretty woman. I'm going to introduce you to Velma when you're in Atlanta. You'll like her. She is classy like you."

"Ok," I replied because I simply didn't know what else to say.

"People used to think Velma and I were sleeping around, I believe her husband, Ted, thought it too at one time, but nothing like that has ever happened. Now one time she told me she always thought she would have married a man like me, which I thought was strange. Don't get me wrong, Velma is a good-looking woman, especially for her age. She is fifty-eight and still looks great, but she was a fox when she first came to work for me. I mean sexy. A lot of other guys on the job attempted to flirt with her, but I never did."

At a loss for words because I was still processing this information I said, "Oh ok." Then after a momentary pause I asked, "So do you and her husband have a relationship now?"

"We tolerate each other now. His ass realized I'm the one who puts food on his table, so we are cordial, but I don't think he really cares for me, and I don't give a shit. I believe he is jealous."

"Oh really? You put food on their table meaning he doesn't work? Is this why you believe he is jealous?"

"He has a decent job; he is a high school history teacher. I believe he is jealous because he isn't an attorney like me. I put food on their table because in addition to paying Velma's salary, I give her half of every bonus check I get. I get a $10,000 check and she gets $5,000 of it. I will always do that because she has always been loyal and good to me."

Now this was some serious 'Sugar Honey Ice Tea' for me to swallow. What did he mean he gives her half!? I definitely had to file this information in my mental rolodex for future reference and visitation because should things move forward with us to the point of marriage that would definitely have to stop.

> *"It's the niceties that make the difference. Fate gives us the hand and we play the cards." - Arthur Schopenhauer.*

Dasht and I had been dealt similar hands as far as life cards were concerned, and we'd both managed to play them well. In getting to know each other he and I both were dropping some heavy hitters on the table. We'd both become comfortable enough to begin revealing our hearts and most protected memories to one another. The core of our foundations began surfacing during our next in-depth conversation.

By this point we'd began learning each other's schedules and synchronizing our daily routines. Dasht typically called while having his evening cocktail. I would be winding down from the gym, and he would be closing out his workday and starting to relax with his beverage.

After exchanging the basic phone pleasantries, Dasht and I began discussing our upbringings, and he shared more insight about his childhood. "My childhood was rough. Daddy left when I was in the third grade."

"I would have never guessed that. I'm sure people assume you're from an affluent background."

"Yes they do, and I don't too much talk about it."

"I can relate. People always assume I came from a well-to-do family, but I come from very humble beginnings that I don't typically talk about either. The funny thing is I didn't know we were poor until I started going to school. Kids are cruel, and it wasn't until I was exposed to teasing and bullying that I realized we were economically disenfranchised."

"Yeah I got teased a lot in school, and that stuff has an effect on you." His voice trailed off as if he was thinking back to being teased as a child.

"It does." I said in agreement momentarily reflecting on my own childhood experiences of being harshly teased and feeling inadequate.

He took a long sip of his cocktail, "Yeah we had some hard times. Sometimes we didn't even have food to eat, holes in our shoes," he paused. "I hated my Daddy for leaving us like that."

"He just left?"

"Well I was really young at the time, so there was nothing that would have let me know he was leaving. I just remember coming home one day, and he was gone. Now that I'm an adult I realize that was the point when they separated and subsequently divorced, but from my eight year old perspective he just left us. He left because he didn't love us anymore."

"You never saw him after that?"

"We would see him during the summer. I loved those summer visits, but that ended by the time I was twelve. My sister got killed that fall, and we never went back for a summer visit after that."

"Why?"

"Who knows? I believe my parents weren't getting along, and as a result my sister, brother and I always suffered. It just got worse after Camille passed away."

"Dang. I'm sorry," was all I could manage to say.

"Yeah. I made amends with my Dad before he died though."

"Well that's good."

"Yeah I guess so. I'm good now. What about you? What was your childhood like?"

"My childhood was difficult. I grew up with two parents. My biological father was never in my life. I knew who he was, saw him three, maybe four times in my entire life. He died seven years ago. I don't remember my legal father. He divorced my Mom when I was two years old. My Daddy, the only father I know, married my Mom when I was five."

"Your Mom was married three times?"

"No. I don't know all the details. You know Southern families are known for keeping secrets, which is why you hear about so many scenarios of someone finding out their big sister is their mother or cousin is their brother."

"That is so true," he interrupted.

"The details weren't really discussed much. Most of what I know was learned from angry, drunk outbursts from my Aunts when they and my Mom were arguing about something. So apparently my Mom and my legal father were engaged, but my Mom was cheating on him with her high school sweetheart."

"Damn! Now that's some funky shit," he interrupted in a tone that while unfamiliar to me I knowingly knew expressed strong judgment and disdain.

I wasn't at all surprised he would strongly disapprove of any suggestion of promiscuity in a woman because that's how I'd known all men to be, especially Southerners, even when they were promiscuous themselves. However, I didn't approve of him passing judgment on my Mom, and I ensured I firmly expressed my disapproval. "I know society frowns on women and holds them harshly accountable when they have affairs, which is so hypocritical, but I understand how women find themselves in these types of predicaments. I don't think badly of my Mom because all she was ever taught was to find a man and marry him. Unfortunately for her, the man she loved wasn't interested in marriage. So even though she didn't love my legal father she felt pressured to be with him because everyone in her family recognized him as a "good man" whom "she was lucky" to have. So when he proposed, she accepted. Even though Ole High School, that's what I call my biological father, didn't want to marry, he just wanted to screw. She was a young woman in love. She just gave in to her heart's desires. I honestly don't know because we've never talked about it, but as a woman now I understand her plight. I believe she either planned to stop sleeping around with Old High School after she married Legal Daddy, hoped Old High School would fall in love and marry her, or hoped she would get pregnant and prompt or force Old High School into marriage. Fortunately and unfortunately for her, Old High School did get her pregnant."

"Old High School, that's funny," he half chuckled. Then in a tone that still conveyed his disapproval but lacked the venom of his previous response he asked, "How was that fortunate?"

"Fortunate because she had me, which not only made her the mother of his first born child but also allowed her to always have a piece of her first love." This was a belief I held that made me most empathic and sad for my Mom, and I could tell my heartfelt emotion had been expressed in my tone when he responded.

"Damn women do go through some shit." He paused briefly as if both pondering his and my last comments while forming his next statement, and I heard the thump signaling the release of a cork followed by ice clinking into a glass. "You know I've heard of some situations of people stepping out on their relationships," he paused for a sip, "and we do," he swallowed. "Us men, we do come down hard on women who step out of their relationships. We tend to not frown on stepping out as much when men do it because for a man it's just sex."

I rolled my eyes and let out a loud sigh of irritation before interrupting him because this double standard and baseless justification that afforded men an imaginary instinct of immorality was irritating and archaic to say the least. "It's always a higher standard for women. To hell with the Golden Rule. After all everyone knows Jezebel was a whore, but no one talks about who she was whoring with. The scarlet letter is always on the woman."

"Well yeah but no, no, no. Hold on that wasn't what I was going to say. Just let me finish. Please."

"Ok. I'm listening," I replied in a tone that let him know I was a staunch opposer of the double gender standard and advised he choose his next words wisely.

I could tell he was smiling when he started talking, which somewhat began to lighten my mood. "What I was going to say is men, at least I or any of my friends to my knowledge, don't really think about the pressure on women to marry. I mean I know a lot of men who were, or at least felt, pressured to marry for one reason or another," he sipped his cocktail, "and as a result ended up stepping outside the marriage. Hell, myself included. I never looked at them as bad guys. I just believed it wasn't their fault because they weren't ready to do the deal, or they'd gotten tied down with the wrong woman. Until you said what you said about your mother, it never even dawned on me this happens to women too. You really just taught me something."

I smiled as I responded, "Yeah the way we are socialized is, for lack of a better expression, more than a notion. You're forced to be something before you ever even know what it is to just be."

"Gabby baby I am really enjoying this conversation. I mean I really love talking to you, but I've got to get me a quick bite to eat. Do you mind if we pause this, so I can eat and then call you back?"

"Oh no, not at all. I actually need to call Tippy because she's called twice since we've been on the phone."

"Who is that?"

"My sister, Tiffany."

"Oh? What did you just call her?"

"Tippy. We call her Tippy."

He laughed. "That's cute, but why do y'all call her that?"

His laugh was contagious, and I laughed too. "We call her that because she can't stand for her feet to touch the floor or ground, so if she isn't wearing shoes, she tip toes across the floor, and it rhymes with Tiffany."

He laughed that deep, throaty, infectious laugh I'd started to both enjoy and become accustomed to. "Aww that's cute, and it fits her too."

"Yes it does," I said smiling inside and out at the memory of my little sister tipping across the floor as a toddler that had led to her nickname.

"Ok. I'll call you back shortly. Don't forget where we are in this conversation because I want us to continue."

As soon as we disconnected, I called Tippy.

"Hey Tippy!"

"Hey Gab. I was about to put an APB out on you. I said if I call one more time and she doesn't answer," she joked. "What are you up to?"

"I was on the phone with Dasht."

"Umm hmm," she teased. "I figured as much. He is taking up all of your phone time these days."

"I know," I chuckled. "He is eating dinner now, and he is going to call me back when he finishes."

"Dang girl! So y'all are really hitting it off?"

"Yeah, actually we are. We are having some really deep conversations. It's a lot, but it is really good and significant information to know about a person before you get involved in a relationship. A big mistake I made in the past."

"Haven't we all. It's good you all are getting down to the nitty gritty of things before getting into a relationship. Even though things are great with Joseph and me, if I had to do it all over again,

I'd do it differently because it would have made things a lot easier. I just thank God we were able to get things right early on."

"I know. I'm determined to not make the same mistakes I made in the past, especially after dating that psychopath Adam."

"Oh yeah, he was awful. I never liked him. I thank the Lord you got away from him."

"Hallelujah!" I joked, but there was an abundance of truth in my gist. "Talk about dodging a grenade, but enough about that. Guess who has lost six pounds!"

"Alrighty now! That's awesome."

"Yeah I'm determined to get this weight off."

"You will."

"Girl Dasht is calling, so let me talk to him. I'll call you tomorrow."

"Okay girl. Tell your 'Boo Thang' I said hello," she teased.

"I will," I answered between my giggles as I switched the lines to answer Dasht's call. "Wow that was fast."

"Yeah it was. I just needed to get some food in me really quick, but I wanted to get back to our conversation. Where were we?"

"We were talking about my childhood, specifically my father situation," I replied.

"Yeah, yeah. That's a lot. So, your stepfather raised you? Is he still around?"

It was customary for Dasht to ask multiple questions at once. "He is not my stepfather, well technically he is, but we don't use that term. I call him Dad because he is the only father I know. My parents are divorced, but they are friends and can coexist, which makes it good for us."

"Cool. How long have they been divorced?"

"Well they separated when I was sixteen, which is how I got pregnant while in high school, but they didn't divorce until eight years ago." In our very first conversation after revealing my age I had told Dasht that I'd had my son, Brian, prior to graduating high school.

"Oh yeah you told me you had your son at a young age. Tell me about that," he requested as he sipped his cocktail.

"Well my Dad was very strict. He didn't allow us to hang out, and my Mom pretty much defaulted to him to make all the decisions about everything. Whatever he said went, and I hated it. When they separated we could basically do whatever we wanted. I was in high school dating a senior from a neighboring high school who was a football jock and succumbed to his pressuring me to have sex. Afterwards, I didn't really like him because the experience was too much for me at such a young age. Most people give me an eyebrow raise when I tell them this, but we only had sex once. The next time I had sex my son was three years old."

"Damn!" He interrupted. "You mean to tell me you got pregnant the first time you all did the deal? Wow!"

"Yeah talk about getting screwed," I half-joked out of fear over the possibility of this information changing his opinion of me, but more so to calm the stomach churns I was feeling due to my own self-judgment. "My parents were totally engrossed in their marital issues, so I was five months pregnant by the time they found out."

When he responded, I could tell he'd stopped mid sip of his cocktail to express his thought, "You mean you didn't know you were pregnant until you were five months?" I could tell by his tone he was asking this question in somewhat disbelief, which I'd expected.

"No, I pretty much knew something was wrong within the first week. Being totally honest, I was in denial at the possibility of being pregnant. I was very skinny at the time, which made the weight gain a tell-tale sign, but my parents didn't notice. I'd gained about twenty-two pounds, but they never said anything. When I was about three months or so my Grandmother had made a comment that I might be pregnant because I'd been sleeping a lot. Of course I denied there was even remotely a possibility that I could be pregnant, and my parents being consumed with their own stuff took me at my word."

"So how did they find out?" He asked in a tone that let me know I had his undivided attention.

"It's kind of funny actually. I was crying for pancakes. I wanted them so bad, but at the time I couldn't make them so my sister, Michelle, made them for me. I threw up immediately after eating them, and that's when my Mom asked me if I was pregnant. I told her I didn't know, and she slapped me. Then she asked me had I been doing anything to get pregnant, and I told her one time. She slapped me again and accused me of lying. Later that week she took me to get an abortion, and we were told I was too far along in my pregnancy."

"Aww Baby. I'm sorry you had to go through all of that." His response was so sincere, and I could tell he'd become sad.

Wait, did he just call me Baby? I caught it, but the conversation was going well so I just allowed his flirting to slide. "It's ok. Having Brian was the best thing that ever happened to me. So much good has come to my life because of my son."

"Yeah?" He interrupted.

"Yes. It made me responsible because I learned at an early age that I was not invincible. Besides, if I had not had Brian at such a young age, I wouldn't have any kids right now, and I'd probably be like so many of my friends who are either trying to have kids now or regretting not ever having any children."

"Really? You think so?"

"I know so," I answered plainly. "I never wanted children, but after having my son my maternal instinct kicked in. The plan was originally to put him up for adoption because I didn't want to marry his father. Lord knows, I'm so grateful my Mom stood up for me and said I didn't have to marry him because my Dad was going to make us get married," I paused to choke back the emotion that was welling up as I mentally replayed the events, "but after Brian was born, my Dad saw me crying." I paused to gather my composure. "When he asked me what was wrong, I told him I didn't want to give my baby away. My Mom was adamant about my not having to sacrifice my high school experience and subsequent graduation. At some point shortly after I told my Dad I wanted to keep my son, my parents met with my son's father's parents and they worked it all out. Both families pulled together to help with babysitting and finances, which allowed me to complete both high school and college."

"Damn Baby, that had to have been hard for you."

"Yes," I said while still mentally reflecting back to that time in my life, "but I am grateful that is one of the few times my Mom stood up to my Dad. In the end it all worked out, and God used it for my good."

"So where is your son, what's his name again, Brian? Where is he now?"

"He lives in Atlanta. He goes to school at Georgia Tech. He's somewhat of a career student."

He laughed a little clearly still enjoying his cocktail, "Career student, huh. That sounds like Dana, my daughter."

Grateful for his lightening the mood I laughed a little, "Really?"

"Yeah, but finish telling me about your son. We can talk about Dana later. Trust me it's plenty to talk about with her. How old is he again, and what is he getting his degree in?"

"He is twenty-nine and majoring in Computer and Information Sciences. He takes a class here and there, which pisses me off because he is smart. Just spoiled, and that's partly my fault."

"Dana is rotten too."

"I believe being spoiled is pretty much inevitable if you're an only child."

"Perhaps, but you're from a large family. It was only three of us, but it was six of y'all," he said this without pausing for me to respond, so I concluded this repetition was his method for committing this information to memory. "So now you're the oldest and Tiffany is next to you in age, correct?"

"I'm the first born, but my sister Michelle is the oldest," I said jokingly.

"Huh?"

"That's just a little family joke. I always say my sister Michelle is the oldest because if you saw us together you would think she was the oldest child. She doesn't look old, but she has an old spirit. Then there is my oldest brother, Jacob, Jr.; next to him is Tiffany, then my brother Jordan and my baby brother Joshua."

"Ok, so you're the only one with a different father, which I would have never known because you and Tiffany look just alike."

"No. Michelle's biological father is my legal father. My Dad is Tiffany's and my brothers' biological father."

"Oh, ok. So you have no full siblings, only half-siblings?" I heard ice being dumped into the sink and water running.

"I have no siblings of which I share the same biological father, but I have no half-siblings. They are my brothers and sisters. We don't refer to each other as steps and halves in my family."

He yawned. "Really? I always thought if you had a different parent, whether it was the mother or father that made you a half-sister or brother?"

"Well technically it does, but we don't do that. We just weren't brought up with separation like that between us. Besides my Dad is the only Dad any of us has ever known."

"Ok cool. Well Baby, I'm getting sleepy, but I've really enjoyed talking to you. Seriously I'm enjoying getting to know you Gabby. I don't stay on the phone like this, but now I've got to hit the sack because that Z-monster is on my back and my eyes are heavy."

I smiled at the compliment and yet another one of his sayings, "Yeah I've enjoyed our conversation too, but it is getting late, and I have a full day tomorrow, so I need to get to sleep as well."

"Well we will definitely talk tomorrow."

"Yes."

"Ok, good night Gabby."

"Good night Dasht."

"When I was a child, I talked like a child, I thought like a child, I reasoned like a child..." 1 Corinthians 13:11

It was quite apparent that we were building a rapport and starting to really like one another in a non-platonic way, and Dasht confirmed this during our daily conversation one Wednesday evening when he told me how much of a little joker he'd been as a child.

"Hello Gabby!" He said in an extremely chipper tone that made me somewhat giddy.

"Hello Dasht. How are you today?"

"You know, I'm great," he sipped. "I'm really great."

"That's wonderful," I responded while waiting for him to tell me what had him so chipper.

"Yeah, I'm really great, and you probably won't believe this, but I'm great because of you."

"Really?" I was smiling like a kindergartner who'd been chosen to lead the lunch line. "How so?"

"I'm just enjoying our conversations, getting to know you and really looking forward to meeting you in person."

"That's really sweet. I'm actually enjoying our conversations too. We are getting close to meeting one another. I will be in Atlanta before you know it."

"I know. I'm in countdown mode. Eight days, I will meet you face to face in eight days."

I giggled a little, "Yes you will."

"How do you feel about it? Are you excited?"

"I am excited, but also a little nervous." I was actually giddy like a schoolgirl, but I dared not tell him that.

"I'm nervous too. Today I told Velma I'm really looking forward to meeting Gabby."

In all honesty the mention of her name somewhat dampened the mood for me, but I suppressed those emotions and asked, "What did she say?"

"She is super excited for me, and she can tell I'm happier since we've been talking and getting to know each other. Like I told you before Velma is my best friend. She has been with me a long time, so she has seen me go through some rough times in both my personal and professional life. Velma is the kind of woman I believe my sister Camille would have become had she lived," he paused to reflect and then I heard ice hitting the glass signaling he was about to refresh his cocktail. Attuned to the downward shifting of the mood, I pounced on the opportunity to redirect the conversation to happier topics.

"I've actually already started packing for next week."

He swallowed before responding, "Really. That's early." He paused abruptly, "Hey, whose picking you up from the airport?"

"No one. I land in Birmingham and drive to Atlanta. One of my sorority sisters whom I pledged with lives there, and I usually visit her when I'm on that side of the country. Besides the airport there isn't as busy and, I need a rental car while in town anyway, so I may as well get it in Birmingham."

"You make that drive alone?"

"Yes. It's only a little more than two hours. I'm used to being in the car for long periods of time. I typically spend one to two hours in the car driving five miles an hour in this area daily."

"Damn, that's got to suck. I would lose my mind. I couldn't deal with that type of traffic. Hello no."

"It used to annoy me but being annoyed isn't going to change it. So rather than allow it to be time wasted, I just attempt to utilize my time wisely when in the car. That's typically when I catch up on my phone calls."

"That's smart, but I couldn't deal with that."

"Yeah, it gets old, but it is what it is because as long as I live in the DMV, I have to deal with it. Complaining about it or getting upset is just a waste of time and emotions."

"You're always so positive. Why is that?"

"I wouldn't say I'm always positive. That would be a lie. I'm human just like everyone else, and I have human moments. I just don't allow myself to stay stuck. I've learned to seek optimism over pessimism because in the end things work out. That's why I really try to see the good in everything."

"That's a good attitude to have, but most people including myself lose their package first and then don't see the good, if there's any good to see, in things until later." He paused and sipped his cocktail. "Much later. People always say there is good in everything, but I'm not so sure there is good in everything." His tone of voice in his last statement sounded as if he were speaking to himself more so than speaking to me. It was as if he was thinking out loud unconsciously, a Freudian slip.

"Well there isn't necessarily good in everything, but God can use every situation for your good."

"You really believe that?"

"Yes. Absolutely," I responded without hesitation. "Every single time something bad has happened in my life it has made me better. I either learned a life lesson and if it was an instance of loss, whatever I lost was replaced with something better."

"How so?"

"Well for example, when I divorced, we had a beautiful, brand new, five thousand square foot, custom built home that we'd only had for a year and a half when we filed for divorce. Because of the divorce we had to sell the house, but the house I have now is better. Unlike the home I had with my ex-husband, my current home is peaceful, and it's built on truth and self-love. At the time of the divorce, I was crushed and felt that it was a loss but living in that house would have been a constant reminder of my failed marriage and all the heartache associated with it. Of course at the time I couldn't see myself where I'm at now, but in spite of all that bad I wouldn't change a thing because it brought me to the good I have right now."

"Ok, I get it. I can see how in the end you can see the good, but while you're in the deal it's kind of hard to maintain your package."

"Your lingo is hilarious, all your deals and packages." I giggled before continuing, "When you're in the midst of something it can be hard to see the good in it, but it's best to not make a habit of complaining because no matter what the situation is, it could be worse. That in itself is the good."

"I guess you have a point. I've never really thought about it like that, but listening to you has me thinking a little, and I can see how some things have worked out for my benefit or could have been a lot worse in my life. I just never thought about it like that, but now that I'm thinking about it a lot of stuff could have been really bad. It's just hard to think that way when you're going through it."

"Yes. If you honestly think back over the course of your life you'll realize, we're really all just one decision from our lives being totally different and not necessarily in a good way."

"You know.... that's true," he took a rather long sip of his cocktail as he organized his thoughts. "Damn, that's true. My life could have been totally different."

"How so?" I asked.

"Well I've never really told anyone this, but I used to sell drugs when I was in college. I'm not proud of this, but I did what I had to do to survive. Thank God I never got caught because I never would have been able to become a successful attorney."

"Oh my. Why? What made you do that?"

"I needed the money. I needed it really bad. I mean there was no money for my tuition let alone food and other things."

He sounded both sad and angry as he reminisced about that time in his life, and I honestly felt sad for him. "That is really messed up. I'm sorry that you had to endure that, but glad that you survived it without your life being ruined."

"Yeah like you said, one decision from my life being totally different."

"In the end look at the good. In your profession how many young offenders have you been able to defend with compassion because unbeknownst to them you fully understood their situation."

"You know, that's true. Damn that's true. You're good girl. I just love your mind...I do...I love the way you think. You're smart. That's why I enjoy talking to you so much. I could talk to you all night. Shit, I've never been on the phone with anyone like this."

I snickered a little conveying the smile that was both in my heart and on my face. "I enjoy talking to you too, but it's getting late. Talk to you tomorrow?"

"You'll definitely be talking to me tomorrow and guess what."

"What?"

"You'll be seeing me in a week."

I smiled inside and out, "Yes, I will."

"I'm looking forward to it."

"Me too," I replied.

"Good," he yawned.

"Good night Dasht."

"Good night Gabby."

> ***"The joker is a wild card because he's always guaranteed a score."***

I was surprised when my phone rang as I pulled into my driveway. He was calling much earlier than normal.

"Hello Dasht."

"Hey Gabby! What are you up to?"

"I'm actually just getting home."

"Oh yeah?" He asked rhetorically. "What are you getting into on this Friday evening?"

"I have no major plans. I typically just relax on Fridays."

"Me too. I used to go to the bar years ago, but now I just relax at home."

"I'm not and never have been a bar person, but I love Fridays and being at home."

"I love Fridays too. Friday is my favorite day of the week." He sounded like he was smiling.

"Why is that?"

"Well on Saturday you have stuff to do around the house and errands to run; Sunday you're catching up on work so you can be fresh and prepared for the week; Monday through Thursday is work and getting prepared for the next workday. The Friday workday usually ends early then your time is your time to go to happy hour, go out to dinner, spend time out with friends or just relax at home. You know?"

With a slightly raised eyebrow I asked, "So you don't go to church and have family time on Sunday?"

"Church really isn't my thing. I mean I believe in God and all that and pray, but I can't get with the whole church thing. It's not really my deal."

"Hmm," I thought out loud. "I grew up in church it's just in me to attend. I'm not a fan of 'church people', but I feel off balance if I don't attend church regularly."

"You go to church every Sunday?"

"No, I can't tell that lie. I try to go regularly though. I don't currently have a church here because I moved, but I watch the church service there via the internet, and when I'm home I attend church with my family."

"What church does your family attend?"

"We attend Word of Praise Non-Denominational Church."

"Oh, I've gone there before."

"Oh wow. Wouldn't it have been something if we'd run into one another there."

"Yeah," he said as he sipped his cocktail. "It would have been, but you probably would have been all funny bunny towards me."

I laughed a little and dismissed his attempt to take the conversation in another direction. "You didn't go to church as a kid?"

I detected the slight hint of disappointment he tried to hide when he responded, "I mean my Mom took us every once in a while, but for the most part no. It was always all about money." He sounded annoyed. "After I was an adult, my Mom used to go to church a lot. She went to The Temple of Worship. I don't really care for the pastor over there. He is all about money."

"Yes, I've heard some things about that church."

"Yeah I can't stand it. My Mom used to give all of her money to that church and then expect me to pay her bills." He paused for a sip of his cocktail, "I hated that shit."

"That was rather harsh," I thought to myself. Attempting to mask how stunned I was I asked, "You hated that your Mom gave all her money to the church?"

"Yes," he replied rather angrily. "I hated that she gave all her money to the church, at least all that she didn't gamble away, and I hated that she was always asking me for money. I can't stand for a woman to ask me for money. I hate people who beg all the damn time."

It was clear that he'd become lost in his thoughts to the point of emoting, and his emotions were strong. I struggled to find the words to say because I'd become somewhat uncomfortable. "Have you had to deal with people asking you for money?"

He finished his sip before responding, and for the first time I could hear the effect of the alcohol on his speech when he responded, "I think I told you I grew up poor, like really poor. After my Dad left things just got bad. He didn't do shit for us so a lot of times we had to go without." He paused and sipped again. "My Mom was always bad with money. She ran the streets with my Aunt Judith and gambled a lot before she got into the church. There was never enough money. Once I got old enough to work, I was determined not to have to ever go without. I picked up odd jobs anywhere I could find one. I mean I did everything, cut grass, raked leaves, tossed newspapers, took out garbage, washed cars, bagged groceries, stocked shelves, you name it. If I could earn a dollar doing it, I did it." I could hear the ice clinking into the glass signaling his refreshing his cocktail.

"You've been working pretty much your entire life," I said for no other reason than to break the awkward pause.

"Yes, I have. I had to grow up fast, especially after my sister got killed. It's like I became the man of the house. My Mom had boyfriends, but they never stuck around, and they took more than they ever gave. Hell by the time I was sixteen I was paying the rent."

I was stunned, "Did you say paying the rent? How?"

"Yes! I had to pay the rent." He said rather sternly and then paused for what seemed like an eternity but was actually no more than five seconds before continuing, "Well that's actually how I got involved in selling drugs, and I had to do it until I finished college because there was no money for Mom's bills or my tuition."

Wait, he'd previously told me he sold drugs in college? Now was he saying he started doing that in high school? I decided to let the discrepancy in his chronology slide and focus my response on the sympathy I was feeling for him. "Dang," I sighed. "That's so sad. That had to be hard."

"Yeah it was," he took a long sip of his cocktail. "It was. Those were bad times for me. That's why I hate my Aunt Judith. She wasn't my real Aunt, but my Mom made us call her Aunt Judith. I blame her for a lot of what happened."

If she wasn't a real relative why did he still refer to her as Aunt Judith was the question I'd initially poised myself to ask, but then he made his last statement and my focus shifted. "Why? Did she live with you all or something?"

"No she didn't live with us. She was always hanging around. She wasn't really my Mom's friend, but that's how she tried to make it seem. She was a loose woman who was always getting money from random men. She got my Mom involved in that shit," he paused then sipped his drink. "I believe wholeheartedly it was her fault that my parent's divorced."

"How so?"

"I believe she was a bad influence on my Mom. Now that I'm an adult and think back on those times, I believe she was jealous of my Mom because my Mom had a husband and she didn't. She hung around influencing my Mom to do bad shit."

I dared not ask what he meant by that. We were both silent until he finished sipping and continued to speak.

"She was always taking my Mom out to meet men. I hated her ass. I still do."

My heart ached for him because I could hear both the hurt and anger in his voice. "Where is your Aunt Judith now?"

"She's dead."

Desperate to find a silver lining in all he'd just told me I asked, "Did your relationship with your Mom improve after you got older?"

"I mean it was up and down. It's kind of hard to explain, but I loved and hated my mother."

"Hate is such a strong word."

"Maybe it is, but that's how I felt. She did some real bad stuff."

There was no way I was going to ask him to clarify what he meant by that, so we were again both quiet until he spoke again.

"My relationship with my Mom just messed me up. I believe that was a big part in my marriage failing. It's hard to explain, but it is what it is. You know?" Not only was he about to abruptly change the subject, which I'd become attuned to, but his tone of voice signaled his snapping out of the period of reflection he'd unintentionally slipped into.

Rather than pry, I obliged his obvious desire to change the subject. "Well they say what doesn't kill you definitely makes you stronger, and you have a wonderful life now."

"True, true," he said with a little extra maple syrup on his baritone. He was clearly tipsy. "My life is good for the most part, but I need me a good woman."

He was flirting again. "Really?" I asked playfully.

"Yep! I do, and I'm starting to believe you're the good woman I need."

"I'm smiling," I said, and I really was.

"Good. I'm smiling too," he paused, and I could tell he was smiling and thinking. "You're easy to talk to. Hell, too easy to talk to. I'm telling you shit. I mean stuff. I don't ever talk about."

"Hmm," I thought out loud. "How do you feel about that?"

"Surprisingly, I feel good. I feel really good. I feel good about everything."

"Aww you're so sweet. I feel good too."

"I might be sweet and all that, but I'm serious. I feel really good about you, and I haven't felt this way...," he paused to think, "ever. I haven't ever felt this way to be honest with you."

"This is different for me too," I divulged. "I've never met anyone this way, but I have to admit I'm really enjoying it."

We skirted on flirting and light banter for another ten minutes or so before calling it a night, and for the first time I added Dasht specifically by name to my prayers.

CHAPTER 5
Kings, Queens and Jacks

"Every house of cards is home to at least one knave who speaks lies and lacks moral character."

We were six days from our first face to face meeting. Our conversations leading up to that day were mostly focused on expressing our mutual excitement and hopes of having as much physical chemistry as we had experienced intellectually via our phone conversations.

On Saturday Dasht called me early in the morning. I was surprised, pleasantly but still surprised because we didn't typically talk early in the day. As if the morning call wasn't surprise enough, Dasht shocked me even further when he put his daughter, Dana, on the phone with zero warning.

"Good morning Gabby!" He cheerfully exclaimed.

"Good morning Dasht."

"What are you up to?"

"I'm just finishing up my coffee and getting ready to get my day started."

"Dana is here with me. Hold on let me let you speak to her."

"Huh?" I was thinking this to myself when she said, "Hello," in a voice that was both raspy and squeaky.

"Hello. How are you?" I replied.

"I'm good, just busy moving."

"You're moving?"

"Well I'm helping my girlfriend. She is moving in with me."

I said, "Oh, ok. Moving can be hard work," because I literally didn't know what else to say.

"It has been back breaking, but we're getting it all done." She replied, and I could tell this conversation was awkward for her as well.

"That's great."

"Yeah. Hopefully everything will be in place by the time you get here so we can have you over for a visit because I'm looking forward to meeting you."

"I'm looking forward to meeting you as well."

Before handing the phone off to Dasht she said, "Well let me get going. It was good speaking to you."

"Likewise," I answered.

"Gabby, let me walk Dana out, and I'll give you a call back."

"Ok."

I was taken aback at the way Dasht had just put me on the phone with his daughter and couldn't really make sense of it. It was just awkward. I immediately text Tippy to tell her what had just happened. Before she responded Dasht called back.

"Ok Baby. I'm back."

"Ok?"

"Dana just stopped by to pick up a drill and of course ask me up for money."

"Oh yeah," I said rather quickly because he was talking super fast.

"Her girlfriend, Lena, is moving in with her, and I'm glad."

"You are?"

"Yeah! That will take some of the pressure off of me. Dana is a lot to deal with. She is always in my pockets. Maybe she and Lena will get married, since it's legal now, and then they can be each other's responsibility."

A part of me sensed that Dasht was trying to feel me out to gauge my opinion about Dana being gay without directly asking, since he'd never mentioned it before. However, I wasn't going to take the bait because I honestly had no opinion. I'd learned long ago to not cast stones on someone else's choices, especially when they didn't directly affect me. I wasn't sure of Dasht's position on Dana's sexuality, but I also wasn't going to provide a platform for him to express or vent about it to me. I changed the subject by inquiring about her employment status. "I thought she was an attorney too?"

"She has a law degree, but she doesn't work," he said bluntly.

"Oh, ok?"

"Yeah, so what are you getting into today?"

Once again, he'd changed the subject abruptly which alerted me to his discomfort and disapproval of his daughter's lack of employment and his desire to not talk about it.

"Queens don't get lost in the shuffle."

It was an overwhelmingly beautiful day in the DMV. Rather than go to the gym, I'd decided to go for a long walk through my neighborhood. Dasht called while I was walking and conversing with him made the five mile trek a hop, skip and a jump. He was witty in a way that kept me laughing and all too often took the focus off what he was really saying.

"Hey Gabby! What are you up to?"

"Good morning Dasht. I'm power walking in the neighborhood this morning. How are you?"

"I thought you would be at church. Power walking huh? You exercise a lot."

"Why'd you call if you thought I was going to be at church?" I teased.

Laughing he said, "Well you got me, but I honestly had you on my mind and wanted to just tell you that. Yep, I just wanted to tell you that you were on my mind, and I'm thinking of you."

"Aww that's sweet, but no, I'm obviously not at church. I thought I told you that I don't have a church here. I've recorded today's service from Word of Praise, and I plan to watch it after I finish working out. I used to watch it while at the gym, but I need to devote my full attention to the message so I get the most out of it."

"Yeah you did tell me that. You watch Word of Praise from there every Sunday?"

"Yes. It makes me feel closer to home and allows me to hear the same sermon my family hears. So in a sense it's like I attended church with the family."

"Ok, ok. Makes sense." He paused momentarily and then said, "Yeah you have been on my mind a lot today. I was talking to Carol this morning and telling her how happy I am now that you've come into my life."

"Carol?"

"My friend Carol. I told you about her right?"

"No?"

"Aww damn. I can't believe I haven't told you about Carol. Carol and I grew-up together. We were neighbors. She is one of my best childhood friends."

"No. You never mentioned her."

"She is one of my good friends, and I was telling her about you this morning."

"Ok..."

"Yeah, I was telling her how we've been getting to know each other, and I'm going to meet you next week."

"Hmm..."

"Carol lives in Miami now. She married a guy in the Air Force and never looked back."

"Oh, I see."

"Her Mom still lives in the house she grew up in. Mr. Harris, her father died about three years ago, but she comes home to check on her mother, Mrs. Harris, often. So we've always kept in touch."

He was talking fast, and I really didn't see a need or even know how to respond. At this point I was primarily in listen mode due to my spidey senses being activated because there were more than enough female "friends" to remember.

"When we were growing-up, I was the only boy that was allowed to visit in the Harris household." He laughed, "Carol and I never dated or anything like that. We kissed once when we were in eighth grade. It was awkward as hell, so we never attempted anything romantic wise after that. I've been telling her all about you, and she is really happy for me."

"That's nice," was all I could muster to say.

"There are always significant events from the past that are represented and continue to rule us in the present like the four kings in a deck of cards."

It was the Monday prior to my meeting Dasht, and my week had begun with a true manic Monday. As much as I wanted to just go home and sleep I couldn't. I was nervously running around doing last minute packing and self-maintenance because I wanted to be as fresh as possible when we went on our date on Thursday. I was busy ensuring I'd packed all the shoes I'd need for the week when he called.

"Hey Gabby!" He exclaimed in his extra cheerful tone.

"Hello Dasht. How are you?"

"I'm great because you'll be in my city tomorrow."

"Yes, I will. God willing."

"Are you ok?"

"Oh yes. I'm well. I'm just ensuring I've packed everything."

"Oh, ok. You want to call me back?"

"No, I don't need to call you back. We can talk."

"Great. What do you want to do while you're here?"

"Well we're going on a date on Thursday, right?"

"Yes. I am going to take you to dinner, but I want to know what you want to do the rest of the week."

"I honestly don't know. I guess we should see how the first date goes before we plan more?"

"You might have a point, but I already like you. I'm hoping you like me too." He paused to sip his drink, "I think you're going to like me though," he half teased.

"I believe I'm going to like you too," I giggled and teased back.

"I told my god sister, Jeannie, about you today, and she wants to meet you while you're here."

My shock got the best of me and before I could silence my thoughts I responded, "Huh? Wait. Who? What?"

"My god sister wants to meet you."

Still somewhat discombobulated I questioned, "Your god sister wants to meet me? Why? I didn't know you had a god sister."

"Yeah Jeannie. I thought I told you about her."

"No, you didn't."

"Well I've been telling her about you and how well our conversations have been going. She is super excited for me. I told her you were going to be in town this week, so she wants to meet you too. I just text you a picture of her."

"I just received it," I acknowledged while looking at the photo he'd just text. "She is pretty."

"Yeah, that's an old photo from when we were in college. She doesn't look like that now," he laughed. "She was always a pretty girl, but she's gained some weight, a lot of weight," he chuckled.

"I don't have any recent photos of her. I guess she is still nice looking, just big." He emphasized the word big. "We grew-up in the same neighborhood. She is a couple of years older than me. She was Camille's best friend, and we all hung out when we were kids. Our parents were really close too so we were always at one another's homes for one thing or another. Jeannie doesn't have any siblings so after Camille passed away she and I became even closer. She is somewhat like a big sister."

"I see."

"I've been telling her about you and showing her your pictures. Today while she was here cooking, she said she wants to meet you."

"Wait," I thought to myself, "did he just say cooking?" Rather than ponder this thought in my head, I repeated what I thought I'd heard him say in a questioning tone, "Cooking?"

He jovially answered, "Yeah. She comes by twice a week and prepares my meals."

At this point my brain was spinning as if I had a bad case of Vertigo. I didn't want to jump to conclusions, but this wasn't setting well with me. My female intuition was on high alert. "So she cooks for you, and you have a housekeeper?"

"Yes Jeannie cooks for me and Val, my housekeeper, cleans and does my laundry."

"Is she a professional chef? Do you pay her to cook?"

He let out a hearty laugh, "No she isn't a professional chef, but she is a damn good cook, and yes, I pay her to cook for me."

"Ok mister high maintenance," I said sarcastically because something about this just didn't sit well with me, but I didn't want to come across as being accusatory.

"Aww stop it," he teased. It was clear that he was oblivious to my apprehension.

In an effort to subside the unease that was stirring in my gut I said, "Well before I meet her, I need to first meet you."

"And you will meet me." I heard the ice falling into the glass signaling the preparation of another cocktail. "You will meet me soon," he paused to pour then sip his drink, "and I'm truly looking forward to our meeting."

PART TWO
The Brood & The Bunny

CHAPTER 6
Face-to-Face

I was actually nervous. "What if he didn't like me? What if I didn't like him? What if we had no physical chemistry?" These thoughts had been running through my mind all day. In an effort to calm myself, I prayed as I headed to the airport.

I immediately called Dasht once I got off the plane to tell him I'd arrived safely. He was openly excited that I'd arrived. We stayed on the phone for two hours chatting about the events of my trip, our mutual anxieties and anticipation over finally meeting one another and how fond we'd become of one another over the past couple of months. The conversation had slightly tamed the butterflies floating around in my stomach.

We were scheduled to go on our first date two days after my arrival, but Dasht said he couldn't wait to see me. I'd ensured I was well primped and polished prior to my arrival, so moving our first meeting to an earlier date didn't cause me any anxiety other than the jitters over us meeting for the first time. It was a Wednesday, but I had the house smelling like a traditional Southern Sunday because I had spent the day cooking, which was what I normally did when I came home to visit. The house was filled with the aroma of fried pork chops, smothered chicken, collard greens, spicy fried cabbage, whipped potatoes, wild rice, hot water cornbread, my often requested cream cheese pound cake, and our normal family excitement. My nieces and nephews were so happy I was home, and the house was full of friends and family.

Dasht had called to see how my day was going and to tell me how excited he was to finally meet me face to face. He had a meeting about forty-five minutes away and was coming to see me afterwards. I anticipated he'd arrive around 6:30-7:00pm. I took care to select a dress that wasn't revealing but made a statement. Pretty dresses and high heels were my signature, and I wanted to present my true self to him. It was a cute, sleeveless, A-line with pockets, covered in a beautiful array of pastel florals that stopped right above the knee. I paired it with a pair of four inch, strappy sandals. My hair was in curls, which was convenient because of the body it gave my hair. I pinned my curls to ensure they'd be fresh when he arrived.

I was headed downstairs to relax and spend a little time with the kids when Dasht called to say he was at the gate entering the subdivision. That literally meant I had three to five minutes to get my dress and shoes on and unpin and comb my hair. Thank God, I wasn't too much of a make-up girl because there was no time for that. As I hung-up the call I rushed up the stairs in a panic. I ran in the bathroom and unpinned my hair first. Then I jumped out of my lounge wear and slipped into my dress while yelling down the stairs for Tippy to please come up and help. She ran up and helped me zip my dress and buckle my sandals. As we were strapping up my left shoe, I heard the doorbell ring. My sister looked at me and said, "Gab, relax. He can wait. You look pretty." Then she headed down the stairs.

I ran in the bathroom and put on a little mascara and lip gloss. As I put on my earrings, a simple pair of gold hoops, I thought, "This is a perfect look because I want him to see me." I was still staring at myself in the mirror when I heard his voice, and surprisingly it put me at ease. It was familiar. I smiled as I gave myself a last quick glance to ensure my hair and lip gloss were perfect. I stepped back into the bedroom, but before I opened the bedroom door to head down the stairs I fell to my knees and prayed: "Heavenly Father, I come to you thanking you for everything. I thank you for bringing Dasht into my life. Please order my steps and help me to stay in Your perfect will for my life. I ask that if he truly is the man you have designed for me that You help me to be the woman you designed me to be for him. If it is not that then please let us continue to be friends. Amen." I stood up and headed down the stairs. My sister later described my ascension as being like a bride walking down the aisle to meet her groom.

He was sitting at the kitchen table with his back to the stairs conversing with my sister, her friend and her friend's teenage daughter about college life and choosing a major. As I came in clear view the room became quiet. All eyes in the room except his had focused in on me. The abrupt silence and demeanor of everyone in the room caused him to stop talking and turn around to see me. Immediately his eyes enlarged and told the story of his thoughts. He was definitely pleased with what he saw. He stood up instantly, flashed that billion dollar smile and said, "Hey!" As I reached the bottom of the stairs, he pulled me in for a hug and kissed me on my cheek. I inhaled his scent, a light mixture of tobacco, grapefruit and lavender then exhaled some of the anxiety that I'd been hording. I was relieved and overwhelmed with emotion to the point that I felt like crying.

Dasht was everything I'd imagined and hoped he'd be. He was slimmer than he appeared to be in his pictures, but his appearance was immaculate. He wore a navy blue suit that fit as only a tailored suit could, a crisp white shirt and a fashionable yet conservative tie. His nails were manicured to perfection, his face was clean shaven, and his shoes were expensive and shined. He had a presence that filled the room. His eyes were truly the window to his soul because they betrayed all his attempts to be stoic or play it cool. They were an odd honey brown shade that was actually pretty. He had the smallest pupils I'd ever seen; they were almost nonexistent. I could tell that his stare could be piercing, if he'd been able to maintain it, but he kept flashing that amazing smile and looking away. He had some of the thickest most pronounced eyebrows I'd ever seen, but strangely he had little to no eyelashes.

After our initial embrace we sat alone at the kitchen table engaging in small talk for about twenty minutes. Everyone had left the immediate vicinity of the table but lingered in the kitchen and hearth room both in earshot and view of us.

He started, "I'm so glad you're finally here." Then his eyes darted to his right apparently focused on nothing.

"Me too," I answered.

He looked at me again briefly, flashed that smile and looked away again. Still looking away he said, "You're really pretty. I mean really pretty."

He'd focused on his hands, and all I could think to say was, "Thank you."

"Your pictures don't do you justice."

I smiled, shrugged, and said, "I guess that's a good thing because it would be bad to look better in pictures and disappoint in person." We both laughed at my comment.

He inhaled the air, "What's the name of your fragrance, it's intoxicating?"

I let out a girlish giggle. "You like it?"

"Yes. It is lovely," he widened his eyes and allowed a flirtatious smile to spread across his handsome face.

"Good," I said flirting back.

"So what is it," he asked again?

"I'm not telling you," I teased, but I was serious.

"Why not? I may want to buy it for you."

I was unable to suppress my giddy giggle. "Thank you, but I have plenty of it. I buy it in bulk."

His eyes continued to momentarily fixate on me and then flit away quickly throughout the remainder of our small talk. By now everyone was staring at us and clearly observing and listening to our conversation. He confirmed his awareness and angst over our audience when he said, "I need a cocktail."

"There is no alcohol in this house other than beer because no one here is really a drinker."

"Oh no, I need a scotch. Would you like to go somewhere and have a cocktail where we could talk without all the ears?" He smiled and winked.

"Sure," I said as I smiled and winked back.

As we left, I could feel my family members watching us through the window. Of course, he was a gentleman and opened and closed my door for the short ride to the bar.

He'd chosen a local watering hole that it was clear he frequented regularly because when we walked in it was like walking into Cheers. Everyone literally knew his name. We sat in his normal booth, and the bartender, waitresses and bar owner came out and doted over him. We sat in the bar for a little more than an hour engaged in surface conversations about my travel, the weather, our adult children all while trying not to stare at one another. We were like two teenagers, and I was really enjoying our meeting. I could feel the chemistry between us, and it felt good.

When we returned to Tippy's the house was still filled with family and friends, and all eyes were still on Dasht and I. He didn't seem as affected by it as much as he had initially. He seemed to enjoy being the center of attention and was all smiles as he joked with Tippy about us finally meeting. It was getting late so he didn't stay long. Keeping my end of our deal, I prepared him a to go plate ensuring he had lots of collard greens in exchange for my chess lesson. As he prepared to leave for the evening, he gave me a warm hug and a light kiss on the cheek as he asked, "Can I call you?"

"Sure."

"Ok. I'll call you after I finish eating," he said smiling from ear to ear as he headed out the door.

He was barely out of the driveway before Tippy and I began giggling and recapping the evening's events.

More to tease me than for me to respond, giggling she asked, "So do you like him?"

Thoughtfully I said, "Yes, I do...I really do."

"Aww this is too sweet," Tippy said.

Smiling inside and out I replied, "I know."

"So what time is your date tomorrow," she asked.

"Well we're going to dinner tomorrow, but I'm not sure of the exact time. He is going to call me in a little while so I'm sure we'll talk about it then."

With a huge smile on her face Tippy said, "This is so exciting."

As promised, Dasht called and gave me rave reviews on the food, and like two teenagers we stayed on the phone until we were both on the verge of falling asleep.

CHAPTER 7
The Perfect Card

Dasht had been listening during our phone conversations. When he arrived to pick me up for our first official date that Thursday night he was standing with his hands behind his back. Later in our relationship I would learn that he would put his hands behind his back or shove them deep in his pockets when he was nervous or frustrated; it was his boyish side coming to the surface. To my surprise when he removed his hands from behind his back, he presented me with a stuffed baby giraffe in a basket of gardenias with a red bow around its neck. Talk about a score! I'd told him in one of our many phone conversations that for as long as I could remember red was my favorite color, gardenias were my favorite flowers, and I'd always had a fascination with giraffes. He could have easily shown up with flowers or nothing at all for that matter, but he'd not only surprised me with the giraffe; he'd shown me he listened to me when we talked. That made me smile inside and out.

Just as the previous day, I'd taken detailed care in putting myself together. I'd chosen one of my favorite ensembles, a green, floral, silk Cynthia Rowley kimono dress paired with a pair of t-strap wedges I rarely wore because I'd purchased them in Europe and they were irreplaceable. Once again, I wore my hair in curls and kept my make-up light wearing only a little mascara and lip gloss. As for jewelry I kept it simple with just diamond solitaires. Dasht was just as dapper as he'd been the day prior. He was wearing another tailor made suit paired with a crisp white shirt, conservative tie and shoes shined to perfection.

When we arrived at the restaurant the hostess greeted him just as the staff at the bar had greeted him and informed him his requested waiter would be taking care of us as she escorted us to his preferred table. As promised the waiter came over and greeted him by name, "Hello Mr. Spelbender. How are you and your lady friend today?"

"I'm well. Ken this is Gabriella."

The waiter politely acknowledged me. "Good evening, Ms. Gabriella."

"Good evening," I responded just as politely.

The food was fantastic as most Southern cuisine is. The dinner conversation had been just as pleasant and intellectually stimulating as our phone conversations. Dasht was obviously smitten with my presence, and I really liked that and the feelings it gave me. He would stare at me momentarily and then dart his eyes away in the shyest but cutest way. I wasn't nearly as nervous as I'd been the day prior. There was no doubt or denying that I liked him, and he liked me. We ended our date with him walking me to the door, giving me a hug that wasn't too tight but was just tight enough to let me know he had enjoyed my company, a peck on my cheek and a plan to see each other the next evening. That night I fell asleep like a happy baby holding the baby giraffe he'd given me.

"I now know firsthand why the queen has the power to move in any direction she chooses."

Dasht was extra casual in navy blue slacks, a royal blue Ralph Lauren polo, a straw fedora, and cognac colored oxfords that were nicely shined. I was casually cute as well in an off the shoulder, seer sucker sundress that I'd paired with gold hoop earrings and a pair of Sam Edelman, 4" mules. I'd resounded to maintain my fresh face throughout my visit, so I again only wore mascara and lip gloss.

When I answered the door, he greeted me with that million dollar smile that I was quickly becoming a sucker for and a warm hug. He was noticeably excited. As he escorted me to the car he said, "You look pretty." He inhaled deeply before he said, "And we've already discussed that amazing fragrance you're keeping a secret. Intoxicating."

"Thank you," I replied with a shy smile that widened when I noticed the bouquet of white roses mixed with gardenias lying on the passenger seat when he opened the car door. "Thank you Dasht."

He winked and smiled as he closed the door. Once he was seated behind the steering wheel he asked, "What do you want to do today Gabby? We can do whatever you want."

"Well, I don't really have anything in mind other than you teaching me how to play chess."

He laughed his deep, throaty laugh before saying, "Ok I can definitely do that. Are you hungry?"

"Not really."

"Well I am. Want to just order something and eat at my place?"

"That's fine."

On the short, approximately ten minute drive to his house Dasht and I engaged in small talk about the songs on the radio while his eyes scampered between looking at me and watching the road. He lived in a gated community, which was no surprise. As we rode down the main street, I admired the large, Victorian style estate homes that I didn't typically see in the DMV. The homes were at least half an acre apart and sat on two to three acre sized lots. Most were hidden from their neighbor's view by privacy lines created by trees or vine laden brick walls. I was not at all surprised when we turned onto a private drive to see a large wrought iron gate adorned with an Edwardian Script style S where the gates connected, which no doubt represented Spelbender. At the end of the driveway stood a grand red brick Victorian style home. A veranda supported by eight stone columns extended across the front of the house. Potted ferns hung between each column, and the grand etched glass double door was complemented on both sides by a pair of giant urn style flowerpots that held Vignettes and ivy. Ten arched, floor to ceiling panel windows encased in black molding created the illusion of multiple doors. As we entered the gate the private, cobblestone drive extended another fifty feet or so leading to a side driveway that steered to a four car garage that in addition to the black, Mercedes S 560 Sedan we were in stored a black, Mercedes GLS 550 SUV, and a black, 1989 Mercedes 560SL. Dasht told me he'd bought the SL when he won his first case. This was something else we had in common, we both liked cars and were partial to Mercedes. The house backed to the lake, which apparently coincided with the name of the subdivision, Lake Woods Estates. Apparently Dasht had one of the largest lots or two lots because there were no neighbors within view on either side, even beyond the iron fence. It was at least four acres. When we pulled inside the garage, I could tell Dasht was peripherally watching me to gauge my reaction. From what I'd seen thus far I thought the home was beautiful, but I wasn't necessarily impressed. I'd seen grand estate homes before. Heck most of my friends in the DMV lived in estate homes with electric, wrought iron entry gates, so this was no biggie to me. Besides, this home was quite ostentatious considering he lived alone. Striving to be mindful of my thoughts, I quickly reminded myself not to judge him for how he lived, especially since I had no detailed history as to how he'd arrived at living here. For all I knew he could be like me and need to do everything within reason to avoid shelling more than his fair share of his earnings over to the IRS.

"Ok we're here," he said as he looked over at me with a big grin on his face.

"Yes, we are," I replied with a smile.

He hopped out of the car and came around to open my door. As I exited the car, he quickly shut the car door behind me and moved in front of me to unlock the door, so we could go inside. "Come on in," he said still smiling as he gestured for me to walk through the mud room door as he held it open. Standing close enough behind me for me to feel his body without him actually touching me, he followed me into the chef's kitchen. Once we entered the room, I stepped aside to allow him to lead me.

"Welcome to my home Gabby," he said with a huge smile on his face, and I smiled back. "Would you like a tour?" He asked as he removed his fedora and placed it along with his keys on a nearby counter.

At this point I was honestly indifferent to the house, and I was willing to bet taking women on tours of his home was typical in his efforts to woo them. On the other hand, I knew he wanted to show me, and I did want to see. Besides at this point I believed there was potential for us to continue down the path of embarking upon a relationship. "Sure."

"Well let's start right here. This is the obviously the kitchen." He gestured with upward facing palms for me to take in the view of the room.

"It's lovely," I said, which was an understatement. The newly renovated kitchen was absolutely amazing. The mahogany hardwood floors held a free standing, seven burner, double oven, gas stove with a griddle, complemented by a pot filler extending from the wall and covered by a custom hood. To the left of the stove were two additional wall ovens and a huge built-in subzero refrigerator. The ginormous center island with hand washing sink accommodated four tufted, leather bar height chairs, and housed an extra dishwasher and the microwave. The custom, white cabinets were paired with a smoke gray, glass subway tile backsplash, Carrara marble countertops, and over and under cabinet lighting. A wall of floor to ceiling windows allowed natural light to flow through the room and brighten up the breakfast area, which had seating for six. I loved to cook, and this was my dream kitchen.

Still attempting to gauge my opinion of his home Dasht asked, "Could you see yourself making one of your delicious meals in here?"

Determined to maintain my slightly cool but cute composure, without looking at him I smiled with a slightly raised eyebrow as I responded with a simple, "Perhaps."

Five bedrooms, five full bathrooms, a master suite complete with his and her watering closets and a California Closet, two powder rooms, an office adorned with mahogany paneled walls, a man cave, formal living room and dining room with seating for twelve off of a grand foyer with a double staircase, and an unfurnished outdoor living area with a pool later we ended the tour back in the dream kitchen.

"So, this is where I live," he said with his chest slightly puffed out.

"I see," I said with a slight smile and a pleasant but stoic facial expression.

"All by my lonesome," he said with a flirtatious smirk and eyes that were clearly searching my face for insight into my thoughts.

With confused eyes that questioned his questioning gaze and a slightly flirtatious smirk I said, "Ok."

He gave me a sly smile and ran his tongue across his teeth. "So, what are we eating for dinner?" He asked as he pulled take-out menus from a drawer in the island.

"I defer to you because I'm not really hungry."

"Hmm well you're a vegan, right?"

"No. I'm a pescatarian."

"We can do fish?" He said with somewhat questioning excitement.

"Sure. I love fish, which is why I'm not a vegan," I said with a smile.

He slid the menus over to me. "You pick. I'm going to make me a cocktail. Would you like one?" He asked as he pulled out a bottle of McCallan 18 from a cabinet.

"I don't drink. I told you that," I responded without looking at him to hide my annoyance.

"Yeah that's right. No wine or anything?" He asked as he filled his highball glass with ice.

"No not really. I may nurse an occasional glass of champagne or wine in social settings, but I'm not a drinker." I responded with raised eyebrows because I'd told him this information already.

"Ok." He responded while focusing on the splash of water he was adding to the scotch. Now again looking at me as he sipped his cocktail he asked, "So did you decide what we're eating?"

I handed him the takeout menu for the restaurant I'd chosen.

"Good choice," he commented with a flirty flash of that smile I liked and took another sip of his cocktail while he walked over to the phone. "What are you having Ms. Gabby?" he asked as he dialed the number to the restaurant.

"I'll have the Salmon salad with no dressing, please."

"Healthy eater," he teased with a wink and a tongue poke as he ordered the food. After he finished placing the order, he refreshed his drink and said, "So I owe you a chess lesson huh?"

"Yes Sir. You do."

"I'll be right back," he said and returned in less than five minutes smiling with the chess board. "So you've never played?" he asked.

"No. I don't know how."

"Ok," he said while setting-up the board. Dasht patiently explained how each piece moved across the board, and then we practiced playing a couple of times. Once I convinced him I understood and believed I had the hang of it, he refreshed his drink before we played a game. "Are you sure you never played before?" Dasht asked with a raised eyebrow during our second game when I took his knight with my rook.

"I'm sure. Honestly, I've never played."

"Damn. Ok I see you. You catch on fast. I've got to watch you. You're smart," he said still staring at me with raised eyebrows as he sipped his drink.

I responded with raised eyebrows, and our momentary, flirtatious stare down was interrupted by the doorbell signaling our food had arrived. Dasht answered the door and returned to the kitchen with the food. He sat the bag on the counter and began unpack it. "Ooh baby, we have a lot of goodies here," he said as he inspected the containers. "You want to take a break from the game and eat now or later?"

"I'm following your lead."

"Ok, let's take a break from that," he pointed to the chess board, "and eat."

"That's fine."

He moved the chess game to the breakfast table, then pulled some placemats from a cabinet under the island and plates from a nearby cabinet so we could eat sitting side by side at the island. "You want to make our plates Baby?" he directed in a questioning tone.

"Sure," I said and moved over to the hand washing sink at the opposite end of the island. As I turned on the water to wash my hands, I noticed Dasht was about to make another cocktail, so I asked, "Are you going to be able to drive me home?"

"I was hoping you'd spend the night," he said slyly.

"Nope. I won't be spending the night," I responded bluntly with a smile to soften my tone.

"In due time," he smiled seductively as he left the bottle of scotch and opened the refrigerator to secure two bottles of Evian water instead.

"Sunday is always a new beginning, a fresh start and an opportunity to learn something new."

I was still in bed when Dasht called to tell me he wasn't going to join me and my family for church and Sunday brunch as we'd previously planned. I was a little disappointed but gave him a pass because he said he needed to go visit his brother, Gary, since he hadn't seen him all weekend. As consolation, he invited me over later in the afternoon for dinner and more chess. When he arrived that afternoon to pick me up he was dressed in a burgundy, short sleeved Ralph Lauren polo, jeans and chocolate brown oxfords. I was glad he was casual because I'd pulled my hair up in a high ponytail and was wearing a white, pocketed A-line sundress that was covered in big yellow roses that hit about two inches above the knee and white, four inch, wedge sandals. Dasht had told me that he loved my legs, so it was no surprise his eyes kept fixating on them and darting away as he admired my outfit. On the ride to his house he told me that his daughter might stop by during my visit.

Over three games of chess Dasht and I conversed about how much we were enjoying getting to know each other and were both relieved our face to face meeting and subsequent dates were going well. Dasht showed no mercy for my being a novice at the game and continuously beat me. Having said that, I noticeably got better with every game, and was confident that in time I would eventually master the game and potentially beat him one day. We were about to start another game when Dana and her girlfriend, Lena arrived.

Dana was taller in person than she appeared to be in pictures. She stood about 5' 7" and weighed no more than a hundred and fifty pounds. She had the same pronounced eyebrows and honey colored eyes as Dasht and the blackest hair I'd ever seen in my life leading me to believe it wasn't her natural hair color. Her hair was pulled away from her face and secured at the crown of her head with a clip that allowed it to flow down her back in loose, wavy curls. Even though she wore bright red lipstick, her lips were almost non-existent because they were so thin. Her make-up was pretty but a little heavy in my opinion. She wore a Kelly green empire waist halter dress and dainty, gold sandals. Her fingernails and toenails were decorated with a deep red nail polish that complemented her lipstick. She was quite dainty and girly and by all social standards pretty. Lena was approximately 5' 9" and super thin, about a hundred and thirty pounds. Her strawberry blonde pixie cut complemented her perfectly arched eyebrows and large dark brown eyes that were draped with long, thick eyelashes. Her super pointy nose made me wonder if her plump, nude lips were a gift from Mother Nature or the result of modern enhancements. Quite the opposite of Dana, she wore very little make-up. I admired the frilly, sky blue romper and Chanel espadrilles she was wearing. They were clearly lipstick lesbians.

Throughout the evening the four of us laughed and engaged in casual conversation while Dana thoroughly inspected me with her eyes.

It was getting late, so Dasht invited them to join us for dinner. Dana polled the three of us to assess our appetite for sushi. The three of them were playfully mortified but seriously stunned when I informed them I'd never eaten sushi.

"Baby are you serious?" Dasht asked.

"Yeah. Really?" Dana chimed in sarcastically before I could answer Dasht.

Somewhat laughing at them as well as myself I confirmed my never eating sushi. "I'm serious. I've never eaten sushi."

Lena smiled at me with widened eyes, while Dasht and Dana looked at each other and laughed.

"Aww Baby you don't know what you're missing, but that's ok. We're just going to have to do something about that," Dasht said rather matter of fact. "Are you willing to at least try it?"

"Sure, I'm not opposed to trying it as long as it isn't raw."

"Cool," Dana chimed in as Lena continued to observe all of this with wide eyes and a smile that expressed how entertained she was.

"Are you all ok with us ordering in and eating here because it's cocktail time, and I don't feel like driving?"

"Hell yeah," Dana responded without hesitation.

"Sounds good to me," Lena said with a smile.

Somewhat taken aback by Dana's response I said, "Sure."

Dasht went to the same drawer he'd gone to a couple of days earlier and retrieved the takeout menus. Dana hastily took them from his hand and intently began sorting through them.

"Here, let's order from here," Dana coerced as she held up the takeout menu she'd chosen.

"Oh yeah, they have great sushi," Lena stated while nodding.

I shrugged my shoulders signaling my indifference because I had no clue or opinion on the matter.

"Ok let's make it happen," Dasht said as he reached in a nearby cabinet for a highball glass.

"Pour me one too Dad," Dana stated while perusing the menu with Lena.

"Would you like a cocktail too," Dasht asked Lena.

"No thank you Sir. I don't drink," Lena said.

Lena's statement prompted Dasht to look over at me with a smile and wink, while adding ice to the now two high ball glasses he'd secured.

"She's my baby and my designated driver," Dana said as she wrapped her arm around Lena's waist and pulled her close, so she could kiss her on the cheek.

Dasht recommended I try the *California Roll* and *Teriyaki King Salmon Roll*, and Dana convinced me to try something called *Monkey Brain* as she picked-up the phone to place the order. While we waited for the food to arrive, Dasht pulled out a full set of silver chopsticks from the butler's pantry and gave me a lesson on how to use them. The four of us laughed at my struggle to use the chopsticks, but I eventually got the hang of it. Once the food arrived we conversed and laughed about Dana's childhood antics and Dasht's responses to them. It was good getting to know her because it helped me know Dasht better. Aside from her lack of employment, Dasht seemed to be extremely proud of Dana.

In spite of his strong conservative stances he seemed both accepting and supportive of her relationship with Lena, which made me more aware of his paternal strength and commitment to unconditional love for his daughter. They had a super friendly relationship, one that wasn't in line with what I knew a typical parental relationship to be, but it seemed to work for them. I was all too aware of Brian's drinking and smoking habits and was pretty sure he cursed, but I couldn't fathom him engaging in those behaviors in my presence. We were friendly enough with one another and could talk about anything, but I required him to exercise respectful decorum when we interacted, and I was the same way with my parents. I would never be comfortable with Dana cursing when speaking to me. Every time she'd dropped an F-bomb or referred to someone or something as a bitch I'd internally cringed. I just didn't like it. Dasht had quickly become attuned to my not being comfortable with profanity and attempted to adjust his use of it to the point it was noticeable. However, Dana was either oblivious or just didn't care because she cursed like a sailor. In my opinion, it wasn't at all lady like. I wondered if her Mom spoke that way.

After Dana and Lena left, Dasht and I were still sitting side by side at the kitchen island when he turned my chair around so he and I were sitting face to face. He gently cupped my chin and leaned in and planted a soft, sweet kiss on my lips. Still holding my chin and looking directly into my eyes he said, "You know Gabby we have something special. Do you know that?

I smiled and said, "Yes, we do."

He paused and looked away as if gathering his thoughts before he continued, "You know, I want you to be my girlfriend. Will you," he paused, "be my girlfriend?"

I smiled as I maintained his gaze and to his surprise asked, "What does that mean?"

"Huh, what do you mean?" He asked in a tone that expressed his being somewhat perplexed and slightly annoyed.

"I believe it's important to be clear and synchronized, so what does it mean exactly to be your girlfriend? What does that entail exactly?"

Dasht let out throaty laugh as he momentarily darted his eyes away from mine. Returning his gaze, he said, "It means I'm with you and you're with me. It means we're not going to fuck this up. I don't mess around on you and you don't mess around on me. We're in a monogamous, committed relationship. You're my Bunny!"

"Ok," I responded slightly apprehensive.

Attuned to my apprehension he said, "What is it?"

"I believe we do have something special, it's just that I live so far away."

"Oh Bunny, I'm coming to Maryland. We've got something special. God has blessed us, and we're going to keep our deal rock solid. I don't want us to go more than ten days without seeing each other. I'm going to fly there when you're not here. I'm so happy," he stopped as if he was pondering his last words then said, "I'm really happy with you. You just don't know how much you've changed my life." He took another short pause and then continued, "For the better. Yeah, we're in this. You're my girl, my Bunny," and he leaned in and kissed me on both cheeks, first the left, then the right and then on the lips.

CHAPTER 8
Gabby's Beau

My remaining days in Atlanta were spent cooking family meals and spending evenings with Dasht. It was always hard for me to leave and head back to the hustle and bustle of the DMV, but now it was especially hard. I was smitten to the point of giddiness over Dasht.

It was late in the evening, around 6:45pm or so when we returned from my niece's soccer game. It was my last day in town, but Dasht and I wanted to see one another. Fully aware by now of his routine of indulging in a stiff, daily cocktail by 5:30pm I offered to drive myself to his house. I'd never driven there and because I hadn't lived in the city for over twenty years Dasht was concerned if I would be able to navigate my way there. Not only had I paid attention on the trips we'd taken there together, but I also reminded him I had access to GPS.

Just as I'd expected, Dasht was staring at his laptop and indulging in a cocktail when I arrived. He greeted me with a hug and a kiss and welcomed me in. We played two games of chess to which he beat me, but also acknowledged that I was getting better and better each time we played.

"Girl you're smart as hell." He sipped his drink. "Damn! Smart as hell. You catch on fast. I have to watch you."

I chuckled as I responded, "Yes I catch on fast. I've always wanted to learn the game, and I'm enjoying playing."

As he packed away the chess board he yawned. "Bunny I'm getting a little sleepy, let's go upstairs and relax and talk."

"Oh, I can leave if you're going to bed."

"Now you need to stop acting like that. You're my girlfriend now, so come on and relax with me."

"Dasht, I'm celibate," I reminded him.

His irritation was visible by the harsh eye roll he displayed as he said, "I know where you are."

I was shocked and disappointed at his display to the point of not even being able to respond. Oblivious to my shock, disappointment and lack of response Dasht stood up from his seat at the kitchen island and took me by the arm leading us towards the staircase.

"I just want you to relax with me and rub my shoulders. You're my girlfriend now, so come on and stop acting all funny bunny."

"Dasht I'm not acting any kind of way. I'm serious about my celibacy, and I want to ensure you manage your expectations."

In a somewhat sarcastic tone he said, "I hear you," as he led me by the hand up the stairs.

Once we were in the bedroom just as I had feared Dasht reverted to a horny teenage boy and tried to pull up my dress. Here I was a forty-six year old woman wrestling like a fifteen year old girl trying to protect her virginity. "Stop Dasht. What are you doing? We talked about this," I said as I jumped off the bed and sat in a nearby chair.

Dasht was unmistakably angry and attempting to roll his eyes without my seeing, but I saw. "Yeah we did," he said in a tone that further expressed his annoyance as well as his desire for me to leave.

Not one to stay anywhere that I wasn't wanted, I stood up and said, "Well it's getting late, and I need to pack so I can get to the airport bright and early tomorrow morning."

Dasht was still lying on the bed staring at the ceiling when he simply said, "Ok," without moving.

"Are you going to walk me out?" I asked with a half-smile solely to release some of the thickness of the tension that had engulfed the room.

Pouting with anger and still staring at the ceiling he said, "Yeah, come on let me walk you out." Then he paused a moment clearly mumbling something under his breath before he lazily rolled off the bed. When he stood, he jammed his hands in his pants pockets and didn't even look at me as he headed towards the bedroom door. Stunned and appalled, I reclaimed my seat in the chair and observed while trying to process all of this. I couldn't believe this fifty-three year old man was acting like an eight year old spoiled brat. At some point he paused from his childish huffing, puffing and mumbling long enough to notice I was sitting in the chair. To my further disappointment, he turned, frowned, rolled his eyes and said, "I thought you wanted me to walk you out. Come on so I can go to bed." Now he was being rude.

"Wait, why are you being so rude?"

"I'm not being rude. I just don't like bullshit."

My head was spinning. I had never imagined he would behave this way. Furthermore, what was he talking about and why was he even upset? I'd told him from day one that I was celibate, and even if I wasn't celibate (in my mind) there was no way he could have ever expected me to sleep with him. Heck we'd just met. "Dasht first of all, please don't speak to me that way, and second what do you mean? I don't understand your demeanor nor the harsh way you're speaking to me."

"You know," he paused and rubbed his forehead before continuing, "I don't have time for this, and I'm not going to go into a long diatribe. Bottom line is I'm a grown ass man, and you're my girlfriend. I mean, damn. Do you expect me to be celibate?"

"Wow," was all I could manage to say.

"Yeah wow is my thought too," he said harshly.

"Dasht I honestly don't understand. I told you I was celibate. This isn't new. So why are you acting surprised?"

"I know you said that, but now you're my girlfriend...or so I thought."

"Yes. You asked me to be your girlfriend, and I said yes. However, I never said I was giving up my celibacy. When you asked me to be your girlfriend you said we were going to be in a monogamous relationship. To me that meant you were willing to practice celibacy for the sake of our relationship. I apparently misunderstood."

He curtly changed the subject. "I'm sleepy. Are you ready to go?"

"What just happened?" was the question that was running through my mind, but I was truly ready to leave at this point. Rather than prolong the uncomfortable conversation any longer I stood up and walked to the door. Once we reached the mudroom door, he gave me an apathetic hug and a peck on the cheek.

"Good night Dasht."

"Good night." Not only did he not say my name, Dasht didn't even wait for me to pull out of the driveway before he let the garage door down.

When I arrived at Tippy's house I text Dasht to say I'd made it home safely. He simply text back, "Great." My feelings were hurt, and I was totally confused. Where had all of this come from, and who was this person because he definitely wasn't the man I'd been getting to know over the past month. I finished packing and prayed myself to sleep that night. "God I believe You brought this man into my life, but I don't understand his behavior tonight. If I'm making a mistake by allowing him into my life please help me to get on the right path, the path that is in line with Your will for my life. I don't want to make a mistake or waste more time getting to know him if he isn't the man for me. Please God don't let me be making a mistake. Amen."

The next morning as I headed to the airport I was surprised, comforted and confused by a text message from Dasht that read:

> *Good morning beautiful. I'm sure you're either at the airport or headed there. I'm so glad we finally met, and even more happy that you're my girlfriend now. Have a safe flight and let me know when you land. Dasht.*

He'd also included three kissy face emoji. I instinctively smiled as I read the text then quickly allowed my thoughts to fleet back to the previous night's events. I decided I needed to process all of this more, so I waited until I was all checked-in and at my gate before I responded.

> *Good morning Dasht. Thank you for the text and the wishes for safe travels. I enjoyed meeting you too and will let you know when I arrive in the DMV. XOXO, Gabby.*

I didn't want to be rude, but I didn't want to pretend that all was well between us because I still wasn't comfortable with the way he'd behaved last night.

Once I landed, I text Dasht, but he didn't respond until more than an hour later and when he did, he simply replied with a thumbs up emoji. I didn't spend too much time pondering it. It was obvious that he had taken issue with my celibacy the night before, and apparently in spite of his sweet morning text he was still sulking. I planned to address this when or if we spoke in the evening. At this point I wasn't sure where we were or what to expect from him. However, in keeping with what had become our norm Dasht called me while he was having his evening cocktail.

"Hello Gabby!"

"Hello Dasht."

"What are you up to?"

"Nothing much. Just relaxing after this long day of travel. You?"

"Sitting here thinking about you."

"Really? What are you thinking exactly?"

"I'm thinking about how much I miss you."

"Hmm, ok."

"No really, seriously. You've been on my mind, and I miss you."

"Ok..."

"What? Why do you say ok? You don't believe me?"

"It's not that I don't believe you. I'm just a little surprised."

"Why are you surprised?"

"Well," I paused to adjust my tone so as not to come across confrontational. "You seemed kind of annoyed with me last night."

"Yeah about that. I was a little pissed off. I can't lie about that. I mean damn, you're my girlfriend now, and I'm attracted to you."

"Yes, I'm your girlfriend, and I am attracted to you too." I paused. "I am also very celibate."

"Well we're going to have to work on changing that."

"I made God a promise Dasht, and I intend to keep it. It will change when it's supposed to change. In God's timing."

"Ok. I hear you, and I get it. Are you happy to be home?"

I smiled at how he'd abruptly changed the subject. "Yes and no. It's always good to sleep in my own bed, but its back to the hustle and bustle tomorrow."

"I have a busy day too, but I want you to do something for me."

"Ok," I said cautiously, "What is it?"

"Check your schedule and let me know a good time to come up and see you."

I let out a lighthearted laugh and said, "Ok. Will do."

"I'm coming to Maryland. I'm serious Bunny, we're going to keep this going. I believe we have something good here."

I was still reeling internally over his temper tantrum about my celibacy, but I thought it was sweet of him to want to visit me and decided to table the needed more serious conversation about my celibacy and his reaction for when we were face to face. "I will check my schedule and let you know tomorrow."

"The one who is willing to travel in exploration of fulfilling strong urges and desires often wanders in lust...wanderlust."

Turns out my schedule was open enough to accommodate Dasht's visit within the next two weeks. He was openly excited when I told him. He took the first available dates I'd offered him and booked his ticket the very next day.

"Hey Bunny!

"Hi Dasht. How are you today?"

"I'm great. I'm coming to see my Bunny!"

"Really?"

"Yep!" He exclaimed. "I had Velma book my ticket and make the hotel reservations today."

I smiled inside and out, "That's awesome."

"Yep! I'm excited."

"Me too."

In a somewhat seductive tone he asked, "So what are we going to do while I'm there?"

"There's a lot to do here in the DMV. It's nice out, a little hot, but nice so we can get out and do quite a few things. I will plan us some fun activities."

"We don't have to rip and run. As a matter of fact, I'd prefer that we didn't devote all our time together trying to do a bunch of activities. I just want to have some good food and spend some quality time with my Bunny."

I let out a little laugh that was more me verbalizing my smile than anything else, "Ok."

"Why are you laughing?"

"I'm not laughing. I'm smiling out loud. Trust me, it's a good thing."

"Ok smiling out loud," he paused as he pondered what I'd just said then said, "I like that. Smiling out loud. Yeah, I like that. I'm smiling out loud too."

"If you play with dirt it will get in your eyes."

I was in Fort Lauderdale, Florida, with Tippy, her husband, Joseph, and their children visiting my younger brother Joshua and his family the week prior to Dasht's visit. I spent the majority of my time on the phone with Dasht when we weren't out and about sightseeing or engaged in a family activity.

As I was leaving the kitchen heading to the patio while answering the phone to engage in my daily evening conversation with Dasht, my younger brother Joshua said, "Dang Gab, you stay on the phone. I've never seen you like this," he teased. "Who is this guy?"

"Yeah Gab," My brother-in-law, Joseph, chimed in. "Tell Dasht he will see you next week. It's family time now. Let's go smoke some cigars like we used to before you started spending all of your time on the phone."

Dasht asked, "Who is that? What did he say?"

"That's Joseph and my little brother Joshua teasing me about being on the phone."

"Yeah I caught that, but did he invite you to smoke a cigar?"

Slightly embarrassed I said, "Yes. It's not something I do often, but I sometimes drink a glass of red wine and smoke a cigar with my brother-in-law."

"Hmm. You didn't tell me you smoked cigars and drank red wine." He sounded a little offended. "I just learned something new about you."

"Well I don't really smoke cigars Dasht," I said in a mildly defensive tone. "It's just something I've indulged in from time to time with my brother-in-law. It's not a habit, and it's nothing I'd do around or with just anyone. As for the wine drinking, I thought I told you I drink a glass of wine periodically or when in social settings. I do occasionally enjoy red wine, preferably port wines with popcorn or cigars when I'm home. I'm not a drinker though"

"Ok. I see you've got a little Olivia Pope in you, a little scandal," he paused to sip his cocktail, "and guess what Bunny."

Rather than attempt to guess I simply asked, "What?"

"I think it's sexy that my Bunny has a little scandal in her."

I laughed because his comment was both corny and cute and it had shut down my defenses. "Well that's good to know."

In a sheepish tone he asked, "Will you smoke a cigar with me?"

"Do you smoke cigars Dasht?"

"Like you I smoke them from time to time and in certain settings, but it's not a habit. I'd love to smoke one with you though since you won't smoke anything else," he added slyly. "Will you," he paused to sip, "smoke one with me?"

"I don't know. Maybe one day. We'll see."

Both seriously and playfully pouting he said, "Hmm my feelings are hurt."

"Don't be hurt. It isn't personal. It's just not something that I do often."

"Ok," he said still in a playful but disappointed tone. "Will you at least have a glass of wine with me when I'm there?"

"Sure Dasht. I will have a glass of wine with you."

"Great. That makes me happy."

"Well I'm glad. So how are you today?"

"I'm great now because I'm talking to you, but it has been an interesting day."

"Really? How so?"

"Well," he paused and took an extra-long sip of his now refreshed cocktail before continuing. "Ok we said we were going to be straight with one another, right?"

"Yes," I answered cautiously because I had no idea where he was coming from or where this conversation was going.

"Ok so I struggled over whether I should tell you this, but I want to ensure that I'm being straight with you."

"Ok..."

"So, there is this lady that I'd been seeing. Now I haven't seen her since we've been together, so let me be clear about that first," he paused to sip his drink. "Hell, I hadn't spoken to her or seen her for over three months before I started talking to you." He stopped talking and there was a period of silence that could have been construed as awkward. "Hello Gabby. Are you there?"

"Yes, I'm here. I'm listening to you."

"Oh, ok. Well like I was saying, there was this lady whom I'd been seeing a while ago. I met her for lunch today and told her I couldn't see her anymore because I'd met someone whom I really like and want to have a real relationship with."

I was caught off guard and didn't know how to respond. On the one hand I felt as though he should not have asked me to be his girlfriend if he had loose relationship ends that he needed to tie-up, but on the other hand he was being honest. "She was your girlfriend?"

"No, we were just dating," he answered somewhat bluntly.

"But you all hadn't spoken or interacted three months prior to our meeting, which actually would mean you all hadn't spoken or interacted in a little more than five months?" I asked while simultaneously processing what he'd said and doing the math both in my head and out loud.

"Yes, that's correct," he responded as he took a sip of his drink.

"What made you have lunch with her today to tell her about me?"

"Well she had called me a couple of times since we've been in our deal, and I've just been ignoring her calls and texts," he paused to drink, and I waited for him to continue explaining. "I'm really happy in my relationship with you, and I believe we have something special." I remained silent. "Bunny?"

"Yes. I'm here."

"You're so quiet."

"I'm listening to you Dasht."

"Oh, ok. I just wanted to tell you that because I want to always be straight with you."

"Ok. I appreciate that. I'm still not clear as to what prompted you to have lunch with her today to tell her about me."

"I just told you Bunny. She's been calling and texting me. Even though I've been ignoring her, I felt like I needed to just be straight with her and tell her I'd met someone."

"Ok. So, it's all taken care of now?"

"Yeah she was crying and asking me a lot of questions?"

"Like?"

"She wanted to know who you were and how and when I'd met you," he paused to add ice to his glass and refresh his cocktail. "She asked me what did you have that she doesn't have."

"I'm sorry, but I don't understand. If she wasn't your girlfriend and you all haven't spoken or had any dealings in over five months, why does it even matter? Maybe I'm confused," I said trying to hide my annoyance and ignore the uneasy feeling that was forcing its way into my gut.

"Well that was our deal. We had a sort of on-again, off-again type of deal. She is basically someone that has always just kind of been around, but she was never my girlfriend," he paused, and I remained silent. He drank more of his cocktail before continuing, "She wanted to be my girlfriend, but I didn't see her like that."

"Why not?"

"I just never did. She's someone that I've known for a long time and about a year or so ago we were at the same place for a social event, and things just sort of happened. Afterwards we talked and agreed we'd always been fond of each other, so we decided to date. You know how that goes?"

I didn't want to sound annoyed, but I was both annoyed and confused. This wasn't making any sense to me. I didn't see the value in him telling me any of this or understand why he hadn't ended this relationship with this person before now or at least before asking me 'to be his girlfriend, in a monogamous, committed relationship.' Rather than confront him or interrogate the issue any further I simply said, "Actually, I've never experienced a relationship scenario such as the one you've described so I don't know how that goes."

"Well Bunny, it is what it is, and it's over now. I just wanted to let you know I'd broken things off with her, and I'm all yours now," he said in an awkwardly prideful tone. It was as if he was giving me a gold star or a prize.

As I sat on the patio staring at the peanut shells all over the stamped concrete that I was just noticing for the first time, "Thank you for telling me," was all I could say that wouldn't prolong this topic of conversation and add to the tightening of the knot that had firmly planted itself in the pit of my stomach.

"A boy has two jobs. One is just being a boy. The other is growing up to be a man." – Herbert Hoover

As usual, time had flown by, and Dasht would be arriving in two days. I was super nervous because this was his first time visiting me, and I truly wanted his second first impression of me to be just as, if not more, positively lasting as our actual first meeting had been. Needless to say, I had a million and one things to do prior to his arrival. I had planned a solid itinerary.

"Hey Bunny!" Dasht exclaimed.

"Hey! How are you?" I responded just as enthused.

"I'm great. I'm almost all packed up and headed to Washington, D.C. to see my Bunny."

"Yes, you are," I said smiling.

In a still slightly excited but also seductive baritone, he asked "So what are we going to be doing while I'm there?"

"I've planned a really fun itinerary that I hope you enjoy."

"Oh really?" He asked with extra maple syrup on that Southern drawl that always warmed my heart.

"Well when you get here on Friday, we'll get you all checked-in at The Gaylord, then I want to show you my house, so you can see where I live. Afterwards we'll go back to National Harbor for dinner and a movie. On Saturday I'll pick you up and we can spend the day at my house, have a light lunch and just hang out. You can change here, and then we'll go into the city for a dinner cruise along the Potomac on the Spirit of Washington. On Sunday we have a reservation at Georgia Brown's for their jazz brunch and afterwards we can tour a couple of the Smithsonian museums. I figured we'd spend Sunday evening just relaxing on the deck at my place, maybe toss something on the grill. Then early Monday it's off to the airport."

"Damn, you've got us busy."

"Well I didn't want you to be bored while you're here or say you flew all the way here, and I didn't have anything planned."

He laughed. "Well I'm happy with us just spending time together and going out for dinner. I really just want to see my Bunny."

I giggled, "I want to see you too Dasht."

"We'll just play the itinerary by ear, but I do want to go to Georgia Brown's because I've heard the food there is good."

"It's delicious. I took Brian and his girlfriend at the time," I paused and let out a slight chuckle as I privately reflected on Brian's last visit.

"What's funny Bunny?"

"Nothing. I was just thinking about Brian and that girl he brought here when he came to visit. I'm so glad they broke up because she was not the type of woman I would want to have as a daughter-in-law. She had absolutely no class, so when we went to Georgia Brown's she was stumped over the two forks on the table. God forbid I'd taken them to a five or seven course dinner. Bless her heart."

"Aww Bunny. Was it really that bad?"

"Sadly yes, but they're no longer together. Thank God."

"Would you make fun of me if I didn't know what fork to use?"

"Oh Lord," I thought to myself and then quickly deduced he was chastising me because he had to know what fork to use. "No, I wouldn't make fun of you, but I'd stop seeing you because you're an adult who should know basic etiquette. Besides I'm not interested in raising or training a grown man."

He finished sipping his drink and half swallowed as he responded, "Damn you're cold and hardnosed as hell!"

"I'm not cold nor necessarily hardnosed. I do, however, have high standards, and I just don't have patience for foolishness or want to do a science project. My ex-husband was my science project. I've made my contribution to society. I'm not raising or training another grown man. I read my Bible faithfully, so I know what God designed a man to be. I'm not buying into the low standards society has set for men and brainwashing women into accepting them under the premise that we have no other choice because of this faux man shortage. I don't want a male, I want a man, and I want to be equally yoked. The man in my life needs to be God fearing, a provider, a protector, and a leader who knows how to speak, dress himself, conduct himself and feed himself."

"Damn, ok. I hear you, and Bunny I am all those things, so you don't ever have to worry about training the Dash-Master."

Just like that he'd lightened my mood because the thoughts of my ex-husband had begun to usher in a small rain cloud of disappointment.

"The sophisticated and conceded are often awkwardly revealed. Pay attention, listen and learn."

I was exhausted, but I was ready for Dasht's visit. I'd accomplished everything I'd wanted to do. From what I knew thus far, Dasht didn't eat a lot, but he was definitely a food connoisseur, so I'd stocked my refrigerator and pantry with a variety of food items. I'd hired a cleaning team to come in to ensure there wasn't a trace of dust or a cobweb in sight. I'd had both my cars washed and detailed, and the yard was freshly cut, and the hedges trimmed. There was no time for a spa day, but my hair, nails, and eyebrows were all freshly done. I was as ready as I could be, or so I thought.

"Hello Dasht. How are you?"

"Hey Bunny! I'm over the moon," he exclaimed. "What about you."

I giggled like a blushing schoolgirl as I answered. "I'm well, a little tired, but well."

"Why are you so tired?"

"For starters I had a long day at the office. Then I had a few errands to run in preparation for your visit."

"Oh yeah?" He asked as he sipped his drink.

"Yep."

"So, are you ready for me to arrive?" He asked playfully flirting.

I decided to affectionately address his flirting. "You are such a flirt, and yes I am ready for your arrival flirty guy."

"Hell yes I'm a flirt. I'm damn sure going to flirt with you. Hell, you're my Bunny. I'm supposed to flirt with you," he paused to take a sip of his drink, "and do other things with you too."

While staving off a strong urge to yawn I said, "Yes it is appropriate to flirt with your girlfriend, but I dare not seek clarification as to what other things you're supposed to do with me too."

He let out a little halfhearted chuckle, "We can talk about those other things when I get there tomorrow."

As I climbed into the bed and allowed my head to sink into the pillow I said, "Oh I forgot to tell you, you will need to bring some nice slacks, a dress shirt and a sports jacket because I believe there is a dress code for brunch on Sunday."

"Hold up. Who the hell do you think you're talking to? I'm not a damn country bumpkin."

Not only was I caught off guard, I was totally confused. Was he serious? "Dasht, I was just saying,"

He cut me off before I could finish my sentence, "You've taken your ass to D.C., and now you think you know everything and those of us in Atlanta are country bumpkins who need you to come back and teach us how shit goes. I don't need you to teach me a damn thing. I'm not that guy."

"Dasht I never said,"

He cut me off again. "I know what you said, and I don't appreciate it." At this point I was still confused but also becoming upset at how mean and disrespectful he was being. The thought of him being a country bumpkin had never crossed my mind, and I honestly didn't understand where his hostility was coming from. Rather than add fuel to the fire and subject myself to being cut off mid-sentence again I chose to just be quiet, and as I remained silent Dasht continued to vent. "People get under my skin with that shit. Move away from the South and start believing they're better than the rest of us. You're from Atlanta the same as me, and you didn't grow up with a silver spoon in your damn mouth." He paused to make a drink all the while breathing loudly and mumbling vulgarities under his breath. "I don't believe this bullshit. Thinks she has to tell me how to properly dress when I've been dressing myself my whole damn life." He sipped his drink before he began actually talking to me again, "What kind of men have you been dating that need you to tell them how to dress?" I regarded this question as rhetorical and remained silent, and apparently my silence prompted Dasht to continue his tirade. "Well, I'm not that guy. I'm just as polished and just as proper as your ass is."

At this point my feelings were hurt, my woman's intuition sensors were on high alert, and my blood was starting to heat up. In a firm but nonconfrontational tone I said, "Dasht I didn't mean to offend you."

"Well you did," he interrupted angrily.

In a desperate haste to try to calm the situation I said, "I apologize because that was not at all my intention. I was just simply trying to ensure you had everything you would need while you're here."

He took a long sip of his drink before he said, "I get it, but I don't need you to tell me what to wear. I'm not a country bumpkin or as you say a science project. Look let me stop because I need to calm down," he paused and took a deep breath, exhaled, took another deep breath and exhaled again. "Let me stop talking before I say something," he stopped short of finishing his sentence. "You're my Bunny," he paused and took another deep breath. "You're my Bunny, and I need to calm myself down. Yep, I need to pause for a second. You're still my Bunny and I care about you Gabby, so let me calm myself down, and I'll call you back. Ok?" He asked but didn't wait for a response before continuing. "Yeah, let me call you back. I'll call you back." Then he became silent.

Not wanting to press anymore of his buttons or prolong his tirade I said, "Ok."

"Look, I'm not angry and you're still my Bunny. Ok?"

Again, I gave the only response that I'd become convinced would suffice, "Ok."

"Ok, I'll call you back. Bye," and he hung up.

I lay there trying to process what just happened. It was beyond bizarre. I replayed the entire conversation in my head at least three times before I gave in to the tears that had welled up in my eyes to provide an outlet for me to release my confusion and frustration.

"Men are like steel. When they lose their temper, they lose their worth." – Chuck Norris

I was running around like a mad woman checking off last minute tasks on my to-do list to ensure everything was as perfect as possible for Dasht's arrival. I'd changed my mind and my clothes four times before being forced by time to choose an outfit and stick to it. I was grateful that I'd been in the gym and my consistency and efforts were paying off. I loved the way I looked in the lavender, red and taupe pleated, maxi skirt and matching camisole style top that I paired with nude, four inch stiletto, peep-toe mules. I opted to wear my hair bone straight with my signature middle part swept behind each ear to show my diamond solitaires. I kept my make-up light applying only mascara, a light dusting of bronzer, blush and lip gloss. I'd achieved the effortlessly, stunning look I wanted. After a final inspection in the mirror, I headed to the airport to pick-up Dasht.

In an effort to calm my nerves and put to rest the butterfly squadron that was doing flight stunts in my stomach as I sat in the pickup terminal waiting for Dasht I stared at my nails questioning the glitter sparkles in the polish I'd chosen. I briefly paused to look up and spot Dasht amidst all the arriving travelers. He was as handsome as I remembered. He was wearing a black tailored sports jacket that had a navy and burgundy plaid pattern, black slacks, a black dress shirt and black shoes that were superbly shined. As he walked closer to the pickup lane, I could see his head and face were clean shaven. His eyes were hidden behind those classic aviator shades as he kept moving his line of sight between his cellphone and the pickup lane. I pulled over and stepped out of the car. He immediately spotted me, flashed that gorgeous, toothy smile and walked in my direction.

"Hey Bunny!" He exclaimed as he and I met at the rear of my car where he was lifting his bag to place it in my already opened trunk.

"Hello Dasht. Welcome to the DMV," I said with a grin as I leaned into his wide opened arms for his embrace. The familiarity of tobacco, grapefruit and lavender scented cologne filled my nostrils taking me back to our first face to face meeting. He smelled absolutely wonderful.

"Yep I'm here, and it's good to be here," he said with a wink and a grin as he released me and headed to the passenger side of the car.

As I buckled my seatbelt, I snuck an admiring glance at him. I was tingling with excitement over Dasht being here and having him in my car. As he fastened his seatbelt, I noticed his nails were perfectly manicured, something I absolutely loved and required of a man. Then I noticed he was admiring me peripherally too, and we both smiled and looked straight ahead as I pulled into the traffic. "So how was your flight?"

Dasht let out a chuckle before he said, "You know it was actually really nice. I'd planned to do a little reading over some work I brought with me, but I sat next to this lady with the cutest little girl. For some reason that baby kept wanting to sit in my lap," he chuckled. "Her mom was apologizing and pulling her away, but she kept crying to sit in my lap, so I just put the work away and let her sit in my lap."

"How sweet. How old was she?"

"She just turned two a couple of weeks ago," he answered still chuckling.

"You're too tickled."

He was borderline giggling at this point. "Yeah. It really was the funniest thing. I'm not at all a baby person, but she was the cutest little thing, and for some odd reason she wanted to sit with the Dash-Master."

"Cute."

Still smiling he said, "Yeah. It was cute." Then with that syrupy, baritone drawl he said, "So Ms. sweet smelling Gabby what are we getting into this evening?"

Smiling I said, "I like your smell too." We exchanged flirty glances before I continued, "I thought we'd get you all checked-in at the hotel and then we can go to my house, so I can show you where I live. Afterwards we can grab dinner somewhere at the Harbor."

"Yeah about me getting checked-in at the hotel. I planned for you to stay with me at the hotel. I booked us a suite and everything. I didn't travel this far to be in a hotel alone."

I felt the butterflies that had been floating in my stomach turn to rocks as I thought to myself, "Please not this again." In an attempt to maintain the upbeat vibe I'd been enjoying I playfully said, "I wasn't planning on staying, BUT I would love to hang-out with you at The Gaylord as long as you promise to behave," and I looked over at him with a slightly raised eyebrow and half-smirk.

"Aww Bunny you need to stop all that now."

"Stop all what?"

"Stop being like that," his voice trailed off momentarily before he continued, "stop being all stiff and acting all funny bunny."

"Dasht I'm not being stiff, and I'm not acting. I'm being myself, and I'm serious about my celibacy."

Pouting he said, "I hear you, but I want you to stay. I came here to spend time with my Bunny, and it makes no sense for me to be sitting in a hotel room alone. Hell I could do that at home."

I was slightly annoyed at his pouting and found it disheartening that I was once again having to remind him I was celibate, but I really did like him and wanted us to have a good time during his visit. "Ok I will hang-out with you at The Gaylord this weekend as long as you behave."

His eyes literally lit up, he sat straight up, revealed a wide grin and said, "Thank you Bunny! That makes me happy."

"I bet it does," I said coyly as we pulled into the valet lane at the hotel.

The consummate gentleman when required, Dasht waited for me to meet him on the other side of the car and holding my hand, escorted me through the lobby of The Gaylord.

"Wow it is really pretty here in Maryland," he said smiling and taking in the view of the Potomac River as we approached the front desk.

"Yes, it's especially beautiful here this time of the year."

Slightly squeezing my hand, he said, "And you're beautiful too," before turning his attention to the front desk clerk.

"Good afternoon Sir. Welcome to the Gaylord. How may I help you today?"

"Good afternoon. I have a reservation. The name is Dasht Spelbender."

"Yes Sir. I see we have you booked for three nights, checking-in today and departing on Monday in a one bedroom, river view suite."

He looked at me, smiled and winked before looking back at the front desk clerk. "Yes. That is correct."

"Mr. Spelbender, I do apologize. I can check you in now, but unfortunately our cleaning staff is running a little behind schedule, so your suite won't be ready for another two hours."

I was not at all prepared for Dasht's abrupt and angry response. "What do you mean it isn't ready? I made these reservations over a week ago, and you all don't have my room ready?"

"Sir I do apologize."

She'd barely finished her sentence before Dasht started speaking. "I've flown over six hundred miles, and I'm ready to get settled in my room and relax," he huffed.

"Sir I do understand and again, I do apolo…"

Dasht didn't even allow her to finish saying the word apologize before he snapped, "Your apology isn't helping the situation. What am I supposed to do for the next two hours while you all are getting it together?"

Visibly taken aback at his harshness and struggling to maintain her professionally calm composure she said, "Sir we do have a lobby bar as well as our National Pastime Sports Bar and Grill where you can have a drink and maybe enjoy a nice meal while you wait. There are also some other nice restaurants and shops here at the Harbor that may be of interest as you pass the time. I do apologize, but Sir there is really nothing else I can do."

At this point Dasht was visibly irate. He'd now stopped holding my hand and was rubbing his forehead and gritting his teeth. I was confused, mortified and embarrassed. The front desk clerk darted her eyes at me, and I managed to give her a half smile and an apologetic look before she was forced to turn her eyes back to Dasht as he indignantly said, "Will the damn room even be clean?"

Even though Dasht's question was rhetorical, the clerk nervously answered, "Yes Sir," which apparently further irritated him.

"This is bullshit!" he spewed. "Get me a manager now!"

I felt like disappearing. His anger was totally unwarranted, and his rudeness was shameful. Fearful the situation would escalate due to his baritone voice and the acoustics of the lobby I felt desperate to calm the situation. I reached for his hand and said, "Baby it will be ok. We can just go for a ride to my house, you can see where I live and see some of the city. At least we're together." As I spoke Dasht was unable to maintain eye contact with me, so I reached up and cupped his chin and gently turned his face towards mine and smiled. "We're together and that makes me smile. I would hope it would make you smile too."

He huffed a little, rolled his eyes and let out the slight smile he'd tried to suppress. "Oh Bunny."

Just as he was smiling the manager arrived. "Mr. Spelbender?"

At the sound of the manager saying his name Dasht instantly reverted to his angry demeanor. "Yes. I'm Mr. Spelbender. Are you the manager?"

"Yes Sir. How can I help you?"

"You can help me by helping me understand why you all failed to have my room ready and think it's acceptable to ask me to wait two hours after I've been traveling all day. I'm spending a lot of money to stay here, which warrants top notch service. You all are off to a bad start."

"Yes Sir. I understand, and I do apologize for the inconvenience. I've instructed the front desk to adjust your bill making tonight's stay complimentary and made a dinner reservation for you and your wife to have dinner on us this evening at the Old Hickory Steakhouse here on the property. While this in no way excuses our failure to have your room ready upon your arrival, I sincerely hope this in some way expresses our appreciation for you our customer."

"Hmph. Thank you because I'm not happy."

"Yes Sir. I understand. I will also see to it that housekeeping gets to your room immediately, so we can get you up as soon as possible. It won't be two hours, I assure you."

"Ok. What's your name?"

"I'm Chad Jones."

Dasht reached out to shake his hand, "Thank you Chad."

Slightly glancing over at me Chad obliged Dasht's handshake. "You're welcome Sir. Is there anything else I can help you with?"

"As a matter of fact, there is. Can you have them take my bags up to my room?"

"Absolutely."

Still authoritarian but in a somewhat better mood Dasht said, "Good deal."

I could tell the manager was slightly annoyed at Dasht's thankless disposition and lack of regard for his effort to rectify the situation when he simply said, "I hope you enjoy your stay."

As Chad walked away, Dasht took my hand and said, "So Bunny, what are we about to get into?"

Still disturbed by the way he'd lost his temper and the rude way he'd spoken to the hotel staff I thought to myself, "What am I getting into with you?" Rather than speak my thought out loud I suggested we take a drive out to my place and prayed the suite would be ready and spotless when we returned.

CHAPTER 9
Love Naked

"...because when we are clothed, we will not be found naked."
2 Corinthians 5:3

Dasht and I returned to the hotel after a flirtatious dinner at the Harbor. At his request, I'd packed an overnight bag when I'd taken him to tour my home.

"Gabby we've got to have a talk, a serious talk."

"Let's talk."

He hesitated, looked at the floor and then looked at me again as he asked, "So what's the deal with this celibacy?"

"There is no deal with it Dasht. It is what it is."

"But why? I mean what's the reason?"

"Hmm. Well, as I've become older and wiser, I've developed an understanding of what it really means to be in love. I believe in God and, therefore, I believe in the words written in the Bible."

With a confused look on his face he said, "I believe in God and the Bible too. What does that have to do with us? You're a woman, and I'm a man. Hell, you're my woman, and I'm your man."

"Yes, I'm your woman as you put it, but we're still getting to know each other. Having said that I don't want to just get naked and have sex. I realize that has become socially acceptable, and it's pretty much the norm for people to be quick to take their clothes off and jump in bed and have sex, but even undressed they aren't naked. I want to be able to be truly naked, the way God intended for me to be. Then and only then will I be sexual with a man."

"Hmm, so what to you is naked?"

"In my opinion to be naked is to be free. When God created Eve for Adam, they were both naked. It wasn't until they sinned that they realized that they were naked and began to cover themselves.

They began to hide. We live in a world where people are in relationships where they take off their clothes and have sex, but they are hidden from one another. In some cases, they even hide from themselves. So many people have become so hidden from others and themselves that they've started to believe in the facades they parade around as representations of themselves. A bunch of fragile human begins with faux existences sustained by social media posts and likes, followed by DM hook-ups, serial on-line dating, affairs and one night stands."

"Damn!" he exclaimed.

"Yeah damn is right because in my opinion that is a sad way to live. Sadly for them, they're never really naked and, therefore, never really free. No thank you. I don't want that. I can get a rush of dopamine from eating a doughnut and just like that is only a temporary pleasure with consequences so is meaningless sex. Once it wears only emptiness remains and then it's off to the next conquest for another fleeting high. Now don't get me wrong I'm not judging anyone. I'm just saying it isn't for me."

"It sounds like you are," he interrupted.

"Perhaps, but I'm not. Honestly, I'm not. It's just not for me. I want more than sex. I want to be naked the way God intended. I want to be free."

With a semi scowl on his face he asked, "So are you saying we have to be in love to have sex?"

Looking directly in his eyes I said, "Yes because I don't want to just have sex. I'm not going to just have sex."

With raised eyebrows he said, "Well you just said a mouthful." His expression softened, and he smiled slightly as he continued, "But really, you can be free with me. I promise you can be free with me."

Not at all amused I asked, "Can I?"

"Yes, you can," he said in a somewhat joking manner.

"Can you be free with me Dasht?"

It was clear he was still focused on sex when he flashed a wide grin and said, "I'm ready to strip down right now," and he pointed to the erection that was forming in his pants.

I was slightly put off at his crassness but stayed focused on the topic at hand. "Ok let's start shedding layers."

His eyes and his smile widened with excitement. "Now you're speaking my language. Tell me what you want me to take off first."

"Let me see your cell phone."

Needless to say, his enthusiasm dissipated and was replaced with confusion. "What?"

"Let me see your cell phone."

At this point he was almost snarling. "See my cell phone? For what?"

"You said you could be naked with me. I mean just a minute ago you were ready to strip down to your birthday suit. So, if you're willing to let me see you naked surely, you're willing to let me look in your cell phone. After all what could be more private than showing me your penis?"

"You seeing my dick is no big deal. What does my cell phone have to do with me taking off my clothes?"

I closed my eyes, slightly pursed my lips before letting out a closed mouth, throaty laugh that wasn't at all humorous but more reflective of the sadness and disappointment I was feeling at how common he'd just shown himself to be. "Dasht I'm not sure if you realize it, but you just proved my point."

Clearly irritated he asked, "What point?"

"I've long been puzzled at how it has become totally common for people to share their bodies, the most private and sacred parts of their body with someone in a sexual way but regard their cell phone, money, credit score, etc. as too private or too valuable to share. Yet they'll take off their clothes and share the most intimate parts of their soul and allow a random stranger to leave traces of their DNA lingering forever. That just doesn't make sense to me..." my voice trailed as I pondered my own thoughts. "I guess I was just raised different."

In a judgmental and questioning tone, he asked, "So you mean to tell me you've never had a one night stand or just had sex with a friend?"

I was somewhat insulted by his question, and I wondered if he was intentionally trying to insult me, but rather than shift the conversation to clarify his intentions I simply answered, "No I've never had a one night stand."

"Never?" He said clearly unable to hide his shock.

"No never."

His demeanor had become serious but subdued. "Damn. That's actually admirable."

"I don't know if it's admirable, but it's true."

"No, it really is. I don't know anyone, including me who hasn't had a one night stand at least once in their life. Damn," he said apparently still surprised at my revelation. "Have you always been this way?"

I chuckled, "Well I'm no angel, and I'm not a virgin."

He flashed a huge smile as he let out that deep, infectious laugh that I loved. "Aww Gabby. Hell, you were married so I know you're not a virgin."

I joined in his laughter a little before continuing, "So you know I'm no angel. Even though I had Brian at a young age I've never been promiscuous, and even though I've been married, I've never been sexually free."

"Hmm interesting," he said paying full attention to my every word. "Are you sexually free now?" At the mention of my sexuality his mind had wandered back to sex and he was flirting again.

I let out a half chuckle as I said, "I'm more focused on being totally free."

Now that I'd once again snuffed the wind out of his sexually intrigued sails his serious demeanor had returned. "What led you to be this way?"

"Well a little more than two years ago I vowed to break my cycle of failed relationships. I went on a personal journey to get naked with myself. I had come to the realization that in order to have the love I was designed to experience and deeply longed for I had to get naked, and before I could sincerely undress and be free with someone else, I had to first become truly stripped down and free with myself. I had to come out of hiding. I had to stop hiding from myself."

"Ok..." he unintentionally interrupted because of his being totally engrossed in what I was saying.

Breaking away from my thoughts I smiled to acknowledge him before continuing. "I realized I was hiding not only from the world but also hiding from myself. I was running inside myself from myself."

"What do you mean? Why?"

"I was ashamed. I was crippled by the power of shame."

Sympathetically confused he asked, "Gabby you're a beautiful, accomplished, and successful woman. What were you ashamed of?"

"I was ashamed of so many things that were at the core of who I was, who I am, and who I will possibly always be."

"Meaning?"

"Some things that I've genetically inherited, some outside of me and my choices or control, but the most shameful things were of my doing. I was crippled by my choices, my repetitions of destructive cycles, my own indiscretions, my scarlet letters so to speak." I paused to choke back the lump that was forming in my throat before continuing. "My biggest and most crippling shame was my previously failed relationships. I was stuck. I couldn't understand what I was doing wrong. I worked, I contributed financially, I cooked, I cleaned, I smiled, I was amenable, I exercised, I took care of myself, I dressed well, I ensured we had sex regularly, I compromised to the point of conformity. I conformed to the brink of losing myself, but it was never enough. None of it was enough. I wasn't enough."

Dasht furrowed his brow, looked away, looked back at me, looked away again and cupped his forehead before he said, "You actually thought you weren't enough? How is that even possible?"

"I was lying to myself and hiding from the men I'd been in relationships with. In order to come out of hiding I had to get to the root cause of what was causing me to hide. I had to answer the question: Why was I hiding? Bottom line is I needed to identify and face what I was ashamed of in order to take back the power I'd given shame over me?"

"And how did you do that?"

"I stripped myself down figuratively and literally."

In his jokester way, he sat straight up, opened his eyes extra wide and flashed a super wide grin over my saying I'd stripped. "Oh really?"

Ignoring his attempts to shift the conversation to a joking posture I maintained my serious tone. "Seriously, I needed to determine why I was hiding. I had to ask myself some hard questions and answer honestly. Most times painfully honestly. Was it because I really wasn't enough? Did I believe I wasn't enough, or did the scars I carried make me too much?" I paused as I reflected on those questions. "I needed to identify what I was ashamed of, what feelings of doubt lingered and what power I had given to doubt, shame and subsequently fear? Then and only then could I determine how to deal with it and render it powerless in my life going forward."

"So are you out of hiding now?"

"Yes, I think so. I know I'm still a work in progress, and I'll never be perfect, but I'm happy with me. I love myself. That's something I can't honestly say was always the case, but now I do love me and the woman I've become. Loving myself has made it possible for me to walk in my truth, and walking in my truth has helped me to know my worth. Now I'm not willing to settle for less than what I want and deserve or compromise to the point of losing myself to be in a relationship."

"What do you want?"

"What do you mean?"

"You said you're not willing to settle for less than what you want and deserve. So, I'm asking. What do you want?"

He listened intently as I answered, "I want to be naked and subsequently free, meaning I want my partner to be my safe place. I'm a woman in the business arena, so I have to navigate the politics of that landscape all day every day. I have to speak, dress and operate a certain way if I want to be accepted, taken seriously and successful. When I'm with my partner I want that to be my home. My place of solace. I want him to be the person who really sees me. The person who is privy to all of me and loves all of me just for me. I want him to accept and love the good, the bad, the ugly, the pretty, the broken, the repaired, the uncivilized, the refined, the light and dark places of me because he knows the sum of it all amounts to the complete puzzle of me. That to me is true love, and that is what I want."

There was a brief but powerful silence allowing my words to marinate in the air between Dasht and I as we stared into each other's faces exchanging stoic but simultaneously questioning glances. Then without warning his words pierced the silence like a clap of thunder on a cloudless day. "Do you want to be naked with me Gabby?"

I smiled, "Well I'm enjoying getting to know you and so far, it seems like we may be on the path. Now where the path will lead remains to be seen."

He kept his eyes locked with mine for a few more seconds before he let go of a sexy, half smile. Then he stood, walked over to me, pulled me up by my hands and placed my hands around his neck. He wrapped his arms around my waist, pulled me in close enough for it to be affectionate but not sexual and kissed the top of my head. I closed my eyes and allowed my body to relax against his and rested my head in his chest. He inhaled, cleared his throat, and in the sincerest tone I'd ever heard from him he said, "I want to be free too...let's make working on being naked and free together our deal."

Without breaking our embrace, I smiled inside and out, "It's a deal."

> **"Stripping to a tuneless song while dancing down a street called Love hoping to find our way home."**

I began to strip down for Dasht in our daily conversations during his visit, each day shedding off more layers. We were sitting in the living room area of the suite when my independence became the topic of conversation.

"Bunny you know one of the things I really admire about you is your independence?"

"Really? That's interesting."

"Why is that interesting? I'm serious. You're a real go-getter. You get things done."

"Hmph. It's been my experience that most men don't really care for a woman to have my level of independence, at least not when it's inconvenient for them."

"Well it doesn't bother the Dasht-Master. I find it admirable and sexy."

There he was flirting again, but I'd began to like his flirting. "You're a mess," I said playfully.

"I'm your mess," he said eyeing me as he sipped his cocktail.

"Yes, you are, but seriously for me independence is a means to an end, so it isn't something I can or want to turn off and on at someone else's convenience. My independence has served me well."

"I can see how it can be advantageous but tell me why you say that."

"I had to grow up fast. Too fast."

"Oh yeah because you had a baby."

"Well my becoming a mother at an early age definitely required me to mature, but even before that I had to grow up. Before I even started grade school."

"How so?"

"Well from as far as I can remember my sister, Michelle and I had to do things for ourselves. Shucks, I could tie my shoes at age three and was shopping for groceries at age five."

I could tell he'd almost choked on his drink when he spewed out, "What!? Wait. Come on. You're pulling my leg. Groceries?"

"Seriously. My Mom would give Michelle and I a list and a book of food stamps and Michelle and I would hold hands and walk to the store. Back then it seemed so far away, but now I realize it was about two blocks or so, which is still too far for a four and a five year old, especially girls, to be walking alone."

Clearly mortified at the thought he said, "That is crazy! Why would she do that? You couldn't even read a damn list at four or five?"

"You know Dasht, I honestly don't know the why, but actually I could read the list. My Mom started teaching me to read when I was three, and she would go over the list with me before we left so I had it pretty much memorized by the time I got to the store. At the time I didn't see anything wrong with it because that was all I knew. But now I realize how dangerous that was and thank the Lord nothing ever happened to Michelle and I when we made those trips to and from the store."

"Dangerous for you and your sister and irresponsible of your Mom. Not to disrespect your Mom, but that was wrong. Hell, that's child abuse." He stood up and walked across the room to secure the ice bucket and the bottle of McCallan he'd purchased earlier that day.

Sadly, I said, "Yes, I know...," and I let my voice trail off as I visualized Michelle and I holding hands going up the dirt road and then struggling to carry the brown paper bags of groceries back home. I took in and then let out a deep breath before continuing.

"I don't judge my Mom though. There's no such thing as a perfect parent."

As he poured his drink he said, "Another part of you I respect is your positivity. You always seem to find the good in things."

I chuckled, "I'm not always positive, but I do try to not make complaining a habit. To me that's just a waste of energy because it won't change the past or the situation. I'm honestly not even mad about it because it made me who I am today and trust me life has taught me it's a blessing to be able to stand on your own two feet."

"My soles are attached to my soul. I want, no I need my shoes."

I stripped off a major layer of insecurity that had long haunted me when Dasht questioned my shoe affection. At his request we were sitting on my deck smoking cigars and having cocktails, me wine and he McCallan 18 of course.

As he cut and lit his cigar he asked, "Bunny do you really need a hundred pairs of shoes?"

"No, I don't need them, but I want them," I teased as I poured myself a glass of red wine.

"Gabby do you even wear all of them?"

Sarcastically joking I said, "Well not all at the same time, but yes I wear them."

"Seriously Bunny that's a lot of shoes and a lot of money."

"Dasht I can afford my shoes."

"Bunny I'm not saying you can't, but wouldn't it be a better use of that money to invest it or save it."

"He's asking me this as he pours a $250 bottle of scotch like a $2 bottle of water," I thought to myself. I fully exhaled the smoke from the coffee infused cigar I was enjoying before I said, "I save and invest, but I also live. I work hard so I enjoy some of the fruits of my labor. Besides you can't take any of it with you when you leave this world."

"I understand that because I work hard too, and I like nice things as well." He paused to collect his thoughts and take a sip of his cocktail. "That's just a lot of shoes."

"I guess, but I love my shoes. Besides I have to switch it up to match my clothes."

"I hear you," he joked halfheartedly.

"It's also necessary to have more than one pair of the basics like black and brown because those are the go-to colors, and I don't like to wear the same pair over and over and have them get worn down. I can't stand to have worn or raggedy shoes."

He was seductively looking at my toes when he said, "You could just walk around bare foot. It's almost a sin to keep those beautiful feet of yours covered up in shoes."

I playfully rolled my eyes as I smiled and shook my head over Dasht's foot obsession that I'd learned about in an earlier conversation. "You are such a card."

He let out a deep, hearty laugh. "I may be a card, but I like what I like." He took a sip of his cocktail, "and my Bunny has everything I like." He looked over at me with wide eyes, raised eyebrows and flashed a grin before he took another sip of his cocktail. Then smiling and dancing his eyes across me he said, "Pretty hair, beautiful face, nice smile, killer curves, gorgeous legs, and pretty feet. Umm hmm, everything the Dash-Master likes."

I giggled as I said, "I take care of myself which includes taking care of my feet. Walking around barefoot, yuck, is not an option." I made a face of repugnance and then laughed and winked as I said, "Thus the need for good shoes."

Laughing too he blew cigar smoke as he said, "I hear you, but you don't need that many pairs of shoes. I've never known a person that had that many pairs of shoes."

"True I don't need them, but I want them. As I said, I love my shoes...," I paused mid thought and took a sip of my wine.

"Seriously, why is that? You have a lot of clothes too, but the shoes are ridiculous. Why do you love shoes so much?"

"When I was five my parents bought a new house in Smyrna. I don't know why, but they left Michelle and I in Grove Park with my Grandparents. From that point we primarily lived with my Grandparents until my Grandpa died when I was seven. I don't know why, but we didn't really see my parents during that time. My Grandpa didn't have a car, but he used to take the bus to go shopping for our clothes and shoes. My Grandmother couldn't go because she'd had a stroke before I was born that left her unable to walk." I took a long draw on the cigar and exhaled the smoke. "Grandpa had Alzheimer's disease and it got really bad my second grade year. He used to wander off and get lost. So that year Michelle and I had to wear the same clothes to school every day because no one was there to go buy us clothes." I stopped, closed my eyes, took a deep breath and opened my eyes and looked at Dasht as I exhaled. He was leaned back in the chair with his hands clasped together under his chin and an intense expression that let me know he was taking in my every word, spoken and unspoken. I looked away and focused on the tree line across the yard in front of me and continued, "I don't remember my parents coming to check on us or my Grandparents that entire school year."

With furled brows and a tone that communicated disgust and disbelief he said, "Are you kidding me!?"

Solemnly I said, "No I'm not kidding. I wouldn't joke about my parents like that." I puffed the cigar then blew the smoke out of my mouth. "I only had one pair of shoes, one dress and one pair of underwear that fit." Still focusing my eyes on the tree line, I paused to take a long sip of my wine. "My Grandma would handwash our clothes in a bucket every night and hang them on a window fan to dry. We would sleep in our Grandpa's t-shirts because we didn't have nightgowns." I stopped because the vision of my Grandma in her wheelchair washing our clothes by hand had covered the trees I'd been staring at like a movie screen. It was like I was seven years old again sitting watching her wash our clothes. I looked over at Dasht, who was totally transfixed on me. "My Grandma had to cut the toes out of my shoes because my feet had grown to the point of my being unable to walk in my shoes. My socks didn't even fit me anymore," I sighed as I reached for the wine.

"Damn Bunny."

"Yeah...damn."

Sympathetically shaking his head, he said, "I get it. I totally get it. We went without too. Not to the point where the toes had to be cut out of our shoes, but there were some rough times."

"Well they say what doesn't kill us makes us stronger."

"Yeah that is what they say," he said while sipping his drink.

> *"I always knew looking back on my tears would bring me laughter, but I never knew looking back on my laughter would make me cry." - Cat Stevens*

It was Dasht's last day in the DMV and neither of us were excited about his departure. We were back at The Gaylord, and at Dasht's request I was staying there with him. Dasht was in the shower when I had an epiphany. His clean, light scent ushered him into the room. I snuck an admiring glance as he walked over to the sofa. A pet peeve of mine was a man who looked at the ground and dragged his feet when he walked. So, I both liked and appreciated the way he held his head high, stood tall and took commanding strides. He looked refreshed with his clean shaven head and face. Dasht really was handsome by all standards. He'd just sat down with a fresh cocktail when I said it.

"Dasht let's have a naked talk."

"Ok Bunny. What do you want to talk about?"

"We can talk about anything but," I paused momentarily, "I want us to take off our clothes and sit facing each other and talk."

His eyes widened, and he swallowed hard. "Say that again."

"I want us to strip down and literally have a naked talk."

Surprisingly he seemed shy as he stared at me and smiled. "Are you serious?"

"Yes."

"Ok," he said staring at me with questioning eyes while taking another sip of his drink.

Taking the lead and proving I was serious I stood up and pulled the t-shirt I was wearing over my head feeing my breast. I tossed the shirt to the side without looking at him as I stepped out of my sweatpants. I picked the pants up from the floor and placed them on top of my shirt. Then I stepped out of my slippers and stood in front of Dasht and said, "Your turn."

His eyes betrayed him as they revealed he was both stunned and pleased. I continued to stand in front of him and allow him to repeatedly run his eyes across every inch of my body. Dasht sat literally clutching his drink for a moment. Then he took a long sip before sitting the glass on a coaster on the coffee table. He swallowed the scotch, wiped his hand over his face and then stood up and removed his t-shirt to my surprise revealing a tattoo over his heart. We locked eyes as he stepped out of his moccasins. Then he flashed a shy smile and broke eye contact as he removed his lounge pants. He paused and took a deep breath before removing his boxer briefs. Dasht collected his clothing and placed it neatly on the sofa before looking over at me again. I remained in my same spot and waited for his eyes to once again meet mine. When our eyes met, they smiled at each other. A few seconds passed before he smiled, raised his brows, widened his eyes and said, "Well we're naked now."

"Are we, or are we just undressed?"

He laughed, "Shit I'm naked," he said as he covered his penis.

I smiled then looked away from him as I retrieved two of the sofa cushions and placed them on the floor for us to sit across from one another. As I sat, I motioned for Dasht to sit on the cushion directly in front of me. Once he sat, I asked, "Are you ok?"

His eyes questioned mine as he let out a deep, nervous laugh. "I think so. I mean, this is different, but I think I'm ok."

"I want you to see me,"

"Oh, I definitely see you," he interrupted.

"And I want to see you."

"Well shit, here I am."

I allowed his nervous laughter to subside before I spoke. Looking deep into his eyes I asked, "What's on your mind?"

"Bunny you are beautiful! Damn, you are gorgeous girl."

"Thank you," I said with a sincere smile.

"No, I'm serious. Whew! Beautiful."

"Thank you Dasht. I'm glad you think so."

Raising his eyebrows and nodding in my direction he said, "Shit, I don't think so. I know so. I'm looking at you."

I smiled and said, "So what else is on your mind?"

For the next two hours we sat unclothed engaged in naked talk. I told him how I'd left home with no plans to ever return to Atlanta or the state of Georgia for that matter ever again. I shared with him how I'd married out of desperation to live up to social requirements rather than for love. As the memories came back, I shared. I wanted him to see all the layers, so he could know me, so he could really see me and see my heart and feel my soul.

From the expression on his face, I believe Dasht was somewhat surprised when I stood up and began stepping back into my sweatpants at the end of our naked conversation. However, I noticed him stepping into his boxer briefs as I pulled my t-shirt over my head. Once we were both dressed, he walked over to me with open arms, and I met him walking into his embrace. He hugged me in a way that made me feel both safe and protected in his arms. It felt good, and I needed it. Dasht kissed me on the top of my head, then gently reached up, cupped my chin and turned my face up to his and locking eyes kissed my lips before he said, "I love you Bunny."

"I love you too."

"So there, we've said it."

"Yes, we have."

"I do Gabby. I love you."

"I love you too Dasht."

"From now on when you come home, you're staying at home with me. No more of this staying at your sister's house. You're with me now. You're my Bunny, I love you, and I want you home with me. Where you're supposed to be."

Maintaining his gaze, I smiled inside and out and simply said, "Ok."

CHAPTER 10
Abracadabra: A Flying Dove

Thankfully the hustle and bustle of everyday life in the DMV had made the two weeks until my next trip to Atlanta seem more like two days. Both Dasht and I were super excited about seeing one another again.

"Good morning Dasht."

"Hey Bunny! Are you headed to the airport?"

"I am actually here and walking to my gate."

"That's great. I'm really looking forward to seeing you."

Smiling I said, "That's a good thing because I'm looking forward to seeing you as well."

He let out a throaty chuckle as he said, "Yeah it is a good thing. Are you nervous about staying with the Dash-Master?"

"A little," I chuckled.

"Why? I promise I won't bite, unless you ask me to."

I laughed out loud as I said, "You are such a card."

Laughing too he said, "Why do you always say that?"

"Because you're always flirting."

"I'm supposed to flirt with you. Hell, there's nothing wrong with me biting my Bunny."

"No biting," I said in a tone that was playful enough to stave off any tension but serious enough to convey my intentions were not aligned with what I thought he was suggesting.

"Ok I hear you," he said sounding slightly deflated. "Is there anything you need or would like for me to have here for you?"

"No, I don't think so."

"Are you sure because you have some strict eating habits, and what about your coffee?"

"Oh, that's right. You're not a coffee drinker. Yes, I would like some coffee and fresh fruits please."

"Just text me a list of everything you want, and I'll have Jeannie pick it up, so it will be here when you arrive."

"Aren't you thoughtful?"

"Yeah I've got to take care of my Bunny. I may not be here when you arrive because I have a meeting with a client that may run a little long, but I'm going to text you the alarm and gate codes and leave the garage door opener in the mailbox for you, and you can let yourself in."

"Are you sure? I can go to Tiffany's house until you're done."

"Stop it. You're my Bunny, and you're staying with me. It's bad enough that you don't allow me to pick you up from the airport. I can't have you waiting outside or at your sister's house until I get home. Nah you're my Bunny, and I love you, so you can just let yourself in."

"Ok."

I was boarding my flight when he texted me the codes to the entry gates and the house alarm as promised. I couldn't believe how easily he was giving me free reign of his house.

"An open door and an open heart are not one in the same".

My heart rate increased as I pulled up to Dasht's private gate. With all of my senses heightened because of both the giddiness and angst going on in my body the smell of the fresh cut grass was both sweet and nauseating. Before I entered the code to open the gate, I stopped to retrieve the garage door opener from the mailbox. As I got back into the car, I told myself to get a grip because if I was this anxious now, I would be a nervous wreck by the time he came home. After pausing to take three or four deep breaths I punched in the code, 0*4*6*3*1*0, for the private gate and waited while the "S" on the gate parted to allow access to the driveway. I slowly drove down the driveway taking in all the air my lungs could hold and exhaling slowly in an effort to slow the pace of my heartbeat. As I pulled up to the garage and opened it, I decided to leave the rental parked in the driveway. Even though he'd given me carte blanche, it just didn't seem right to park in the garage. Still a ball of nerves, I walked into the open garage. Despite his welcoming posture I felt a little strange, like an intruder entering Dasht's house alone. I slowly turned the knob and was relieved to find the mud room entry door unlocked as he'd promised. I quickly entered the alarm code, which oddly was the same as the gate code, and thankfully got it right on the first try. Now somewhat relieved I walked into the kitchen and stood in place for what couldn't have been more than five minutes taking it all in. The air in the room smelled like cleaning products signaling the house had been freshly cleaned. The kitchen seemed a little larger than I remembered. A heartwarming smile spread across my face when my eyes focused on the vase of fresh gardenias and large bowl of apples and pears sitting on the island. Jeannie worked fast. Feeling my nerves subsiding I walked over and opened the subzero refrigerator and inventoried its contents. Other than being stocked with the fresh melon and the almond milk I'd requested; it was pretty much empty. There was an array of salad dressings, sauces, water and cocktail mixers but no real food. Apparently Dasht survived on the nutrients provided by the meals ordered from his drawer of take-out menus. I grabbed a bottle of water before peeking in the cabinets. There were only paper products and a few sad mismatched plates and saucers. The cabinet that housed the drinkware, however, was filled with crystal high ball glasses, red and white wine glasses and champagne flutes. "He is really a bachelor," I thought while tip-toeing into the formal dining room that I was willing to bet he hardly, if ever, sat in. Even though I absolutely loved the stately furniture the room felt unwelcoming and cold. I didn't feel any laughter in the walls from holiday meals with family and friends or love from romantic candlelit nights for two. I pondered my own thoughts momentarily before I fixated on the teal accent wall that didn't seem to fit his personality. Without warning fantasies of Dasht and I sitting at the grand table conversing and dining by candlelight took over my thoughts. Totally enjoying the moment, I decided to have a seat at the massive table. I attempted to pull out a chair only to be immediately discouraged by the weight of it. I gave the room another glance over and made a mental note to ensure Dasht and I had dinner in there during my visit.

I headed over to the formal living room, and there was no doubt in my mind that this space had never been occupied by anything or anyone other than the luxurious furnishings. I sat in one of the palatial, armchairs and admired the displayed photos of Dasht and Dana. Remove their gender and age difference and they were almost twins. Even though they were arched, it was clear she had inherited his pronounced eyebrows as well as his eye color, nose and smile. My staring at the photos was interrupted by my phone ringing. I rushed into the kitchen to retrieve it, and it was no surprise to see Dasht's name on the screen.

"Hello Dasht," I answered.

"Hey Bunny! Where are you?"

"I'm standing inside your home."

"Oh," he said enthusiastically. "I see you were able to get inside."

"Yes," I answered smiling.

"Do you need anything?"

"No, I'm fine. Thank you for getting fruit for me."

"You're welcome Bunny. Would you like me to pick anything else up for you on my way in?"

"No thank you."

"I'm so glad you're here."

"Me too."

"I can't wait to see you Bunny!"

"Ditto, I'm looking forward to seeing you too. Is it ok if I take a shower and get comfortable?"

"Of course. Bunny my home is your home. Make yourself comfortable. I should be home in the next hour or so."

"Ok thank you. I'll see you soon."

"The magic that sets you free is unveiled in the melodies that tickle your heart and move your feet."

"Hello! Is there a Bunny in the house?" Dasht called out as he entered the mud room.

"Hello," I responded with a smile as I slid off the bar chair and walked towards the mud room to greet him.

He met me with open arms, "Look at my pretty Bunny." He embraced me tightly as he sincerely said, "It's so good to see you."

Hugging him back I said, "It's good to see you too."

"I'm so happy you're here," he said as he kissed both my cheeks, first the left and then the right, and then my lips. "Umm you smell good. Lord, I love that scent. Makes me want to bite you," he playfully snapped at me, and I giggled like a schoolgirl. "What do you want to do this evening? We can do anything you want to do."

Looking deep into his eyes I said, "I'm happy I'm here too. I just want to spend time with you."

"I'm really happy Bunny."

"I'm happy as well."

"No, I'm really happy. I feel like dancing." He was smiling from ear to ear.

I chuckled a little and smiled.

"Seriously Bunny. Do you want to dance with me?"

I wasn't sure if he was serious, but I was pleasantly surprised because even though I wasn't the best dancer I loved to dance. "Sure Dasht. I would love to dance with you."

"Ok Bunny." He was still smiling as he hung his suit jacket on a bar chair and then pulled out his cell phone, which was connected via Bluetooth to a surround sound system and speakers in the ceiling that I hadn't noticed until Stevie Nicks' voice came blaring through them. He placed the phone on the island, reached out and took my hand, and twirled me to pull me closer to him so we could dance. We danced around the kitchen smiling and laughing, touching and hugging, and petting and flirting. Dasht leaned in and sang softly in my ear, "Tell me Bunny you are mine, all mine?"

He was light on his feet, and I was floating.

> **"If I was to wake-up tomorrow morning and decide that I really wanted to write about love, my first poem, it would be about you." – Rudy Francisco**

I'd learned that Dasht was an early riser by nature; however, I was determined to get up earlier than him today. It was August the second, Dasht's fifty-fourth birthday. I'd set my alarm to ensure I would be staring at him bright-eyed and fresh-faced when he opened his eyes. I was too pleased when just as I'd planned "You're the Inspiration" by Chicago floated through the alarm at 4:30am. To my surprise and delight Dasht began singing along with the band as he awoke. He yawned before he opened his eyes.

I met his eyes as they opened with a huge smile and said, "Happy Birthday Dasht."

Shyly smiling wide he said, "Aww thank you Bunny."

I was excited about being able to spend the day with Dasht. While he was in the bathroom, I placed my first birthday card and gift, a book he'd mentioned he planned to read, on his pillow. Then I headed back to the guest suite to finish getting dressed for the day's events. I'd convinced Dasht to take the day off, which was no easy feat. Dasht was a true workaholic so the theme for his fifty-fourth birthday festivities was serene relaxation. Dana had taken the initiative to find me via Facebook, and the two of us had connected and planned Dasht a day of birthday festivities culminating with a surprise birthday dinner party. I knew he didn't have a clue and would be totally surprised with our collaboration as well as the dinner party. I just hoped Dana had invited the right people.

Connecting with Dana was optimal because I wanted to ensure Dasht was away from the house when the patio furniture he so badly needed arrived. He had an amazing outdoor space that provided a breathtaking view of the man-made lake, but it was clear he never enjoyed it because there wasn't a stitch of outdoor decor or furniture. Aside from the sad, tiny college dorm style grill there was nothing that signified him ever utilizing the space. He seemed to enjoy sitting on the deck when he visited my house, so I decided to surprise him with some patio furniture. Based on the emptiness of the space, I'd concluded it wasn't' something he'd planned to purchase for himself, and I knew the only way he'd accept it from me was as a birthday gift.

Dana and Lena were taking him to his favorite barbeque restaurant for lunch. The delivery and set-up would be complete before he returned. Dana had added the icing on the cake by purchasing him a stainless steel, five burner gas grill. Dasht would see his new outdoor set-up when he returned from their birthday lunch. The plan was for Dana to invite him to join her outside for a cold beer where I would already be waiting to share in the surprise. However, as with all the best laid plans, this one went off course.

"Aww Bunny. Thank you." Dasht called out as he noticed the birthday gift I'd left on his pillow.

"You're welcome." I smiled as I stood in the doorway watching him read the first of the cards, I'd planned to give him throughout the day. In each card I'd added stanzas from "If I Were a Love Poet" by Rudy Francisco.

Walking towards me he said, "Bunny this is so thoughtful, but you didn't have to give me anything. I'm just happy you're here with me." Then he embraced me in a warm hug.

"I'm happy to be here with you too." Then I pecked him on the lips.

Smiling slyly with raised eyebrows as he looked directly in my eyes he said, "You know what the best birthday gift would be?" With raised eyebrows he began running his fingers up my spine.

I reached behind my back and restrained his hands, "You're so frisky." I parted his hands, so I could step out of his embrace.

Dasht let out a disappointed sigh and walked across the room and said, "So Ms. Gabby, at your request I've taken the day off," as he placed the card on the nightstand.

"Hmph so I'm not Bunny; I guess he's peeved," I thought to myself. Holding back my disappointment about his reaction, I smiled and said, "Yes I did, and thank you for obliging. You shouldn't work on your birthday."

"Why not?"

"Because you should be celebrating. Do you normally work on your birthday?"

"Well yeah. I mean in the past when I was younger in my twenties and thirties I used to party, but I've always worked."

"That's sad."

"Why is that sad?"

"I understand working, but it's important to take time to enjoy life. You know, have balance?"

He let out that deep laugh I loved, "Ok balance. I get it. You make a good point. So how are you going to balance me today?"

"I'm going to help you relax and enjoy your day."

"Hmph I offered to let you relax me a few minutes ago, but you're stuck on being celibate."

"Was he back here again? Dang does he always have sex on the brain?" I thought to myself. I smirked as I slightly rolled my eyes, "Stop it Dasht. I'm serious."

"Shit, I'm serious too," he thwarted while giving me an under eyed glance.

Ignoring his advances, I said, "You're going to be glad you took the day off because you're going to have a fabulous day."

"Am I really?" He asked teasingly.

"Yes," I answered confidently.

"So, you've got it all planned out?"

Smiling like a grade school kid who'd just been told a secret I nodded and simply replied, "Umm hmm."

"Well I don't know exactly what you have planned for us, but Dana called and said she wants to take me to lunch for my birthday."

"Oh, that will be fun."

"Does that fit into the plans for today?"

"Oh yes. I expected she'd want to do something with you. I wasn't going to be selfish and book the entire day. Lunch is actually perfect because we have dinner reservations this evening."

"Great. You can go to lunch with us."

"YIKES!" I thought to myself. "No Dasht. Enjoy your time with your daughter."

"I want you to go too. It's my birthday, and I want to spend it with both of you."

"Dasht..."

"You're going." He walked over to me and kissed me on the top of my head. "You're going with me. You're spending the day with the Dash-Master."

I smiled to hide how mortified I was inside. "Ok Dash-Master," I teased to hide my tension. "Let me finish getting dressed." I scurried to the guest room to text Dana and tell her Dasht had invited me to lunch. Then I started to text Tippy to let her know I needed a huge favor. As I was texting Tippy, Dana responded to the text I'd sent her.

NO!!! I DON'T WANT YOU TO GO TO LUNCH WITH US!!!

Whoa. I understood her being off kilter because this wasn't what we'd planned, but I didn't understand the all caps nor the, "I don't want you to go with us." That to me was unnecessarily harsh. I didn't have time to ponder nor address it, so I simply text.

> *I'm trying to get out of it because as you know I need to be here to take delivery of the furniture and grill as well as supervise the set-up. He is insistent. I'm trying to get my sister to help me have something else to do. I will keep you posted.*

To my further dismay Dana text,

> *Well figure it out because I want to spend time with my Dad without you.*

"Damn!" I thought. I definitely needed to convince Dasht to go without me because not only did I not want to go, I didn't want to be around Dana at all if this was her attitude. Her tone also made me leery and somewhat fearful about how the rest of the day's activities we'd planned together would play out.

Tippy wasn't responding to my text so I called her office. "Hey Gab. How's it going?"

"Hey Tippy. It's not going as planned. I need a huge favor."

"Oh Lord. What do you need?"

"Dasht wants me to go to lunch with him and Dana."

"Oh no. What about the furniture delivery?"

"Right. So, I need you to need me to help you with an urgent matter, and if that doesn't work I'm going to have to give you the code to the gate and house so you can be here when the furniture arrives. I don't know what else to do. I'm stressing."

"Ok. Don't stress. I hate to lie on my kids, but you can need to pick Isabella up from her dance workshop because she isn't feeling well, and I am stuck in a meeting?"

"Dang I hate to lie on them too, but I'm desperate. Can you call me in about ten minutes and say that you need me to pick her up?"

Giggling she said, "Yes Ma'am. Dinner is at Canoe at five-thirty, right?"

"Yes, and don't forget to pick up the cake and bring it with you."

"Gotcha. Talk to you in ten."

"Don't forget Tippy."

"I won't. Wrote it on a sticky and posted it on my monitor. Call Gab in ten."

As planned Tippy called me in exactly ten minutes urgently needing my help. Visibly disappointed Dasht accepted I wouldn't be able to accompany him. Whew saved by my little sister. Once he left to meet Dana, I text her to let her know all was well and Dasht would be meeting her alone as planned.

> *Hi Dana. Crisis averted. I will not be accompanying Dasht to lunch.*

I was pissed when I read her flat out rude text response of: *GOOD.*

"I hope you wish for me the way I wish for you, for us, for a lifetime, for love."

I'd remained pleasantly cordial but pretty much avoided any conversation or one on one interaction with Dana when she and Lena returned with Dasht. He was totally surprised when she walked him outdoors to see the new outdoor set-up. To my dismay she presented it as if it had been all her idea and she'd purchased all the items. Needless to say, Dasht knew that wasn't true because she was unemployed and literally didn't have a pot to piss in unless one of her parents gave it to her, and the likelihood of her Mom giving her that kind of money for a gift for her father was both unrealistic and unlikely. She'd seemed so amenable when we'd spoken via phone to plan the day, but now she was being a total brat. I'd even noticed her glaring at me a couple of times while we sang happy birthday to Dasht as I hung the 'kiss the cook' apron I'd gotten him around his neck and gave him the second of my birthday cards. I hoped whatever was bothering her would have subsided by the time we arrived at Dasht's birthday dinner.

Dana and I had chosen to host Dasht's dinner party at Canoe because of the peaceful natural scenery the location provided and the palate pleasing cuisine. I'd never eaten there, but Dana had said it was one of Dasht's favorite restaurants. I faintly remembered him mentioning the restaurant and how he loved the crawfish tortellini in one of our conversations. Even though I was quite confident Dasht would approve of the restaurant choice, I'd decided to keep the location of our dinner reservation to myself. After all, I was enjoying his astonishment.

At a little after three when we should have been getting dressed, Dasht unknowingly attempted to throw another curve in the plan when he said he didn't feel like going to dinner.

Pulling me close into an embrace he said, "Bunny I appreciate all you've done for me today. It has been a wonderful birthday."

"Aww you're welcome Dasht."

"Seriously, I've really enjoyed myself, and I appreciate everything you've done."

"You're most welcome, but the day isn't over," I said as I kissed him on the lips.

"About that, would you mind if we skipped dinner and stayed in? I don't feel like going to dinner. I'm tired."

"Oh no, not again," I thought to myself. I kissed him and said, "Come on Baby, I'm really looking forward to us going to dinner. We won't be out long." I jokingly made a pouty face.

"Bunny I'm tired. It's been a long day for the Dash-Master, and I'm still full from all the barbecue I ate during lunch."

"Dasht I haven't eaten since breakfast. I'm literally starved." This time I pouted for real.

"We can order in Bunny."

Pulling away from him I said, "No Dasht. I don't want to order in. I want us to go out."

He seemed stunned at my taking a stance. Grudgingly he said, "Ok."

"Whew! Thank God," I silently prayed. "Don't get a bear on you. We're going to have a good time."

He laughed a little at my using one of his references. "You're the one who was getting a bear on you."

"Perhaps," I giggled.

"I don't want to be out too long Gabby."

"We won't be long. I promise," I said over my shoulder as I sauntered to the guest room to get dressed for dinner.

I knew Dasht would be drinking, and I didn't want to drive the economy rental I had so I'd ordered car service to take us to dinner. The car arrived promptly, and we were on our way. Dasht's demeanor was still slightly begrudging on the ride to the restaurant, which annoyed me. Rather than allow my annoyance with his attitude to surface to the point of being noticeable I chose to smile and ignore it. As a gesture of reassurance, I reached over and held his hand gently stroking his fingers with mine. As we pulled up to the restaurant, I was mildly disappointed that Dasht's disposition seemed to worsen. I'd anticipated him perking up once he realized we were having dinner at Canoe. I was on the verge of becoming totally frustrated with him. At this point I just hoped he would be happy when he saw his daughter and friends were joining us.

"I didn't know we were coming to Canoe," he said as we exited the car.

"You weren't supposed to know. It's a surprise." I winked.

"Yeah it is," he said in a tone that gave me pause. "This is actually one of my favorite places."

Still struggling to suppress my growing frustration I forced myself to smile as I playfully said, "Really?"

"Umm hmm," he replied rather stoic.

Dasht was borderline being a jerk, and it was becoming arduous for me to ignore. In an almost defeated desperate effort to stifle the tension that was growing between us and salvage the evening, I reached down and grabbed his hand. I felt my heart sink a little when he didn't oblige my attempt to make eye contact with him as our hands met and fingers intertwined. We both looked straight ahead as we entered the restaurant hand in hand.

"Hello," the hostess said in a perkier than professional tone as soon as she saw Dasht.

I felt his body tense and through my peripheral noticed his jawline tighten. It was obvious he and the hostess recognized one another.

Attuned to his demeanor she went from briefly visibly being put off and puzzled to noticing me and becoming professionally polite. "Good evening. Welcome to Canoe. Do you have a reservation?"

"Good evening," I said forcing her to lock eyes with me. "Yes, we do. Franklin party." Dasht relaxed his hand almost letting go of mine, but I tightened my fingers forcing him to maintain the grip.

"Yes, I see you right here," she said looking at the computer screen. She nudged then nodded towards the other hostess standing beside her, "Bianca will take to your table." She looked at Dasht, who was looking straight ahead and said, "Enjoy your dinner." Her tone was pleasant, but her eyes were terse. Dasht didn't look in her direction or say a word to acknowledge her.

"Thank you," I replied once again forcing her to look at me, and she did so with a borderline glare.

As we followed Bianca away from the hostess station, I could feel her eyes piercing our backs. "You know her?"

"Who?"

"The hostess. I believe her name is Jill, at least that's what her name tag said."

"I mean I've seen her a couple of times when I've been in here, but I don't know her," he said defensively.

Still determined to salvage the evening I chose to let it go, but there was a tiny knot in the pit of my stomach that advise I remember her name, her voice and every detail of her face.

"SURPRISE!!!!!" Everyone yelled as Dasht and I entered the private room. Finally, to my delight I looked over and saw he was grinning from ear to ear and uncontrollably letting go of that deep laugh I loved so much. He was genuinely happy and surprised. I breathed a long sigh of relief. Mission accomplished.

Other than Tippy and Joseph, Michelle and Paul, I'd left the extension of invitations to Dana. It was a nice intimate group and Dasht seemed really pleased with the faces in the room. Along with herself and Lena, Dana had invited Velma, Dasht's executive assistant and her husband Ted and Dasht's friend and law partner, Carlton and his wife Barbara. Velma was nothing like I'd imagined her to be. Based on Dasht's raving about her, I'd pictured a curvaceous, polished, drop-dead gorgeous sophisticate. Quite the opposite, she was an extremely tall, slim, homely plain Jane, and her husband Ted was a pudgy, nerd. Carlton did not fit any of the typical lawyer stereotypes but rather looked like a professional football player. He stood well over six feet and was all muscle, which I'm sure caused women to regard him as handsome. However, it was my opinion that other than his stature there was nothing about his face or features that would make him memorable. His wife, Barbara was what my friends and I referred to as a Franken bride, meaning it was obvious she'd been nipped and tucked as many times and ways as her plastic surgeon could nip and tuck her without killing her. She was probably pretty once upon a time, but now she had boobs that were much too large for her frame and a catlike face that I didn't find at all attractive.

Shortly after Dasht and I greeted all the guests and had taken our seats I accidentally made eye contact with Dana whose demeanor while not as curt as earlier still seemed quite cool. For the life of me I didn't understand her attitude towards me. While placing our drink orders I noticed an empty seat. As I was leaning over whispering with Tippy about the cake, I caught a glimpse of Dana smiling slyly as she glanced towards the entry to the private room. I turned to see what had Dana amused to see a very well dressed, petite woman entering the room. As her presence became noticeable everyone in the room except for me, my sisters and brother-in-laws seemed to recognize her, and Dasht, Carlton and

Velma seemed terrified. Dana gleefully stood up and welcomed her with a hug and then pointed her to the empty seat.

"Everyone this is my Aunt, Lillian." Then pointing out everyone at the table, Dana continued the introductions. "Lillian you know Carlton, and that's his wife Barbara." Carlton nodded in acknowledgement and took an extra, long sip of his drink as his wife, who'd obviously became aware of the tension, leaned in and whispered in his ear. I was sure everyone knew Dasht's sister was deceased so I'm willing to bet she was asking the same question I was thinking, "Why is her mother's sister here?" Lillian glanced briefly at Carlton and Barbara, flashed a fake smile, darted her eyes at me and then Dasht before focusing back on where Dana pointed. Dana jovially proceeded, "You've met Velma, Dad's assistant, but I don't believe you've ever met her husband Ted." Ted and Velma politely smiled in acknowledgement towards Lillian. Nodding towards my sisters Dana said, "Those are Gabriella's sister's Tiffany and Michelle and their husband's Joseph and Paul." Michelle and Tiffany nodded gracefully in her direction and then obscurely looked over at me with questioning gazes. It was obvious Dana was being mischievous and absolutely up to no good when she glared at me as she continued to speak, "And as you know that's Dad, the birthday boy, and that is his new girlfriend, Gabriella."

In spite of the lack of oxygen in the room due to everyone staring at Dasht and I with bated breath, I smiled and said, "Hello Lillian. Nice to meet you."

It was undeniably evident that her smile was forced, and she was lying through her teeth when she said, "Why hello Gabriella. It's nice to meet you as well." Catching everyone, including me, off guard she said, "You're beautiful," in a decisive but disapproving tone.

"Thank you," I said in a timbre that while polite was not at all grateful.

Without taking her eyes off me and still maintaining her strained smile she saucily said, "Happy Birthday Dasht."

Even though there was no doubt her sentiment wasn't sincere, I was confused when I turned to look at him and saw his brows furrowed and eyes burning a hole through Dana. Through slightly clenched teeth he flatly said, "Thanks Lil."

Why would Dana invite her mother's sister to Dasht's birthday dinner? That made absolutely no sense to me, especially since it was obvious Dasht wasn't fond of her. Why would Dana want to taunt her Dad? As I was about to get lost in my thoughts the waiter's entered the room and began taking our orders. Thank God their presence shifted everyone's attention from Lillian to the food and temporarily elevated the mood in the room.

Other than Dana continuously shooting me the evil eye as she drank way too much and Lillian attempting to engage Dasht in verbal sparring, dinner went well. After the wait staff removed the dinner dishes, the lights were dimmed and Dasht's gourmet, three-layer, German chocolate, birthday cake clad with sparkling candles was brought into the room as everyone clapped and sang Stevie Wonder's rendition of "Happy Birthday".

Gushing Dasht said, "Aww guys, this is too much." He looked down to shield the emotion that was forcing its way across his face. Once he was confident he was in control of his composure, he smiled wide and exclaimed, "This has been great!"

As the lights went up in the room I reached out and took his hand in mine and said, "Happy Birthday Baby." Dasht stared deep into my eyes, winked at me, released his hand from mine and placed his arm around my waist pulling me in close to him. Still locking eyes with him I said, "Blow out your candles." He gave me a wink before he broke our gaze to focus on the candles. As he leaned in to blow, I said, "Make a wish Baby." Even though I was speaking to him the intimacy of the room made everyone privy to my statement. With his arm still snuggly wrapped around my waist Dasht closed his eyes momentarily to make a wish before sucking in all the air his lungs could consume and successfully blowing out the candles.

Everyone's cheers and clapping were momentarily interrupted when Lillian resentfully said, "I sure hope your wish comes true."

The miniature devil that more often than I liked managed to perch on my left shoulder poked me in the neck with her pitchfork as she encouraged me to go over and slap Lillian across the face and tell her to get her unwanted, unwelcome ass out of here. However, the pristine angel perched on my right shoulder gently stroked my cheek as she praised and confirmed the value of my restraint and composure. My angel's guidance was confirmed when Dasht acknowledged Lillian's statement by pulling me into him with both arms in a loving embrace and looking deeply into my eyes as he said, "I hope it does too." Then he kissed me sweetly and gently.

To add insult to her injury I held his gaze just long enough to make her uncomfortable. Solely to ensure she understood I was aware of her intentional malice, didn't appreciate it, and that if provoked could be noxious, I looked her straight in the eyes with no hint of a smile on my face or in my eyes. Then I flashed a smile of amusement and panned the room allowing myself to momentarily lock eyes and exchange a fleeting, heated glare with Dana before I turned a softened gaze to Dasht and lovingly said, "Now you know why I was determined for us to come out for dinner, and I hope you're glad we didn't stay in."

"I'm more than glad. This was awesome. Thank you, Gabby. This has been the best birthday celebration I've ever had."

Except for Lillian and Dana, everyone was applauding and smiling in celebration of Dasht's happiness. Lillian was breathing with nostrils flared like a dragon releasing flames as she clapped unenthusiastically, and Dana who was noticeably inebriated was sulking.

"If you fall off the wagon don't lay down in the street."

I was grateful the car ride home was much better than the previous ride had been. Dasht was happy to the point of being giddy. We sat in the backseat of the Town Car cuddled-up like two teenagers leaving prom reliving all the events of the day. As much as I wanted to assess if Dasht had noticed Dana's behavior and inquire about Lillian, I wanted to savor the moment more. There would definitely be a discussion about both of them, but it had to be postponed for a later time.

Once we were back at Dasht's we were both still naturally high from the day. Overall it had been spectacular.

"Bunny I'm not ready for this day to end."

"It doesn't have to."

"You aren't sleepy?"

"No, not at all."

"Want to play a game of chess?"

"Sure. That would be nice, but I'd like to get comfortable first."

"Me too."

This was the perfect opportunity for me to get changed and give him my last card and gift. I changed into some comfy loungewear that was effortlessly sexy and rushed down to the kitchen and took a seat at the island. Dasht came in almost immediately after me clad in pinstripe pajamas carrying the chessboard. Once he'd set up the board instead of moving my first chess piece, I handed him my last card and the silver gift box that held two airline tickets to Dallas and two tickets to see Chicago and the Doobie Brothers in concert.

"No Bunny. Not another gift. You've already gone above and beyond with the cards, patio furniture, dinner...," he paused.
"Bunny this is too much," he blushed.

"It's never too much when you're in love," I said with a toothy smile.

"Aww Bunny this is so sweet," Dasht gushed as he read the card.
"I get it now. All the cards go together."

"Umm hmm," I smiled.

"Bunny you're a wonderful writer."

"I can't take credit for the poem. It's not mine."

"Well I like it. Thank you," he leaned over and kissed the top of my head.

"You're welcome. Open your gift."

"Bunny you really have gone above and beyond. You didn't have to do all this," he said as he removed the bow. Once he opened the box Dasht's knees buckled and he was visibly overwhelmed with joy to the point of totally losing his composure. "WOW!!!! DAMN!!!! BUNNY!!! WOW!!!! Oh my God, I don't believe this! Chicago!? I love Chicago!" He had tears in his eyes. I stood with my hands clasped together as if in prayer smiling from ear to ear. I'd knocked it out of the park. Not only had I surprised him, I'd made his fifty-fourth birthday one to remember. Dasht wiped the tears from the corners of his eyes, shook his head again in overwhelming joy and disbelief before walking over to me and hugging me so tight he lifted me off my feet as he said, "Thank you so much Bunny. I love you. Damn, I love you."

I managed to say, "I love you too Dasht," just before we engaged in a deep, fiery, passionate kiss that led to touching and groping that felt way too good. One to take full advantage of an opportunity, Dasht seated me on the island and stood between my parted legs squeezing my behind as we maintained our sultry lip lock. What we were doing was definitely jeopardizing my celibacy. Maybe it was the taste of the alcohol he'd been drinking or simply the manifestation of my fantasies and subsequent mounting desire I had for him that made me feel justified in continuing to participate in the intense foreplay. I was actually enjoying making out with him, but when he began to pull my lounge pants down my body tensed and my eyes popped open. "We better stop."

"Why? Come on Bunny stop being that way?"

"Dasht we need to stop before we go too far."

Obviously disappointed and borderline angry he said, "We're just kissing. Damn."

"Dasht we're doing more than kissing."

"So, what if we were? Hell, I'm your man, and you're my woman. I'm attracted to you," he paused and then gesturing towards his subsiding erection said, "I want you."

"Yes, but I'm celibate."

"Well I'm not," he responded dryly.

Taken aback by his brashness I simply sat where he'd sat me.

He stared at me momentarily, wiped his face with both hands and flashed a slight smile. I softened my expression and allowed a flirty smirk to form on my face. Now he was the one attempting to salvage the mood. Still standing in front of me he reached over and rubbed his hands up and down the outside of my thighs then cupped my chin in his hands pulling my lips into his. He didn't kiss me but rather brushed his lips across mine moving his head from left to right inhaling through his nostrils the breath that escaped my slightly parted lips. Then he released my chin and grazed the back of my neck with his left hand and cupped my left breast with his right hand. Before I could tense up to pull away, he gently held the back of my neck in his hand and leaned in to whisper, "I want you so bad. Please Bunny, let me have you," in my right ear. He didn't wait for a response before he ran the tip of his nose down the side of my neck, across my collar bone all the way to my shoulder. "Please let me have you," he whispered as his tongue ever so lightly repeated the pattern in reverse going from my shoulder back to my neck.

"Oh my God," I whispered. His touch felt so good and I silently prayed and asked God to give me the strength to resist.

Still caressing my left breast and slightly pinching my nipple, he ran his other hand up the back of my neck gently gripped my hair and pulled my head back to allow him to softly kiss and exhale his warm breath up my neck to my chin, and I didn't resist. He ran his tongue across my bottom lip before we locked into a long passionate kiss. Our eyes met in a lustful gaze as our lips parted. "Can I Bunny? Can I have you?" His voice was almost pleading.

"Dasht," I paused to take a breath, "Baby I want to. I do, but I can't. I'm celi…"

He cut me off before I could finish the word, "Yeah, yeah, yeah, you're celibate." He pulled his hands away, sucked his teeth and stepped away from me.

"Really?"

"Gabby you're pissing me off. Do you want me?"

"It's not that I don't want you, it's just that I made myself a promise."

"No answer the question. Do you want me Gabby?"

Conflicted with myself I hesitated to answer. I could feel the air thickening between us. I closed my eyes, clasped my hands together as if praying in front of my face, and exhaled deeply before I said, "Dasht I do want you." I took in another deep breath before I met his gaze.

He stepped back into the spot between my thighs he'd abandoned, stared deep into my eyes with a longing and questioning gaze. The silence between us became loud as we both searched the windows of each others soul. He took my hands in his. "Come on. Let's go upstairs Bunny."

I woke-up the next morning feeling conflicted. I loved him and enjoyed our lovemaking, but I'd failed myself by breaking the promise I'd made to myself two years earlier. In an attempt to make myself feel better and subside the guilt I mentally began rationalizing the night's activities. Staring at the ceiling while attending my personal, internal therapy session I told myself this was supposed to happen. After all it was fate that brought us together. "Lord please forgive me, and please let him be my soul mate."

PART THREE
Tuskers

CHAPTER 11
House Keeping

As I lay next to him taking in every detail of his face, I felt my anxiety over our love making deteriorating. I really loved him, and I felt good about it. I'd been staring for almost an hour when he started to wake up. I wanted to be looking in his eyes when he opened them. However, to my dismay he seemed stunned rather than happy to see me when awoke. He looked at me and then he rolled over, turning away from me without saying a word. "Damn," was all I could think as I turned my eyes back to the ceiling and felt my previously deteriorating anxiety returning. A part of me wanted to get out of the bed and run, but more of me wanted him to roll over, pull me in close to him, kiss me and tell me he loved me. He must have sensed my angst because while I was lost in my thoughts and the ceiling, he'd rolled over and was now staring at me. I allowed my eyes to meet his momentarily, and my nervousness pushed an appeasing smile across my face before I focused my eyes back on the ceiling.

"Good morning Bunny."

His calling me Bunny sent a mild wave of relief through me. Without looking at him, I graciously said, "Good morning."

Propping himself up on his elbows he said, "Ok look at me," and I obliged. "How are you feeling?"

Breaking our eye contact, I closed my eyes as I responded, "I feel fine."

"Ok, ok, open your eyes and look at me. Let's talk about the elephant in the room." Once again, I complied and looked at him as he continued. "We did the deal, and it was great. It was time for us to make love." He reached over and cupped my chin, "I enjoyed you, and I hope you enjoyed me too." He paused as he stroked my chin with his thumb. "We're rock solid Bunny. Ok? We're rock solid. This was good for us"

I allowed a smile of relief to spread across my face but remained silent because good or bad was something only time would tell.

"First there's quiet and calm, and strangely it is this peace that ushers in a raging storm."

I was sitting alone in the kitchen enjoying the view of the property while I drank my coffee. Dasht was still upstairs, but I could hear his baritone laughter as he spoke to someone on the phone. His laughter made me smile. I was relieved he'd addressed my broken celibacy vow and referred to our relationship as being rock solid. I was daydreaming about Dasht and I when I was startled by the sound of the front door opening and then closing.

It was a good morning until she walked in the door.

Her energy proceeded her. It was like an evil cloud that took all the air and light out of the room. I felt her negative energy before she appeared in the doorway where I first actually saw her. Once I saw her face the room became even darker. She was not at all attractive, and her ugly demeanor made it worse. She appeared to be in her mid to late sixties. She had these huge, thick drawn on eyebrows that took up most of her forehead, two of the oddest gray ponytails I'd ever seen, and her glasses were super thick, and they made her extremely dark eyes look humongous. Some of her teeth were missing and the ones she had were broken or jagged and sharp like fangs. She stood about 5'7" or 8" and wasn't fat, but she was far from skinny. She was what my Grandmother would call stout. She wore dungaree style jeans, a t-shirt with an open plaid button down, and what appeared to be orthopedic sneakers. She gave me an angry look and rolled her eyes so hard I was amazed that they didn't get stuck in the top of her skull. Then she introduced herself with a tone that conveyed I needn't forget who she was. Her voice was a deep not at all feminine pitch, and she spoke with what us Southerner's commonly referred to as a thick tongue. Every word had a 'th' included in it whether it belonged there or not (Thello, Gooth morthin...).

"Good morning, I'm Valerie," she said as she glared at me with a look of resentment. "And you are?" She questioned with a tone of authority.

"Hello, I'm Gabriella, Dasht's girlfriend," I replied with a smile.

At this point Dasht emerged from upstairs all smiles, "Hey Valerie! How are you this morning? Did you meet Gabby?"

"Hmph," she sighed then quickly said, "Yeah, I met your little friend," with a severe scowl on her face.

"Valerie, Gabby is my girlfriend," he said quite matter of fact.

"Oh" she said, as if this shocked her while continuing to sneak glares at me.

After our brief introduction, she stomped up to the master bedroom and literally snatched all the covers off the bed and threw them out onto the hall floor. Apparently, this was not her normal routine because Dasht had headed up the stairs after her, and I'd followed him. However, once we saw her angrily disassembling the bed that had been made prior to her arrival, we'd both stopped in our tracks. Dasht looked at me with a puzzled look on his face and asked, "What the hell is going on? What is she doing?"

I returned his puzzled gaze with an equally puzzled stare and shrugged my shoulders because I had no idea what she was doing or why. Her actions and her presence made us both uncomfortable. The air in the house was so thick with tension that both he and I left the house. She was dragging the bed linens down the stairs as we were leaving. In a sadly feeble and disingenuous attempt to return the stolen oxygen and light back into the house she called out, "It was nice meeting your little friend. Y'all have a nice day."

We both stopped, and Dasht for the second time clarified, "Valerie, Gabby is my girlfriend."

It was clear her referring to me as his "little friend" was a not so subtle attempt to disrespect me, which was baffling to me. Why would the housekeeper be disrespectful towards me?

"When lightning strikes be still and watch. Sit in silence and listen when the thunder claps."

Two days later Valerie was back and back with a vengeance. She'd entered the house in the same manner as before, and I felt her maleficence before she was in plain view. Valerie was visibly miffed to find me sitting at the kitchen island staring at my laptop while enjoying my coffee, and she made no attempt to mask her irritation. I looked up from the computer screen to meet the daggers she was shooting in my direction from her eyes. I exhaled and silently asked God for strength as I feigned a smile and said, "Good morning Valerie."

"Hello Gisela," she venomously replied while still murdering me with her eyes.

"It's Gabriella." Suspecting she'd addressed me by some other name intentionally, I smiled politely before I reiterated, "My name is Gabriella."

She sucked her teeth and waved her hand in a gesture of dismissal. "Hmph, whatever. I need you to get out of the way because I need to get in here and clean."

Stunned by her total disrespect and rudeness. I shook my head like a boxer shaking off an unexpected punch before I asked, "Pardon me?"

Before she could answer Dasht sauntered into the room, "Hey Valerie!"

I was totally put off when she batted her eyes and flashed a snaggle toothed smile at him as she said, "Good morning Dasht."

Seemingly oblivious to the bubbling hot tension he'd just walked into he flashed a toothy grin back as he asked, "How are you today?"

She let out a sigh of sadness, "Well things haven't been going too good for me lately.

"Really? What's wrong Valerie?" He asked in a manner that I felt was a little too overly concerned.

I was confused, annoyed and borderline angry at this point. They were interacting as if I wasn't in the room. Something was off. I had concluded Valerie was just not a nice person and potentially had a crush of some sort on Dasht, but I couldn't decipher his position towards her. Just two days ago he seemed both stunned and displeased with her violently stripping the bed, and now he was totally engrossed with her to the point I'd become invisible. He was either clueless or intentionally ignoring the tension between she and I that he'd walked into. I sniffed in the flames that were sparking in my nostrils causing them both to stop their banter and acknowledge my presence. Dasht looked both stunned and slightly uncomfortable while Valerie looked infuriated at my interrupting their conversation. It was clear Dasht had recognized her irritation, but rather than address it he quickly left the room. I was baffled when she icily looked me up and down and then huffed as she called after him and headed in his direction. I could hear them whispering as I sat at the island trying to process what I'd just witnessed. I reasoned there was no way he'd had any sexual encounters with her, so what was her issue and why was she so brazen? My head was still spinning when he walked back into the room with his head down and a somewhat cagey look on his face. The expression gave me pause, but the words that came out of his mouth sent a simultaneous heat and chill through my veins.

"Uh Gabby, can you, uh move out of Valerie's way so she can get in here and clean?"

At that moment I know I went deaf and mute because there was literally not a sound in the room, and I couldn't form my lips to part to verbalize a response, so I just stared at him without blinking.

His face became childlike as he said, "Can you just go to your sister's house, umm so you won't be in her way? I mean...," he paused. "Well she has to do her job."

Now my hearing had returned, and through my peripheral I saw Valerie emerge in the doorway to observe Dasht and I. I was overwhelmed with emotion as I continued to stare at him. Without breaking eye contact or uttering a sound, I closed my laptop, secured it under my arm and slid off the bar chair. He broke my gaze and dropped his head and eyes towards the floor. As I brushed past him my eyes met hers, and she revealed that atrocious smile coupled with a spiteful gawk of victory. Before I walked out the door, I looked in his direction once again to see he was still standing at the island looking down towards the floor. My feelings were hurt, and I was confused. "Why did I have to leave the house he'd so freely welcomed me into?" I pondered. It wasn't right, but I obliged and left without uttering one word. As I drove down the driveway I reasoned, "Valerie looks like death warmed over two times, so there is no way he is attracted to her, but something isn't right." It was obvious he felt the tension when she was around, and it made him uncomfortable too. There was an elephant in the room, I just couldn't put my finger on what it was.

"There's always wind and rain accompanying the storm."

Over the next two months whenever I was in town we did the strained routine of Valerie showing-up to clean the house while killing me a hundred and one times with her eye rolls, intentionally butchering my name, and making sly, hateful and curt remarks, Dasht looking confused and rushing out the door and me avoiding her like the incurable disease I'd began to regard her to be. The tension was mounting, and to my surprise Valerie decided she needed to 'have a talk' with me about it. Once again, I asked myself, "Why do I have to accommodate and maneuver around the housekeeper?" As I was walking out the door, she literally stepped in front of me, blocked my path and said, "Gabriel we need to have a talk."

I was perturbed at her sabotaging my name, stunned at her approaching me and mortified by her level of aggression. Rather than respond with an equal level of aggression, I ignored her referring to me as Gabriel, stood still and listened to what she had to say. She began by giving me permission to be in the house. I thought to myself, "What the hell? Who are you to give me permission?" However, I didn't respond but rather continued to listen. She went on to tell me how Dasht was "a good man," I was "lucky to have him," and she and I were "going to work together and help each other." To this I thought again, "What the hell? Does she expect us to be sister wives?" Yet, I remained silent and allowed her to continue to speak. Out of nowhere she burst out crying, and at this point I became slightly afraid and was literally ready to run away from her. Continuing to block my path to the door, Valerie proceeded to tell me how her husband had passed away four years prior and "the Lord was going to bless" her with another husband. The light bulb in my head lit all the way up! She does have a crush on Dasht, and she'd thought her dusting and polishing the furniture would eventually lead to her polishing his knob. This was disturbing. Rather than respond to any of the craziness she'd just wasted my time telling me, I just smiled at her and told her I had to go. Before she would move out of my path, she demanded I give her a hug. I was mortified inside because I didn't want her touching me and passing off her evil spirit, but at this point I resolved she was a basket case. I hugged her with minimal contact, which literally made my flesh crawl and headed out the door. I could feel her eyes all over me as I walked away, and it gave me the creeps. As I walked outside, I saw the garbage can in the driveway, so I pulled it to the back of the house.

Apparently, Valerie had been watching me through the windows the entire time because she ran out and brought me a wipe for my hands and informed me that was her responsibility. I smiled, thanked her, and took the hand wipe. As I drove down the driveway, I could see her in the rearview mirror. She stood in the driveway watching me drive away. "What a psycho," I thought to myself.

> *"I hear the howl of the wind that brings the long drear storm on its heavy wings." – William C. Bryant*

As time went on Valerie's behavior became more aggressive, disrespectful and abusive. Dasht attempted to ignore it, but she was becoming more blatant and had begun doing it in his presence. I'd been in Atlanta the week prior and had just returned to the DMV when he opened the door for us to speak about it during our usual evening conversation.

"I miss you Bunny," he said before taking a sip of his cocktail.

I could picture him standing in the kitchen either looking out the window or sitting at the island in front of his laptop, as he typically did when he'd just gotten home and made a stiff wind down the day drink. "I miss you too Dasht."

"You know, I love you girl. Damn, I really love you."

"I love you too," I replied.

"The strangest thing happened today," he said.

"Really? What?" I asked.

"Valerie called me and told me she had a talk with you," he said in a questioning tone that let me know he had some concerns and wanted to know the details of the conversation but wasn't quite sure how to ask.

I laughed in a tone that conveyed I was entertained but not at all tickled before I said, "Yes she told me I could ask her to do some things around the house or for me if I needed it and she, I quote "will let you know if I will do it." This isn't the first time she's had a talk with me. Awhile back she gave me permission to be in the house. She also refuses to say my name correctly. She always calls me Gisela or Gabriel. I know she is doing that on purpose because I've heard her call me Gabriella when she was speaking to you."

I could hear both him adding ice to his glass to make another drink and the discomfort in his voice, "I don't know what her deal is, but I'm disappointed in how ugly she's been acting."

"Well I don't know her, so it's hard for me to gauge her actions, but they are ugly," I replied. I wanted to see how far the conversation went before I told him I believed she had a crush on him.

Oddly he didn't acknowledge my comment but rather reiterated his previous statement. "I'm just so disappointed in how she's been acting, but you stay calm," he paused to take a sip of his drink. "Just don't say anything to her."

To this I thought to myself, "What am I missing?" Rather than ask him that question directly, I chose a more passive aggressive route. "Well it's clear she has a crush on you," I said.

He verbally dismissed this remark and expressed disgust, disbelief and mortification at the thought of her. "What the hell? Aww hell no. Val!? Aww no, no, no. I would never... She is not my type. Not at all. I would never ever. Please don't say that...don't ever say that again..." It was odd how his voice had trailed off. Then as if a silent warning of some sort went off in his head, his tone changed, and he said, "She just wants to be included," he took another sip from his drink before continuing, "you know be part of the family."

His attempt was an epic fail as far as I was concerned. Rather than smooth things over, he'd began to piss me off. I didn't even acknowledge his statement. I refused to dignify his foolery with a response.

It was clear my silence had made him uncomfortable, when he said, "Just get to know her. Be her friend."

Had he lost his mind? Or did he think I was stupid? Heck I didn't know what he was thinking, but there was no way I was going to be silent and afford him the opportunity to misconstrue my silence as compliance or consent. I tried my best to hide my frustration as

I spoke, "I didn't have a problem with her, but it's clear that she believes she has the right to have one with me. Up to this point I had shrugged her shenanigans off to her just being batty, hoping that over time whatever issues she had would subside. At this point, I have no desire to even know her let alone be her friend. Besides she is not someone I would befriend in any other situation. I will be cordial, but that is all she will ever get from me." My tone was both sincere and firm. I honestly couldn't understand Dasht's reaction, and it was gnawing at my gut.

When Dasht started talking again my eyebrow raised. "You know Valerie has been good to me." He paused to take a long sip from his drink. "When I had to have my knee surgery last year and no one was there for me, not even my damn daughter, Valerie was there, and she took good care of me."

"Wait a minute." I thought to myself. "Hadn't he hired her via a home healthcare service when he had the knee surgery? She was a paid employee so what was all this praise about?" I silently asked myself as he kept talking.

"I will forever be grateful for her. Val walked with me, drove me places, she stayed with me. Valerie was there for me, and I appreciate her...," he paused slightly. "I promised her that she would always work for me. I told her she would always have a job as long as I was alive."

At this point I could tell he was pausing for my reaction. My head was spinning as I was attempting to make sense of what, but more why he was telling me this. Was he trying to tell me that he'd promised her forever employment, and she couldn't be fired or worse, that she would always be around? His words and the thoughts running through my head had my emotions escalating to a level that was not ideal for me to provide a non-confrontational response, so I said nothing.

I'm not sure if it was nervousness or ignorance, but whatever it was it prompted him to continue his diatribe. "Val used to be on drugs. She started out popping pills, but eventually hit rock bottom and started using cocaine." At this point he didn't pause for me to respond, as I guess due to my previous lack of response, he surmised I wasn't going respond. I heard ice clinking into the glass again, which meant he was making yet another drink. I understood that, as this conversation was about to drive me to pour a glass of wine for myself. He continued, "I know that probably shocked you, but she told me she started going to church and just like that God helped her," he took a sip of his drink before continuing, "and she turned her life around."

My head was full of thoughts, but I filtered them and chose my words carefully because I wasn't at all surprised at the revelation that she was a drug addict, and I was convinced she'd used more than cocaine. I'd venture to say she was more of a meth or heroin addict. I was somewhat puzzled as to why he would have a known drug addict in his home at all let alone unsupervised and in possession of a key. "No, I'm not surprised at all. I'm not being mean, but Valerie looks like a hard drug user. Her teeth were a telltale sign for me that she was addicted to drugs at some point in her life, and as far as drug addiction is concerned once an addict, always an addict."

I could tell by the grunt he let out in reply that he didn't expect nor too much like my response. He abruptly changed the subject, and I was all too glad to talk about something else, but deep in my bones I knew there was more to be said about this, and it was only a matter of time before the conversation resurfaced. The Valerie Norris mastodon was getting bigger, and it was starting to haunt me.

> **"There are some things you learn best in calm, and some in storm." – Willa Cather**

My trips to Atlanta had become longer and more frequent. I was there at least ten days of the month, and my extending presence was annoying the heck out of Valerie. She worked on Monday and Thursday, so to minimize my contact with her I'd intentionally arrived on Tuesday. I was in the kitchen looking for a storage container to put away the leftover tuna salad I'd purchased for lunch. I rolled my eyes as soon as I opened the cabinet. The disarray of the cabinets had long annoyed me. It was as if all the cleaning products and storage containers were just thrown in the cabinets. It was normal to have a lid or plastic container come falling out whenever I opened a cabinet door. I had some time, so I decided to organize the cabinets. After all, this was becoming my home away from home, and I was establishing myself as the woman of the house. I was not expecting to find what I found in the cabinet under the sink pushed far in the back corner. It was a pair of Dasht's underwear and one of his t-shirts. They weren't old and apparently hadn't been washed as they still reeked of his body odor, cologne and soap. What in the world was this doing here? Was this psycho practicing some type of witchcraft? It's not uncommon to find persons, especially women, in the South who dabble in voodoo, and Valerie definitely fit the stereotype of a voodoo priestess with her over exaggerated drawn on eyebrows, thick tongued speech, and weird, gray hairdo. I had always felt squeamish about her doing any of the laundry, but I specifically took issue with her washing Dasht's underwear, and this confirmed my need to feel the way I felt. I threw the underwear away without mentioning it to him.

Committed to being inappropriate and bold, Valerie confronted me about the missing underwear the following Thursday. As usual, her wicked spirit filled the room before she was visible, and she strained a "Good morning" while killing me a thousand ways with her eyes.

"Hello," I returned the greeting as I shook my head, chuckled under my breath and went on with my morning treadmill run.

After I finished my run, I was headed to the kitchen for a bottle of water. As soon as I walked into the dining room to cut across towards the kitchen, she beelined for me and with her thick tongued speech and masculine voice she began confronting me. "I had my apron in the laundry room and some dust stuff I use to clean the mirror in the cabinets under the sink. Did you move my stuff?"

I half glanced her way all the while continuing my stride towards the kitchen and simply replied, "No." I didn't feel the need to respond further because first off as far as I was concerned she didn't have any "stuff" here and secondly, she doesn't have the right to question me. She stood in place continuing to stare at me, and then I heard her mumble something as she stormed off. Ooh she was mad, and I was too tickled about it.

"A hurricane can create a path of tornados."

Monday morning, I was running on the treadmill looking out the window when I saw her drive up. She literally got out of her car, headed up the walkway, turned around and got back in her car. She sat for a few minutes and got back out again only to turn around and walk back to her car before she made it half-way up the walkway. On the third attempt she stood in the middle of the walkway and looked up at the sky as if she were talking to God or in her case the devil because after all at one point Satan was an angel too. She paced in a semi-circle. I thought to myself, "This woman is certifiably crazy." At some point she came to terms with whatever issue she had and entered the house. Just like a nerve agent, I could feel her presence. The next thing I knew the door was being slammed to the room I was in. "Did she just shut me up in here?" I thought to myself. I stopped the treadmill, got off and opened the door to see not only had she closed the door to the room but had also closed the door to the hallway on this side of the house totally closing me off from the rest of the house. "Who the hell does she think she is?" I asked myself out loud.

I opened both doors and walked into the kitchen to find her perched in a bar chair watching television. I spoke, and she grunted a hello and began her normal act of murdering me with her eyes. Dasht was upstairs in the bedroom on the phone chatting it up with his buddy. I poured myself a cup of coffee to let her know I wasn't leaving the kitchen, so she could stop gawking at the television and get to the mediocre cleaning job she did. She stood for a moment and stared me up and down. It was clear she wanted to say something but resolved it was in her best interest to keep quiet and start pushing the broom across the floor. I continued to stand in the kitchen drinking coffee and watching the morning news. Once the news ended, I shut the television off and headed to the office to begin my workday. I heard the vacuum cleaner as she began vacuuming the tile floor, which totally annoyed me because who vacuums the tile? I wasn't at all impressed with her cleaning. I began to hear banging over the roaring of the vacuum and then a crash. She'd knocked something down. Then the vacuum shut off and she started crying and singing an old gospel song. "This joy I have," she paused and let out a string of loud sobs, "The world didn't give it to me," followed by more sobs and sniffing. I thought to myself, "I couldn't make this psycho **S**ugar **H**oney **I**ced **T**ea up if I tried." This was crazy. She continued this way until Dasht exited the bedroom and came down the stairs. I heard his footsteps heading into the kitchen and then him saying hello to her. She mumbled what sounded like hello and something about knocking a picture down. I couldn't decipher the rest of their conversation, but it seemed shorter than usual. Within two minutes of their mumbling ending, Dasht rushed into the office where I was asking me what was wrong with her.

"Hey Bunny, what's wrong with Valerie?"

I was annoyed at this, but I masked my annoyance with indifference. I shrugged my shoulders and asked, "What are you talking about?"

"I don't know. Valerie is being really short with me. It seems like she is upset about something."

"Really? I hadn't noticed anything different. She is always short with me."

He seemed bothered and uncomfortable, and he quickly kissed me goodbye and rushed out of the house as if the fire alarm had gone off.

Valerie continued to cry and sing the gospel song until she apparently couldn't stand being in the house with me any longer. She yelled rather curtly to me that she was leaving. "Hey Gabriel, I'm gone for the day."

I walked to the door to say goodbye.

Instead of saying goodbye, she complained about having brought her lunch. "I brought my lunch," she gestured at the bag in her hand, "but I guess I'll just take it home and eat it."

I ignored her complaint. "Have a great day."

As I locked the door behind her, I thought to myself, "She is not my friend and she'll never be my family."

"Sometimes we don't know we're standing in the eye of the storm."

When Valerie arrived on Thursday it was obvious she had not expected to see me, and she'd had enough of my presence. The feeling was mutual because I didn't want her around either. As usual, Dasht was in the bedroom getting dressed for work and talking on the phone when she arrived. I knew she wouldn't expect to see me because I was typically gone after a week. To antagonize her, I intentionally sat in the kitchen enjoying my morning cup of coffee and thumbing through a magazine. When she walked into the kitchen I cheerfully said, "Hello," without making full eye contact.

She let out a grunt followed by a long sigh before she said, "Hello Gabriel."

I flashed a smile that wasn't the least bit jovial as I said, "There isn't much for you to do today. I would just like for you to take out the garbage and clean the bathrooms."

In a tone an octave below yelling she said, "What about the laundry?"

Still smiling I said, "No, there is no laundry. Please just take care of the bathrooms and the garbage. Thank you."

She stormed towards the mudroom, and I heard her open the door to the laundry room. The next sound I heard was the cabinet doors being opened and shut, and then I heard her crying. As I sat there literally shaking my head, I heard Dasht's footsteps coming down the stairs. She apparently heard them too.

As he walked into the kitchen he said, "Bunny, I'm about to head out."

"Ok. Did you…"

Before I could finish my sentence, Valerie emerged and interrupted, "Good morning Dasht."

"Hey Valerie. I didn't know you were here?"

"Why wouldn't I be here? It's after nine. I'm always here by nine," she said rather curtly.

Clearly taken aback he said, "Oh ok. Are you ok?"

She looked at me with disdain and then turned her eyes towards him as she said, "Where is the laundry?"

Dasht literally took a step back as he said, "Huh?"

My blood was boiling. How dare she try to usurp my authority? In a polite and firm tone, I said, "Valerie I told you there is no laundry today."

She didn't acknowledge me but rather continued to glare at Dasht, who was looking at the floor with eyes so wide one would think the floor was tiled with $100 bills. There was an awkward momentary silence before Dasht spoke in a tone that mirrored the meekness of a five year old, "Valerie do what Gabby says. Ok?" It was almost as if he was pleading with her.

She looked at me with eyes of hate and rage before turning her burning gaze back to him. Then she stormed out of the room.

Once he thought she was out of ear shot he said, "What's her problem?"

"Dasht I was going to ask you the same question?"

Totally catching me off guard, he waved his hand in a gesture of dismissal and said, "This is women shit. I'm going to leave you all to deal with that. I have to get to work."

"No Dasht. What do you mean by that, and what is that for you to say? This is your crazy housekeeper?"

"I don't know why she is acting this way. Just ignore her. Ok? I've got to go." He hurriedly pecked me on the lips then the forehead, and he rushed out the door.

My stomach was churning, and I was becoming nauseous. Why did she think she could challenge me? She was bold enough to do it in my face, and Dasht seemed afraid to chastise her. This was too much. My thoughts were interrupted by her whimpering and slamming something. I turned on the television to drown out her sobs. As I was flipping through the channels my phone rang.

"Hey Tippy."

"Hey Gab, what are you up to?"

"Nothing much. Sitting here drinking my coffee and laughing at this psycho housekeeper." I'd told both Michelle and Tippy about

Valerie, and they both agreed she had a crush on Dasht and needed to be fired.

"Oh. How's that going?"

"Tippy it is getting worse. She is too bold. I told her to just clean the bathrooms and take out the trash, and she had the nerve to question both of us about the laundry."

"What!? She questioned you?"

"She questioned both of us."

"She is out of line. She needs to go."

"I know." At that moment I heard Valerie coming down the stairs. "Hold on Tippy."

"Bye Gabriel. I'm leaving," Valerie called out from the foyer.

Still holding the phone to my ear, I walked into the foyer as she was opening the door. "Did you clean the bathrooms?"

"I cleaned Dasht's bathroom and took out the trash like you said."

"Valerie I would like for you to clean all of the bathrooms?"

"I'm not here to clean after you or have you giving me specific things to do!!!"

"Is that the housekeeper talking to you that way," Tippy asked.

Valerie was still standing in the doorway glaring at me, and I was glaring back. "You heard her?"

"Uh yes I did. Who wouldn't have with all that yelling?"

"Hold on Tippy."

"Valerie please clean all of the bathrooms?"

Valerie slammed the door shut, threw her purse down on the floor and stomped up the stairs.

"Gab I think you should have just let her leave because she sounds crazy."

"Yeah you're probably right, but she needs to do something around here to earn her pay."

"I understand that, but I don't feel good about you being in the house with her alone. Especially with her yelling at you that way."

"She is always rude to me."

"Really? I didn't realize it was this bad. Does Dasht know?"

"I've told him. She does things in front of him too, so yes he knows."

"Then he needs to fire her."

"Yeah, I'm glad you heard her because now I have a witness. I'm going to talk to him this evening because she definitely needs to go." Just as I finished my sentence, I heard glass shattering.

"What was that?" Tippy asked.

"I have no idea, but clearly something is broken. This psycho has to go."

CHAPTER 12
Yoked

Both of us were cautious because of our failed marriages and disappointments in previous relationships, but despite our prudence we were becoming closer and our relationship was growing stronger. Each day we were falling deeper in love. As happy as we were, we apparently both struggled with the same internal conflict because we'd both quietly kept our individual lives separate from our relationship. Other than Dasht's surprise birthday dinner, I hadn't met any of his friends and he hadn't met any of mine. I had mentioned him to Brian in passing, but they'd never met. We hadn't gone out together since Dasht's birthday dinner. I also hadn't crossed paths or communicated with Dana since then. When we were in Atlanta we never went out, and when he visited Maryland despite my planning outings for us, he preferred we stay in.

Dasht wasn't really family oriented, which I found a little disheartening at times, but I attributed this to him having such a small family and the family hardships he had endured. Even though I was close with my family and ensured I spent time with them when in Atlanta, Dasht rarely if ever joined me. He most often opted to stay at home and work. A couple of times I'd brought my niece, Isabella and nephews, Joseph II and Benjamin over, and even though Dasht didn't complain he seemed a little uncomfortable. The kids were uncomfortable too because the house wasn't kid friendly.

We spent most of our time together away from the rest of the world. This pattern of hibernating was an arrangement that I wasn't accustomed to, and I didn't like it. Had we lived in the same city this shunning the world would never have materialized because there was no way I would have consciously agreed to this. However, by the time I recognized it and deemed it odd it had become our norm. I'd always been advised the way you start a relationship was the way you would finish it, and I didn't want this to be our finish.

> *"Sometimes people hide from the light because the light will expose the dark."*

Since the beginning of the year I'd been planning the signature fundraising event for one of my social organizations. This was an ideal opportunity for Dasht and I to get out in the public eye and for me to introduce him to my friends.

"Have you gotten your plane ticket?"

"Damn. Is it time for that already?"

I was a little put off by his brashness but chalked it to his potentially staring at work while we chatted. "Yes," I answered politely.

"I'm just so busy. I've got a lot going on here in Atlanta," he paused. "This will have to be a short trip." He seemed irritated, but he knew not attending was not an option.

I continued to choose not to acknowledge his irritation with inquiry and instead said, "That is fine. Remember I was planning to fly back next week for Dad's birthday, but I can leave earlier. If the tickets aren't too outrageous, I may be able to change my flight, and we can fly back together."

"Oh, ok. Hmm. I didn't know your Dad's birthday was this month. I guess that would work," he said as he took a sip of his drink.

"You guess? Dasht I told you months ago that I was coming home for Dad's birthday. Do you not listen to me when we talk?"

"Yeah, it's good Bunny. Look I'm listening to you. I'm just a little swamped with work. Why don't I just put you in charge of plane tickets. Yeah, you handle all that."

I was becoming annoyed with his dismissive attitude and it came out in my response. "Thank you for putting me in charge of doing what you don't want to do."

"Aww Bunny, stop it. Don't be that way. I put you in charge of this because you're better at this type of stuff."

"Umm hmm. Ok Dasht," I sarcastically quipped.

"The funny boyhood bullying, bad tempers and tantrums aren't so funny when they transition into manhood."

I was staring at the ceiling, listening to the birds chirping and mentally mapping out my day when the phone startled me. It was Dasht calling to tell me he'd made it to the airport, or so I thought.

"Good morning," I answered.

"This is FUCKED-UP!" he yelled in my ear.

"Huh? What? What's wrong?"

"I'm here at the airport, but this asshole won't let me get on the plane."

"Ok, calm down. What do you mean he won't let you get on the plane?" As I finished stating the question, I heard the ticket agent tell Dasht to step away from the counter.

"No, I'm not going to step away from the counter. My girlfriend booked this ticket, and she's on the phone now. You need to tell her what the damn problem is."

"Dasht. Calm down. What's the issue?"

"I don't know, something about me being booked on another flight."

"Ok, calm down. Let me call the airline, and I'll call you back."

I was online reviewing the itinerary while I was holding for an agent when I realized, I'd made a typo when I booked his ticket. Needless to say, Dasht had missed his flight. Thankfully, the agent was able to assist me and ensured Dasht was booked and checked-in on the next flight. I hung-up with her somewhat relieved, but I was not at all prepared for the follow-on conversation with Dasht.

"Hello," he barked angrily into the phone and before either of us could say anything else, I heard a male voice in the background say, "Sir if I have to ask you to step away from the counter again, I will call the cops."

"Dasht, what's going on?"

"This asshole made me miss the damn flight, and he won't answer my questions."

"Dasht please just walk away from the counter. You've been booked on the next flight leaving in an hour. So please just calm down because the last thing we need is for you to get arrested."

"I'm pissed. What the hell happened?"

"I made an error in the booking, but it's all taken care of now. You're on the next flight."

"I should just go home because I'm mad as hell."

"Really Dasht? You're being extreme. It's all taken care of, so just relax. We're going to have a wonderful weekend."

"Yeah, I hear you. Let me try to calm down. I'll text you when I get on the plane."

"Hey, I'm looking forward to seeing you."

"Yeah me too. Let me calm myself down. I'll let you know when I'm on the plane."

Feeling deflated I said, "Ok."

This was not the way I wanted to start the weekend, but there was nothing else I could do. I just prayed that he would make it safely and the weekend would go smoothly.

> ***"There's no running to escape from you because when you're alone the four walls of truth will close in on you."***

When I picked Dasht up from the airport he seemed a little standoffish when he got into the car. I chalked it up to him being embarrassed at how he'd behaved earlier.

"You made it," I said cheerfully, trying to lighten the mood.

He avoided eye contact as he said, "Yeah I did. Hell, it wasn't easy but I'm here."

"Well are you happy to be here," I asked with questioning eyes that were softened by the half smile on my face.

"Aww Bunny, of course I'm happy to be here. I'm happy to see my Bunny," and he leaned over and gave me a dry kiss on the cheek then pecked my lips. "What was the deal? Why couldn't I get on the first flight?"

"Dasht can we please talk about that later. You're calm, and I want you to stay calm. I want us to enjoy our weekend."

He looked perplexed but smiled and said, "Ok Bunny. Ok."

We engaged in superficial chatter about the weather and the details of the event as we drove to the hotel. Once we arrived and got all settled in, Dasht approached the subject of his flight again, "What time do I leave on Monday?"

"Geesh, please drop it already," I thought to myself before I exhaled and said, "Dasht you leave at 2pm."

"I can't leave that late. I need to be home earlier in the day. I have things to do," he said in a huff.

"Really Dasht? Are you just determined to be a grouch?"

"I'm not being a grouch.," he said defensively. "I just don't like getting home late in the day. I don't want to spend the entire day traveling."

I was annoyed to the point of becoming angry, but I was also desperate to salvage the mood. He was going to meet my friends, and I didn't want there to be tension between us during the meeting. I exhaled and chose my words carefully, "I'm afraid to change the ticket because of the debacle we had earlier today, but if you want to take a chance…," I shrugged my shoulders as my voice trailed off because of the lump forming in my throat.

"Bunny, I'm sorry. Come here," he came over and pulled me into his arms and for the first time since he'd arrived, he looked into my eyes. "I'm sorry Bunny.

I half smiled and stared back into his eyes.

"I'm sorry for being a jerk. Ok? I was just really pissed off, but I'm better now. Ok?"

Still unable to a suppress my annoyance to the point of allowing a genuine smile to cross my face I pursed my lips, half smiled again and said, "Thank you for apologizing Dasht. Your temper is something we're going to have to talk about because you could have gotten arrested today."

"Aww Bunny…" His phone rang before he could finish his statement, and his body stiffened, brow furrowed, and he released our embrace as he looked at the call screen. He turned his back to me as he whispered, "What the hell," before he answered the call. "Hey you ok?" He paused to allow the caller to answer then said, "I'm in Maryland, but I'll call you when I get back to Atlanta." He listened to the caller intently before he said, "Ok, bye." Once he hung-up the phone he was strangely awkward. Rather than return to our embrace he walked to the other side of the room, sat in a chair and became preoccupied with the television remote.

"Wow," I thought to myself. There was no way I could allow the awkward silence to fester. As I was pondering ways to spark a conversation, my phone rang. Thank God for Tippy.

Dasht and I spent the remainder of the evening watching movies and engaging in superficial conversation while pretending we didn't see the elephant sitting in the middle of the room. Prayerfully he'd be in a better mood tomorrow when he met my friends and my fundraising event would be a success.

"FUNdraising"

As usual, Dasht got up super early. I was a little surprised he opted to go down to the hotel gym for a work out instead of lounging on in the room and watching television. I couldn't join him because I had to meet the hotel staff in the grand ballroom to ensure everything was properly set-up for the fundraising ball.

I was pleasantly surprised when Dasht appeared in the ballroom to help me set-up.

"I thought you were working out?"

"I was but I needed to come and help my Bunny. I'm here to spend time with you."

He seemed to be in a good mood, and I was relieved. He must have really wanted to make amends for his previous behavior because he stayed and helped throughout the entire set-up. He even helped carry a few boxes. Once the ballroom was finished, Dasht and I went to the hotel restaurant to have a light lunch before heading to our room to relax a little before the fundraiser. To my surprise we bumped into my friends Nikki and Tabatha as they had just checked-in and were stopping at the bar for champagne and appetizers.

"Well hello Gabriella," my friend Tabatha cheerfully said as soon as she and I made eye contact.

Nikki joined her saying, "Hello Mr. Spelbender. It's good to finally meet you."

I was blushing like a teenage girl. "Dasht these are my friends Nikki and Tabatha."

He flashed that toothy, million dollar smile that melted me like wax before he said, "Hello ladies. It's good to meet you."

"What are you two lovebirds about to get into," Tabatha teased.

"We were about to grab a light lunch before we head upstairs to get dressed."

"Mind if we join you so we can get acquainted with Dasht," Tabatha asked?

"Sure," Dasht obliged without hesitation.

Dasht was both charming and cordial throughout lunch, and I was pleased. He seemed to have enjoyed conversing with Nikki and Tabatha.

"Places everyone! Lights! Camera! And ACTION!"

My schedule was tight. I was scheduled for make-up and hair at the hotel spa at 4:00pm, and I had to be dressed and in the ballroom at 7:00pm. I'd gone over the schedule with Dasht numerous times to prepare him for the pace of the evening.

To my dismay when I returned from having my hair and make-up done, Dasht was lounging on the sofa in his pajamas dividing his attention between ESPN and his cell phone.

I was rushing to get into my ballgown, and he wasn't moving. "Dasht can you help me with my zipper?"

He put the phone in his pocket and with his eyes still focused on the television, he stood and zipped my dress. Then plopped back down onto the sofa.

"Dasht," I took a deep breath to soften my tone before I continued, "we have to be downstairs by seven."

He looked over at me with an expression of annoyance. "The games are on. How long do we have to be down there?"

I was beyond annoyed, I was pissed. The primary purpose of his trip was to attend the gala with me, and now he was pulling this stunt. I said a silent prayer and asked God for wisdom and patience before I responded. "Which earrings do you like best the pearls or the diamonds."

His annoyed expression softened to one of confusion and slight shock. "I like the diamonds."

"Me too," I said turning to face the mirror and put on my earrings. I watched him put his head in his hands as if trying to understand what was happening.

He abruptly hopped up and started getting his clothing. "I don't like to be rushed, so I don't know if I can be ready by seven."

I smiled and said, "It's ok. We'll just be late together." I was smiling on the outside, but I was screaming on the inside. He was testing my patience, but I refused to lose my cool or entertain his shenanigans. It was clear he was trying to start an argument. I just didn't understand why. While I sat waiting for him to get dressed, I text Nikki to let her know I'd be a few minutes late.

At 7:15pm Dasht and I stepped onto the elevator with an awkward tension between us. Rather than focus on the tension, I focused on how handsome he looked in his tuxedo. "You look handsome."

"Thank you," he said as he allowed a huge grin to spread across his face and unconsciously poked out his chest.

We walked right into my friend Tabatha on our way to the grand ballroom.

"Aren't you all adorable. Stop, let me get a picture."

Tabatha's compliments and us pausing for the photo melted the tension between us, and we entered the ballroom all smiles and holding hands. Once we got to my table directly in front of center stage, I introduced Dasht to my other friends. He was charming and supportive. He started off the mobile giving with a $10K donation. Throughout the evening he was the epitome of a supportive boyfriend. I was on cloud nine. There were over three thousand people in attendance and, we raised slightly more than $500K for scholarships. Now it was time to dance the night away.

"This was great Bunny. I'm so proud of you."

"Thank you, Dasht. Let's dance," I said as I stood up.

"Aww no, not now. Maybe later. You go dance. Have fun with your friends."

I wasn't expecting that, but I wasn't going to let him ruin my natural high, so I strutted to the dance floor alone. I danced with my friends until my feet hurt. When I walked off the dance floor Dasht wasn't at the table. I assumed he'd gone back to the room. I was headed in the direction of the elevator when I noticed him sitting at the hotel bar with Nikki and my other friend Beth. The three of them were quite tipsy.

"Hey Bunny," Dasht almost slurred as he noticed me walking over to the bar.

"This guy is hilarious," Nikki giggled.

"Yes, we love him," Beth gushed.

I was glad Dasht was having a good time with my friends and they liked him. I was also irritated that he'd chosen to sit at the bar drinking rather than dancing and spending time with me. However, true to what was becoming the norm for this weekend I sucked my feelings into my lungs with the long breath I'd just inhaled and smiled. "Yes, he's quite funny."

"His sayings are outrageous. Lose your package, get a bear on you," Nikki said as she continued to giggle.

Dasht was grinning too as he ordered another scotch. I was ready to go, but the fresh drink prompted me to slide onto the bar chair next to him. We sat for what seemed like an eternity but was only twenty minutes or so with the three of them laughing like old friends.

"This was fun, but I've got to get going before my husband puts an APB out on me," Beth said as she gulped down the last of her drink and slid off her chair.

"Thank God," I thought to myself because I was annoyed, and my feet hurt.

"It was nice meeting you Dasht. I'm sure we'll be seeing you again soon. Take care of our girl," Nikki said as she slid off her bar chair and exchanged a friendly hug with Dasht.

"It was good meeting you ladies too," Dasht said as he hugged Nikki then Beth.

I exchanged hugs with Nikki and Beth as Beth said, "Great event."

After Nikki and Beth walked away, Dasht chugged down the last of his drink before he asked, "Ready to call it a night?"

"Yes, I'm pooped."

Dasht slid off his bar stool, kissed me on the top of my head before he reached down and held my hand. As we walked across the hotel lobby holding hands he said, "Bunny, this was fun."

"I'm glad you had a great time."

"I did. I really did. And you, Bunny I'm so proud of you. The way you stood up there speaking in front of all those people like it was nothing. I felt like I was with a superstar. I can't believe you planned all this. I'm really proud of you."

"Aww thank you."

"You act like it's no big deal."

"It went well overall, but there are some things I could have done better. I wish I would have rehearsed my remarks more so my delivery would have been smoother. I will definitely have to make some tweaks for next year."

"Well I thought you were great. You have really made a life for yourself here. I'm so proud of you. So proud of my pretty Bunny standing up there commanding the room and looking like a doll. You're gorgeous girl." He blew me a kiss. "My girl is a superstar. My beautiful Bunny. I love you girl. Damn I love you."

"I love you too Dasht." I blew him a kiss. "I'm happy you're here with me, and I'm glad you had a good time."

CHAPTER 13
1224 Euphoric Lane

Time really doesn't wait for anyone because it seemed as if the holiday season appeared almost out of nowhere. My sister Michelle typically hosted Thanksgiving for our family, but I was going to break tradition because this was the first major holiday celebration for Dasht and I. Michelle being the supportive sister she always was understood. I had planned every detail of the day from the menu to the décor. I was actually glad Dasht didn't have dishes suitable for the occasion because it gave me the opportunity to purchase the china I liked as well as have a real presence in his home and my add persona to the décor.

Dana had still been pretty much nonexistent since Dasht's birthday, but I wanted us all to get together for the holiday. This would be the perfect setting for Dasht and Brian to formally meet, and for our children to have a safe space to meet one another as well. Afterall, Thanksgiving is all about family.

Dasht was supportive and openly happy about my taking the lead on planning our dinner. He helped me with the menu and once he saw the table setting insisted his friend Carlton and his wife Barbara be invited to join us. I'd chosen a peacock patterned china trimmed in gold, which I complemented with gold, teal, and purple beaded placemats because it went well with the teal accent wall in the dining room. My centerpiece of teal glass pumpkins complemented the teal and gold pumpkin place card holders I'd luckily stumbled upon at a trip to a local HomeGoods store. To finish off the table setting I purchased gold flatware, ivory table linens and the Waterford Markham crystal drinkware collection. I used the same pumpkin place card holders to identify the dishes on the buffet I planned to set-up on the kitchen island with the polished silver Crown chaffing dishes and gold serving utensils I'd ordered.

"Bunny this is awesome. This is going to blow their socks off! I'm proud of you girl."

I had to agree it was nice, but I didn't necessarily expect anyone to be blown away. "We're always eating at the island, but I love to set my table especially for the holidays."

"You do a hell of a job, and I love it. I can't wait for Barbara to see this."

"Why?" I asked before I could filter the thought. Why would he want Barbara to see this?

"Because she thinks she is every man's ideal woman, but I've never seen their table look like this."

I was almost dumfounded by his statement because from what I remembered of her at his birthday dinner she was a lush who'd had too much plastic surgery. Of course, I wasn't going to say that, but I couldn't stifle all of my thoughts. "So, it's a competition?"

"Hell no. It's not a competition, not even close because she can't compete with my Bunny. I do want to see the look on her face though because she always has some sort of sarcastic comment for me, and she is always saying I'm too picky and that's why I'm single. She thinks she knows everything."

"That's interesting," was all I could muster to say that wouldn't prolong the conversation that I was now becoming uncomfortable with.

"Two is company, three is a crowd and four sucks all the air out of the room."

Ironically the first to arrive for dinner was Barbara and Carlton. Dasht rushed to take her coat and escort her into the dining room. Carlton followed behind them with an awkward look on his face that made me slightly uneasy as I felt obligated to tag along.

"Barbara look at how beautiful Gabby has the place decorated," he bragged.

"Well this is lovely," Barbara said in approval.

"Thank you," I said with a polite smile.

"Dasht she might be worth keeping," she teased Dasht as if Carlton and I weren't in the room.

"Yeah she is," Dasht said with a huge grin while staring in Barbara's face longer than platonically acceptable.

Carlton observed in silence with an odd but unreadable expression on his face.

The energy in the room was eerily off, but I couldn't discern why. I once again attempted to get Barbara's attention. "Thank you for the compliment on the décor. It's nice for you all to join us."

As if she'd been abruptly snapped out of a trans, she looked at me with a dazed and slightly annoyed expression on her face before she allowed a tight, physically strained smile to form. Dasht looked like a kid who'd gotten caught eating candy before dinner. The questioning thoughts that were forming in my head were interrupted by the doorbell. Dasht hurriedly walked out of the room to answer it, leaving the three of us standing in awkward silence.

I was relieved to see my son walk in behind Dasht when he returned. I walked over and gave him a hug and then formally introduced him to Dasht who introduced him to Carlton and Barbara.

"Hello son," I said with a smile as we embraced. "Dasht this is my son Brian. Brian meet Dasht."

"It's nice to finally meet you Brian. I've heard a lot about you."

Laughing Brian said, "I'm sure. I hope it was all good. It's nice to meet you as well."

"Brian, this is my friend Carlton and his wife Barbara."

While the introductions were ongoing, the alarm system signaled someone entering from the mudroom, which meant Dana had arrived. I was expecting Lena to be following behind her, but when Dana entered the room she entered alone.

"Happy Thanksgiving," she called out to everyone as she walked over to Dasht and gave him a peck on the cheek. "Hey Daddy."

"Happy Thanksgiving Dana," I said walking over to embrace her. The tension between us was like static, but I smiled to ensure it didn't register on my face. "Dana this is my son Brian."

I was stunned at the way she made goo-goo eyes at him as she said, "Well hello. It's nice to meet you handsome."

Brian chuckled under his breath as he and I quickly exchanged questioning and disapproving glances before he said, "Hello."

Still sneaking lustful glances at Brian, Dana strolled over to Barbara and then Carlton and exchanged friendly hugs.

"Where's Lena," Dasht asked?

"She's having dinner with her family," Dana said with apathy.

"Well dinner is ready," I said because it was, and I wanted to clear the tension Dana was brining to the air.

Dasht directed everyone to the kitchen where the Thanksgiving buffet lined the island.

"This is fancy," Dana said while still sneaking glances at Brian between reading the buffet cards.

Barbara offered a back handed compliment, "Umm, everything smells wonderful Gabriella. Hope it tastes as good as it smells."

"Yes, it does smell delicious," Carlton awkwardly agreed.

Brian and I stood in place as everyone else began piling food on their plates and moving towards the dining room. After exchanging a questioning glance with Brian, I walked over to Dasht and whispered in his ear. "Baby are we going to go around the room and give thanks before you bless the food."

Dasht first looked confused then annoyed. "No, we're not doing all that. I mean we can pray over the food if you want us to, but we're not doing all that other stuff. That's just too much."

With a raised eyebrow I said, "Ok..., well can we at least bless the food. I mean it is Thanksgiving." This time I wasn't able, nor did I really want to stifle my irritation and concern.

Dasht glared at me before turning his back to walk towards the dining room. I inhaled and exhaled a deep breath before following behind him.

"Damn, we have assigned seats," Dana quipped as she looked at the place cards.

"Gabby wants us to pray over the food because it's Thanksgiving," Dasht announced with emphasis on my name. "I'm not much of a praying man, so Barbara since you attend church every Sunday, why don't you say a Thanksgiving prayer."

I was mortified, confused and pissed. What the hell was going on? Why did he need to announce that "I" wanted to bless the food? Blessing the food was a Thanksgiving tradition as far as I knew. And why in the hell would he ask Barbara's plastic ass to pray? I snuck a glance over at Carlton, who was just standing behind his chair with his hands in his pockets looking void of emotion as if he had been lobotomized. Was I the only person feeling leery about all of this? I bowed my head, closed my eyes and said my own silent prayer, for the patience and strength to get through this dinner with grace, while Barbara rendered the blessing.

> **"There is something to be said about good food and how it brings people together and cures all ills."**

The tension that had been festering before we sat down to eat seemed to somewhat subside as the turkey was carved and gravy was poured over the mashed potatoes. Dasht continually raved over the food. "Bunny this duck dressing is phenomenal. It's moist and seasoned just right. You did a good job," he said blowing me a kiss.

"My Mom's cooking is one of the things I miss the most since I moved away from home," Brian chimed in.

"Yeah it is good," Dana praised grudgingly.

"This green bean casserole is delicious. I've never had it like this," Carlton complimented.

"It is tasty. Gabriella you must share the recipe," Barbara said

I regarded her compliment to be as fake as her breast because she was primarily picking over her food as she drank her weight in wine. I responded with only a smile and continued to focus on my plate as I thought to myself, "You're not my friend, and there is no way I'm sharing my recipes with you." It was obvious Brian was attuned to my thoughts as we exchanged conversational glances and chuckled under our breaths.

With the exception of Brian and I, everyone in the room was inebriated by the time dessert was served. Barbara was slurring her words as she continued to converse with Dasht as if she and he were the only people in the room. Carlton was almost mute throughout dinner but now appeared to sneak lustful glances at me. I didn't like being around those two. They made me uncomfortable.

> *"A classy woman exudes the same level of poise whether she's clothed or unclothed."*

When Dasht and I had first met he'd mentioned he attended an annual holiday ball, and he'd always attended alone. The few lingering thoughts I had about his true commitment to our relationship dissolved when he asked me to accompany him. We were both excited as we Facetimed while I packed.

"I can't wait to see you Bunny. Are you all packed?"

"I'm looking forward to seeing you too. I'm almost done. Just have to pack my dress for tomorrow night."

"What are you wearing?"

Somewhat perplexed by his question I answered, "A ballgown."

"What color?"

"I haven't decided yet."

"What do you mean you haven't decided yet."

"I have a lot of formal gowns, and I haven't decided which one I want to wear."

"What colors do you have?

He sure was asking a lot of questions and seemed overly concerned about my attire I thought before answering, "I have every color?"

"Are you serious? Girl you have a lot of stuff. All those shoes and purses. You have clothes in every closet of that house. We're going to have to do something about that because you don't need all that stuff."

Rather than respond I just smiled because I wasn't at all fond of his constant commenting about my clothes and shoes.

He gave me a look that led me to believe he sensed my feelings on his constant commenting about my clothes and shoes before he said, "I want you to wear black because I love the way black looks against your skin."

Determined to avoid an unnecessary confrontation I lied and said, "That's funny because I was leaning towards wearing black."

He flashed a big smile as he said, "Great minds think alike. Let me see the dress."

"Do you want to see it on me?"

"Yes."

He was really getting under my skin. "Ok, hold on for a second while I put it on." I laid the phone on the nightstand and moved to the other side of the room out of view. I stripped completely out of my clothes before I returned to the camera. Dasht was totally shocked when I picked up the phone again.

With extremely wide eyes he exclaimed, "Ooh Bunny!"

"You approve," I asked with a raised eyebrow and a seductive smirk.

"I do...I do," he smiled as he sipped his drink.

"We are dressed to the nines when we dress up in love."

Our entire weekend was packed with events. We were attending the ball tonight and Dasht's holiday social for his law firm on Saturday. For two people who rarely went out at all attending two back-to-back outings was a lot. Once I landed in Atlanta, I literally hit the ground running. My schedule was tight. I went straight from the airport to the beauty salon to have my hair curled.

Once I left the salon, I met Tippy to grab a quick lunch. By the time I arrived at Dasht's house I only had time to quickly unpack, shower and slip into some sweats before the make-up artist arrived.

She was adding the finishing touches to my make-up when Dasht came rushing in through the mudroom door.

"Hello," I called out pleasantly.

"Hey Bunny," he said as he came over, rubbed my shoulder and kissed me on the top of my head. "Hello, Dasht Spelbender," he introduced himself to Eva.

"Hi, I'm Eva. Nice meeting you Sir," she said without looking at him as she continued to put the finishing touches on my face.

"Bunny, are you going to be ready because have to leave soon."

"Yes. Once Eva finishes my make-up I just have to put on my dress."

"Ok, let me get dressed," he said as he headed upstairs.

Thirty minutes later Dasht and I were gathering our coats to head out the door.

"Bunny you look stunning," he said with a huge grin. "You're a gorgeous woman. Humph," he wiggled his eyebrows and blew me a kiss. "I love you girl. Damn, I really love you."

I let out a girlish giggle and smiled as I said, "Thank you. I love you too."

The evening was beyond wonderful. The entire event was lovely from beginning to end. Dasht was the consummate gentleman, introducing me to the legal who's who of Atlanta. Most of the lawyers he'd attended law school with were now judges. This prompted me to ask him if the judgeship was in his future. I was stunned when he expressed that he had no interest in becoming a judge, but even more confused by his rationale.

"Hell no, I don't want to be a judge. They dig too deep through your private life. Besides, I like to make money."

Our private conversation was interrupted by one of his colleague's approaching. I spent the remainder of the evening engaging in friendly chatter and smiling cordially, but something in my gut wouldn't let his opposition to becoming a judge rest.

On the ride home, Dasht turned to me and said, "This was the most fun I've ever had at this event. I'm so glad you're in my life Bunny."

"Aww Dasht. You're so sweet. I'm grateful God brought us together," I said smiling inside and out.

"We're going to be great together. We're going to be powerful together," he grinned and reached over and held my hand as he turned his eyes back to the road. "Yeah we're going to be great."

"Don't let face and ass be all you bring to the table."

As always, time had flown by and it was Saturday morning. We were both getting dressed when Dasht said, "I know I said this already, but I have to say it again you looked absolutely gorgeous Thursday night."

I let out a little shy giggle before I said, "Thank you."

"So, what are you wearing tonight?"

"Dasht why do you always ask me what I'm wearing?"

"I just want to see so I can ensure it's appropriate, and I like you in short dresses. You have gorgeous legs girl," he added attempting to deflect the tension that was seeping into the room.

"Thank you for the compliment, but what do you mean you need to ensure it's appropriate? I know how to dress myself."

"Bunny I didn't say you didn't know how to dress yourself. I just want to see. Can I see please?" There was a brief silence between us before he said, "Come on Bunny, let me see?"

There was a part of me that was offended, but this wasn't worth an argument. I went to the closet and returned, "I brought these four options."

"They're all red. I wanted you to wear black."

Now somewhat taken aback I said, "Dasht it's the Christmas season, and I want to wear red."

Visibly disappointed he said, "Hmm, I guess. Let me see them again."

Now I was annoyed, but as was now becoming all too common I suppressed my feelings and obliged Dasht's request. I allowed a faint smile to form across my face as I showed Dasht the dresses.

"Hmm, they all seem nice. Which one were you thinking?"

"I like this one best," I said dangling a red lace, sheath dress with nude lining.

"Yeah that one is nice, but it looks a little long. I like the shorter one. You know I like things that show off your legs. Let me see what you look like in them."

I rolled my eyes and let out a long sigh. "Really Dasht?" I asked before I headed towards the bathroom to comply and model the dresses.

"Let's wake-up to a sunny Christmas song."

This had been one of the best Holiday Seasons I'd ever had. I loved being at home with Dasht. I was happier than I'd been in a long time. Everything in my life was perfect. I had my family, the perfect job, and the perfect man. After the social Dasht had become full of the Holiday spirit. I'd suggested we put up a Christmas tree and was pleased to the point of squealing when he suggested we go out and purchase one. I went a step further and purchased Christmas themed dishes and décor for the house.

Dasht and I had finished decorating the tree and were practicing for the annual Christmas Eve karaoke party Tippy hosted for my family. We were singing Bill Withers' Lovely Day, which we'd decided was our song. We were practicing our harmony when his phone rang. I was used to him getting calls after he came home from work, but it was well after 9pm, 9:24pm to be exact.

"What the hell?" Dasht asked no one in particular as he hurried over to answer the phone. Something about his demeanor and body language was off. "Hey are you ok?" I could hear the person laughing as he walked into the bathroom. "Are you sure you're ok?" He asked again. "Well let me talk to you later." He came back into the room with a cat who ate the canary look on his face. "Where were we," he asked looking at the floor.

"Who was that Dasht?"

"No one. Just one of my friends. So where were?"

"Excuse me," I said as I got up to leave the room. He didn't say another word or try to stop me. There was a knot in the pit of my stomach that made me slightly nauseous. Something about that phone call wasn't right, and I knew it. I closed the bathroom door, sat on the toilet and prayed. "Lord I know something isn't right, so I thank you for the spirit of discernment. Please give me wisdom on how to address this situation. Amen." I sat for a few moments longer. Then I took a few deep breaths before I walked out of the bathroom. When I walked back into the room, he said nothing and avoided eye contact with me.

I inhaled before I spoke, "Dasht when we first met, I asked that you not bring any foolishness to my life, and I promised you that I wouldn't bring any foolishness to your life.'

"Yeah," he said with widened, guilty eyes.

"That phone call was foolishness."

"You're being silly!"

"Silly?"

"Look we're having a great time. Don't ruin it."

"I'm not ruining it. However, I'm not going to pretend the phone call didn't happen."

"You're making a big deal out of nothing." He paused and put his hands up before he said, "You know what, just forget it. I don't want to practice, and I'm not going to talk about this anymore.

I'm going to bed," he said harshly and abruptly headed for the stairs.

I sat in a nearby chair and replayed the conversation in my head. Something about that phone call just wasn't right, and Dasht was overly defensive because he was lying to me about it. I couldn't in good conscious let the conversation end without some resolution. I couldn't force Dasht to converse further, but I could say what I had to say. I resorted to writing him a note expressing my feelings about the situation. I slid the note in the outside pocket of his briefcase deep enough to prevent it from falling out but shallow enough to ensure he wouldn't overlook it.

"You're the dean and a student at the University of Y-O-U; admission is a privilege, so grade accordingly and enforce your standards."

I tossed and turned all night. Going to bed without resolution had heightened my anxiety. I got up earlier than normal and went to the gym to avoid a confrontation with Dasht. I was relieved when I returned from the gym to an empty house even though I knew I wouldn't be able to dodge the conversation once he came in from work. However, I hoped reading my note would help him understand my feelings and opinion about the situation, and we could have a meaningful conversation to ensure we established some agreed upon standards and boundaries for our relationship.

I'd volunteered to chauffer my niece and nephew to their after school activities, intentionally ensuring I was out when Dasht got in. When I walked into the kitchen he was sitting at the island, sipping his cocktail and staring at his laptop screen.

"Good evening," I said.

He kept his eyes fixated on the computer screen as he flatly said, "Hey. I ordered some dinner. It's in the oven."

"Thank you. Have you eaten?"

"Yes."

I took a deep breath, "Dasht we need to talk about last night."

"Yeah, we do." He gave me a spiteful under eyed glance before continuing. "The way you behaved last night was really ugly and unnecessary."

I was taken aback by his attack, and immediately became defensive. "What? Dasht that's a crock of crap."

"Call it what you will, but you didn't have to behave the way you did."

"Behave? Ok," I paused to steady my tone. "I simply told you that I don't believe it's appropriate for your phone to be ringing at nine o'clock at night when it isn't an emergency."

"That is ridiculous," he huffed. "I know a lot of people, and people call me for advice."

"Really Dasht? What type of advice is someone calling you for after nine o'clock?" I asked sternly.

"That was my friend calling," he made an awkward face, then attempted to stifle a smile as he said, "She was just calling to get some advice concerning a situation with her fiancé."

I let out a sigh of frustration before I said, "Really Dasht? Well you and I both know the best way for her to rectify a situation with her fiancé is to speak to him, not you. Besides you're not a counselor."

"I don't have to be a counselor to give my friend advice," he snapped. People always ask me for advice. I know lots of people, and I help people. That's what I do." He paused for reaction, but I didn't respond, so he continued at a tone slightly above a mumble. "I had a life before you. I'm going to get phone calls."

I inhaled a deep breath and exhaled as I made firm and direct eye contact with him before I said, "Dasht I had a life before I met you as well. However, I've made room in my life for you, for this relationship. I realize you will get phone calls." I paused to steady my tone and gather my composure. "There is a time and place for everything, and you and I both know that phone call last night was inappropriate. It was foolishness."

He rolled his eyes, huffed and turned his gaze back to the computer. "You will never tell me who can call my phone," he scoffed in a venomous tone I'd never heard him use before.

His words landed hard, and I literally felt my body shudder from the verbal blow. I felt like I'd been punched in the gut. "Wow that was harsh," I thought to myself as I bit my lip to choke back the harsh, retaliatory words that were dancing on my tongue and the tears that were attempting to well up in my eyes as a result of both hurt feelings and anger. The air was thick with tension and the silence was becoming so loud it was deafening. I wanted to leave, but I knew we couldn't allow this to fester another day. I swallowed so hard it hurt my throat before I spoke. "Dasht do you have room in your life for a serious relationship, for me, for us?"

He grimaced as he asked, "What do you mean? Why are you asking me that?"

"I'm asking you because I want to know. Do you have room in your life for me?"

"Do you think I would have you here, in my house if I didn't?"

"I don't know Dasht, that's why I'm asking. Why am I here?"

"You're here because I want you here."

"You still didn't answer my question Dasht. Do you have room in your life for me, for us, for a serious relationship?"

He looked confused, "I did answer you. I told you, you already. Hell, all of this over a damn phone call."

I was becoming more annoyed with every word he spoke. This conversation was going downhill. "Since you won't answer, I'll answer for you. The answer is no," I said as I turned to walk out of the room and hide the tears that I could no longer stop from flowing.

"Bunny," he called after me, but I kept walking because I could no longer choke back the tears, and I didn't want him to see me cry. "Bunny, wait," he said in a heartfelt tone as he slid off the bar chair and walked over to where I'd stopped with my back still turned. He put his hand on my shoulder, and I instinctively reached up and placed my hand on his as I steadied my breath to silence and swallow the sobs that were brewing. "Bunny...look at me." I closed my eyes as the tears made their way down my cheeks. Dasht attempted to turn my body towards his, but my feet were planted. He slid his hand down to the center of my back, wrapped his arm around my waist as he came around to stand in front of me. With my eyes still closed, I dropped my head down towards the floor to hide my tears. Dasht gently caressed my chin and attempted to lift my face up to his, but I pulled away.

"Stop Dasht," I said weakly.

"Bunny, he sighed. "Bunny look at me, please," he paused, and I kept my eyes closed and my head down. "Come on Bunny, stop all of this." He caressed my chin again and this time I opened my eyes and allowed him to raise my face towards his. "I love you girl. You understand? I love you. You're my Bunny. I want you to be my wife," he stopped as he searched my face for my reaction to his revelation of matrimonial desires, but I gave none. "Did you hear me? I want to marry you. I'm going to marry you. Now stop all this nonsense and overthinking every little thing. Come here," he pulled me in close, hugged me tight and kissed the top of my head. "You're going to be my wife so stop getting all upset over nothing."

I allowed my head to rest in his chest not in agreement but rather from emotional exhaustion. I knew I wasn't upset or overthinking. He'd avoided answering my question and gone to the extent of faux proposing to deflect my attention from the phone call. I stayed in his embrace and that knot of uneasiness stayed in my stomach.

"It was the night before Christmas..."

It literally was 'the most wonderful time of the year' for my family because everyone was home for the holidays and family fun was in full swing. Tippy had suggested I invite Dana and Lena over for our annual Christmas Eve karaoke, which I sincerely appreciated. I was sure Dasht and I would be the best act because we'd practiced until we perfected our harmony. It was going to be fun.

Dasht was sitting in his usual spot at the kitchen island enjoying a cocktail and staring at his laptop screen. "What time are we supposed to go to Tippy's?"

"I told her we'd be there no later than six-thirty."

"How long are we staying?"

"Well, we normally stay up all night on Christmas Eve."

"What? Oh no, I can't do that," he balked.

I laughed, "Dasht I don't expect us to stay over all night. I was just saying that's what we normally do. I was planning on us coming home around ten. You're funny," I said still laughing.

"Hmm, ok. Well that's almost four hours. That's still a long time."

My laughter faded, "Well everyone is going to be there, and I want to spend time with the family."

"Bunny, I know you do, and I do too," he paused. "I just don't want to be there for four hours. I have some work I want to look at."

"Dasht it's Christmas Eve."

"I know. I'm not saying I'm not going. Why don't you have Tippy pick you up, and I can join you in a couple of hours."

"No Dasht. It's Christmas Eve. The laptop is getting put away today and tomorrow." I was putting my foot down, and he apparently knew it because he closed the laptop, took the last sip of his drink, and stood up to get prepared to leave without any further resistance.

"Now we are family, and to be family is to be everything."

"Bunny that was so much fun!" Dasht exclaimed as we got into the car.

"I'm glad you had a good time," I said smiling wide inside and out.

"Bunny it was great," he said with a huge grin. "I have never had a Christmas Eve or a Christmas, for that matter, like that. Everything was perfect, the food, your family, and I love your brothers. Both Dana and Lena seem to be having a good time too, but I need to call her and tell her not to overstay her welcome."

Dana and Lena had arrived around 8pm and surprisingly she seemed to have enjoyed herself. It didn't hurt that she and Lena had been the best at karaoke.

"Oh Dasht, Dana and Lena are fine. Leave them alone. Like I told you we typically stay up all night. They have to wait for the kids to go to bed, so Santa can come."

"The kids still believe in Santa."

"Yep," I smiled and winked.

He let out that heartfelt laugh I had fell in love with when we first met, "That's funny and cute."

I smiled, "Perhaps. Let them enjoy being kids for as long as they can."

"You know that's a good way to think about it. Keep the Christmas spirit."

"I'm glad you enjoyed yourself."

"I did. I truly did." I pulled into the garage, and as I put the car in park, he leaned over to kiss me on the cheek. "I love you girl. I really love you."

"I love you too Dasht."

We walked into the house holding hands like two teenaged lovers.

Rather randomly he asked, "Are you sleepy?"

"I'm fine. Why?"

"I'm not sleepy either. Want to play a game of chess?"

"Sure, I'd love to play, but I want to change and get comfortable first."

"Yeah, let's get comfortable," he agreed giving me a frisky glance.

When I came downstairs from changing, Dasht had set-up the chessboard on the island, and was standing at the counter sipping a cocktail and smiling.

"You know I love you Bunny."

"I love you too Dasht."

"No Gabby, I really love you."

I smiled inside and out. "I really love you too Dasht."

"No Bunny. You don't understand. I love you," he paused, looked down and shook his head as if he were shaking off a knock-out punch. "Damn I love you girl. Believe me when I tell you, I have never felt this away about anyone, and to be honest it was almost love at first sight. I've been in love with you for a long time," he paused to sip his drink and I stood in place smiling. "I told you I was going to marry you. Do you remember me telling you that you were going to be my wife?"

I smiled inside and out as I said, "Yes, I remember."

He took a long sip of his drink and then stared at me long and hard. "Go into the dining room, there is something in there for you"

I looked at him with a confused but excited look on my face.

"Walk into the dining room Bunny."

I slowly walked into the dining room and there it was, a stuffed giraffe that stood well over five feet tall with a giant red bow tied around its neck. "Aww this is so cute." I'd told Dash I always wanted a giant stuffed giraffe. Like a big kid I wrapped my arms around the neck to reach around to hug the giraffe, and something hard hit my arm. My heart dropped to the pit of my stomach. The mahogany ring box was secured at the neck of the giraffe in the giant red ribbon. My eyes welled up in tears as Dasht walked over to me and put his arms around me.

"Are you going to marry me Bunny?"

"Yes," I sobbed, "Yes." I gave him the ring box.

He opened it and slid the ring onto my outstretched hand.

"You're my soulmate, and you're going to be my wife."

"Yes, I am," I said as I wiped away the happy tears and smiled inside and out.

CHAPTER 14
"ME" for "WE" is a Tusky Tango

My trip to Atlanta was coming to an end, and it was going to be two weeks before I returned. Dasht and I were spending the evening sitting on the patio with cigars. Furnishing his patio was a great idea. It was the most relaxing seating area in the house. I was glad we'd added the fire pit coffee table because it allowed us to use the space all year.

"Bunny I love having you here with me."

I smiled inside and out and said, "I love being here with you."

He furrowed his brow as he cut the cigar and said, "I feel funny when it's time for you to leave me."

"Me too," I pouted, "I don't like leaving you. It's getting old."

"Yeah it is. We've got to put some things in motion so we can get you here permanently and move forward with our life."

I smiled and took a sip of my coffee as I watched him stare at the lake as he blew smoke from his cigar.

"The first thing we're going to have to do is get rid of all that stuff you have." He took a sip of his cocktail, "Get rid of some of those clothes and all those shoes."

I was stunned to the point of being silenced. I thought to myself, "What? How did we come to me getting rid of all my things?"

He continued to puff his cigar and verbalize his thoughts, "I know you like having a convertible, and I'm ok with you keeping that, but you don't need two cars. We need to figure out when we're going to ship that one here and what we're going to do with the other one."

At this point I had to say something, "Really Dasht? You have more than one car."

I'd barely finished my sentence before he rather dismissively said, "Yeah, yeah, yeah I hear you," while still puffing his cigar and staring at the lake. "I was initially thinking of allowing you to keep the car because I was leaning towards us keeping the house," he paused and took another sip of his drink. "I thought it would be kind of nice to for us to have a place in Maryland because I love it there, but I think it would be best to sell the house," he stopped and puffed his cigar. As he exhaled the smoke he said, "I really like the National Harbor, so maybe after we sell the house, we can buy us a condo there."

I wasn't really sure if he was speaking to me or at me. "Dasht don't you think we should start with me getting a job in Atlanta first?"

Still looking out at the lake he said, "Bunny that's something else I wanted to talk to you about."

I thought to myself, "Oh we're talking? I thought you were talking, and I'm listening." There was no way I could say that and keep the peace though. So, I sipped my coffee while he continued to talk.

"You don't have to work because I can take care of us. I understand you want to work, and I support that. I just want you to know you don't have to worry about any of that. I'm ready for you to be here with me all the time, so maybe you should just resign."

"Dasht I can't quit my job. I have bills to pay, and I also want to ensure I'm never a burden on Brian."

"Brian is an adult. What do you mean you don't want to be a burden on him," he asked as he finally looked at me with a slight scowl?

I was seeing a side of him I hadn't really seen before, and it wasn't resonating well with me. "Dasht what I'm saying is I don't want to be a burden on my son in my old age."

With his focus back on the lake he exhaled the cigar smoke, let out a condescending chuckle and then said, "Aww Bunny you shouldn't worry about stuff like that. First of all, nothing is going to happen to you and like I said, I can take care of us. You don't have to ever worry about that. Let me handle all of that."

As far as I was concerned this conversation was going nowhere fast. I didn't like how dismissive he was being. It was borderline disrespectful. I wanted our visit to end on a high note, so rather than continue to allow this conversation to proceed and rain on our love parade, I took a page from his book and changed the subject. "Aww you're so sweet. Thank you. On another note we need to synchronize our social calendars."

"Well Bunny you're the socialite. I don't really get into all of that. We've already gone to everything I wanted us to go to." He blew a smoke ring.

I have a few things that I must attend in the upcoming months in the DMV, and I would like for us to attend them together.

He gave me a look out of the corner of his eye that landed like a small dagger, took a sip of his drink, pursed his lips as he swallowed, then sorely asked, "What is it?" Then as if hearing his tone caused him to chastise himself, he looked at me and in a more cordial tone of voice said, "I mean tell me about these events you want me, you want us to attend."

I exhaled slowly before I spoke because I was agitated with Dasht to the point of wanting to get up and leave. He had been quite cantankerous, but I was committed to leaning on the mantra that love conquers all. So, I continued to force myself to keep a positive attitude and pleasant tone as I spoke. "There are three events that I absolutely want us to attend. The first is my friend Delilah's birthday party in March. You may not remember her, but you met her at the fundraiser. She is also an Atlanta native who relocated to the DMV. The next event is a wedding," I said with a smile, widened eyes and raised eyebrows. "My sorority sister Kiersten is getting married in April, so we must attend that. The last event is with my friend Nikki, whom I'm sure you remember. She invited us to attend the Washington Ballet's Annual Spring Gala. This is one of the big annual events in DC, and she is a sponsor. That will be the last thing we attend in DC before we're married because our wedding is the following weekend," I ended happily.

He smiled a real smile when he said, "Of course I remember Nikki. I like her a lot. Now, Delilah is the one who is married to the alderman right?"

"Yes," I smiled.

"Yeah, I remember her. Did I meet your sorority sister?"

"No, Kiersten wasn't at the fundraiser because they had another commitment. I've never met her fiancé, but I'm really happy for her and want to celebrate her on her wedding day."

He'd gone back to puffing on his cigar and staring at the lake, "So we will be going to something every month?"

"Yes," I smiled. "That's the life of a socialite."

He rolled his eyes and sucked his teeth as he secured the bottle of scotch, he'd carried outside to refresh his drink. "Yeah I hear you, but you're going to have to let all that go."

"What do you mean, let all that go?"

"Bunny I'm not into all this going here and there all the time. I like a nice easy life. I like to be at home."

"Dasht I love being at home too; however, there needs to be a balance. I don't want to always be locked away from the world. There is a time to be inside and a time to go out." As much as I'd tried to temper my growing frustration my tone had conveyed it, and I could tell Dasht recognized it when he responded.

"Ok, tell me about this birthday party."

Just thinking about Delilah's party made me cheery. "It's going to be so much fun. It is a nautical themed party because it's on a yacht. Delilah is requesting we wear nautical attire in shades of blue and white with little pops of red."

He abruptly cut me off, "I don't want to go to that."

I was caught off guard by his abruptness and confused at his not wanting to go. "Why not?"

He finished sipping his drink before he spoke. "Look, I've gone to all kinds of parties. I'm not interested in attending a yacht party. You go to that one without me."

"I don't want to go without you," I said with my disappointment, confusion and irritation laced in my tone.

He was visibly annoyed, and he wasn't trying to hide it when he sucked his teeth before he said, "Look, I'm not going to all three. I'm being nice to you by going to two because I'm really only interested in going to the thing with Nikki. You pick the other one, but I'm not going to all three."

"Dasht?" I questioned as I demanded face to face contact from him by leaning forward, cupping his chin and turning his face towards mine. "What is going on with you? Why are you being so difficult?"

My feelings were hurt when he pulled his chin away from my hand, turned back to the lake and coldly said, "Oh I'm being difficult because you can't have your way? Hmph. There's nothing going on with me. I just don't want to go. That's not my thing, and you're going to be with me now, so you need to let all that go."

"Let all that go? Dasht why do you keep saying that, and what do you mean let all that go? My marrying you does not mean I stop being me." I was failing miserably at keeping my cool. The air between us was getting thick, but I couldn't yield to what he was saying and wasn't going to allow my silence to misconstrue consent.

Maybe the reality of my becoming frustrated as expressed in my tone prompted him to attempt to lighten the mood because he responded, "Tell me about the event with Nikki."

I was extremely aggravated, but I exhaled and said, "It's a black-tie dinner with cocktails and dancing."

"We can definitely do that one, but I don't want to go to a wedding or a stupid nautical party."

"Stupid? Dasht, stop it. You're being unnecessarily cruel."

He scowled at me and then yelled, "I don't want to go to that shit ok? I've done all of that dumb stuff, and I don't want to do that now. Damn."

"Dasht you're being disrespectful. Don't speak to me that way," I said firmly.

He put down his drink, placed the cigar in the ashtray, reached over and took my hands, but now I was the one looking away and staring at the lake. "Look at me Bunny, please," he said in a suave tone and I grudgingly obliged.

"Bunny we're getting married. You're going to be my wife. You don't have to do any of that stuff anymore. You're going to move here and have a life with me. We're going to start our life together. You're with the Dash-Master now," he attempted to joke to soften the mood before he continued. "I love you and you love me, right?"

I softened my expression and nodded in agreement before I said, "I love you Dasht."

He flashed that toothy smile that he knew I loved. "And that's all that matters. You're going to move here. Our life is going to be great. We're going to have a great life together. You can work if you want to or not work. We're going to be great. I'll support us, and you'll take care of everything else like the house and stuff."

Just like that we were back to my giving up everything about my life in the name of loving Dasht. I was emotionally frustrated and exhausted with the entire conversation. I knew if we continued the discussion, we were going to end up having an ugly argument, but I also knew I couldn't just sit back and accept this. I said a quick silent prayer for wisdom and then chose my words carefully. "Dasht, my love, I love you, and I am looking forward to our life together. Just as you, I know we're going to have a great life. We have to figure out how to bring our lives together to build a new life that we are both comfortable with." I sensed him tensing up as he attempted to let go of my hands, but I wouldn't allow it and tightened my grip. He broke eye contact, but eye contact wasn't his strong suit when things between us were normal, so I wasn't offended that his eyes wandered now. "It's not about me fitting into your life or you fitting into mine. It's about us bringing our lives together to build a life together that works for both of us."

"I'm not asking you to fit into a box," he said harshly as he jerked his hands away.

I was at my limit. "Oh no? Well it sounds that way to me. Everything you've said this evening has involved me giving up something. Sell my house and move here, get rid of my clothes and shoes, stop attending my friends' events, and oh you'll let me keep my convertible but sell my other car. You even want me to quit my job." I stopped abruptly because I could feel the tears forming, and I didn't want to cry.

"Gabby we don't need all those cars, and there's no space for them," he said while pouring himself another drink. "I was trying to be considerate by allowing you to keep one. I have three cars. You could really just use one of those."

"What did he mean allowing me?" I silently asked myself. I knew if I asked him that question it would come across as a confrontation and rightfully so, but confrontation was not my goal. So instead I said, "Dasht you're being ridiculous, those are your cars. I know you can take care of us," I paused to steady my breathing and maintain a calm tone. "I appreciate your being willing to provide for all our needs, but I want to work. I'm going to work and have my own car," I said now slightly rolling my eyes.

"Keep the cars," he said between puffs on his cigar. Then squinting from the cigar smoke, he looked over at me and said, "You're going to be my wife, so that means letting some of that stuff go. That's your old life. You're with me now. You're going to be Mrs. Spelbender."

I was bothered with this entire conversation. This was a side of him that was new to me, and I didn't like it. He was being stubborn, controlling, mean and selfish. Everything was about him, and what he wanted. Even though Dasht denied it, he was expecting me to give up my entire life and fit into the box he'd designed for me. He'd started out with trying to dictate how I dressed. Now he was planning my future, and he apparently believed he had the right to do so without my input simply because he'd proposed to me. I was all for loving and taking care of him, but the sole purpose of my life wasn't to cook, clean, run errands for and be supportive of him. I had my own life and my own identity. I was starting to wonder if marrying Dasht was going to cost me too much me for us to become we.

PART FOUR
A Headless Giraffe

CHAPTER 15
My Funny Valentine

I flew in Friday and surprised Dasht. He wasn't expecting me until Saturday, but I had a free day and wanted to get a jump on wedding planning because May would be here before we knew it.

As expected, the garage door opened at half past five, and a couple of minutes afterwards Dasht walked through the mudroom door with the phone to his ear.

I flashed him a wide smile as I stood up to kiss him hello. I pecked him on the lips then the cheek and leaned in and whispered, "Surprise," in his ear. His eyes revealed he was truly surprised, but something in his expression and the stiffness of his body language made me believe he wasn't happy about it. He signaled with his pointer finger for me to give him a minute to complete his phone call and left the kitchen. I returned to my seat at the island and waited.

When Dasht returned to the kitchen, he glanced past me as he beelined toward the cabinet, secured a glass, grabbed a bottle of scotch, and moved towards the refrigerator to fill the glass with ice. Staring at the glass he said, "So Ms. Franklin you decided to just show up and surprise the Dash-Master huh?"

He'd never referred to me as Ms. Franklin. "Ms. Franklin? You've never called me that."

Dasht looked at me over the rim of the glass as he took a long sip. He swallowed before he sarcastically said, "Hmph. It's your name, Ms. Franklin."

I felt my brow furrow as I quipped, "Yes, it is, Mr. Spelbender."

His eyes widened and a smirky smile formed across his face in acknowledgement of my mockery. "What made you come home a day early?"

"Well I didn't have any meetings, and I wanted to work on our wedding plans. But if this is my home, I should be able to come and go as I please?" I questioned.

"Hmph," escaped his lips and that same smirky smile reappeared as he raised his glass to take the last sip of his cocktail. "You're right. You can come and go as you please. I just wasn't expecting to see you sitting here when I walked in the door today."

"Well aren't you happy to see me?" I asked bluntly.

"Oh, stop all of that. You know I'm always happy to see you."

I stared at him with a slightly raised eyebrow and questioning eyes.

With his eyes focused on the fresh drink he was making he said, "Is this because I was on the phone?"

"Is what because you were on the phone? You're always on the phone." I felt slight annoyance at his deflective accusation. He'd been condescending and sarcastic since he walked into the room.

His smirk disappeared, his brow furrowed, and he rolled his eyes as he walked over to the refrigerator to add more ice to his glass. "Is this what we're going to be doing all weekend?"

I was becoming thoroughly annoyed with Dasht at this point. Out of spite, with a confused look on my face I asked, "What are we doing?"

He chuckled to himself as he poured more scotch over the fresh ice. "What would you like to eat for dinner?"

Just like that he'd changed the subject.

"When all your moves are executed with strategy the pawns can be powerful too."

The tension that had manifested earlier was still lingering after we finished our dinner. I wanted to talk about what had transpired, but I knew the conversation would have to wait because Dasht had drank at least five cocktails. In spite of his inebriation it was apparent he was cognizant of the tension and wanted it to dissipate when he walked over to where I was seated and placed his hands on my shoulders, kissed the top of my head, struggled to look in my eyes, and asked, "You feel like playing a game of chess?"

I felt a conciliatory smile spread across my face. "Sure."

Dasht's suggestion to play chess worked at changing the aura in the room. Our competitive spirits seemed to cause us both to forget about our earlier tiff. He was all smiles as I laid my king down in surrender to his being victorious in our first game. Over our second game we began having an actual conversation, and the topic became exes and liars.

"I hate lying," Dasht said vehemently.

"Me too," I agreed.

"I just don't understand it," he said as he slid his rook across the board.

"Me either, but I believe it's worse when a person believes their own lies. I believe that makes them dangerous," I said as I hopped two squares back and one to the left to capture his bishop with my knight. "Your move," I said with a wink and a playful smirk.

"Ok. I see you. Good move," he paused, "damn good move." He paused again to assess the vulnerability of his remaining pieces. Still studying the board, he asked, "Why do you say that makes them dangerous?"

Staring at the chessboard I said, "It's been my experience that pathological liars begin to believe their own lies. Their lies become their truth and it causes them to lose touch with reality. They will defend those lies, and in some cases become violent in defending them…" my voice trailed off as my mind wandered to a time before I knew him. When I looked up, Dasht was looking at me with a questioning and slightly concerned expression on his face.

"What happened Bunny?"

Apparently, my face had betrayed me as my mind drifted back to one of the most miserable times of my life. I took a deep breath before I spoke. "I don't like to dwell in the past or talk about exes, but one of the reasons I took a long hiatus from dating was my ex."

"I know about exes and how that can make you gun shy," he said as he slid the chess board to the side and reached over to caress my hands. Dasht was a real sweetheart when he wanted to be. "Jewel wasn't a liar, but she just wasn't the woman for me. We shouldn't have married. We weren't ready, and we definitely shouldn't have stayed married as long as we did," he paused as he pondered his last statement. Then as if snapping himself out of a daze he abruptly said. "But finish telling me what you were saying about lies."

"He was just a liar," I said matter of fact. "Everything about him was a lie. He would lie about the simplest things. It was as if he couldn't help himself. I thought because we went to church together and he prayed and read the Bible all the time that he was an upstanding person." I paused, "But after being with him I learned firsthand that even the devil can sit in church and pray."

Dasht was stunned. With widened eyes he asked, "What do you mean the devil. Damn, was he that bad?"

"Yes, he was. He was evil. I didn't realize it at first, but time has a way of revealing things. He was very quiet, but I made him talk to me."

"Oh, I'm sure you did." Dasht said jokingly, but I wasn't in a joking mood. "I'm sorry, finish telling me."

I smiled politely before speaking. "Every time we went to church he would cry. He would cry like a child almost. It was weird. Then when his lies were exposed, and the truth came out it made sense. His entire life was a lie. From the number of times he'd been married to the number of children he'd fathered. But even with the truth in his face he continued to lie and defend his lies to the point of being violent."

"He hit you?"

"No, he never hit me, but he did hold me hostage with a knife for a couple of hours, threatening to stab me if I attempted to leave."

"What? That's crazy."

"I know."

"Bunny I'm sorry you had to go through that." He caressed my hand. "Damn. I would never treat anyone that way."

"Yeah, it was bad. This was the one time in my life when I know without a shadow of doubt the devil was present. It seemed like the truth would kill him. He was pure evil. That experience is why I truly believe the devil walks amongst us. Call me crazy, but I know what I know. That's why when I refer to him, I say I danced with the devil, and I managed to avoid getting burned."

The look on Dasht's face puzzled me. His posture stiffened, and his eyes somewhat glossed over as if he was about to either cry or have an out of body experience. It wasn't surprise, it wasn't confusion, it wasn't the sympathy that was previously there. It was something that I couldn't identify, but whatever it was, it made my spine stiffen and the hair on my neck stand up. True to what had become his normal passive aggressive manner he abruptly changed the subject.

"Damn! That's a funky way to put it, but forget all that," he waved his hands dismissively. "It's over. You're with me now." He winked and flashed a half-hearted smile as he slid the chess board back in between us. "Let's get back to this game."

The air became thin as the elephant sashayed into the room. All I could think was, "Why did he just shut down like that?" But I went along to get along and allowed the conversation to end.

We spent the rest of the evening discussing the news over the game of chess, which I won with two pawns, a bishop and a rook.

You're getting good at this," he paused. "You're really getting good. Hell, too good. I'm going to have to put these drinks down and pay attention."

"During the day I don't believe in ghosts, but at night I'm a little more open-minded." - Unknown

I woke up out of my sleep abruptly. Dasht was snoring loudly, but it wasn't his snoring that woke me. There was a strange air in the room. I was about to roll over to flip on the lamp when I saw the silhouette. I stilled my body, held my breath, closed my eyes, and exhaled slowly as I re-opened them hoping my half asleep vision was blurred. But it wasn't. I wasn't seeing things. There was someone in the room and they were backing out slowly. My heart was racing so fast it was hard to keep still as I strained to watch the movement of the intruder. And then I recognized her. "No, it can't be." I clenched my teeth to stifle the, "Oh my God," I screamed in my head as I recognized the ponytails. "That's Valerie." I was mortified as the questions ran across my mind like the five o'clock news ticker tape. "What is she doing here? Why is she here? Has she lost her mind?" She stood in the doorway staring at us for a few more seconds before she inched towards the staircase. I moved closer to Dasht as I continued to watch her tip towards the stairs. I kept my eyes fixed on the bedroom door for what seemed like an hour but was only about three minutes. Once I heard the door shut, I slid out of bed to quietly hurry over to the window. My heart fell into the pit of my stomach as I watched her car go down the driveway and through the gates. I continued to stare out the window as the flood of questions continued to run through my mind. "Why would she come here this late at night? What was she doing in the bedroom? How long had she been in the house before I awoke? Did she know I'd seen her?" I was overwhelmed with emotion. I was confused, annoyed, but more than that, I was now afraid.

"Money can dress insecurity in beautiful things, but it will never make it beautiful."

Dasht was already downstairs when I awoke. I was surprised I had gotten any sleep at all as I lay there reflecting on what I'd seen last night. There was no more skirting around the issue. Valerie had to go. I laid there staring at the ceiling asking God to give me the words to say, and the temperament to say them in a manner where Dasht would be receptive. I finished praying and went to the bathroom to do my morning hygiene before taking the nervous walk down the stairs to tell Dasht about Valerie's intrusion. I could smell the coffee Dasht had brewed for me which made me smile in spite of the ensuing conversation. My smile, however, was replaced with a questioning gaze when I walked into an empty kitchen. I went to the garage to see the 1989 Mercedes 560SL, which he rarely drove, was missing. As I walked back into the kitchen I wondered where he'd gone this early?

I was still sitting at the island drinking coffee when Dasht returned looking wide eyed and confused. There was a rigidity that I didn't understand.

"Good morning sleepy head," he said in a mildly condescending tone.

Conscious of the tension and focused on discussing Valerie's unauthorized visit I pleasantly responded, "Good morning. Thank you for making my coffee."

He seemed vaguely annoyed but managed a semi smile before he said, "You're welcome." There was an awkward silence between us as he began setting up his laptop on the island.

Desperate for a way to start a conversation that would segue into discussing Valerie, I said, "I see you took your baby out for an early morning spin."

Dasht kept fidgeting with his laptop as he grunted, "Yeah I had to meet Velma at the office to pick-up some files."

Before I could stifle it, my thought flew out of my mouth, "This early on a Saturday?"

He sucked his teeth then said, "Look I'm a lawyer. I don't just lounge around on Saturday or any day for that matter. I have to work."

The anxiety over Valerie's intrusion and his unprovoked rudeness got the best of me. "Dasht, there is no need to be rude. I'm simply trying to make conversation with you, but since you're determined to be a jerk, I'm going to let you do your work." I stood up and walked over to the sink to dump my coffee. I'd had enough. As I headed towards the stairs, I could feel him sneaking glances at me as he huffed under his breath and allowed a few brusque sighs to escape.

"I know how to hide, even when I'm sitting in clear view, right in front of you."

After I showered and dressed, I felt lost. I was on the verge of mental exhaustion. I was dreading going downstairs because Dasht had been so pissy. However, I couldn't hide out upstairs all day because we had wedding planning to get done this weekend. Besides hiding out would only add to the already mounting tension, and I still needed to tell him about Valerie's intrusion. My thoughts were interrupted by the roaring of the landscaper's lawn mower. I walked over to the window and stared out at the property while silently asking God to give me clarity, patience and wisdom. Unfortunately, the tranquility of the beautiful grounds was invaded by the vivid memory of Valerie's car driving down the driveway in the wee hours of the night. The more I replayed the vision of her silhouette backing out of the room the faster my heartbeat. I was consumed with confusion, anger and fear. I inhaled and exhaled, intentionally pacing my breathing. As I steadied my breathing, I felt my heartbeat tempering, and my eyes became fixated on a cloud formation as I once again silently asked God to give me clarity, patience and wisdom. I stood at the window for a few more minutes before I closed my eyes, took a deep breath and exhaled, then headed towards the stairs.

When I reached the bottom of the stairs, Dasht was still sitting at the island staring at his laptop screen. To my surprise he said, "My goodness, girl you smell good. I love your smell." Then he turned away from his laptop and reached out for me to come close to him.

I tried to smile but there was no smile to be found as I obliged him and walked into his now outstretched arms.

"You know I love you right?"

"Yes Dasht, I know you love me."

"And you're going to be my wife."

"Umm hmm," was all I could muster.

Dasht gently grasped my arms and walked me a step back until I was arm's length and looking at him face to face, "Ok, look I know you've been in a huff about some things, but it's ok. You're my Bunny," he paused and stared at me clearly searching my face which was void of expression. "And we're solid."

"What? Wait? Did I miss something?" I silently asked myself. I took a deep breath as I consciously masked my inner confusion to avoid it appearing on my face. "Dasht I haven't been in a huff. Things have been awkward between us, and I've been trying to understand why."

He looked slightly confused as he released my arms. He first glanced at his shoes then turned his eyes and his body back to the laptop screen and said, "Yeah the air has been thick." There was an awkward momentary silence between us before he said, "Bunny we do need to talk about some things."

"You think?" I thought to myself as I slid into the bar chair next to him in preparation for the conversation and replied, "Ok?"

"Yeah there are some things I've been wanting us to discuss before we tie the knot," he paused still staring at the laptop screen. Then he abruptly turned his eyes to me and continued, "I think it's important for us to discuss our insecurities, unresolved issues, money and marriage counseling. I want us to resolve any issues we may have before we're married because I want our marriage to work."

"I agree those are definitely important topics for us to discuss, and there are a few that I'd like to add myself, but we can start with the topics you just stated."

"Swell. Write your list out and we can talk about it tomorrow. I need to finish this document I'm working on right now."

I was utterly confused. The manner which Dasht had addressed wanting to have a conversation was random to say the least and now he we wanted to postpone the conversation. His passive aggressiveness was irritating the heck out of me. "Dasht why would you say we needed to talk if you weren't prepared to have the conversation?"

"Because we do need to talk, but that doesn't mean I have to talk at this very moment," he snapped.

"Then why bring it up? Why not wait until you're ready to engage in the conversation."

"I wanted to give you some time to prepare yourself," he said staring at the laptop screen.

"I don't need time to prepare. I'm prepared to talk now," I quipped.

"I can't do it right now because I need to get this document done, but I'll be ready to talk tomorrow."

I didn't appreciate his tone which had become slightly raised with the baritone of his voice lowered an octave. I purposely allowed my face to convey my disapproval as I slid off the bar chair to leave the room.

Something wasn't right. Dasht always worked, but now he was hiding behind his work, and I didn't know why.

"Some people never stop to see and smell the roses, and they end up missing all the sweet things in life."

Dasht and I had spent the night basically avoiding one another, so the aroma of constriction that was becoming all too familiar was permeating the air when morning came. As usual, I woke-up to an empty bed and Dasht talking and laughing with someone on the phone. The amount of time he spent on the phone was starting to irritate me. Lately, if he wasn't working, he was on the phone, or staring at a *Lifetime* movie while having a cocktail. We were in the same space, but we weren't in the same place. He seemed totally uninterested in planning our wedding, and he was obviously avoiding any meaningful conversation. We hadn't made love once since I arrived. There was so much we needed to do, so much we needed to discuss, and we had so little time to do it. As if that weren't enough, I still needed to tell him about Valerie's Friday night intrusion. For the life of me I could not fathom why she would be in the house at all, let alone standing over us. Just the thought of it caused goosebumps to form all over my body. All the thoughts became overwhelming and as the tears filled my eyes, spilled down my cheeks and ran into my ears, I felt the need to get out of bed and pray.

"Lord, I come to you with a heavy heart and a confused mind. I believe you sent this man to me, and I thank you for him. I love him so much, and I believe he is my husband. Please don't let me mess this up. Please God, give me wisdom, understanding and patience. Please help me to be the woman that I am supposed to be for him. Give me the words to say and guide me so I'll know when it's the right time to say them. Lastly, I ask that you protect us from Valerie and don't allow her to come in here and hurt us. Amen." As I got up and headed to the bathroom, I could still hear Dasht laughing and talking on the phone.

My feelings were somewhat hurt when I walked into the kitchen and not only was there no coffee, but Dasht didn't even acknowledge me. He actually seemed miffed that I'd entered the room. I attempted to make eye contact with him as I walked over to the sink to fill the coffee pot, but he avoided my doing so. As if that were not insulting enough, he added insult to injury as he got up and walked out of the room to continue his jovial phone conversation. My heart was hoping for us to have a loving and productive day, but my head said this was going to be another long stressful day.

I was still standing at the island, drinking my coffee and staring at nothing when Dasht returned to the kitchen.

"Good morning Ms. Franklin," he huffed.

"Ms. Franklin," I repeated then let out a soft sigh before I asked, "What's going on Dasht?"

"What do you mean," he asked sarcastically.

"You know what I mean. You've been quite terse, and I want to know why?"

"Terse," he chuckled mockingly. "You're so snooty."

He was attempting to avoid answering the question by insulting me, but I wasn't having it. "Dasht that's not nice," I scolded. "However, that is a prime example of what I'm speaking of. What is going on with you? Why are you being so brusque?"

"Brusque," he said, this time visibly mocking me. Then he let out a spiteful giggle.

"Stop it Dasht."

The ornery grin disappeared from his face, his eyes momentarily reflected shock, then his brow furrowed as he glared at me with a stare that I couldn't define. He looked me up and down before he walked over to the bar chair to take his normal seat at the island in front of the laptop that was conveniently sitting there.

"I'm waiting for an answer Dasht."

He glared at me momentarily before opening the laptop to stare at the screen.

"Dasht?"

"Gabriella, I can't talk to you right now. You're pissing me off."

"First of all, don't speak to me that way. What do you mean I'm pissing you off? You're pissed off because I asked you about your behavior towards me? That makes absolutely no sense Dasht, and you know it," I huffed.

"I said I don't want to talk about this, but you're still pushing me."

"Pushing you? Dasht who do you think you are, and what has gotten into you?"

He shot me a look of sheer rage as he yelled, "Look god dammit! I said I don't want to talk right now and that's what I mean." Then he turned his attention to the laptop screen.

I stood there momentarily, then I walked towards the stairs. Once upstairs, I went to the bathroom to cry. I didn't understand his behavior. It was erratic to say the least. He had been cold and mean for no reason. I sat at the vanity sobbing for at least ten minutes before I looked up and starred at myself in the mirror. I was supposed to be here planning our happily ever after, but instead as I looked into my eyes, I could see my heart breaking. Then I went from being sad to angry. I was angry at Dasht for being a jerk, and I was angry at myself for allowing him to treat me this way. That was when I decided I wasn't going to spend my day being ignored and mistreated. I stood up and washed my hands and my face. I grabbed my purse and headed down the stairs and out the door without saying a word to Dasht.

"The creeping plants kill the flowers."

When I returned home Dasht was drunk, but he was too glib to be sloppy about it. He was posted in his usual position at the island staring at his laptop. I didn't have the energy nor the desire for more confrontation. I took a deep breath before I said as cordially as possible, "Good evening."

"Hey Bunny," he smiled. "Have you eaten?"

"I'm not hungry. I'm just going to go to bed."

"Come sit down and talk to me."

"I'm tired Dasht."

"Come on Bunny, stop all that. Come sit down with me." He motioned for me to sit next to him.

I hesitantly obliged and walked over and slid into the bar chair next to him at the island.

"First I want to give you these." He handed me a bouquet of magnolias, red roses and white hydrangeas. "I wanted to give you these tonight instead of tomorrow." As I reached out to accept the bouquet, he leaned over and kissed me on the cheek. "Happy Valentine's Day."

"Thank you Dasht."

"Ok look, I know I was a little harsh today, and I apologize. Ok? I love you. You hear me?"

"Yes, I hear you," I answered without emotion.

"I love you, and you love me. So, stop all this pouting. We're getting married." He smiled as he paused for me to respond, but I didn't have anything to say. "I know you want to work on the wedding plans and we're going to do that. I just couldn't do it today because I needed to concentrate on this big legal issue I've been working. I need you to be understanding when it comes to my work because I'm making money, money for us." His phone rang and I saw the name "Danica Edwards" scroll across the screen. "Oh, I have to take this," he said abruptly as he answered the phone. "Hello, did you get my email? Great, have you had an opportunity to read it over? Ok, read over it and we'll talk tomorrow. Ok. Good night." He hung up and said, "So, where were we?"

"Who is Danica?"

"She is a young lawyer that I've been mentoring. I'm just helping her with her cases. But let's get back to us. That's what's important. I love you girl. You're my Bunny. You're going to be my wife, Mrs. Spelbender." He looked at me and smiled. "Damn I love you girl."

"I love you too Dasht," I responded still void any enthusiasm.

"Ok, let's talk about some of the things we need to discuss."

"Dasht you've been drinking."

"I'm not drunk," he said defensively.

"I didn't say you were. It's a serious conversation that I believe should be had when we're both one hundred percent cognizant."

"Hmph," he let out a mildly annoyed sigh before he said, "Ok how about this? I take tomorrow off and stay at home with my Bunny for Valentine's Day. Would you like that?"

I felt a smile forming on my face. "I would," I answered softly.

"Great," he flashed a toothy grin. "We can talk and do some wedding planning."

I felt a wave of relief come over me as I smiled inside and out.

"Courage is choosing to use your voice to own your words."

I woke up early and decided to start the week off right. I was putting on my sneakers to go for a quick run when Dasht rolled over.

"Bunny?" He questioned peeking at me as he awoke.

"Good morning Dasht."

He rolled over on his back yawning as he asked, "What are you doing up so early?"

"I haven't worked out in three days, so I wanted to get a run in before we got our day started."

"Oh, that's good," he yawned. "I'm proud of you and how you work to stay fit. "He yawned and stretched. "That's one of the things I love about you," he said as he climbed out of bed.

I was relieved and glad the energy was good between us.

When I returned from my run Dasht was in the kitchen chatting with Valerie. I had forgotten she was coming today. I still hadn't had an opportunity to tell him about her standing over us Friday night. She accidently made eye contact with me as she gave me a dirty look when I entered the room.

"Good morning Valerie," I said in acknowledgement of her glare. Then to both her and Dasht's surprise I said, "I forgot you were scheduled to come today, but we won't be needing you. I'm sorry you drove out here, but we'll pay you for the day so you can leave now." They both stared at me in shock. Then Valerie looked at Dasht with pleading eyes, but he looked away. "That's right," I thought to myself, "you'd better look away." But she was not accepting my sending her home.

"Dasht?" she questioned.

I was thoroughly perturbed with her bold and blatant disrespect. "Valerie, we won't be needing you today," I reiterated without waiting for Dasht, who was visibly uncomfortable, to respond to her.

Valerie glared at me briefly before she turned to him and said, "Well I guess I'll see you Thursday."

Without looking at her Dasht defeatedly said, "Thank you for everything Valerie. I'll talk to you later."

She glared at me once again before she left.

As soon as the door clicked Dasht turned to me and angrily asked, "Why did you do that?"

"I did it because I wanted her to leave. There isn't much for her to do today. Furthermore, this is our day. You and I are supposed to be planning our wedding and having a detailed discussion, so we don't need Valerie hanging around. Besides she is one of the issues I would like to discuss with you."

"What do you mean she is one of the issues you want to discuss with me?"

"Dasht I've told you how Valerie has been disrespectful, which you just had another opportunity to witness firsthand."

"What!?" He cut me off. "How was she disrespectful? She didn't do anything. You're the one who sashayed in here and told her to go home for no reason."

I felt my blood starting to heat up. "Dasht why are you being so snippy with me over the housekeeper?"

He seemed insulted when he questioned, "Housekeeper?"

"Yes, housekeeper. She is the housekeeper?"

"You don't have to belittle her and call her that," he snapped.

"How am I belittling her? That is her job."

"Yes, she cleans the house, but you don't have to call her the housekeeper. Valerie has been good to me." He placed his head in his hands in frustration.

I didn't care that he was becoming frustrated. I was frustrated too, and I'd had enough of Valerie and enough of him defending her. "Good to you? You pay her to do a job that she isn't even good at. How is that being good to you?"

He raised his head and glared at me as he said, "What do you mean she isn't good at it? Valerie keeps this place clean, and she is my friend."

"Dasht, there was a spider's web hanging on the dining room chandelier that had been there since I first started spending the night here. You know when it was wiped away?" I asked rhetorically. "When I cleaned it off so we could have a nice Thanksgiving dinner in there. I've come in several times to find Valerie sitting in front of the television watching soap operas. Hell, one time she was sitting on our bed watching television." I stopped because I could hear my voice raising.

He again dropped his head in his hands as he said, "I told Valerie she could watch television. What's the big deal?"

"The big deal is she is inappropriate and unprofessional. The big deal is she is disrespectful. The big deal is I don't want her here anymore. The big deal is she makes me uncomfortable. The big deal is I woke up to her standing over us at almost midnight Friday night!" That wasn't how I'd planned to tell him, but I'd become angry and it slipped out.

"What do you mean she was standing over us? That didn't happen," he balked as he gazed at me with an expression of both shock and distress.

"Oh yes it did happen."

"You're crazy!"

"Dasht Spelbender don't you dare speak to me that way! I am not crazy, and I don't appreciate you calling me out of my name," I said sternly.

"Well why would you say that?"

"Say what? The truth? Because it happened, that's why I would say it. I said it because I woke-up to that psycho standing over us, and I don't want her in this house anymore." I felt the lump forming in my throat as my anger, sadness and confusion collided like locomotive trains. Dasht was staring at his shoes and rubbing his head. I inhaled and swallowed hard to try to dissolve the lump before I continued to speak, "I've been wanting to speak to you about it, but you've been so irritable. I was trying to wait for the right time for us to talk about it."

He placed his head back in his hands as he said, "Are you sure?"

"What do you mean, am I sure? I know what I saw Dasht."

"Why would she do that?"

"That's the same question I ask, but there really is no answer that would make it right. She needs to go. No, she has to go."

His head popped up like a jack in the box as he scowled at me with piercing eyes. His lips curled and he almost snarled as he said, "Are you giving me an ultimatum?"

"No because if I have to give you an ultimatum then we have nothing else to talk about. I need to go." I'd reached my limit. I was putting my foot down.

"Go where?" he asked in a challenging and contemptuous tone.

"Go home, that's where. If I need to give you an ultimatum about the person who is here to mop the floors, then I'm the one who needs to go because I'm the problem. Maybe you should be marrying her." I stopped because the tears were coming.

"Don't' say that," he spat. "You're being ugly. Me marry Val...don't say that." He rubbed his head as he shook it in disgust. "Damn, I hate this. Val..., I can't believe she would," he stopped short of completing his sentence. "I'm so disappointed in her." He covered his face with his hands as if he were either hiding or crying. Then he wiped his hands over his face, shook his head in disbelief as he opened his eyes to meet my tearful gaze. "Ok...damn. I'll let her go. But I have to do it my way."

"I don't care how you do it. I just want her gone."

"Some stench is stronger than soap and water."

I stood in the shower allowing the hot water to run over my head as I tried to release the multitude of emotions about what had transpired. Why would Valerie even think she could disrespect me the way she had, and why had Dasht been so defensive? I could understand if she was the housekeeper he'd grown up with or they had some type of family relationship. But I didn't want to spend the day stressing about it. I wanted her gone, and he said he was going to let her go. The fact that he was so distraught about it wasn't sitting well with me, but he'd agreed to let her go I reasoned to myself. Besides Dasht had taken the day off, which he rarely did, and we were going to work on planning our wedding. "Yeah," I thought to myself, "focus on the wedding." The goal was to get rid of her, and he'd agreed. She was gone and that was that. I smiled determined to focus on the positive as I turned off the water.

After I dressed, I joined Dasht in the kitchen where he was staring at his laptop as usual.

"Happy Valentine's Day," I said cheerfully as I handed him a card and slid into the bar chair beside him.

A wide, boyish smile spread across his face as he took the card. "Bunny, you didn't have to get me anything." He opened the card and sat and read it intently. "Aww Bunny," he leaned over and kissed me on the cheek. "Thank you."

"You're welcome."

"You're good girl. You think you know the Dash-Master."

I giggled, "I'm trying."

"No, you're doing more than trying. You really get me." He leaned over and kissed me on the cheek again. "I love you Bunny. Damn I love you." He looked down at the card. "Yeah, you're my Bunny. We're good, rock solid. We're going to be good together."

"I believe so," I said in agreement.

"You know how to deal with me, and you do a good job of keeping that bear off my back." We both laughed. "So, do you want to have our talk first or do some wedding planning?"

"I think we should do the more serious stuff first and save the wedding planning, the fun part for later."

"Wedding planning is fun huh? If you say so." He smiled and then looked at me with raised eyebrows before he said, "I hope you aren't planning on having us spend a lot of money."

"No, classic and chic is what I'd like, but let's talk about the things you wanted to talk about. I believe you said money, insecurities, unresolved issues and marriage counseling?

"Wow you remembered all that. You have a great memory. I have to watch what I say around you because you remember everything," he joked halfheartedly.

I winked as I flirtatiously said, "I remember what I want to remember, but I make it a point to remember what you say because I love you."

He blew me a kiss, and I winked and blew a kiss back before I said, "So, lets disconnect from the world." I reached over and closed his laptop and slid it to the side.

"What are you doing?"

"I'm giving you my undivided attention, and I want you to give me yours."

"I'm just monitoring my e-mail. I'm waiting on a message about something I'm working on."

"Dasht you said you were taking the day off so we could talk and plan our wedding. Now I understand you may not be able to totally disconnect, but while we're having a serious discussion about our future, I would like for you to please silence your phone and divert your eyes and attention away from the computer screen, please."

He looked dumbfounded as all the blood drained from his face. "I don't' understand why I need to turn off everything for us to talk."

"Dasht," I said calmly, "We're planning our future."

"I know," he huffed. "Ok," he silenced the phone, "let's talk."

"Our life together," I continued calmly as I reached over and turned the phone face down so he couldn't monitor the screen. "Don't you think that deserves our undivided attention?"

He took a deep breath before he said, "Ok," in a ruffled tone.

"Are you getting a bear on you?" I teased to lighten the mood.

"Stop teasing me," he pouted in a childlike manner,

I playfully tickled him in his side, "You know you want to smile."

"Come on, stop it," he blushed. "Let's talk."

"Whew, I'd dodged a bullet," I thought to myself. "Do you want to start with money and the prenup?"

"Sure. Sounds like a good place to start."

I had taken the time to compile a list reflecting all my assets as well as liabilities, which I slid over to Dasht for him to observe.

"I didn't know we were giving a financial report," he said.

"Well since you'd given me time to prepare for the conversation, I thought this was the easiest way for me to capture everything."

Dasht studied the list as he said, "You've done well for yourself Bunny."

I was somewhat taken aback when Dasht wasn't as forthcoming about his finances. Especially since he'd initiated this conversation. As if that weren't stunning enough, he'd postponed under the guise of giving me time to prepare yet he had nothing prepared. Every number he provided was an estimate, but I wasn't overly concerned about his finances. I had my own money, and we'd agree to have a prenup. As we transitioned to the topic of insecurities Dasht began fidgeting with his phone.

"Can we take a break? I need to return these phone calls I've missed." He said while looking at his phone.

I was visibly annoyed. "Dasht you said…"

He cut me off before I could finish, "Look I'm a lawyer. I can't turn off my phone and ignore phone calls. Clients depend on me."

And just like that all the tension that had come and gone was once back again. "You said you wanted to talk. Then you said we had to wait until today to talk. Now you won't take the time to have the conversation."

He was still looking at his phone when he slid the laptop over and opened it, "I need to check my e-mail. Can we please just take a break."

"Fine Dasht," I huffed.

He seemed oblivious to my disappointment as he diverted his attention between his phone and the laptop. Then he dialed a number, "Yeah, I got your message. I can meet you in about twenty minutes. Will that work? Ok see you shortly." He hung up and then turned to me, "I need to run to the office, but we can finish this conversation later."

I was beyond peeved. I was pissed, confused and emotionally exhausted. I stayed seated as Dasht packed-up his laptop, kissed me on the top of my head and walked out the door. I heard the door click, then the hum of the car engine, the garage door opened and then it closed. I continued to sit in the same place engulfed in a tornado of emotions. Elephants blocked the windows dimming the light and sucking the air out of the room. What a way to spend Valentine's Day.

"Let the ManGo."

I was sitting at the island thumbing through a magazine when Dasht sauntered into the door a little after 5pm with the phone glued to his ear. He flashed me a smile as if everything was great between us as he rushed to the cabinet to grab a glass and begin making himself a cocktail.

I was trying to be understanding. I was trying to stay peaceful. I was trying, but I was leaving pissed and rounding the corner to flat out angry as I continued to watch him unpack and open his laptop while he continued to chat on the phone. After about ten minutes or so I couldn't take it anymore. I went upstairs, grabbed my purse and left.

Once I got in the car, I called Tippy.

"Hey girl," she answered cheerfully.

"Hey, what are you up to?"

"Oh, just the usual, call me kiddie chauffer," she joked. "I just dropped Isabella off at dance, and I'm on my way to pick-up the boys from Kumon. What are you all getting into for Valentine's Day?"

"You know Valentine's Day isn't really my thing. I don't want that once a year love."

"Tell me about it," she said in agreement.

"We decided we weren't going to make a big deal out of it but, Dasht gave me some flowers yesterday, and I gave him a card this morning."

"Joseph and I just exchanged cards this morning. I prefer to spend the money on a vacation rather than get a piece of jewelry that I'm not going to wear."

"Ditto," I said as I stared at the stoplight.

"How's the wedding planning going?"

"It's not," I said. "Dasht doesn't even seem interested in planning this wedding. He's been very standoffish since I arrived," I paused to choke back the tears. "I don't know what is wrong with him."

"What happened?"

"We were supposed to spend the day together today talking about money, prenup, marriage counseling and insecurities, a conversation he said he wanted to have. Then we were supposed to work on the wedding plans, but he left earlier to do something for work. When he came back, he had the phone glued to his ear as usual. Then he started drinking and hoped on his laptop, so I just left."

"What did he say when you left?"

"I honestly don't think he even noticed. He was talking on the phone."

"Hmm, that would piss me off."

"I am pissed off."

"You're going to have to talk to him about the phone and how much he works when you're here. You fly here and take time away from work to be with him. He needs to be appreciative of that and not take it for granted."

"Yeah, I know. But now he's drinking so talking about anything serious will have to wait until tomorrow."

"I don't like this, and I don't like the way you sound."

"I'm ok, just irritated. I'm sure we'll work it out."

"Speaking of working it out, have you all spoken about what's her name, umm Vickie?"

"Vickie?"

"The housekeeper."

"Oh, her name is Val. Funny you should mention her. That was a huge source of contention yesterday. She was her normal disrespectful self, and she did it in front of Dasht. I told him she has to go, and he was in a huff about it but said he's going to let her go."

Tippy bluntly said, "Well good because it's about time he recognized how she was treating you. She needed to go."

"Yeah," I said as I continued to drive with no destination.

"So where are you going?"

"Honestly nowhere. I just needed to leave to clear my head because I don't want us to spend our time arguing."

"Want to meet me somewhere? We can go for yogurt or something. I would say dinner, but every restaurant is probably crowded."

"I'm not really hungry, but yogurt sounds good. I could use a treat right about now."

"Ok, I'll swoop the kids up and take them home then I'll meet you at Sweet-Stack Creamery."

"Sounds like a plan."

When I arrived Tippy was waiting inside. "Hey Gab," she smiled and gave me a hug.

"I knew you were going to beat me here," I teased so I could force a smile to form on my face. "Ma'am this is not yogurt."

She playfully batted her eyes as she said, "Umm, they have dairy free ice-cream."

"Dairy free or not, it's still ice cream, and it will still make me fat."

"There is nothing fat about you, and one treat is not going to kill you."

While we perused the menu I teased, "I should order two scoops of the Let the Man Go."

Giggling Tippy said, "I can't believe that is on the menu, but we all feel that way at times. That's probably why it's on there because women do eat ice cream when we go through a break-up. But you're not going through a break-up, so take your mind off of that. Order something else."

"Hmm I think I will indulge in a scoop of Cuban Coffee Cream."

"Just one scoop?" She questioned. "Well I'm going to have the doughnut stuffed with Sweet Dreams ice cream."

I playfully scolded, "I don't think there's anything right about a doughnut with ice cream stuffed in it."

Licking her lips, she said, "It's probably not right, but it's going to taste oh so good going down. Besides what's the point in coming here if you're not going to enjoy yourself. If you're going to do it, you might as well go all out."

I laughed a real laugh, "Makes sense, but I can't go all out. I'm sure I've gained weight just from walking in here and inhaling the air." We both laughed.

"Yeah you've got to fit into a wedding dress."

I felt my somber return as I said, "Maybe, maybe not."

"Gab it's going to be alright. You all are just going through a rough patch. It happens. Everything is going to work out."

"Yeah, I know," I said as I paid for the ice-cream.

Tippy and I had been sitting in the ice-cream restaurant for a little over an hour when Joseph called. As she answered her phone it prompted me to check to see if I'd missed a call or text from

Dasht. My heart sunk when I saw there was no missed call or text from him, but I was surprised to see a missed call from Dana and a subsequent text inviting me to have lunch.

Once Tippy finished her call I showed her the text from Dana.

Always the optimist Tippy said, "Oh good, she's inviting you to lunch. So, she's been acting better towards you?"

"No not really. I haven't spoken to her since Christmas Karaoke. She seemed happy about the engagement."

"She's probably reaching out because she knows you all are getting married, and she wants to be a part of everything."

"I guess. I'll text her later to see if she wants to meet tomorrow."

"Well I've got to get going because my husband is looking for me. What are you about to get into?"

I looked at my phone again to see if Dasht had tried to contact me, but there was nothing from him. I felt my heart sink to the bottom of my stomach as I thought, "Did he even notice or care that I'd left." My sadness had registered on my face.

"So, he hasn't tried to call or text you?"

"No," I said softly.

"Well you can always come to the house. You know the kiddos have been anxious to see you."

"Ok, let me get them some cookies and I'll meet you there."

"Only one cookie each," she scolded.

"Only one cookie each when you just ate a doughnut stuffed with ice cream. Whatever, I'm getting them two each."

She shook her head in surrender as she smiled and said, "I'll see you when you get there."

"He loves me; He loves me not."

After I hadn't heard from Dasht by 9:30pm I decided to spend the night at Tippy's. My feelings were beyond hurt when I rolled over at 6:00am to check my phone and there still was no message or missed call from Dasht. I wanted to call him, but I refused to. If he wasn't concerned about me then I wasn't going to be concerned about him. I text Dana to see if she wanted to meet for lunch. I was surprised when she responded immediately. We agreed to meet at 1:00pm, so I decided to go to the gym to work off last night's ice cream but more so the stress over Dasht and I that was making my neck and shoulder's ache.

I pulled into the parking lot of the Pappadeaux Seafood Kitchen at 12:52pm. Dana hadn't arrived. At 1:30pm I was starting to worry, and as I picked-up my phone to text her she came rushing through the door.

"Hey, sorry I'm late."

"Hello Dana, I said trying to mask my annoyance. "I was just about to text you."

"I got caught up doing something for Lena and lost track of the time. Sorry."

"It's fine," I lied as the hostess guided us to a table.

Once we were seated Dana asked, "Did you tell Daddy we were meeting for lunch?"

"No," I said in a questioning tone. "Was I supposed to?"

"No, I'm actually glad you didn't. He probably would have told you not to come."

"Why would he not want me to come? I'm sure he is supportive of you and I spending time together and getting to know one another."

"Hmph, a normal person would be, but not my Dad."

With a puzzled look on my face I asked, "What do you mean a normal person. Why would you say that about your father?"

"Gabriella, I know you and I really haven't interacted with each other much, but I wanted to invite you out today to let you know that the way I've acted wasn't about you. I know it may have felt that way because in all honesty I've taken it out on you, but it wasn't about you."

"Ok," I said signaling for her to continue.

"I'm not going to lie. I had a problem with you at first because I thought you were just another one of these women who've been chasing my Dad for his money. But after being around you and seeing all the nice things you've done for him like the birthday celebration, and spending time with your family I realize you really love that old hound."

"Dana you shouldn't call your father a hound," I said in gist but also denouncing her statement.

"He's lucky that's all I call him," she said bluntly. "Gabriella, trust me when I tell you, you don't know my Dad the way you think you do." She paused as she looked at me for a reaction, but I gave none. "I told my Mom I was going to invite you to lunch, and she said I should." The waitress interrupted her as she came over to take our drink order. "Let me have a Kentucky Peach Mule," Dana said without looking at the menu.

"I'll have sweet tea, please."

Once the waitress left Dana continued, "I told my Mom that I believe you are a nice person, and you're walking into this marriage blind."

"How so," I obliged.

"Well I don't know what my Dad has told you about me and my Mom, but he is not all he pretends to be when he is around you."

"Dana your father has never spoken ill of your mother. All I've ever been told is they married really young," I lied.

"He doesn't speak bad about her because he can't. He knows what he did to my Mother." She searched my face for expression, but my eyes just invited her to continue. "He treated my Mom like shit. He cheated on her. He beat her, and then he divorced her and left her with nothing."

I couldn't mask the frown and shock that had plastered across my face, "Are you serious?"

"As a heart attack. And if that weren't bad enough, he started dating my aunt a year ago further adding insult to injury."

My head was spinning, "Your aunt?"

The waitress brought our drinks, "Here you are ladies. One Kentucky Peach Mule for you, and a sweet tea for you. Would you ladies like an appetizer or are you ready to order?"

Without looking at the menu Dana said, "I'll have the Oysters Pappadeaux, and The Louisiana Gumbo & Po Boy."

I was still dumfounded by Dana's allegations when the waitress asked, "What can I get for you Ma'am?"

Quickly perusing the menu, I said, "Uh, I'll have the Grilled Shrimp & Grits."

"Ok," she said taking our menus. "I'll have that out shortly."

As soon as the waitress walked away Dana continued, "Yes my Aunt Lillian. You met her at the birthday dinner."

My mouth literally dropped open as I closed my eyes to process what Dana had just said. When I opened my eyes, they locked with Dana's intent stare. "Are you saying Dasht was dating your Aunt Lillian."

"It was beyond dating. They were a thing."

"She's your Mom's sister," I clarified.

"He didn't care." She sipped her drink. "He does whatever he wants to whomever he wants with whomever he wants. He doesn't give a damn about anyone else."

"When did this happen?"

"Well they were still an item until you came into the picture."

"What do you mean?"

"I mean they were still dating, and then he met you and in typical Dash-Master fashion he dumped her for you."

I swallowed hard to fight off the urge to vomit because I was utterly disgusted at this point. "How could he? Why would he?" I questioned to myself. "So...," I struggled to find words. "Is that why she was at his birthday dinner?"

"I invited her to taunt him. In a way I was glad that he dumped her, but I wanted to see him squirm in front of you because I know him. I know he's been putting on this image for you. Like I said, I honestly didn't like you either at first, but then I realized you weren't like all the other ones. I told my Mom you seem to be a nice lady, and he had proposed to you. She said he was going to ruin your life the same way he ruined hers. That's when she and I decided I should talk to you."

The waitress came back and placed the oysters in front of Dana, "Here's your Oyster's Pappadeaux. Would you like another drink?"

"Yes, I'll have another," Dana said as she sucked down the last of the one in front of her.

Once the waitress was out of ear shot, I asked, "So you're telling me this because you don't want me to marry your father?"

"No, I'm telling you this because my Mom and I think you should know. I'm telling you because I know he isn't going to be honest with you. I'm telling you so if you do decide to marry him you will know what you're getting into. I'm telling you so he won't ruin your life like he ruined my Mom's."

Still in a fog over all the information she had shared, I asked, "How did he ruin your Mom's life?"

"First off he treated her like shit the entire time they were married. My Mom said he always had affairs. I remember him always being gone, but I didn't know he was out cheating until I got older.

Then he left her when I graduated high school. She came home and the house was empty."

"What do you mean empty?"

"Just what I said," she slurped the oyster. "Empty. He took everything and moved away."

At this point I was sure there wasn't an ounce of blood left in my face, but as much as I was overwhelmed, I now wanted to know more. "You said he beat her?"

Dana stopped eating and paused before she said, "Yeah, he used to hit her. When I was about twelve, I remember seeing him push her down the hallway into their bedroom, and before he closed the door, I saw him smack her across the head. There were other times that I heard the smacks and her crying," Dana stopped to wipe away the tears that had rolled down her cheeks.

I felt my heart cracking as tears welled up in my eyes and I thought to myself, "She's not lying."

The waitress returned with Dana's drink and our food, "Kentucky Peach Mule and Louisiana Gumbo & Po Boy for you," she said as she placed the items in front of Dana. "Would you like me to take the Oysters Pappadeaux or are you still working on that?"

"You can take it," Dana said.

"Alrighty," the waitress said as she took away the dish. Then looking at me as she placed the hot food in front of me, "And I have a Grilled Shrimp & Grits for you. Can I get you ladies anything else, sauces, refill on the tea?"

"No thank you," we both said in unison.

When the waitress left, I said, "Let's bless the food."

"Ok," Dana shrugged.

I reached across the table for her hands, and we closed our eyes as I prayed, "Dear God thank you for this day, this food and this fellowship. Bless the hands that prepared it. Help it to provide nourishment for our bodies. Amen."

Once we released hands Dana took a sip of her drink, "I know you think I'm lying, but I'm not."

"I don't think you're lying," I said solemnly.

"My Dad really isn't all he wants you to believe he is. He puts on this show for you, like he is supportive of me, but he isn't. When I first told him, I was gay he disowned me."

"Really?"

She let out a contemptuous laugh before she said, "Before you came into the picture, he never invited Lena over. It was all a show for you because you're so liberal." She bit into her sandwich. Still chewing she said, "He acted shocked when I came out, but I honestly don't know why. It's partially his fault."

"What do you mean it's his fault? You blame him for your being born gay?"

"No," she took a bite of the gumbo, then a sip of her drink. "I wasn't born gay Gabriella. I choose to live a gay lifestyle. I became curious about women because of the amount of porn my Dad kept in the house. That is how I was exposed to homosexuality."

"You mean that's how you became aware of women having relationships with other women."

She laughed, "You're so proper. No not relationships, sex and not just women, homosexuality. My Dad looks at all kinds of porn. I believe he is a sex addict and my Mom does too." She took another bite of her gumbo.

I hadn't touched my food, and I feared I would throw-up if I did. This was too much. "I've never seen any porn in Dasht's house," I said somewhat defensively.

"That's because he doesn't want you to see it. But trust me it's there. He has a safe in his closet. I'm sure that's where he's hiding it from you."

There was a safe in the closet, and I'd never thought to ask him what was in it. "So, are you saying Dasht is gay?"

She took another sip of her drink as she motioned for the waitress to come over, "I don't know if he's ever had a homosexual experience physically, but I know for a fact he enjoys watching homosexual sex, both men and women." The waitress appeared and Dana said, "I'll take another," she paused, "no wait I'd better not because I'm driving. I'll just have a Michelob Ultra." As Dana took another bite of her gumbo, she noticed I wasn't eating. "You've lost your appetite huh?"

"Yeah I guess I have," I said looking at the untouched food.

"I'm sorry to have to tell you all this because you do seem like a nice person Gabriella. I would just hate to see him treat you the way he treated my Mom. She and I always joke," she stopped because the waitress returned with the beer.

Noticing the untouched food in front of me, the waitress asked, "Ma'am is everything ok with the shrimp & grits?"

"Oh yes, it's fine."

"Can I get you ladies anything else? Tea refill?"

"No thank you, we're fine," I said while Dana sipped her beer.

When the waitress left, I said, "You were saying?"

"What was I saying?"

"Something about you and your Mom joking?"

"Oh yeah," she said as she popped the last bite of her sandwich in her mouth. Still chewing she said, "My Mom and I always joke that I'm going to get everything he owns when he dies and split it with her."

"You joke about your father dying?"

She finished chewing, took a swig of her beer, swallowed, then looked me dead in the eye and said, "I want him to die. I hate him."

My heart dropped as confusion, sadness and horror flooded over me. "That makes me sad."

"It used to make me sad too, but I'm not sad anymore."

I signaled for the waitress to bring the check. "Ma'am are you sure the food was ok? Would you like a box?"

"Yes, everything was fine. No thank you. I'll just take the check."

After I paid the check Dana and I walked out of the restaurant together.

"Thank you for meeting me for lunch and treating me," she said as she gave me a hug.

"You're welcome," I said returning her embrace.

"Caution: Handle with Care -- Your Bunny is quite cute and cuddly, but if you mishandle her, she will attack to protect herself."

Once I was in the car I checked to see if Dasht had called or text me, and I felt totally depleted when I saw he hadn't. Rather than go home I drove around Atlanta replaying the conversation I'd had with Dana. "Why would Dasht date his ex-wife's sister and why would she date him? When we met, he'd said he didn't have a girlfriend? And what was going on with the pornography? Could it be as bad as Dana made it seem? But why would a heterosexual man want to watch homosexual porn?" All the questions flooded my brain, but there were no answers. I drove and drove trying to make sense of it all. My thoughts moved at light speed until the gas light came on.

Once I finished pumping the gas, I sat in the car and checked my phone again, except unlike the other times I had no expectation to see any contact from Dasht. And just as I expected, there wasn't any. Out of desperation, I closed the text icon and opened my e-mail exhausting my last glimmer of hope that he'd taken the time to write me a sweet, sincere note but there was none. I threw the phone on the passenger seat, and I stared at the 2-carat solitaire on my left hand. The more I stared at it the sadder I became. Then my sadness became anger. "Why was he treating me this way? He asked me to marry him. He asked me to be his girlfriend. He'd been pushing for a relationship from day one, not me. And now he had the audacity to treat me like yesterday's newspaper?" I thought to myself. Then I locked eyes with myself in the rearview mirror and said, "No! Hell no! Dasht Spelbender does not get to treat me this way. He can take this ring and go straight to hell."

I started the engine and headed towards the Spelbender estate. As I pulled up to the gate and entered the code, I made the decision to ring the front doorbell rather than enter because this clearly was not my home. Dasht answered the door with a confused and annoyed expression on his face.

"Why are you ringing the doorbell when you can come in through the garage?"

I held out my hand offering up the engagement ring, "Here, I just came to get my things and give you this."

He threw his hands up dismissively and walked away as he mumbled, "I don't have time for this shit."

"Dasht to whom do you think you're speaking to? I don't know what has gotten into you, but you don't speak to me that way and you don't treat me this way," I said as I followed him into the house.

"You're the one who just up and left, and now you come in here with this bullshit!"

"Dasht don't curse at me."

"Whatever. If you want to leave, then leave. I'm not begging you to stay. Go!" He waved his hand dismissively as he turned his back to me.

"Why would you even ask me to marry you?" I asked as tears ran down my face.

He sat down at the island as he said, "I asked you because I thought I wanted to marry you, but I don't know who you are because this side of you I'm now seeing," he stopped and put his head in his hands.

"You thought...," I said as I placed the ring on the island next to the laptop and headed towards the stairs to get my things.

"Where are you going?"

"I'm going to get my things. It's obvious I'm not wanted here."

"What do you mean?"

"Dasht you have been a jerk since I arrived. You've been condescending and curt the entire time. All we've done is fight or bicker at each other. We haven't done one ounce of wedding planning because you've been either on the phone or hiding behind your work." I stopped to wipe the tears from my face.

"I have not been a jerk," he yelled defensively. "You're the one who wants to have a wedding. I proposed because I wanted to get married. I never said I wanted to have a wedding, that is all you. And as far as us talking, I had to go to work. Why can't you understand that? I'm a lawyer, and when my clients need me, I have to go."

"First of all, you have been a jerk, and I do understand having to work. But you seem to fail to realize that I also have a career, which I've taken time away from to be here with you to plan not only our wedding but also our life together. If I can disconnect from my phone and my laptop so can you. So, I don't want to hear anything about your clients," I said mockingly. "Trust and believe if you died today, God forbid, they would find another way. We're talking about our life together and that will last longer than your career or mine. But after today, I don't believe this is just about your career."

"What do you mean?"

"I had lunch with Dana today."

"And," he questioned with a look of surprise, annoyance and slight concern that he tried to hide.

"She told me about you and Lillian!" He looked both shocked and angry. "How could you? Why would you?" I asked rhetorically.

He stood up so fast it caused the bar chair to flip over. Through clenched teeth he said, "Gabriella that's none of your damn business." He blew air out of his mouth before he said, "That happened before I knew you, so it has nothing to do with you. You and Dana had no business, no right to discuss it," he yelled so loud it scared me. "But I will deal with Dana's ass. You can believe that."

Even though he'd frightened me my anger made me brave as I stood in place and challenged him, "So you don't think you sleeping with your ex-wife's sister is a behavior I needed to know about?"

"What do you mean a behavior," he snarled?

"I mean exactly what I said. I have two sisters. Would you attempt to sleep with them?"

"You know," he grabbed the counter as if he wanted to break something. "You need to stop talking to me before I get angry."

"Who are you Dasht, the Incredible Hulk? I could care less about you becoming angry. Hell! Join the club because I'm pissed off too." He shot me a look that made me remember Dana saying he'd beat Jewel. "Oh, and Dana also told me how you used to physically abuse her mother."

He threw his hands up in disgust, "What!? That's a bold face lie. I never beat Jewel."

"Well your daughter seems to remember you doing so."

He was pacing the floor when he picked up his phone, "I'm calling her ass right now."

"Why would she lie Dasht? Why would she lie?"

"Dana can be spiteful when things aren't going her way. She is more than likely making stuff up because she doesn't want me to remarry."

"So you're saying your adult daughter would make up stories about you beating her mother simply because she doesn't want you to remarry? Do you hear how absurd that sounds?"

"Gabby you don't know Dana like I know Dana."

"Funny she told me the same thing about you."

"Dana put me through hell when she was in high school and college. Hell, it's been some rocky times since she's been an adult. Dana has issues."

"Dasht we all have issues."

"No, you don't understand," he seemed to calm down as he picked up the chair and sat down at the island. "Dana's been on drugs. I mean heavy drugs."

"What? What do you mean she's been on drugs?"

"Dana was on drugs so bad she was in one of those drug houses in Kirkwood." He put his hands on his head, then looked up and stared aimlessly before he began rubbing his head as he spoke, "I had to go and get her. I found her high and laid out on the floor."

I didn't mean to be insensitive but between the two of them they'd bombarded me with too much information, and I couldn't filter my thoughts. "You say she is a drug addict, and she says you're a sex addict."

His anger returned, and he once again picked up the phone as he repeated, "Sex addict! Dana told you that I was a sex addict?"

"Yes, she did," I answered both questioning and matter of fact.

"Damn, my own daughter," he stared at the phone in his hand as he shook his head in disbelief. "She has no decorum. She doesn't know what to say. Why would she say something like that?"

"Well according to her you're the reason she is a lesbian."

"What!?" he asked angrily as he stood up again.

"Yes, according to her you have an addiction to homosexual pornography, both male and female, and that is how she became exposed to it."

"Don't tell me anymore. I don't want to hear anymore because it is making me mad," he said as he walked over to the cabinet, got a glass and begin making a drink. "You believe what you want to, but Dana is telling lies."

"You're saying she was she lying about you and Lillian?"

He turned his eyes to the scotch as he said, "I already told you that has nothing to do with you. Dana talks too much."

"What do you mean it has nothing to do with me? You don't think I have a right to know that you had an affair with your ex-wife's sister?"

"I didn't have a damn affair. We dated and that's our god damn business. What's the big fucking deal!? Damn!!!!"

"Dasht Spelbender you don't speak to me that way ever."

Mockingly he said, "Well how would you like for me to speak to you when you've come in here starting shit with me telling me all this bullshit you and Dana have been talking about."

"Dasht you're being disrespectful." He rolled his eyes as he went back to his seat and begin sipping his drink. "I didn't ask for any of this! Dana contacted me asking to have lunch. You asked me to marry you. I have been honest with you about everything," and once again the tears came.

"Look, stop all that crying, and calm down. Come sit down and let's talk."

I didn't move but rather stood staring at him.

He took another sip of his drink before he said, "I did ask you to marry me because I want us to get married. We can't allow Dana and her shenanigans to come between us." He looked at me with questioning eyes clearly trying to gauge my thoughts, but my face was void. "I love you, and you love me. Yes, things have been a little stiff between us, but life isn't going to be perfect. You understand?" He asked without waiting for an answer. "We're going to have tough times, but we shouldn't be fighting over conjecture, and that's what all of this is about." He picked up the engagement ring and twirled it around in his fingers. "Are you willing to walk away from the love we have over some nonsense that Dana told you?"

"It's not just what Dana said that is bothering me Dasht. You've been cold and outright mean…"

He cut me off before I could finish my sentence. "Look I know I can be cantankerous at times, but that's my personality. It doesn't change the fact that I love you, and you love me. You do love me right," he asked as he slid off the chair and walked toward the refrigerator to fill his glass with ice for another drink.

"Yes, I love you Dasht, but this isn't..."

He stopped me again, "No it is about love. If we love each other the rest of this BS doesn't matter." He looked up from the scotch he was pouring, smiled and winked at me as he said, "See I said BS because you don't want me to curse, and I love you," he blew me a kiss before he took a sip of his fresh drink. "So, let's stop all of this arguing," he said as he walked back over to the island and took a seat. "Why are you still standing there pouting? Stop it and come sit with the Dash-Master." He motioned for me to sit next to him.

Still whirling with emotion, I slowly walked over and sat in the bar chair next to him. Once I was seated, he leaned over and kissed me on the cheek. "You're my Bunny. You hear me?"

I turned to meet his gaze as I said, "Yes Dasht, I hear you."

He picked up the engagement ring from the island, "And here, give me your hand."

I didn't move my hands, instead I just looked at him.

"Come on, stop being a brat. I know you have a bear on you," he made a joke, "but that's going to happen." He stopped to sip his drink. "And guess what, I'm going to help you get that bear off your back, the same way you help me. Now here," he thrust the ring in my direction. "Give me your hand, so I can put this back where it belongs. I paused a few seconds before I gave him my left hand and allowed him to slide the engagement ring back on my finger. "Now don't you ever take it off again, deal?"

I stared at him momentarily before I gave in to my emotional exhaustion and in agreement said, "Deal."

> *"All that hate me whisper together against me: against me do they devise my hurt." Psalms 41:7 KJV*

I tossed and turned all night. Even though Dasht and I had somewhat mended our relationship and made it through Wednesday without an argument, I was still reeling with despair over the things Dana had told me as well as how he'd been behaving towards me. I rolled over and looked at the clock. It was 4:12am, but rather than lay there and listen to him snore I decided to get up and pray. I slipped out of the bed and tipped into the bathroom. I sat on the edge of the huge soaking tub and asked God, "Please give me peace. My heart is so heavy. I believe you brought Dasht and I together. I believe he is the man you made for me. I know I've messed up by breaking my vow of celibacy, and I ask that you forgive me. I love him, but I don't want to ruin my life by marrying him. So, if I'm wrong, if I'm outside of your will, God please save me from myself. Please don't let me make a mistake. Amen." I sat there a few moments more pondering how the day would pan out. All the while hoping for the best, but also bracing myself for the worst. "Think positive thoughts," I told myself as I slipped out of Dasht's t-shirt and into my work out clothes. It was too early to drive to the gym, so I decided to hop on the treadmill.

I was on the treadmill running when Dasht staggered sleepily into the room. "Good morning Bunny," he yawned. "You're up and at it early I see."

I slowed the speed on the treadmill to a brisk walking pace so I could hear and speak, "Good morning," I panted. "Yeah I woke-up so I decided to knock out a run."

"I should be doing the same," he said as he patted his stomach.

"Well I'll be done in about ten minutes if you want to jump on."

"I might just do that," he said as he stretched his arms towards the sky. "Bunny, I like having you here with me."

"Do you," I asked?

"Yeah," he yawned. "You've been here with the Dash-Master for a while," he stopped and appeared to be counting. "What seven, eight days now?"

"Seven," I said as I adjusted the incline.

"So, when do you leave, Sunday?"

"Yes, my flight leaves at 1:00pm"

"Hmph. Ok. You know I think I will get on the treadmill when you're done."

"Well I'll be done in about ten minutes," I said as I pushed the button to increase the speed on the treadmill.

Once I finished my run I went into the bedroom where Dasht was still in pajamas lying across the well-made bed reading the newspaper.

Without looking at me he said, "You got up and knocked it out early today."

"Um hmm," I smiled. "I thought you were going to get some steps in."

"I am. I just wanted to read the paper first. You know I have to know what's going on."

"Yes, I know."

"What do you have planned today?"

"Nothing much. I'm going to telework for a few hours, so I won't be so behind when I get back to Maryland. Then I was going to go look for a wedding dress."

He looked up from the paper, "Want to meet me at The Georgian Club for lunch, and we can do some wedding planning while we're there?"

I couldn't control the huge smile that spread across my face as my heart warmed and pumped a sigh of relief. "Sure, that would be nice."

He blew me a kiss, "I love you girl."

I blew a kiss back and said, "I love you too Dasht," as I walked toward the bathroom to shower.

While I was in the shower, Dasht had gotten up and hopped on the treadmill. Once I was dressed, I headed to the kitchen for my morning java. On my way to the kitchen I peeked my head in and gave him a wink and a thumbs up. He smiled and kept jogging. I smiled as I went into the kitchen to make a pot of coffee. While the coffee brewed, I stared out the window admiring the beautiful landscaping and thanked God for changing the atmosphere between us.

I was sitting at the island drinking coffee when I heard Dasht run up and then shortly afterwards down the stairs. Before I could get up to see what he was doing, I heard the alarm chime signaling the opening of the front door.

"Ooh Dasht, you scared me."

It was Valerie. I felt my blood starting to simmer as I thought to myself, "What is she doing here? He told me he was going to fire her."

I heard him whisper, "I'm sorry Val. Here is your check for the week. I won't be needing you to work today. Ok? I'll call you."

I heard her ask, "Are you sure Dasht? What's going on?"

"Yes. I'm sure. Just go. I'll call you later," he whispered as he closed the door.

I was livid and when he walked into the kitchen, I let him have it. "Dasht did you not tell me you were going to fire Valerie?"

"Yes, I said I was going to let her go," he said over his shoulder as he grabbed a bottle of water from the refrigerator.

"What was all that whispering at the door about? Why was she here?"
"Look I said I was going to fire her, and I'm going to do it. I don't need you rushing me," he shouted.

I yelled back, "Rushing you? How am I rushing you?"

"You want me to just fire her without giving her time to find another job. I'm not going to treat her that way. I'm not going to be mean to her."

"Dasht I never asked you to be mean to her."

"No, you didn't come out and say it, but that's what you want."

"No, it is not what I want. What I want is for her to never come here again. You can pay her for the next three months for all I care. I just don't want her in our home ever again."

"I just can't treat her that way," he said angrily as he slammed the water bottle down on the counter.

"Treat her what way? What's so hard about firing the housekeeper?"

"Stop calling her that!"

"Calling her what?"

"The housekeeper. Valerie is like family. She is my friend."

"Well she's not my family, and she isn't my friend." I paused because I could feel the four letter words bubbling up in my esophagus. I took a deep breath before I asked, "What am I missing Dasht?"

He turned his eyes towards the windows before he asked, "What do you mean?"

"Don't play dumb because it is insulting to both of us. You know exactly what I mean. First Valerie is disrespectful to me, then she is hiding your dirty underwear in the cabinets and if that weren't bad enough, I wake-up to find her standing over us in …"

He cut me off, "That never happened. Stop saying that."

"Dasht what makes you believe you can tell me what and what not to say? It did happen. I know what I saw," I yelled. He looked at me, and I could tell from his facial expression he was taken aback by my anger. "You know," I paused trying to steady my temper, but I had had it, "I'm tired of arguing with you about this. It's clear that you have some type of attachment to Valerie that I don't understand. But I'm not going to keep arguing about it. Valerie is not welcomed in this house anymore. I don't want to see her ugly face, hear her thick lisp or hear her name."

"You are being mean."

"Yes, I am because I am sick and tired of people being mean to me! You and Valerie have taken my kindness for weakness, but let me be clear, there is nothing weak about Gabriella Franklin. You're always quick to tell me you're about to get angry. Well newsflash, you aren't the only person who gets angry, and I have reached my limit with this Valerie shit." The four letter word had flown out of my mouth before I knew it.

"Did you just curse at me?" he asked rhetorically. "Not the prim and proper, Christian woman. No not Ms. don't speak to me that way, don't curse at me," he mocked.

"Pressure bursts pipes and saved isn't perfect, Christians curse too."

"Yeah I see," he said in a spiteful and judgmental tone. "And you're right, pressure does burst pipes, so stop pressuring me about Valerie," his voice had lowered an octave. We had a brief stare down before he spoke again, and this time he spoke through clenched teeth, "I said I was going to let her go, and I am. But you don't get to rush me," he spat. "I will do it when I'm ready, and in my own way." As if his words weren't insulting enough, he stomped his foot and pointed at me.

"Dasht you have clearly lost your mind," I said as I slid off the bar chair and walked away.

"I may have been dog walked, but I've never been leash trained."

While I was driving to The Georgian Club, I received a text message from Dasht that read: "I can't make it to The Georgian Club, but I let the catering manager know you were coming. I've booked the date and paid the deposit. I'll talk to you later. Love, Dasht."

I had mixed emotions about him not meeting me. A part of me wanted him to be an active participant in our wedding, but the other part of me didn't feel like being around him right now. He'd brought out the worst in me this morning. But instead of dwelling on it, I focused on the wedding as I smiled at the catering manager while looking at set-up, linen, chair and china options before touring the Galleria Gardens. Afterwards to past the time, I drove to Winnie Couture to look around and confirm my Friday appointment.

Once I returned to the house, I decided to do a Dasht and sit at the island with my laptop and work. I was conflicted as I simultaneously worked on wedding plans and replayed the events of the morning over in my head. "Why was Dasht stalling on firing Valerie? Had he thought I wouldn't hear him whispering to her this morning? Why was he so defensive of her? Why was she standing over us in the middle of the night last Friday?" I stared at the draft wedding invitation attempting to subside the anger that was starting to boil inside of me. Then it hit me, and I wandered out loud, "Had I not been here I bet he was going to allow her to work today." I shook my head at my own revelation as I recalled him asking how long I would be in town this morning. "Oh, so he's planning on having her work when I'm not here," I said as if someone other than me was in the house. I minimized the draft wedding invitation, opened my Outlook calendar and began moving meetings. Once I'd adjusted my schedule, I changed my plane ticket to leave on Tuesday.

As usual Dasht rushed in the door at 5:15pm with the phone glued to his ear and hurried to the cabinet to grab a glass and make a drink as soon as he put his bag down. He ended his conversation with whomever he was speaking to before he took a sip of his drink. Then he said, "Good evening Ms. Franklin."

I reciprocated his sarcasm, "Good evening Mr. Spelbender."

He let out an insolent chuckle as he glared at me before taking another long sip of his drink. "So, did you go to The Georgian Club today?"

Glaring back, I responded, "I did."

"And what did you decide?"

"What do you mean?"

"What did you decide on for the wedding? What are we doing?"

"I didn't make any decisions because we should make those decisions together."

"I don't need to be involved in that. If it were up to me, I would have one of the judges I know marry us. You're the one who wants to have a wedding." He turned to add more ice and then scotch to the glass.

"A justice of the peace wedding is not an option. I'm not getting married in secret."

"Who said anything about getting married in secret? I'm not trying to keep our marriage a secret. I'm just not a fan of spending a ton of money putting on a show for people. This is about us."

"Is it about us?" I asked apparently catching him off guard.

"What do you mean? Who else would it be about?"

"That's the question I would like for you to answer?"

"Gabby you're not making sense," he said rather dismissively.

"Hmph," I huffed. "Welcome to my world."

"What does that mean?"

"It means that's how I've felt all week, like nothing makes sense," I shrugged my shoulders and threw my hands up in surrender before I continued. "Me waking up to Valerie standing over us on Friday night doesn't make sense," he attempted to cut me off, but I kept on talking. "The way you've been hiding behind your work to avoid interacting with me and avoid planning our wedding, makes no sense. The way you've been cold and mean to the point of almost being cruel, doesn't make sense to me."

In a somber tone, he said, "I'm not a cruel person."

Out of everything I'd just said he'd only responded to my saying he'd been almost cruel. "Wow," I thought to myself before I responded. "I never said you were a cruel person, but you have been cantankerous and mean."

He sucked down the last of the scotch before he asked, "Have I really been that bad?"

"Yes Dasht, you have."

He seemed surprised that I'd answered the way I'd answered, "Damn that was harsh." He walked over to the refrigerator to add more ice to the glass, and as he poured scotch over the fresh ice he said, "I'm sorry Bunny." He replaced the cork, placed both hands on the counter, momentarily looked down at the drink, then looked over at me and said, "I never want to be mean to you, and," he paused, "I damn sure don't want to be seen as cruel." He shook his head in rejection of the idea of him being cruel as he continued to stare at the drink. "I'm sorry ok?" He looked over at me, "Do you hear me? I'm sorry."

"I hear you Dasht," I answered without sympathy.

He picked up the glass, took a long sip of the drink then asked, "Want to order something for dinner and work on OUR wedding plans?"

"Sure," was all I could muster in response to his patronizing me.

"I see my dreams with my eyes closed and with my eyes open both in the day and in the night."

I inhaled deeply as my eyes popped open. I blinked a couple of times while I determined if I was awake or still dreaming. Then Dasht's snorted snoring confirmed I was awake. I looked over at the clock 1:03am. I lay there for another moment as the visions of my dream started to resurface. I got up and went to the bathroom to wash my face, and as I stared at myself in the mirror my dream, so vivid, so real came back to me.

I had dreamed I was walking on a dirt path surrounded by a field of some sort. It was a bright sunny day with the clearest and bluest skies I'd ever seen. There was not one cloud in sight. I could see myself happily walking along the path. I felt my own happiness as I observed myself nonchalantly strolling along. At some point I came to a big tree, the only tree in sight where the path ended, and there was a fork in the road. I stopped and stared at the tree before Dasht called out to me, "Come on, Bunny." He motioned for me to come towards where he was waiting for me on the path that veered to the left.

But I didn't move. No longer smiling, I turned to the tree instead as a presence of something I couldn't see enveloped me. Then I heard a voice coming from the right side of the fork say, "I am here." I turned to look down the path, but I didn't see anyone.

"Bunny! What are you doing?" Dasht called out in concern, but I ignored him. I was focused on the presence of something I could feel and hear but couldn't see.

Then the voice said, "The choice is yours."

"Is that you?" I asked as I searched with my eyes for the source of the voice. Then I felt a covering over my body that caressed me like a whisper, and my heart said, "Oh my God. Is it really you…God?"

"Yes Gabriella, I am here. I am always here."

"Bunny, please come on," Dasht called out.

"He is yours if you want him," God said. "I have shown you who he is. You can marry him if you choose. I have shown you what your life will be. You can go with him or you can trust and follow me. There is no wrong choice. I will be with you always. The choice is yours."

"Bunny, I'm waiting for you," Dasht called out yet again. Then there was the most peaceful silence and stillness before he pleaded, "Come on Bunny."

I heard Dasht, but I never looked back to see his face again. I reached out my right hand, and said, "You've never left me, so I'm going to keep walking with You." I felt God take my hand as I walked down the right fork of the road.

I could feel my heart racing as I stared at myself in the mirror replaying the dream. I had prayed and asked God to guide me, and apparently the choice was mine to make. I splashed more cold water on my face, then patted it dry with a towel before I went and climbed back into bed.

My eyes darted between the ceiling and the clock as I continued to think about the dream and try to fall asleep. I rolled Dasht over to ease his snoring which had become excessively loud. One forty-five a.m., 2:01am, 2:14am, I tossed. Then I decided to silently pray myself to sleep. "Lord I know I asked you for peace. You know my heart is not at peace. You know the things I'm struggling with. I do want to marry Dasht, but if he isn't the man for me please Lord…" I stopped my thoughts and opened my eyes to peek at the clock again, 2:17am. I exhaled before I closed my eyes and continued my silent prayer. "If he isn't the man for me please remove him from my life. I want to live in your perfect will and your perfect way. Please, show me if I'm making a mistake. Our Father, whom art in heaven, hallowed be thy name. Thy kingdom…," and I drifted off to sleep only to have another dream.

It was my wedding day. I was in my wedding gown getting ready to get married. The venue was not the Galleria Gardens at The Georgian Club, but rather this huge space with tall ceilings and white marble walls. It appeared to be a train station or maybe a museum. Someone, a woman, whose face I couldn't see was helping me with my dress. Then I saw him, and I tried to hide. "No, you can't see me. It's bad luck for the groom to see the bride before the wedding."

"I don't have to see you to know you're here," he called out. "I know when my wife is present. I can feel you. Even when you're miles away I still see you."

I smiled as I peeked around the corner to see him. He was dressed in a black tuxedo with tails, but he looked too tall. He appeared to be around 6'7", but Dasht was only 6'4". He had hair and Dasht was bald. I never saw his face, but it was clear the man I was about to marry in my dreams was not Dasht Spelbender.

"I'm waiting for you, he called out," and I woke-up. The sun was shining. I rolled over to look at the clock, 7:12am. I heard Dasht laughing. He was on the phone. My heart was heavy as I lay there staring at the ceiling, thinking about my dreams.

I was so deep in thought I didn't notice Dasht had come into the bedroom until he was standing over me smiling. "Good morning Bunny."

"Good morning, "I said, rubbing my eyes and forcing a sleepy smile.

He kissed me on the forehead before he laid across the foot of the bed and began reading the newspaper. "What are you getting into today?"

Staring at the ceiling with the dreams still vividly occupying my mind I said, "I'm meeting my Mom, Michelle and Tippy at Winnie Couture at 10am to try on wedding dresses." As I said it my heart sank because I was no longer excited. The week had taken a toll on me emotionally, and my dreams were adding to the stress.

Oblivious to my mood he said, "Just what you like, girly stuff. Your kind of fun."

"Yeah," I said as I rolled out of bed and headed to the bathroom to shower and get dressed.

When I came out of the bathroom Dasht was on the phone yelling and cursing at someone. "This is bullshit!"

"Oh my God," I thought to myself as I looked at his enraged face with eyes that asked the question, "What is going on?"

He diverted his eyes and shook his head as he waved me off and continued cursing, "What do you mean? How long is all this going to take? This is total bullshit, and I don't appreciate this at all. This is not good. You can't just do this," he paused. "Well do what you need to do!" He stopped as the person talked. "No that's not going to work! Yeah, you call me back, and call me back soon. I mean it." He stopped to listen. "Ten minutes. Okay," he huffed as he hung up the phone.

"What is going on Dasht, and who are you speaking to that way?"

"The lady at the damn bank," he huffed. "They have pissed me off this morning."

I was stunned that he would speak to a customer service representative that way, but more surprised the person hadn't hung up in his face. He was literally spitting mad, so rather than scold him about his behavior I asked, "What happened?"

"It's bullshit!" he yelled. "Just bullshit!"

I was shocked, baffled and concerned. "What do you mean? Tell me what happened?"

He sat down on the bed and placed his head in his hands before he said, "Give me a minute to calm myself down, please…give me a minute."

I stood there watching him as he took in deep breaths and then exhaled as if he were doing some type of exercise. After about three minutes he peeked up at me then said, "I'm fine. I just don't like not having access to my money."

"What do you mean? Why don't you have access to your money?"

Still practicing the breathing and rubbing his head he said, "They've had some type of bank merger," he exhaled. "So, my ATM card and checks are no longer good." He paused for another fifteen seconds or so repeating the breathing exercise. He stood up and began pacing the floor.

Totally taken aback, I said, "Ok, calm down. It's not the end of the world. If you need cash, I have working ATM cards."

"I'm not going to take money from you," he spat.

"I didn't mean to be insulting," I said calmly. "I just want to help if I can."

"I know," he huffed. "I'm not taking it out on you." Then he abruptly yelled, "I'm pissed! I don't like not having access to my goddamn money."

"Dasht, please calm down." His violent anger was starting to concern me because the situation, in my opinion, didn't warrant it. It seemed extreme. "Did the representative say when you will have access to your money? You can also withdraw cash from your credit card, or just go inside the bank."

"I don't want to use my credit cards," he huffed before he plopped back on the bed, lying on his back, rubbing his face. "She is going to call me back. She'd better call me back."

I looked at the clock. I was supposed to be at Winnie's at 10am and it was now 9:25am.

"Are you going to be ok?"

Still covering his face in frustration, "Yeah. I need to get dressed because I have a meeting. I'm fine." Even though he was visibly upset, his tone was now calmer.

"Well let me know if it's something I can do to help," I said more so out of angst than for solution. I leaned over to kiss him on the cheek as I said, "I have to go so I won't be late."

"Ok, have a good…" his phone rang before he could finish the sentence. He sat up straight, "This is the bank. Hello," he answered. "Did you fix it?"

He barely noticed me waving goodbye, and as I reached the bottom of the stairs, I heard him once again yell, "That's a bunch of bullshit!" to the person on the phone.

I shook my head in disbelief as left.

> ***"Everything happens for a reason. Nothing is ever happenstance."***

Dasht was sitting at the island having a cocktail when I walked in the door. He looked up from his laptop and smiled at me, "Hey Bunny." There was that syrupy charm I'd so loved when we first met. It had been missing in action this past week, but now it was back.

I obliged him with a soft smile before I asked, "How are you?"

He looked embarrassed as he said, "Bunny I'm fine. I'm sorry for the way I was this morning. I didn't mean to upset you."

My eyes questioned his as I said, "You were extremely angry. You were literally spitting mad."

He dropped his eyes in shame. "I need to do better with controlling my temper."

"It's not healthy for you."

"I know. I'm going to do better." He looked up, winked at me and blew me a kiss. "You're good for me. Do you know that?"

"Am I?"

"Yes. You are just what I need. You help me. I love you. You are for me." Something about his words was awkward. On the surface they seemed genuine but there was an aura of contrite that impacted their meaning.

The emotional rollercoaster I'd been riding had drained me. His aloofness was still causing me concern, and my mind was still clouded with all the arguments we'd had all week. As if that weren't enough to bear, my heart and soul were disturbed because of my dreams. I wanted to tell Dasht this, but I didn't. I consciously softened my eyes, forced a smile and said, "I love you too."

He stared at me with expressionless eyes as he asked, "How was the dress shopping," before sipping the last of his drink.

I felt myself smiling as the fantasy of the wedding and my being covered in lace and tulle took over my consciousness. "It didn't go as planned, but it went well."

"Tell me about it," he feigned interest as he walked over to the refrigerator to add ice to his glass in preparation for another drink.

I knew he wasn't really interested, but I appreciated his efforts to oblige me. "I thought I'd found something I liked at Winnie Couture, but the dresses I tried on weren't exactly what I wanted."

Without looking up from the scotch he was pouring, he asked, "What was wrong with them? They not fit?"

Talking about the dresses was easing my tension because I unconsciously chuckled, as I said, "It wasn't a fit issue. The dresses fit fine, and they were pretty. They just weren't what I wanted. But luckily Tippy suggested we go to The White Magnolia Bridal Collection, and I found something I really liked there."

He took a sip of his drink before he said, "You seem happy about that so that must mean you bought a dress." He playfully raised his eyebrow and shot me a questioning glance as he took another sip of his drink.

"I am happy," I beamed. "And yes, I bought a dress." Inside one part of me was smiling, and the other part of me was scolding myself over the non-refundable $3000 deposit I'd left at the bridal shop for the special order dress.

"When will I get to see it?"

He had to be joking, I thought to myself before I playfully batted my eyes and said, "You'll see it when I'm meeting you at the altar on our wedding day."

He let out a slight chuckle before he playfully poked out his tongue. "You have a habit of making me wait, and I don't too much like that. But I love you," he blew me a kiss. "Yeah, I love you, so I guess I'll just have to wait."

"You are hilarious."

"You up for a game of chess?"

Somewhat taken aback at how he'd abruptly changed the conversation, but appreciative of how a game of chess always seemed to ease any tension between us. "Sure. Get the board."

"A win is a win. A loss is a loss. A draw is an agreement to quit."

"What did you just do?" Dasht asked in shock as I took his unprotected queen off the board.

I put the queen back in place and replayed the move in which I'd taken his queen with my bishop that I'd strategically placed towards the middle of the board at the beginning of the game. "That's what I did." I flashed a clever smile and wink at him before I once again removed his queen from the board.

He studied the board long and hard searching for a counter opportunity but there wasn't any. It was clear I had him on the ropes and was going to win this game. I was borderline giddy because we had been playing for over two hours, and I had avoided all his typical tricks. "You've gotten good Bunny. Damn you've gotten good."

He gasped when I slid my rook the length of the board to capture the knight he had moved in a desperate attempt to protect his king. "Check," I called out excitedly.

"Hmph." He shook his head as he studied the board before he slid his last bishop over to protect his king and capture one of my sacrificial pawns.

I smiled as soon as he took the pawn off the board because he'd taken the bait, and we were now about to play a game of cat and mouse with the remaining pieces that I was most likely to win. "Check," I said as I moved my knight into a position that was going to force him to sacrifice his rook for the sake of protecting his king.

"Hmph," he smiled an unfriendly smile and shook his head in disbelief before he stood up and said, "Bunny we might as well call this a stalemate because neither of us is going to win. We're just going to be chasing each other across the board all night. Deal?"

Not one to argue or add insult to injury, I agreed because what is understood doesn't need to be explained. It was clear that I could and would win if we continued to play. What I couldn't make heads or tails of was why my winning would be an issue. Even though he won most of our games I'd won quite a few times before. He walked over to the sink to dispose of his glass and then left the kitchen with no explanation. I wasn't sure where he'd gone until I heard his footsteps going up the stairs.

It was something different about his demeanor that I was now fully awakened to. He'd been extremely moody, difficult, distant and cold over the past week. In all honesty his entire disposition had changed since the holidays, since he proposed. What was supposed to bring us together seemed to be tearing us apart. I could feel it in his poise, he'd more than merely left the room, he'd turned his back on me and literally walked away.

But why? What was the reason? What had changed between us since the holidays? I'd tried desperately to discount all the chaos and justify and make sense of it all under the guise of being understanding. But I couldn't step around the massive elephant in the room any longer. The knot in my gut made me nauseous as I stared at the chess pieces. Then almost out of instinct, I reached over and knocked down his king.

CHAPTER 16
Forty-Six, Thirty-One

"I'll be as sweet as you allow me to be."

I woke up with the goal of making today beautiful. As usual, I'd began the day with prayer and coffee; however, today I prayed long and hard because my soul was still heavy, and my heart wasn't at rest. I was still feeling some uneasiness over last night's chess debacle, but I was determined to put forth the effort necessary to change the energy between us. Dasht had once told me he liked it when I was "sweet", so today I vowed to be sweet to him. I'd invested too much in this relationship to just throw my hands up and quit.

After I meditated and prayed, I returned to the bedroom where he was lying across the bed reading the newspaper.

I gently rubbed his back before I asked, "Would you like some eggs?"

He seemed pleasantly surprised as he looked up from the paper and smiled at me. "I could go for some breakfast this morning," he stopped as if collecting his thoughts. "Uh Bunny, I appreciate you offering to make eggs, but I'd honestly prefer an omelet if you know how to make one?"

It wasn't a big deal, but I was somewhat perplexed that he questioned my capability to make an omelet because it had long been established that I could cook. "Of course I know how to make an omelet," I teased. "What would you like in it?"

He flashed that smile I'd fallen in love with and said, "Aww Bunny, you're being sweet to me. I like it when you're sweet to me."

Something in his smile was still distant, but I loved that smile.

Rather than focus on that, I leaned over him and said, "I'll be as sweet as you allow me to be." Then I kissed him on the lips before I asked again. "What would you like in your omelet my love?"

"What do we have?"

"I'm going to the store because there's not much here so you can have anything you'd like."

"In that case," he wiggled his eyebrows playfully before calling out his list of ingredients. "I'd like sausage, bacon, cheddar cheese, tomato, mushroom, onion, and jalapeno," he smiled again before he blew me a kiss. "Thank you Bunny."

I blew a kiss back as I said, "You're welcome." Then I left to go to the store.

I began mentally planning my day, as I rushed through the aisles of the supermarket grabbing the ingredients. "Make Dasht breakfast, tomatoes, onions, work out, fresh jalapeno. Oh yeah, plan Dasht's meals for next week, dang I'm going to have to come back to the store. Might as well grab some potatoes and lamb chops while I'm here. We need to finalize and order the wedding invitations, bacon, sausage," I thought as I put the ingredients in the cart. "Draft the guest list. Oh, I need to exchange my phone, cheese, eggs, butter." I was mentally all over the place. My energy was off to the point of confusion. I felt off balance and out of synch.

I rushed back from the store, and immediately began making Dasht's omelet to order. He was still upstairs apparently talking on the phone because I heard him laughing. I smiled as I plated the omelet and added two thick slices of hickory smoked bacon to the plate before I placed it on the tray. I poured him a glass of fresh squeezed orange juice before I took the tray upstairs and served him breakfast in bed.

"Bunny this is delicious," he raved about the food. "Thank you for cooking for me."

"You're welcome," I smiled.

"What do you have planned for the day?"

"Well I got this phone a couple of weeks ago, but I don't like it so I need to go and exchange it."

"You don't seem sure about it".

"It's not that I'm unsure. I just hate that my information is now in this phone."

"You can just delete it."

I shook my head in disagreement, "Once your information is in a device it can always be retrieved from that device. Please tell me you don't donate or give your old phones away."

"No. I keep my old phones, but you just got that phone so it shouldn't have much information in it."

"Dasht it's been connected to my iCloud, so it has all my information in it. Once you link a device to your cloud it can be used to access your information. Anything with a chip in it is nothing more than a tracking device. A cell phone is basically an ankle bracelet that we wear by choice. I just heard on the news the other day how they solved a murder with a Fitbit."

"What?" he questioned with widened eyes. "Don't tell me anymore," he shook his head. "Stuff like that freaks me out."

"I can't believe you didn't know. Every move you make is pretty much tracked."

"Please stop talking about this," he said nervously. "You're spooking me with all of this talk about tracking people. That's crazy. I don't like the thought of my privacy being invaded."

"I don't mean to spook you, but privacy is pretty much a thing of the past. It's true, big brother is always watching. I don't know why people even attempt to commit crimes because they will get caught."

"That's enough. I get it," he waved his hands for me to stop talking about it.

"Ok," I said nonchalantly because I was perplexed at how anxious he was especially, considering he was always glued to his phone. "You're funny I teased," playfully to lighten the mood before I asked, "What's on your agenda today?"

"Well after eating that delicious breakfast, I want to just lay around and watch television, but I need to get going."

Mildly annoyed I asked, "Are you working today?"

He shot me a look that reflected subtle irritation before he let out a sigh and said, "Bunny don't start that. I'm not going in the office, but I have a brief I need to work on for a few hours later today." He rubbed his stomach and yawned, "That food was delicious. To be honest, I really want to lay in bed and watch the tube all day, but I better get up. I need to check on Gary, and I need to go to the bank before it closes."

"Ok" I said as I collected the breakfast dishes.

"The cloud gives more than rain."

I was still trying to mentally organize my day as I put the breakfast dishes in the dishwasher. Once I started the machine, I walked over to the island to write out a 'to do' list on one of his legal pads.

Dasht had left a mess on the island. There were legal pads and work papers everywhere. I was tidying up the mess and organizing the papers when I noticed his iPad screen light up signaling a text notification from someone named Farah that read, "Are you almost here?" As I stared at the screen it went black. "Who is Farah?" I thought to myself. I went back to stacking the papers as I told myself, "Probably a pesky client." But as I continued shuffling the stack of papers, I felt unease rise in my gut and my intuition pushed me around the corner to suspicion. I sat at the island replaying all the conversations Dasht and I had had over the past 8-9 months and not once did I ever remember hearing the name Farah.

I picked up the iPad and stared at the black screen. I pressed the home button and the screen lit up. I exhaled before I pressed the button again and the keypad for the passcode appeared. I stared until the screen went black again. I thought for a few moments before I pressed the home button again, then again. This time when the numbers appeared, I took a chance and entered his birthday 080266. The bubbles shook signaling that wasn't the code. "Hmm," I thought as I tried the gate and alarm code, 046310 and voila I'd unlocked the iPad on my second try. I immediately went to the text icon to read the full text thread from Farah. I wasn't at all prepared for what I read and what I saw.

DASHT: *I miss you.*

FARAH: *Miss you too. Will I see you today, or is she still there?*

DASHT: *Still here, but I am seeing you today. I can't wait any longer.*

FARAH: *Why is she here so long? Are you going to be able to get away?*

DASHT: *I'm sorry. I didn't know she was going to be here this long. I'm ready for her to leave. Yes. Told her I need to see Gary.*

FARAH: *I bet. You better not be cheating on me with her. LOL.* Tongue poke emoji

DASHT: *LOL, trust me I'm not. I want YOU.*

FARAH: *I can't wait to see you. Let me know when you're on the way.*

DASHT: *I'm leaving in about ten minutes.*

FARAH: *Are you almost here?*

I became lightheaded as I read the text messages. I closed their text thread to scroll through his entire text history. There were text messages from so many women. Farah, Danica, Jeannie, Velma, Valerie, Lillian, Kimberly, Allison, Carol, Tanya, Beth. Some names I'd heard and some he'd never mentioned.

Friday he'd been texting Danica, a name I'd heard before. I recalled him saying she was a young lawyer that he was mentoring but from what I saw on the text preview he was mentoring her on something other than law. I clicked her name and opened the thread.

DASHT: *Hey sweet Bunny. You staying with me tonight?*

DANICA: *Hello handsome. You want me to?*

DASHT: *YES*

DANICA: *I'll be there around 7:30*

DASHT: *I'll see you then.*

DANICA: *Any special requests...*

DASHT: *Thong and heels, nothing else...walk in the door that way.*

DANICA: *Ok. See you tonight.* Kiss emoji

DASHT: *Danica I need to cancel tonight. Something unexpected came up.* Sad face emoji.

DANICA: *Ok. Tomorrow?*

DASHT: *No... I'll call you.*

"I'd ruined their plans when I surprised him on Friday. Now I know why he was so mean to me, and hmph," I huffed. "So everyone is Bunny," I angrily thought to myself as I continued to scroll through the text history. I felt my blood boiling as I came across the name Eva. "No way," I thought as a I stared at the read preview. "It can't be. You've got to be kidding," I asked no one as I clicked Eva to see the text thread between Dasht and the make-up artist, Eva, who'd done my make-up for the ball we'd attended in December. She'd text Dasht immediately after she walked out of the house after doing my make-up.

EVA: *I didn't know I was coming to UR house. I'm jealous. U never invited me over.* Sad face emoji

DASHT: *Shit I didn't either.* Tongue poke emoji

EVA: *I bet she is boring as hell.'*

DASHT: *At times. She is a good girl.'*

EVA: *Good girl=boring.* Eye roll emoji *Ur a bad boy & U like bad girls.* The text included a picture of a vagina with a pierced clitoris. *I bet she doesn't have this.*

DASHT: *Damn, I want that...NOW!* Yummy emoji

EVA: *When does she leave?*

DASHT: *Not soon enough. Damn, you've got me excited. Sunday.*

EVA: *I'll C U Sun night?*

DASHT: *NO. I'm texting you as soon as she is at the airport so you can bring that to me.*

EVA: *Want me to bring a friend?*

DASHT: *You're killing me.*

EVA: *U coming to the club or can I can come to UR house now?*

DASHT: *We'll talk. Gotta go.*

Just as he'd said he would, he had text her as soon as I left, and they'd apparently met as agreed to do whatever they'd done.

DASHT: *Hey Sexy Bunny!*

EVA: *Hey U. Ur girl gone?*

DASHT: *Yep.* Wink emoji. *You still have my address?*

EVA: *Yeah, but I'm doing makeup right now. Will come when I'm done.*

DASHT: *Don't make me wait long and put your tongue ring in!* tongue poke emoji
Just you and me this time.

EVA: *LOL UR a freak* 3 eggplant emojis

DASHT: *Hurry up and get here!*

I felt my body stiffen and my blood run ice cold as I sat scrolling through the text messages. "I can't be here when he comes back," I thought to myself as my throat started to close and the hot angry tears began streaming down my face. I stood up, and the air literally left the room. I became light-headed as my heart swelled in my chest. The knot that had been growing in my gut over the last few weeks was now full grown. It was pushing on my spleen and causing my esophagus to close. "I can't be here," I said to myself again as I stared at the iPad. I wiped my face before I sprinted up the stairs with the iPad. I put the iPad in my laptop bag and hurriedly packed my things.

> *"Broken china like broken hearts when glued back together will still have missing parts."*

Once I reached the bottom of the stairs with my suitcase I stopped and stared around the house. Memories of us and our time together began to flood the space, and then my flesh began to crawl as rage quickly crept across my skin. The longer I scanned the rooms the angrier I became. Then my eyes landed on the photo of Dasht and I smiling at my fundraising gala. Without thought or hesitation I walked over to it, picked it up, stared at it for a moment, and my tears plopped on the glass.

"Bastard," I yelled as I smashed the picture against the wall. I walked over to the broken frame and stomped it repeatedly. "So you like playing games," I said out loud. "You think my life is a game for you to play with," I yelled as my eyes landed in the dining room.

I stood staring at the grand table as I trembled with anger. My mind drifted back to the first time I'd come here alone and fantasized about us having romantic meals in there, and then I thought about the Thanksgiving table setting he'd been so happy about. Almost instinctively, I ran to the butlers' pantry and flung open the cabinets housing the neatly stored china. I picked-up a dinner plate and smashed it to the floor, and it felt good. I picked up three more and walked into the dining room where I tossed them against the wall one by one like frisbees. After I'd broken all the dinner plates, I began collecting the salad plates, which I broke all over the butlers' pantry and the foyer. I sauntered back and forth to the butler's pantry breaking every single piece of the china I'd bought leaving a trail all over the floors. Next, I destroyed every piece of the crystal glassware. Ensuring there was glass all over the kitchen floor.

I stood in the kitchen looking around at the mess I'd made when the flowers Dasht had given me for Valentine's Day caught my eye. I walked over to the breakfast table and slapped the crystal vase sending it crashing to the floor. Flowers, water and blood splattered. I'd cut myself, but I felt no pain. As I looked at the blood covering the diamond on my left hand I cried and screamed, "Why!? Why would he do this? Why did he even ask me to marry him?"

I watched the blood continue to drip over the diamond leaving drops of blood on the floor as I walked over to the sink to rinse the blood off my hand. I snatched a paper towel off the roll to clean the diamond and cover the cut. Looking at the blood made me angrier as my mind wandered back to the night he'd proposed. It had seemed so well thought out, so planned, so perfect. I wrapped another paper towel over my hand before I grabbed a butcher knife from the knife block and ran up the stairs to the guest room where the stuffed giraffe stood. I loved the giraffe. It had been the most thoughtful gift I'd ever received from a man. I walked over to the stuffed animal and stabbed it in the neck. I paused before I plunged the knife into the giraffe again. I screamed at myself, "What's wrong with you? How could you be so stupid?" The stuffing started coming out of the giraffe, and my tears flowed so hard I could barely see. My hand was bleeding again.

I went to the bathroom to wash the blood off my hand and get a bandage. I starred at myself in the mirror as I applied the bandage. "And you were willing to give up your life for him," I said out loud. I walked back into the guest room where the giraffe still stood with its head hung low to the floor, barely hanging on to its body. I ripped the head off then walked down the stairs with it in my hand. I smiled a vengeful smile as I looked around at the mess and said, "Now you can have your precious Valerie clean it all up." I stood a few minutes more before I dropped the giraffe head on the floor and rolled my suitcase out the door.

"Bloody screams speak all the words my heart never wanted to ever say."

I was relieved when I pulled up to Tippy's house and opened the garage to see no one was home. I pulled into the garage, turned the car off and let the garage door down. I sat in the garage staring at the wall until the garage light shut off. When the light went off, I welcomed the darkness. I cried and cried and cried. I heard my phone ringing in my purse. I was sure it was Dasht calling. I blew my nose before I turned on the reading light. I looked at myself in the rearview mirror. My eyes were red and puffy. I pulled out my phone to see six missed calls from Dasht and two from Tippy. I closed the call history and saw I had multiple messages. I opened Tippy's text conversation first.

> TIPPY: *Gab where are you? Are you ok? Dasht keeps calling me. He says you tore up his house and you left? What's going on? Call me.*

I didn't feel like talking, so I sent her a text:

> *Tippy I'm fine. I found out Dasht has been cheating on me and I left. I'm at your house sitting in the garage.*

Tippy responded immediately.

> *What! OMG. Are you ok? We're at Benjamin's basketball game, but I'll be there shortly. Why don't you go in the house?*

I responded:

> *I'm about to go inside. Just sitting here trying to get myself together. I'll see you when you get home.*

I closed Tippy's chat thread and opened the messages I had from Dasht.

> DASHT: *Gabby where are you? What is going on with you? Why did you break these dishes all over the house? What is wrong with you?*

> DASHT: *Answer your phone!*

> DASHT: *Call me Bunny.*

> DASHT: *Please call me. Bunny I'm worried about you.*

I threw the phone on the passenger seat. I sat there replaying all the betrayal, blatant lies, and just dirt he'd done over the last nine months. My heart swelled like an over inflated balloon and to avoid it bursting all I could do was scream. The more I felt tears rolling down my cheeks to my chin and dripping into my chest the harder I screamed. I sat and screamed for what felt like hours until I could taste blood in my throat. "Why? Why? Why!!!?" I asked myself as I stared into my own eyes in the rearview mirror. Then I screamed so loud it made my ears hurt, and as I screamed my heart shattered, it shattered like the china I'd just left broken all over Dasht's floors. Then I slumped over the steering wheel and sobbed.

I was still sitting in the car crying when the garage door opened and Tippy pulled in.

She got out of her car and got into the car with me.

She looked concerned, hurt and angry as she looked in my face. "What happened Gab?"

"He's been unfaithful the entire time."

"What do you mean?"

"I mean from the day he met me, he was seeing other women and he never stopped."

"How did you find out?"

"His iPad...it was sitting on the island and I just happened to be standing by it when a text message came across from a woman named Farah whom he'd apparently gone to see when he left today."

Tippy put her head down. "Gab I'm sorry I introduced you to him."

"Tippy don't do that. It's not your fault. There's no way you could have known. I'm not blaming you, and don't you blame you."

"Have you spoken to him?"

"No. He has called me a bunch of times, but I can't talk to him right now. I just can't."

"He said you tore up his house."

I laughed a spiteful laugh, "He's lying. I didn't tear up his house. I purposely didn't touch any of his things. But I left him a mess because I want him to know..."

"What do you mean?"

"I broke all the dishes I bought and left a mess scattered all over the floor. Then...," I stopped, "then I cut the head off the giraffe."

"Your giraffe? The one he gave you when he proposed?"

"Yes," I felt my lips curl up as the tears trickled down my face.

"Aww Gab, I hate to see you crying."

"It's ok, they're tears. It's better to cry them now. Imagine if I'd married him."

"A picture is worth a million unspoken words."

I laid across the bed tears streaming down my face, sobbing until my body shook. I didn't know what to do, my heart hurt. I felt like I was dying. I got up from the bed and retrieved the iPad from my computer bag. I logged in to see Dasht had text Velma. Apparently, he either hadn't realized I had his iPad, or he'd forgotten the conversation we'd had earlier in the day. I opened the settings and turned off the location tracking. I closed the settings and opened the text messages again.

He'd taken a picture of the broken dishes and the headless giraffe and sent it to Velma.

> DASHT: *Look at this shit!*
>
> VELMA: *What happened?*
>
> DASHT: *I don't know. She isn't here. I came home to this mess.*
>
> VELMA: *Baby please be careful.*

"Baby? What? Lord not her too," I thought to myself as I scanned their text history. He'd met her early Saturday morning to celebrate Valentine's Day. They'd apparently gone to "their spot" in "their car" because she apparently no longer came to the house. I clicked her name, then info to review the images in the text history. My eyes weren't prepared for what I saw. There were over seventy images. Selfies of them kissing, pictures of her posing next to and driving the 560SL, naked pictures of her, pictures of her performing various sexual acts on Dasht and for Dasht. Then I scrolled across it, three pictures of her painting the teal wall in the dining room. I found the text history that coincided with the pictures.

DASHT: *I was thinking about this today.*

VELMA: *That was a great day.*

DASHT: *It was. I've always wanted us.*

VELMA: *You have us.*

DASHT: *Part time...* Sad face emoji

VELMA: *Babe you have the best of me. We have our time when we get away, and we're together every day in the office.*

DASHT: *But you go home to him every night.*

VELMA: *Now you have Gabriella.*

DASHT: *She's not you and he's not me.*

VELMA: *Babe don't do this.*

DASHT: *Goodnight* Angry emoji, Sad emoji, Heart break emoji, Kiss emoji

I closed the thread and stared at the ceiling. So that's why we've never ridden int eh 560SL together and why he'd driven it to meet her Saturday morning. He'd told me he bought that car when he won his first case. I closed my eyes as I thought back to all he'd told me about Velma, "She's like a big sister. She's been with me for over twenty years," then it hit me. "When I get a check, she gets half." Now I understood why. They'd been having an affair for over twenty years. That's why she looked me up on Facebook when he, and I had first met. Then I remembered him saying,

"She's my best friend. I love her." "What a fool I've been," I said out loud to myself.

Pandora's box was open. A part of me couldn't take any more, but another part of me needed and wanted to know. I went through Dasht's entire text history. There were so many women. I clicked on Lillian's name to find more of the same sexual messages, pictures of her spread eagle on what I thought was our bed. There was even a short video of them having sex. I felt the bile in my throat as I clicked the video closed. I scrolled through the text thread and there it was. She was the woman he'd met for lunch to tell her about me. Just as Dana said, he'd dumped her for me.

> LILLIAN: *Why are you ignoring me?*
>
> DASHT: *We need to talk.*
>
> LILLIAN: *That's what I've been trying to do, but you're not answering the phone.*
>
> DASHT: *Can you meet me at 12:30 today?*
>
> LILLIAN: *Usual spot?*
>
> DASHT: *No. Let's meet for lunch.*
>
> LILLIAN: *Ok. Where?*
>
> DASHT: *Georgian*
>
> LILLIAN: *See you there.*
>
> LILLIAN: *I love you Dasht. My heart is broken. I've been waiting all these years for you. First Jewel and now this new woman. I'm tired of being second. All I can do now is try to move on. I will always love you. Forever yours, Bunny.*

"All these bunnies," I thought to myself. I closed the text messages and clicked the photo icon. There were albums that housed two hundred and fifty-six photos and another seventy-six videos. Each album was named after the woman whose photos it held. Tears rolled down my cheeks as I scrolled and clicked. I came across an album labeled Kate. I braced myself for more sexually graphic pictures, but I wasn't prepared for the rest. My tears dried in horror as I came across pics of Dasht and this woman indulging in drugs. There appeared to be cocaine sprinkled over their genitalia. I closed the picture icon and opened the text messages. Just as I'd expected there was a thread that matched her name. I clicked it and as I read their text history my jaws begin to tighten. Christmas Eve the day he'd proposed. "How could he," I asked myself?

> KATE: *This is so us!* Meme picture that read: When you meet your client for a drink but you always end up fucking.
>
> DASHT: *I know.* Tongue poke emoji, Wink emoji
>
> KATE: *Dinner will be ready at 3, but you can come early* Wink emoji
>
> DASHT: *Can I?* Wink emoji
>
> KATE: *Yes and we can smoke this baby.* Picture of a joint.
>
> DASHT: *Don't smoke it without me.*
>
> KATE: *I won't.* The text included a picture of a thin woman in some cheap, raunchy Santa themed lingerie.
>
> DASHT: Wow emoji
>
> KATE: *You been naughty so I'm not gonna play nice.* The text included a picture of some handcuffs and a large black dildo.
>
> DASHT: *I've been really naughty so punish me good.*
>
> KATE: *I will.*

"Hmph, this is why he wanted me to go to Tippy's alone on Christmas Eve." I shook my head in outrage before I continued to read the messages.

Right before we'd left for Tippy's he'd text her:

> DASHT: *Kate I'm not going to make it. Some family stuff came up.*

"Family stuff," I thought. And he'd had the gall to propose to me that same night. I closed my eyes, inhaled and shook my head in disbelief as I huffed to exhale some of the anger I was feeling. "How could he look at me with a straight face and propose knowing all the things he'd been doing? Knowing he wasn't committed and apparently didn't intend to ever commit or conduct himself like a husband. How could he? How could he," I asked myself?

I closed the text thread and went back to the picture album. There was an album labeled Jill. I recognized her immediately, the hostess from Canoe the night of his birthday dinner. There was a video of her masturbating on a weight bench in a location I didn't recognize. Apparently Dasht had recorded it because he could be heard in the background saying, "Yeah baby, do it for me…" I shut it off, dropped the iPad on the bed and ran in the bathroom to throw up.

I lay across the bed mentally and emotionally exhausted. I heard my phone ringing. I looked over to see Dasht was calling. I hit ignore, tossed the phone and picked-up the iPad once again. I'd had more than my share of looking at the pictures so I tapped the message icon instead. I saw the name Patsy, another name I never recalled hearing, so I tapped the conversation.

> PATSY: *When were you going to tell me you were engaged?*
>
> DASHT: *Where did you hear that? I'm not engaged.*
>
> PATSY: *Liar! I saw the purchase!*
>
> DASHT: *WTF! What are you doing going through my bank account?*
>
> PATSY: *You lied! You told me it wasn't serious!*
>
> DASHT: *You don't get to question me.*
>
> PATSY: *Oh yeah? We'll see about that.*

DASHT: *What did you do?*

PATSY: *$10K or I'm telling her!*

DASHT: *Bitch who do you think you're blackmailing*

PATSY: *Make it $15K. I know she's here. I will come to your house.*

"Ahh so this is who he was cursing and yelling at on the phone Friday. She knew about me, but he'd told her it wasn't serious. Wow," I said as my thoughts were interrupted by the ringing phone. It was Dasht calling yet again. I hit ignore and kept reading.

DASHT: *What did you do to my accounts!?*

PATSY: *Apparently you reported your wallet stolen so all of your cards are cancelled. You will need to come to the bank to retrieve funds.*

DASHT: *Bitch!*

PATSY: *And just yesterday I was Bunny.* Bunny emoji

I closed their text history and just sat on the bed thinking about how he'd watched me walk out to the door to try on wedding dresses while he argued on the phone with one of his many mistresses. "Everywhere he goes. He has women everywhere he goes. Work, the bank, the gym, restaurants… I don't know him. I don't know him at all," I whispered.

I opened the photo album with my name on it, and there I was naked. Unbeknownst to me, he'd snapped a screenshot of me while I'd playfully flashed him over FaceTime when he'd asked me about my ball gown. "Bastard," I huffed. Then I became sad as I looked at the pictures we'd exchanged via text when we'd first began talking. I pursed my lips as I came to the picture he'd taken the first time I beat him at a game of chess. I was so happy in this picture. I almost smiled, but I couldn't. My heart was literally aching.

I closed the album and continued to scroll the names and then I saw V-A-L-E-R-I-E. "No freaking way! He wouldn't, he couldn't," I hoped out loud as I opened the folder. There she was in a pink t-shirt, no pants, lying on the floor holding her legs open as Dasht urinated on her. I couldn't take it anymore. I closed the iPad and cried myself to sleep.

"Connected on contact"

"Hello," I answered sleepily.

"Bunny, we…" At the sound of his voice I immediately hung-up.

The fog of sleepiness was replaced with anger. "How dare he call me," I thought to myself as I pressed the home button to check the time. It was 3:19am. I'd fallen asleep in my clothes. I rolled off the bed, grabbed the iPad and put it on the charger before I went to take a shower.

I was about to lay down and try to rest when the iPad flashed a reminder that tomorrow was Jeannie's Birthday. I'd forgotten about her, the cooking god sister that I was supposed to have met when we'd first started dating. I grabbed the iPad and opened the calendar. I clicked the birthday reminder and the contact opened, and I read the notes:

>Nickname: Jean
>Favorite color: Blue
>Favorite flower: Rose
>Favorite Perfume: Flowerbomb
>Bethel Baptist
>Ranking ** 56

"Ranking," I thought and then as fast as I questioned it my mind clarified it. I quickly exited the contact and searched for my contact information:

>Nickname: Gabby
>Favorite color: Red
>Favorite flower: Gardenia, Hydrangea & Red rose
>Favorite Perfume: ?
>Likes Giraffes / Word of Praise when in Atlanta
>Ranking ***** #1 Bunny 46

"So I'm the number one Bunny? Lucky me," I quipped as I scrolled to Velma's contact:
>Nickname: Velvet
>Favorite color: Black
>Favorite flower: Orchid
>Favorite Perfume: Chloe
>Catholic

"No ranking for Velma," I said to myself. "This is some sick <u>S</u>ugar <u>H</u>oney <u>I</u>ce <u>T</u>ea," I said as I clicked on Valerie's contact, to find no notes. "Hmph, I guess he doesn't need a reminder to tell him who he can piss on," I said spitefully. "Speaking of trash let's look up Lillian:
>Nickname: Lil

"I'd actually heard him call her that at his birthday celebration. "Butthole," I said under my breath as I continued to read the contact notes that coincided with her name.
>Favorite color: Peach
>Favorite flower: Lillies
>Favorite Perfume: White Diamonds
>Ranking ** 52

"This is nothing but a game to him," I said as I shook my head and continued to scroll through the contacts looking at the notes on one woman after the next focusing primarily on the names that matched the text threads I'd read. I clicked on Danica:
>Nickname: Nikki
>Favorite color: Orange
>Favorite flower: Sunflower
>Favorite Perfume: Burberry Her or Juicy Couture
>Word of Praise
>Ranking **** #2 Bunny 31

"Wait," I said out loud as I stared at the contact note. "So I'm number one and she's number two and we attend the same church…0*4*6*3*1*, well I'll be damned."

CHAPTER 17
It Is What It Is Because...

"...completing a clandestine mend..."

I heard a light tap on the door, and then my sister calling my name as she gently opened the door, "Gab you awake?"

"Yeah, I'm just lying here."

She came in and sat on the bed, "How are you feeling?"

"I'll be alright."

"I know you will be alright. There's no doubt in my mind, but how are you feeling right now?"

"I'm overwhelmed with emotion. I'm hurt, angry, sad, disappointed, embarrassed, humiliated....," my voice trailed off as I choked back tears. "Even though I know I'm not, I feel like I'm dying."

Tippy looked angry and distraught, "Dasht should be ashamed of himself. He is too old for this type of foolishness."

"He is, but chronology doesn't necessarily guarantee maturity or wisdom. I just thought he was better than this."

"I'm sure he's called."

I nodded yes as I blankly stared at the wall.

"Have you spoken to him."

"Not intentionally. He called around three this morning, and I answered the phone in my sleep. Once I heard his voice I hung-up."

"Hmm, yeah that was not the time to talk I'm sure, but you should talk to him."

I turned my stunned gaze towards her before I said, "For what. I have all the proof anyone could ever ask for. There really isn't anything to talk about."

"Oh no I wouldn't want to hear any explanations either. I agree you have all the proof. But Gabby you do need to talk to him. You need to tell him how you feel. He needs to know the type of pain he has caused you. You've been in here crying all night. I came to check on you, and you were crying in your sleep. Sometimes people don't understand the repercussions of their actions on others. You just walking away, yes that is bad, but he just saw the dishes and the headless giraffe. He didn't see the tears and the hurt he's caused. I saw your face yesterday, and I'm looking at you now. Don't let him get away with never seeing the impact of his actions. Tell him how he made you feel because that bastard needs to know.

"I can't look at him," I paused to choke back the tears. "Tippy there is so much stuff in that iPad. It is awful. I can't be around him."

"I agree you shouldn't be around him. I honestly don't believe he deserves to be in your presence ever again. Next time he calls, because he will call again, tell him how he made you feel and be done with it. After that he never gets to hear your voice again, and that will be his loss. But you owe it to yourself if given the opportunity to tell him how he made you feel. He needs to know."

"I'm going to pray about it."

"I'm going to pray too. When do you fly out?"

"Tomorrow."

> ***"Searching in a bin of dirty rags and fabric fragments, but for what I'm searching I just don't know."***

I looked at my phone to see I had more text messages from Dasht, but I didn't have the stomach to read them. I was done torturing myself with his iPad too. I got up out of bed and took the iPad to the garage where I demolished it with a hammer. I swept all the smashed pieces into a pile, collected them in a dustpan and dumped them into two separate plastic bags. I threw one bag in the garbage can and kept the other bag to toss into a local dumpster.

As I got dressed, I thought about what Tippy had said. I agreed that Dasht should know how I was feeling, but part of me believed he honestly didn't care. He knew what he was doing was wrong, and if the shoe was on the other foot, he'd be mad enough to kill someone. I decided to get dressed and go for a drive to clear my mind and toss the crushed iPad pieces. No sooner than I'd backed out of the driveway Dasht called yet again. Hearing Tippy's words, "Tell him how he made you feel," I inhaled and asked God for strength before I answered the phone, "Hello."

"Bunny please don't hang-up."

"Don't call me that," I spat. "Don't you ever call me that."

"What? What is wrong with you? Why…"

"I know Dasht! So cut the bull. I know all about your little collection of Bunnies."

"What are you talking about?"

"I'm not in the mood to play games with you Dasht. I know all about your harem of whores, and I don't want to be a part of it. I'm taking myself out of the ranking so you can move Danica, or should I say Nikki to Bunny #1."

"Gabby it's not what you think it is…"

"Dasht I saw the photos. I saw the videos. I read the text messages. I saw the contacts, your calendar with trips planned for you and Farah, your ranking system, your pictures with Velma. Dasht I know, so please stop lying. I KNOW."

His voice lowered and I could tell he was angry but struggling to control it, "What did you do?"

I couldn't believe he hadn't figured out that I had the iPad, and even if he had I wasn't going to admit to it. "I didn't do anything. It may be cliché but it's true, what's done in the dark will come to the light, and your chickens have come home to roost."

"Can we meet somewhere so we can talk?"

"I don't think that's a good idea."

"Where are you?"

"My whereabouts are no longer your business or concern."

"Look Gabby, I can explain…"

"What? What can you explain Dasht? How you've been playing a sick, immature high school game for the last nine months? How you callously played with my life? How you were pressuring me to give up everything to move back to Atlanta to be with you knowing full well you had no intention of being a committed or faithful husband? Is that what you would like to explain?"

"Ok, ok. I see where you are. You're angry, but you don't know all the details. Maybe we should talk later after you've calmed down."

"Hmph. You have some nerve. After I've calmed down," I mocked him. "As if my emotions are unwarranted."

"They are! There was no reason for you to break all those dishes and leave that mess all over the house."

"I just wanted to ensure Valerie had something to do when she came to work this morning because I know she's there," I huffed sarcastically.

He almost choked before he said, "Well it's a good thing I hadn't fired her."

"Yes, it is. Lucky you," I spat. "Now you don't have to. Keep her." I felt my blood boiling so hot it was bubbling up in my veins.

"Bun-, I mean Gabby, can you just listen to me?"

He'd almost called me Bunny and hearing it made my heart hurt, "No Dasht, I would like for you to listen to me." I inhaled a deep breath to steady my tone and focused on Tippy's words, "Tell him how he made you feel."

"Dasht from day one I was honest with you. I've never lied to you. Not one time. I've always been honest with you. I told you what I'd been through in my past relationships, and I specifically asked you not to bring any foolishness to my life. Yet here we are."

He cut me off, "It's ok if you hate me. I see where you are."

"I don't hate you, and I won't hate you. I refuse to ever give some that much power over me. Am I angry? Absolutely, but anger towards you is fleeting. It will subside. It's the anger with myself that will linger. I'm more hurt and disappointed with you than anything else. I'm hurt that you would intentionally hurt me. I'm hurt over the reality of knowing you never had any good intentions. You played games with my life, and you didn't care if you ruined my life." I paused to steady my tone and choke down the tears. "You were willing to ruin my life."

"No I wasn't."

"Yes, you were. You were pushing me to sell my house, quit my job, get rid of my things. All the while you were traipsing around with all these other women." I paused as the images of the pictures and messages clouded my vision. "You had no limits to how far you would go. Why and how could you ask me to marry you on the same day you were trying to sneak away to be with another woman? And doing drugs?"

"I don't do drugs."

"Yes, you do. Smoking pot is doing drugs. Snorting cocaine off someone's genitals is doing drugs, and I told you I don't do drugs, never have and don't want to be around anyone who does drugs."

"I wasn't going to…"

I cut him off, "Please stop. Just stop lying. You were going to do whatever it was you'd planned to do, and you didn't care if or how it would impact me. The sad part is you would have still proposed afterwards because it's clear you have no boundaries or remorse."

"It's not what you…," he stopped himself mid thought. "I see where you are."

"I don't think you do, but I clearly see where you are."

"Look I've made some mistakes, but everyone makes mistakes. I'm a man and all men mess up…"

I cut him off again, "Mistake? No sir, you made choices, some very poor, irresponsible, immature, selfish and low down choices. You knew exactly what you were doing. You did what you did willingly and on purpose. And I don't want to talk about what all men do. We're talking about your actions because those are the actions that have impacted me."

"You won't listen. I'm trying to explain but you won't listen because you've made your mind up over some information without having all the facts."

"I don't need any more facts," I said bluntly. "The details are irrelevant at this point."

"So, what are you saying that you hate me, and if you do it's ok."

I let out a condescending sigh over his pathetic attempt to make me feel guilty. "This is sad."

"Yes, it is sad," he huffed. "It's sad that you are willing to throw everything away without allowing me to explain."

"No Dasht, you threw us away. From what I now know you've always treated this relationship like garbage. It meant nothing to you."

"That's not true! I love you."

"No, you don't, well maybe in your mind you do. But as far as I'm concerned this is not love."

"I do love you, and if you really loved me you wouldn't throw our relationship away this easily."

"I love you, but my love for you or your love for me is really a moot point. At this moment I don't like you because of your actions, and I don't respect you because of your lies." I paused as I felt my heart constricting tighter than was comfortable because it was still breaking. I inhaled and exhaled before I spoke, "Loving you doesn't mean I'm supposed to be with you. As much as I love you, I cannot be with you. Not knowing what I know because that would require me to sacrifice my self-respect, self-worth and self-dignity."

"I'm not asking you to…,"

I stopped him. "Correct, you're not asking me. Your actions demand that I sacrifice my self-respect, my self-worth, my dignity, and my love for myself. However, on numerous occasions you have asked me to compromise my values, my morals, my desires, my goals, and I have, which is why you continued to expect me to sacrifice more. As much as I love you, I love myself too much to continue to pay such a high cost to be with a man that has never been with me."

"Gabby,"

"Call me Gabriella. My name is Gabriella."

"So this is where we are?"

"Yes. This is exactly where we are. Right where you've placed us. Right where I've allowed you to place me. I don't want to be stuck in a relationship that is decorated on the outside for all the world to see but underneath is just a pretty box of lies, guilt, and shame. That kind of life is not for me. I just have to be true to myself. I want to be happy, and I want it to be real happiness."

"It's not for me either."

"I beg to differ."

"I'm a good man. I'm a good person."

"I never said you were a bad person. Good people do bad things, and you have done some very bad things. The sad part is maybe if you weren't so satisfied with being good you could allow yourself to be great."

"What do you mean?"

"In spite of all the things that have been plastered in my face about you, I still see all the potential for good in you. But I also see a man who for whatever reason is ashamed of who he really is. While I am disturbed by the drug usage and the numerous women and some of the sexual proclivities, I would have not frowned upon you had you been honest. You are ashamed of who you are and what you like, and that is the cause for concern. It is the shame that has you in bondage. Your shame has become your vice. You don't see the real greatness in yourself because you're cloaked in guilt and you're crippled by it. Rather than be all that you can be and capitalize on all the greatness that is in you, you've succumbed to standards that are so low until now you don't have the where with all to walk alone or in a relationship in standards that are high." I paused to gather my thoughts. "Here you are fifty-four years old justifying your behavior, your choices with an all men mess up and everyone is doing it defense."

"All men do mess up."

"I'm not a man so I can't truly say, but I don't believe that. I won't accept that. A bad choice is a bad choice, and you consciously made them regularly, habitually. It has nothing to do with your gender. It is clear what you were doing is your norm. I'm not the woman for you. I'm not what you desire. You want me because I fit the image you want to project to the world. I compliment the representative, your façade."

"I don't have a representative."

"We can agree to disagree, but you cannot change what you won't acknowledge or fix what you refuse to face. Besides I'm not saying you're bad and I'm good. I'm saying we don't fit, and our love isn't enough. I don't even know you. I only know your representative."

"Stop saying that. You do know me".

"No I only know one persona."

You make me sound like a monster," he said in a tone that conveyed defeat.

"I didn't say that, but the Dr. Jekyll and Mr. Hyde concept certainly applies. You're dressed up on the outside but that's not you. That man is fiction, a character you've created to hide the real you. But I see you now, and you're not at all the man you pretended to be. You look good but your soul is dark and broken. It is painfully clear that you don't hold yourself accountable and you don't allow others to hold you accountable. Like Dana said, you do what you want, when you want with whom you want."

"Don't tell me anything Dana said," he huffed.

"It was the truth. Everything she said, it was all the truth. And here I was wanting and trying to love you up close and personal, but no matter how many times your words invited me into your life, your brokenness found a way to ensure I was never truly welcome in your space."

"It wasn't all truth, but that's neither here nor there. You are welcome in my space. I do love you."

"I was never welcome in your space. I was never in your life the way I was led to believe I was. I was duped, and that is not love. To love someone, in my opinion is a choice. A choice that you never made. However, I chose to love you. I chose to love you," I repeated as the words sank into my soul. I shook my head in disbelief before I continued, "I made a conscious decision to love you. Only to find you were playing games." I paused as the tears flowed down my face.

"I love you Gabriella. Please forgive me. Let's meet somewhere and talk face to face."

"No thank you," I said as I tried to hide my sniffles.

"Bun-, I mean Gabby, I mean Gabriella," he sighed in frustration, "don't cry."

I shook my head in disgust as he struggled with all the pet names. "You're not in a space emotionally to be in a relationship. You never were."

"That's not true," he countered.

"The reality is I can't blame it all on you. If I'm being totally honest the signs were always there, elephants were always in the room, big circus elephants twirling balls and standing on their hind legs."

Angrily he asked, "What do you mean? I was always respectful."

I let out a condescending laugh as I sarcastically said, "By ranking me Bunny number one. Hmph, gee thanks." I sucked my teeth as I rolled my eyes. "There is nothing respectful about infidelity. There's no such thing as respectful cheating. The act itself is blatant disregard and disrespect. When you were plotting and planning your conquests you were disrespectful. When you sat in my face and lied to me, you were disrespectful. But it is what it is because you are who you are. The responsibility rest with me to make a choice as to how I will handle the truth that I now know it to be, and I choose better than this. I choose better because I know my purpose is not to be disrespected, not to be mistreated, not to be handled as less than, not to be treated callously. My purpose is to be honored, loved, respected, adored, desired, cherished, nurtured. My purpose is full of positivity. There is nothing negative about my purpose on this earth. And all of this is negative. I can't and I won't. I choose better than this," I said more so as confirmation to myself than to him.

"You're not perfect in all of this Gabriella," he countered. "You lost your package and broke all those dishes and cut the head off that giraffe. That wasn't right. Not right at all. That is cause for concern because there are some issues there."

"Dasht we all have issues. Our issues become our vices when we don't deal with them and they become our dirty little secrets, and all your dirty little secrets and the shame you carry about them are shackles that have you in bondage. You're in the worst kind of prison because it has no walls and you lie to yourself and pretend to be free. Now that's an issue. But if you want to talk about me, we can because I own my part in all of this, and you're right, I'm not perfect. Yes, I cried. Yes, I lost it. I also compromised to a fault. I stroked your ego and your libido, and this is what it got me. I may have lost my temper, but I refuse to continue losing myself." I stopped and closed my eyes in a feeble attempt to stop the pace of the blinding tears that were flowing freely. "I thought you were my book, but you've proven to be only a chapter, a bad chapter." I stopped to choke my sob that still escaped as a whimper. "So, I'm turning the page and moving on with my story."

"Please can we just meet somewhere and talk this thing out? I do love you. Please…" his voice trailed off as if he was becoming choked up.

"For me this is not about love. Maybe you do believe you love me. That's not for me to confirm or deny. Unfortunately, I don't believe you are at peace with loving me. From what I can tell you never wanted to love me or anyone else for that matter. I believe loving someone scares you. Your intentions as far as I was concerned was to simply add another sexual conquest to your long list."

"That's not true!"

"Hmph. Sadly, it is. But either way, love is not attachment. Just because I love you it doesn't mean I get to be with you or that I'm even supposed to be with you. As I said earlier, I believe love is a choice. I chose to love you, and I can live with that choice. Even though a part of me is dying because I am heartbroken, I can't lie and say I didn't see this coming. I didn't see it at this magnitude, but if I'm being honest, I knew. I knew something wasn't right. I chose to keep ignoring it hoping the elephant would just find its own way out of the room. So now the task for me is to figure out what is so broken in me that I would be willing to give up my entire life just to be married to you." I leaned my head back as the tears rolled down my cheeks, dripped off my chin and onto my chest.

"Don't do this. Please."

I exhaled and tried to stifle the whimper of my sobs before I said, "Goodbye Dasht," and clicked off the call.

In true angry Dasht fashion he called back repeatedly. After I'd ignored his ninth call, he sent an angry text.

> DASHT: *I don't know how you got into my stuff, but just know this I have a naked photo of you, and I will share it if you ever try to blackmail or extort me.*
>
> GABRIELLA: *The picture you took without my permission. I know about that too. Your threats mean nothing to me Dasht. Do what you will! I don't care. Unlike you, I've embraced my TRUE nakedness. I thought it was enough to be naked with you, but maybe I have to be naked with the world in order to walk in my God-given purpose so if God sees fit to allow you to share it, so be it. Because it clearly wasn't enough to be naked in our relationship. I have nothing to hide. I'm prepared to shed my fig leaves because I'm determined to be free.*

EPILOGUE

"The best and most beautiful things in this world cannot be seen or even heard but must be felt with the heart." **Helen Keller**

Six Months Later...

Gabriella,

I have not written a letter to anyone in many years; however, I feel compelled to express my thoughts to you. During our separation, God revealed several things to me. First, I had to become closer to "HIM" to truly understand the meaning of love. I had to learn that my pride means absolutely nothing without having you in my life – God placed you in my life for a reason.

During this separation from you, I've been forced to look in the mirror and hold myself accountable for all of my actions... Losing you forced me to take inventory of my personal life. I realized that I had lost the love of my life, my wife, my friend, my soulmate.

I love you with all of my heart! In fact, I'm "IN LOVE" with you! I simply love the essence of you. I look at you and see the rest of my life in your eyes. It gives my heart joy and happiness to know I am loved by you! I hope and pray you will accept my proposal to be my wife – I promise and pledge to you that I will cherish you for the rest of my life. I will likewise be faithful to you for the rest of my life!!! I have an unwavering commitment to you, our love and our lives together.

I love you Gabby and would love to spend the rest of my life with you. Please forgive me and marry me.

-Dasht

ACKNOWLEDGEMENTS

I would like to begin by thanking God for choosing me and allowing me to live the life for which he chose to be the vessel to inspire this story. Without Him, I am nothing.

Thank you to my Mom who taught me how to read and instilled in me the desire to always want and be the best. Thank you to my Dad for making me read the Bible, teaching me to have reverence for God and to always pray. Thank you to my Grandmother, may her soul continue to rest, for teaching me how to love through your example of unconditional love. Thank you for giving me the knowledge that to be loved was the richest I'd ever be in this world.

To my forever best friends, my sisters Tina and Toni. Thank you for always being there when I needed you. Thank you for your limitless friendship and a lifetime of laughter and love.

Thank you to Olivia Warner my first professional mentor for requiring me to find and use my voice at a most critical time in my development as a woman. You ignited a spark in me that turned into a burning flame. I am forever grateful.

To my sisters from another mister Charlotte and Ginette. Thank you for standing in the gap and being the big sisters I never had. For selflessly sharing your wisdom and sparing me some bumps and bruises while lovingly guiding me along this journey of life.

To my sorority sisters Erica, Robbin, Tammie and Tasha who have crawled, walked and hurdled without hesitation on this journey of womanhood with me. Over the years our experiences and personal stories of happiness and heartache have made us laugh, cry and testify all the while making our bond stronger.

To Mrs. Elnora Jackson, Mrs. Vivian, Lenaye, Roni, Diana and Devron thank you for always being genuinely supportive, encouraging me to leap without fear of a fall and giving me a safe space to cry and be open without judgment or fear of regret.

To my sister and friend Germaine, thank you for your beautiful spirit, consistent inspiration and being an angel in disguise and a catalyst to move this project forward.

Thank you to all young women who ever sought me out and allowed me to serve as a mentor. You opened the windows to my soul and allowed me to see myself through you. Thank you for empowering me to share my stories and lessons learned and encouraging me to write this book. A special thank you Leyah, Ashley N., Skye and the members of Pearls of Perfection (2007-2008) and For Girls' Only (2015-2017).

A special thank you to the Smiley family for your love, support and friendship.

Thank you to my son Sam for your unconditional love and challenging me to be the woman you've always seen me to be. I thank God for choosing me to be your mother. You are forever my purpose. I love you to the moon and back a thousand times.

SHANNA SARSIN is a Shreveport, Louisiana native. Her successful career in executive level positions led Shanna to be sought after as a mentor by young women seeking to establish their professional identities and careers. It was through panel discussions and mentoring relationships that she began sharing her professional navigation techniques. In 2015 she was asked to serve as the Chair of a mentoring youth program for girls from impoverished and unstable homes. It was through this venture that she began sharing her personal journey from humble beginnings in the rural outskirts of Shreveport to a place her five year old mind could only imagine, an office with a view in the NW sector of Washington, D.C. This is when she began to be encouraged to write a book. Realizing her passion for helping others and ability to connect with and inspire widely diverse populations, she decided to put away her business suit and take a hand at writing and the result is her debut novel *ELEPHANTS, BUNNIES & A HEADLESS GIRAFFE.*

Shanna currently splits her time between her hometown of Shreveport, Louisiana and Fort Washington, Maryland where she spends her free time volunteering to promote STEM, the arts, healthy living, financial empowerment and helping to raise funds to provide scholarships for underprivileged children.